SHOOT AT THE SUNSET

CHAPARRAL HEARTS
BOOK FIVE

KATHLEEN DENLY

WILD HEART
BOOKS

Unless otherwise indicated, all Scripture quotations are taken from the Holy Bible, Kings James Version.

Cover design by: Carpe Librum Book Design

ISBN-13:

To my God who sustains me and carries me through the darkest of valleys, and the people He placed in my path to help me along the way. You know who you are.

The fear of man bringeth a snare: but whoso putteth his trust in the Lord shall be safe.

— PROVERBS 29:25 KJV

FOREWORD

Dear Reader,

The story you are about to read involves complex characters facing extremely difficult circumstances. I feel it's important to offer a gentle forewarning about some of the situations they encounter. Through their eyes, you will see discussions and depictions of sensitive topics including abuse, addiction, rape, and Post Traumatic Stress Disorder. While these themes are integral to the narrative and are handled with care, they are also deeply personal subjects that may evoke strong emotions or memories. Skip over those parts if necessary, but I urge you to continue reading. The purpose in including these difficult topics is to bring light and hope to even our darkest moments and to remind ourselves that we are never struggling alone. Our loving God is always with us. I can assure you these characters do find hope and faith along with that oh-so-sweet romantic ending we all love.

Thank you for embarking on this literary adventure with an open heart and mind. May the pages ahead offer insight and empathy. But most of all, I pray this story blesses you with comfort, joy, and hope.

Warm regards,
Kathleen Denly

CHAPTER 1

JUNE 6, 1873
SAN FRANCISCO, CALIFORNIA

"*Y*ou fool."

At the sound of Reginald Green's angry voice, Lucy Arlidge froze midstep in the fifth-floor hallway outside Junior's residential suite in the Green Hotel. Never had she heard her consistently imperturbable employer so much as annoyed. Yet now the hotel owner sounded furious. She wrung her hands. What was Mr. Green doing in his son's parlor? Whenever he wished to speak to Junior, Mr. Green always directed one of the maids to have his son come to him. She couldn't recall a single instance during the two years that she'd been working at the hotel when Mr. Green had deigned to come to his son.

Yet there was no mistaking her employer's voice coming through the slim opening left by the not-quite-closed door. "I told you to keep things with Miss Prichard above reproach. If you'd done as I instructed, none of this—"

"This wasn't about Agatha. This was about the..." Junior's haughty retort cut off, as if he'd thought better of finishing his sentence.

Lucy smiled. Finally, he was taking her advice to heart. Unlike his father, Junior was prone to strong passions that often landed him in trouble. Lucy had been counseling him for months to take a deep breath and think before he spoke. But what were they saying about Miss Agatha Prichard?

Lucy's smile faded. She'd heard rumors along with the rest of the staff that Junior was courting the young heiress, but Junior had assured Lucy that's all they were. Rumors. So why...?

Junior resumed speaking in a calmer tone. "This was about our business dealings." There was a brief pause. "She knew."

Who knew what? Were they still discussing Agatha?

"What? But that's impossible. How could she possibly...?" Mr. Green's bewildered voice turned hard. "What did you say?"

"Why do you assume I'm the one who let something slip? It could as easily have been him." Who was Junior talking about now? Lucy inched closer to the door even as her conscience shouted that she shouldn't be eavesdropping. But if this had something to do with Agatha—if Junior wasn't being truthful with Lucy—she needed to know. "*He* was at Prichard Hall last—"

"Don't be ridiculous." Mr. Green dismissed his son's argument. "Why didn't you just promise to pay the woman?"

Junior released a harsh laugh unlike any she'd heard from him before. "With what money? My tailor has threatened to quit if his bills aren't paid soon, and you can't even satisfy the small sum the Davidsons requested last week."

Couldn't pay? But the Greens were one of the wealthiest and most influential families in the city. How could they not afford any amount owed? And what did Lucy's best friend's parents, the Davidsons, have to do with Agatha Prichard? It was true both families were part of San Francisco's elite, but beyond that, the families were known not to be on friendly terms. Mrs. Prichard had never approved of the Davidson's adoption of Lucy's dearest friend, Biddie, and had publicly snubbed them ever since. She'd even accused Biddie of starting the fire that had destroyed half of Prichard Hall more than a decade ago, forcing the family to rebuild at great expense. Lucy sniffed. As if the Prichards couldn't afford it.

Mr. Green's proud tone brought Lucy back to the conversation happening in Junior's parlor. "Never you mind about the Davidsons. I've just convinced them to leave their money invested longer for a higher return in a month's time."

Junior laughed again. "Of course, you have. The poor saps will never see the end coming, will they? What do we have? A month? Or is it two months before we're out of money and this whole scheme comes crumbling down around our ears? We ought to be selling what we can and planning our escape from this place before it's too late."

Oh no. Lucy had been the one to convince the Davidsons to invest in Mr. Green's railroad enterprise in order to raise more funds for their charitable efforts. At the time, Mr. Green had been new to the city. In her position as a maid in the new Green Hotel, she'd overheard multiple businessmen discussing how, when others struggled, Mr. Green's businesses back east had held steady and even flourished. They'd sounded convinced that Mr. Green was set to do the same in San Francisco. Everyone had exclaimed over his consistently high-earning results. Investing in one of his myriad business ventures had seemed the perfect solution to the ever-growing needs of The Davidsons' Home for Women and Children. The Davidsons had given the gregarious magnate every penny they could spare. Could so many savvy businessmen have been wrong?

Mr. Green's indignant voice rose. "And give up everything I've spent my life building? You truly are a fool. You—"

"You could talk a mule into dancing a quadrille, but you

can't dupe me. And that still doesn't answer how I'm meant to have paid the enormous sum Mrs. Prichard was demanding."

Mrs. Irene Prichard had demanded money of Junior? But why? It was the bride who brought a dowry to a marriage. Not that Lucy believed the rumors. Junior had assured her time and again that he had no understanding with Miss Prichard and didn't intend to enter into one, despite his father's demands. Surely, there was a good explanation for Agatha's mention in this confusing conversation.

"Have I taught you nothing?" Mr. Green's exasperated voice continued. "There are ways of convincing a person—"

"We don't all have your silver tongue."

"Enough." Lucy startled at the sound of a third man's calm but authoritative voice—one she didn't recognize. A strange, muted thumping began in the room, as though a man with a cane were pacing the far side of the carpeted floor. Thankfully, the noise didn't draw nearer. She tried to remember which guests employed the stylish accessory. Too many to guess who the mysterious third man might be. "We'll worry about the money later." The odd scent of rosemary mixed with licorice wafted from the room. "Did Mrs. Prichard say whether she shared what she knew with her daughter or anyone else?"

Junior's response was tense and low. "She claimed to have told no one."

"Good." The thumping stopped, but the unfamiliar calculating voice continued. "That'll make cleaning up your mess easier."

Mess? Was there a mess she or one of the other maids would need to tidy? Lucy leaned toward the sliver of opening between the door and its frame. Then froze.

A clean-shaven man dressed in the latest fashion and holding a fancy cane inspected a woman's still body sprawled across the plush carpet. Mrs. Irene Prichard's unseeing eyes stared straight at Lucy. The powerful woman's chest neither rose nor fell. A strangled breath lodged in Lucy's throat, a shiver coursing through her as a silent scream echoed in her mind.

Dear Lord, what have they done? How could Junior be a part of this?

Suspicions swarmed in light of the conversation she'd been listening to. But no, they couldn't be true. Junior would never... he couldn't—

From somewhere beyond her view, Junior's cold words sliced through her panicked denial. "Can't we just call a policeman? Isn't this the sort of thing we're paying them for? They can rule it a robbery. They're common enough."

"Not at my hotel." Mr. Green's voice soured with disgust. "Besides, they're not all on the payroll, and contacting one of ours will take more time than we've got."

The well-dressed man looked at Junior, his inspection seemingly at an end. "You managed to leave her clothing intact. That's something. I have a trusted resource about her size and coloring." He shook his head as Lucy struggled to remember if she'd seen the dandy before, but her thoughts were a whirling storm of elusive memories and chaotic fragments. "It'll be a shame to lose her, but there's nothing for it. Have your man deliver this to the address on the front immediately." He pulled a sealed envelope from his pocket and held it out.

Mr. Green stepped into view as he accepted the missive.

Who was this stranger that could order Mr. Green about? Not daring to breathe, Lucy crept back, praying the men wouldn't notice her movement in the gap she'd been spying through. Thoughtless, reckless decision. She should have departed the instant she'd realized Mr. Green was in the room, not let curiosity and jealousy pull her toward the crack in the door. Her fingernails pressed into the palms of her hands. She risked a larger step backward. She'd heard too much. If they knew—

Her heel caught on the carpet runner. She stumbled.

The door flew open.

Mr. Green lunged for her.

She spun out of reach and fled down the hall. As she rounded a corner, her heart beat against her ribs as fast as the footsteps chasing her.

"Lucy, wait!" Junior's pleading tone might have fooled her an hour ago. No longer. His handsome face and charm couldn't erase the scene she'd witnessed, nor the cold and calculating words she'd overheard.

A porter appeared at the top of the stairs, directly in her path.

"Stop her!" Mr. Green shouted. "She's a thief!"

Lucy's fists clenched at the blatantly untrue accusation.

The porter opened his arms, ready to catch her, but she ducked beneath them and tumbled down the servants' stairs. She crashed against the wall of the fourth-floor landing.

"Move out of the way." Junior shoved the poor porter into the railing.

Lucy scrambled to her feet. Her ankle screamed in protest as she hobbled down another flight of stairs. She'd never make it to the first floor before Mr. Green and his son overtook her.

Two maids stood like gaping statues on the third-floor landing. As Lucy careened by, she grabbed the wrist of the farthest woman and jerked her against her companion. The two fell in a tangled heap behind her, and Lucy swallowed a pang of regret.

Again, Junior shouted at those in his path.

Lucy didn't look back. She reached the second floor and staggered down the hall. She seized the knob of the first door and yanked. It didn't budge. Swallowing Mama's favorite curse word, Lucy rushed to the next door. It opened to reveal a maids' closet with no other means of entry. Or escape.

Heavy steps thundered down the stairs. She was out of time.

She flung herself into the tiny room and tugged the door

closed. Blackness enveloped her. She shifted her weight off the ankle she'd twisted.

Footsteps drew closer. Had the men seen her?

She groped the cleaning items around her until her fingers clasped the handle of a broom. It would have to do.

The footfalls continued down the hall, then retraced their path.

"She's not there." Junior's voice was breathless and close.

Lucy quieted her breathing, though she could not slow her heartbeat.

"Keep searching," Mr. Green ordered.

A new voice, probably a guest, joined them. "What's the meaning of this?"

"My apologies for the disturbance," Junior said between huffing breaths. "A maid was caught stealing and ran this way. Not to worry, though. We'll soon have her."

Betrayal seared her cheeks. What a gullible sap she'd been, believing his private declarations. No matter his sweet words, deep down, she'd known any man truly in love with a woman wouldn't ask her to sneak around as Junior had. Thank goodness, she hadn't succumbed to his passionate pleas.

When the guest spoke again, his voice had risen an octave. "Stealing? What kind of establishment are you running here? I daresay the Fifth Avenue Hotel would never subject their guests to such vulgarities."

Mr. Green's calm tenor interceded. "And I assure you this is a first and a last for the Green Hotel as well. Junior, please escort this gentleman and his wife to our dining room and see that they are served whatever their hearts desire at the hotel's expense for the remainder of their stay."

Several sets of footsteps faded toward the main stairs.

Lucy didn't dare move as she listened to doors being opened and closed up and down the hallway. As the thuds drew nearer, she readied her broom to strike whoever opened the closet.

Lord, protect me. If not for my own sake, then for the Davidsons who've served You so faithfully for so many years.

She had to warn them. If what she'd overheard was true—and she had no reason to doubt it—the Davidsons' decision to follow her advice by investing in Mr. Green's railroad venture was going to cost them—and those who depended on them—everything. She clamped her lips against a sob. No doubt the Davidsons would be furious with her. And all those women and children would have nowhere to go. All the good the generous couple had worked to accomplish over the years would be undone. What if the Davidsons, the only people who still loved her, rejected her the way Mama had? Perhaps—

"Enough." Mr. Green's order sounded as if he were right outside the closet, startling her into shaking the broom. "We're drawing too much attention."

Dust filled her nose and coated her throat. She fought against sneezing and coughing.

A stranger's low voice joined Mr. Green's. "We cannot let her escape." Was it the well-dressed man she'd spied in the corner of the room upstairs? She shivered with the memory of his cold inspection of Mrs. Prichard's body and the odd scent of rosemary mixed with licorice. Bile surged up her throat and she swallowed hard as the stranger's voice continued. "Didn't you say she's a particular friend of the Davidsons' daughter?"

"No doubt that's where she's headed now. You must stop her from reaching them."

"And if she's not there?"

Mr. Green's voice dropped so low Lucy strained to hear his next words. "Her mother's an opium whore working the Barbary. My sources tell me, Miss Arlidge visits the brothel every Sunday and pleads with her mother to give up that life."

SHOOT AT THE SUNSET

Disdain dripped from Mr. Green's words. "Which means the maid still cares for her mother, but no one else will bat an eye if a trollop goes missing. Capture the mother and the girl will come to us."

The hallway fell silent as the quiet pat of shoes on carpet receded.

A sneeze burst from Lucy's nose, but she smothered the sound with her free hand. She held her breath, though she couldn't stop her body from shaking as she listened for the men's return.

Please Lord, don't let anyone have heard.

Silently, she counted the seconds. A minute passed. Then two. When five full minutes had elapsed with no other sounds, she lowered the broom and sagged against the wall. Despite her aching muscles, she straightened. She had to reach Mama before the men did.

Lucy cracked the door open and peered into the hall. Empty. Thankfully, the brief rest had reduced the pain in her ankle to a mild burning. Ignoring the discomfort, she slunk to the nearest guest room and used her maid's key to gain entry. Riffling through the wardrobe, she chose the simplest and oldest-looking ensemble, which was still worth twice her monthly earnings. She wriggled out of her maid attire and donned the many layers of a well-to-do lady. An oval mirror above the chest of drawers revealed chaotic brown curls that had once been a neat bun. She ran her fingers through her thick locks and tamed them into a soft twist. A beautiful blue hat bedecked with a large white plume and pretty pink rose completed the transformation.

She grabbed a small satchel from the wardrobe floor and stuffed her uniform inside. After a moment's longing for her familiar clothes and other personal belongings in her shared attic room, she snapped the bag shut. There was no time, and nothing up there was worth the risk of Mr. Green and that stranger getting to Mama first.

She lifted a fan from a side table and pressed her ear to the door. No footsteps or chatter sounded in the hallway. She cracked the door for one last check before slipping out and making her way to the main stairs.

CHAPTER 2

*H*ead held high, Lucy kept the fan open and ready. At the first whisper of voices around the next corner, she began daintily fanning her face, hiding all but her eyes from view. Thank heavens for the unseasonably hot weather.

The passing guests disregarded her, and she made it all the way to the first floor, seemingly unnoticed. As she approached the grand entry, an ambitious porter rushed forward, his hand out for the satchel. "Allow me, miss."

Seeing no way to avoid handing over the bag without causing a scene, she relinquished the satchel and allowed him to follow her out the door.

He paused at the edge of the circular, paved-stone drive and considered the two gentlemen engaged in conversation and a third who tapped his foot as he waited for his conveyance to be brought around. "Do you see your companion, Miss...?" The porter leaned to one side in an obvious attempt to see her face and discern her identity.

Lucy shifted, careful to keep the fan between her face and his. She spoke softly and in a higher pitch than her usual voice.

"He'll be along shortly. You needn't wait." She stole the satchel from his grasp and pivoted away in clear dismissal. She sensed his lingering presence and held her breath. No doubt the man was confused by her behavior and disappointed not to receive the customary tip. After a moment, however, his quiet steps pattered back into the hotel.

She risked a surreptitious glance around. None of the gentlemen paid her any mind, but a porter standing beside a pile of luggage behind the two chatting men stared at her with blatant curiosity. Drat. She whirled away and forced herself to breathe slowly. Squaring her shoulders, she strolled along the perimeter of the circular drive toward the arched exit.

Once at the street's edge, she ventured a final peek back. The nosy porter was busy loading the gentlemen's trunk onto a carriage.

She released her breath, turned right, and hurried down the sidewalk as quickly as she dared. It wouldn't do to draw attention now. Occupying the entire block, the opulent hotel loomed beside her like a gilded cage, waiting for another chance to trap her within its walls.

The sharp clatter of a passing horse drawing a passenger-laden car on tracks that ran down the center of the stone-paved street drowned out the rustle of her stolen silk dress. Each strike of the animal's shoes against the rectangular blocks jarred her nerves. Late-morning sunlight flashed off the polished brass fixtures of the horse car, momentarily blinding her as she reached the intersection. She nearly collided with a gentleman in a fine suit stepping onto the granite curbstone.

He leapt aside just in time and raised his stylish hat. "Pardon me, miss."

Beads of perspiration trickled down her back as she clutched the fan, its delicate tines shaking in her trembling grip. She nodded demurely before darting across the road.

Not until the stone-paved avenues and elaborate masonry

buildings gave way to old planks and faded brick facades did she dare to lower her fan.

One block later, she spotted a policeman on the opposite street corner. Should she dash over, confess everything she'd overheard, and beg his protection? Junior's words echoed in her mind. *"Can't we just call a policeman? Isn't this the sort of thing we're paying them for?"* No. She had no way to know if this lawman was trustworthy, and even if he was, she was wearing stolen clothing and carrying a stolen satchel.

She ducked into the nearest alley and hid behind a large stack of empty crates. Heart pounding, she peeked around the pile to see if he'd noticed her. He was gone.

Thank You, Lord.

Something squelched beneath her heel. She looked down. The contents of a chamber pot—likely emptied through one of the windows above—had soiled the beautifully embroidered footwear as well as the hem of the green silk dress. Time to change.

She stepped out of the foul heap and searched the casements facing the narrow space between a pair of two-story buildings. No curious gazes met hers. This would have to do.

As quickly as she could, Lucy exchanged the ruined fancy clothes for her plain black maid's attire and sturdy shoes. She left the white mobcap and apron in the bag, which she stuffed into a barrel at the back of the alley, separate from the crate she'd crammed the stolen outfit into.

She waited for a break in the flow of people walking by before stepping onto the dirt lane. A young boy loitered outside a mercantile two doors down, no doubt hoping to be sent on an errand that would buy him his next meal. Lucy caught his attention and waved him over.

He surveyed the shop door before obeying her summons.

"How would you like to earn a dime?" Lord forgive her for promising payment she didn't have, and taking still more from a family she owed so much. But she had no money of her own, and Daniel Clarke—the older cousin of Lucy's best friend, Biddie, and one of the volunteer staff at the charity home— would see the boy paid.

The boy's eyes widened at the amount she was offering. Then his expression turned cynical. "What do I got to do?"

"Go to The Davidsons' Home for Women and Children and ask Mr. Clarke to meet Lucy at Pete's Palace. Make it clear that he needs to come right away."

The boy's skepticism vanished at her mention of the charity home well known for its generosity. Still, she needed to be sure. "Do you know where that is?"

The kid's chest puffed. "'Course I do. I been there plenty of times."

No doubt he'd gone for the free meal The Home offered street children each Saturday along with a children's sermon given by the pastor of the Davidsons' church. She examined his eyes for honesty. "Then, you'll go and deliver my message? Mr. Clarke will pay you."

"Sure thing." The boy sprinted away.

As soon as he was out of sight, she hurried forward. Cutting through alleys and dodging behind passing carriages every time she spied a policeman meant it took much longer than usual to reach Pete's Palace, the brothel Mama worked in.

Normally, the former card dealer and friend of the David-sons, Fletcher Johnson, would escort her to visit Mama since he visited the hell on earth known as San Francisco's Barbary Coast each Sunday in search of desperate women wanting out of their miserable lives. For years now, he'd made it his mission to help such individuals escape and find respectable positions throughout the city and surrounding areas.

Fletcher's secret forgery skills provided false reference letters which opened the door to a new start for the childless women The Home didn't have room for. After how Mama had left things with the Davidsons, Fletcher was the only one willing to take Mama in, if she ever agreed to quit Pete's Palace and give up the opium.

Today, Lucy wouldn't give her a choice. Mama must leave San Francisco. How Lucy would get Mama to Fletcher's apartment in Sacramento when she had only a half dime in her pocket was a problem she'd solve later.

Lucy hesitated in the alley behind the establishment. She'd never come here without an escort. When Fletcher wasn't available, Henry Davidson or his nephew, Daniel Clarke, would accompany her. Now, she was alone.

She scanned up and down the narrow passage. No sign of Mr. Clarke. Nor any policeman. Just two men lingering near the far end, propped against a building and arguing in a way that betrayed their drunkenness despite the early hour.

Squaring her shoulders, she marched forward and carefully pushed through the back door. The long creak of its rusty hinges made her wince. She held her breath in the relative quiet that greeted her ears as her eyes adjusted to the dim lighting.

She stood in the corner of an L-shaped hall. Continuing straight would bring her into the main saloon. She turned left and crept up the stairs leading to the women's quarters.

Mama's door was second to last. Lucy slowly twisted the knob and inched the door open.

"Not now, Pete. I'm—"

Lucy threw the door wide, cutting off Mama's muffled protest.

Lucy whispered, "It's me, Mama." The ammonia-like stench of opium and the sweet smell of alcohol slapped Lucy in the face as she ducked inside and closed the door. Another breath brought the scent of men's cologne and hair grease mixed with tobacco and Mama's perfume.

"Who're you?" Mama's slurred words emerged from

beneath a stained patchwork quilt made of mismatched scraps. She swatted weakly at the covering until it revealed her wrinkled face and the tattered neckline of her chemise. At only thirty-nine years old, Mama had been aged by her hard life, making her look closer to forty-nine. "Lucy?"

Lucy moved to the edge of the bed, fatigue tempting her to sit but revulsion holding her back. "Yes, Mama. It's me. I need you to get up and dress. We have to go." Lucy reached for her hands, but Mama pulled away.

"Go? I don't want to go anywhere. I'm tired." She rolled over to face the wall. "Leave me alone, girl."

"It's not a good day for a visit."

Lucy jumped and whirled at Moira's voice. How had Pete's favorite prostitute come into the room and closed the door behind her without making a sound?

The curly-haired brunette nodded toward Mama. "She's worse than usual."

Lucy's shoulders sank. Moira was right. She'd never get Mama out of here without alerting Pete, who was certain to object to losing one of his "heifers." Not without help. She eyed Moira, who Mama sometimes referred to as a friend and sometimes with words Lucy wouldn't repeat. "Can I trust you?"

Moira cocked her hip and settled a hand on it. "Depends. What do you want?"

Lucy looked back at Mama, who'd begun snoring. Then turned back to Moira. "There's someone after me and Mama. They're going to be here any minute, and if I can't get her safely away, they're going to kill us both."

Moira blanched and shrank back. "Girl, what have you gotten yourself into?"

Images of the scene in Junior's suite burst through the mental box she'd shut them into. "I didn't mean to. I wanted to see Junior, but then I heard Mr. Green...and I saw...what they're planning..." Lucy swallowed a sob and dug her fingernails into her palms, forcing the memories away. "No. If I tell you, they might hurt you too."

Moira studied Lucy for a long moment, then looked at Mama for another heartbeat before straightening. "I'll help you, but you got to at least tell me who's coming. Is it this 'Junior' you mentioned? Doesn't Reginald Green Jr. manage that hotel you work at? Is that who's after you?"

Lucy clamped her lips shut. She'd said too much already.

Moira crossed her arms. "I can't keep a lookout if I don't know who I'm looking for, now, can I?"

The woman was right. Lucy needed to explain about the dandy since it had sounded as though he intended to hunt them down himself. "Very well, but you must not tell another soul."

Moira jerked her nod in agreement.

Lucy blew out a breath. "I'm not sure who he is. All I know is, he was dressed like a rich man and about this tall." Lucy held her hand about five inches above her head. "He was clean shaven, and his clothes were very stylish." The image of the man standing over Mrs. Prichard's body flashed through her mind, and she shuddered. "And he has a carved wooden cane with an engraved gold top."

"Like a dandy?"

"Exactly. And he seems to be working with Mr. Green and his son, Junior. At least, I think that's who's coming. I didn't actually see who was talking to Mr. Green."

Moira's brows rose and a smirk quirked her lips. "You were eavesdropping?"

"Not on purpose." Lucy lifted her chin. "Will you help me or not?"

"'Course I will." Moira left the room and returned with a ratty towel she'd tied into a sack. "You pack her things. I'll get her dressed."

Lucy took the makeshift bag and scanned the room for

anything Mama would want to take with her. She tossed in a hairbrush and a vial of perfume before passing by a half-empty bottle of whiskey and yanking open the lone drawer under the small table.

A picture of her and Mama lay at the bottom. A gasp caught in her throat. The image must have been taken before the day Lucy revealed the secret that ruined their lives, though she had no memory of posing for the picture. Which wasn't at all surprising considering she appeared two or three years old in the image.

Why hadn't Mama ever shown this to her? Lucy tucked the photograph into her hidden pocket.

Moira retrieved an indecent-looking dress from a peg on the wall. "Sit up now, Opal, and I'll help you put your clothes on."

Mama didn't budge and continued snoring.

Lucy set the bag down, grabbed Mama's shoulders, and lifted.

Mama wailed to stir the lifeless. "Let go of me!"

Lucy's heart leapt into her throat, and she released Mama, who slumped onto the bed.

"Oh! My head!" Mama whined like the toddler Lucy had appeared to be in the photograph. "You're killing me. Why do you hate me?"

"Shh! Mama, shh! You're going to bring Pete."

Footsteps thumped on the wooden stairs.

Lucy clapped her hands over her face. Would nothing go as planned?

Moira dropped the garment and spun for the door. "You calm her down and get her dressed. I'll stall Pete."

Lucy took a deep breath, snatched up the frilly fabric, and bent over her still-wailing mama. "Be quiet." Lucy employed the tone she'd used when she'd still lived at The Home and children younger than her had disobeyed. "Do you hear me? Stop it right now."

Mama's wails finally ceased.

Lucy thrust the garment in her face. "Now sit up and help me dress you."

Mama sat, but was so unsteady, Lucy wrapped her arm around Mama's shoulders and propped her against the wall.

The door flew open, and a red-faced Pete blocked the exit, his large muscles flexing as a vein bulged in his forehead. "What do you think you're doing in here?"

Moira's apologetic gaze caught Lucy's over his shoulder, then she disappeared.

Lord, help.

"I'm, um..."—Lucy tried to hide the dress behind her back—"visiting. As I usually do."

"It ain't Sunday. And I ain't given you permission to be up here." He stepped aside and flung an arm toward the hall. "Get out."

Trembling began in Lucy's limbs, but she raised her chin. "Not without my mama."

Pete's fists clenched. "What did you say?"

She swallowed back the bile and held her face calm, confident. "Mama's done here. She's coming with me."

He stomped forward, his right fist rearing back.

"Lucy?" Henry Davidson's shout rose from below. "Are you up there?" Again, footsteps pounded up the stairs.

Pete's eyes squeezed shut for a moment before his glower returned to her. "If you were anyone else, you'd be dead now. But seeing as you're a particular friend of Henry Davidson's, I'm going to give you one more chance to leave." His glare seared the air in her lungs. "And don't ever come back." He swung sideways, clearing her path to the door just as Mr. Davidson appeared in it.

KATHLEEN DENLY

Mr. Davidson's concerned gaze took in the room. "What's going on here?"

Pete spoke first. "Miss Arlidge was just finishing her *visit*. Isn't that right?" He shifted so that only Lucy could see his left hand clasping the handle of what was likely a large blade tucked into the front of his trousers. The message was clear. If she didn't leave immediately, her life was forfeit, and probably the life of Mr. Davidson's as well since the honorable gentleman would no doubt attempt to save her.

Lucy stared at the filthy wood floor. "That's right. I was just leaving." She gave Pete the widest berth she could manage as she headed out the door.

Mr. Davidson's brow furrowed as he glanced from Lucy to Pete and back. "Are you sure?"

"Yes." She slipped her hand into the crook of Mr. Davidson's arm and all but dragged him down the hall. "Let's go."

Once outside, Henry dug his heels in. "What was that all about? The boy you sent said it was urgent Daniel come."

Lucy latched onto the change in subject. "Where *is* Mr. Clarke? Why didn't he come?"

"He and Eliza and their children are still back East visiting his family in Boston. I thought you knew that."

Lucy almost slapped her forehead. She *had* learned that from her visit with Biddie last Sunday, but in all the chaos and fear of running for her life, she'd forgotten. "I'm so sorry to have bothered you."

Henry patted her hand on his arm and began leading her down the street toward his waiting carriage. "Helping you, my dear, is never a bother. But tell me, what prompted you to call on your mother today? It's Friday. Shouldn't you be at work?"

Lucy used the excuse of watching her step as she entered the conveyance to evade his gaze. "I've been dismissed."

"Whatever for?" He took the bench across from her, and the driver clicked the horses into motion.

20

Mr. Davidson's shock was mollifying, but her heart ached over her failure to rescue Mama. "I'd rather not talk about it just now, if that's all right." She needed to figure out what to do about Mama. Perhaps it would be easier to sneak in at night when the saloon was crowded and noises less noticeable.

"Of course." Mr. Davidson was silent for a moment, then a smile erased his pensive expression. "Today seems to be a day for surprises. I received your message minutes after dropping Fletcher and Katie Johnson at the wharf. They'd come to inform us that Katie is in the family way. After seven years of marriage, I believed they'd about lost hope." His sparkling eyes found hers. "Isn't that wonderful news?"

"Absolutely wonderful." Lucy returned his grin. The couple who risked so much to help women like Mama deserved every happiness life had to offer. Lucy peeked at her watch.

If anyone could get Mama out of Pete's Palace, Fletcher could. The afternoon ferry to Sacramento, where the Johnsons lived, wasn't due to leave for another three-quarters of an hour. If she sent a message with one of the boys from The Home as soon as they arrived, would it reach Fletcher before they boarded?

CHAPTER 3

JUNE 6, 1873
SAN FRANCISCO, CALIFORNIA

a gust of wind pushed at Lucy's back as she followed Henry Davidson up the steps to The Davidson's Home for Women and Children. The front door creaked as they stepped into the sanctuary for unwed mothers and their offspring.

After closing the door, Mr. Davidson hung his coat and hat on the rack in the foyer and adjusted the glasses perched on his nose. He glanced at the mirror on the wall, but, as usual, showed no concern for how his gray-speckled curly brown hair had been mussed by the wind. Warm, dappled sunlight filtered through the lace curtains covering the tall, skinny windows on either side of the front door, lending a sense of comfort to their surroundings. Memories, both bitter and sweet, assailed her as she followed him down the long narrow hallway lined with doors. The walls were adorned with once-elegant wallpaper, now faded by time, and the air held the faint aroma of wood polish and chalk dust.

SHOOT AT THE SUNSET

The first room they passed was filled with young children. The littlest ones sat at desks, diligently learning their letters under the watchful eye of a dedicated teacher, while the older students, probably aged eight through twelve, pored with wide-eyed curiosity over selections from the charity home's collection of books. Their youthful voices followed Lucy as she continued down the hallway.

Another open door on their left revealed a group of mothers, some of whom appeared to be as young as fourteen and others as old as their early thirties. These resilient women, their heads bent in concentration, were mastering the art of sewing, skillfully transforming simple cloth into garments that would support their futures.

As she and Mr. Davidson neared the stairwell, the clatter of pots and pans, the sizzle of food cooking, and the fragrant aroma of a shared meal being prepared wafted toward them from the open kitchen door. Lucy glimpsed a small group of women toiling together, their camaraderie evident in their weary smiles as they chattered.

Mr. Davidson stepped aside and waved for her to precede him up the stairs, but the flutter of clothing pinned across the line outside the kitchen window caught her eye. "Oh, yes. Today is laundry." She smiled. After one of the children had spilled soup on Lucy's brown dress the prior Sunday, the child's mother had insisted that Lucy leave the garment for her to launder. It was the perfect excuse she needed to seek out one of the street children on the back porch. Surely, one would be willing to run for the wharf with her message for Fletcher. Plus, she could change out of her maid's dress.

Rather than taking the first step up the stairs as Mr. Davidson indicated, Lucy moved around him. "I nearly forgot that I left my dress here, last week. I hope you don't mind if I take a moment to change." She gestured to the inevitable grime that clung to the hem of her skirts after any walk through the city, but which was always worse after a visit to the Barbary.

"Of course not." Mr. Davidson's gaze drifted to the women in the kitchen, and his stomach grumbled. His cheeks flushed. "I'm afraid I was in such a rush, I missed the noon meal. Waiting will give me a chance to see if there's anything to spare before the evening meal."

Another twinge of guilt pinched at Lucy as she dashed for the back yard. No doubt rushing in response to her request for an escort was at least partly to blame for the dear man's empty stomach.

As expected, a small group of lads lingered in the packed-dirt clearing behind the building. Three were skipping a length of rope at the far end, while two sat near the back door with a scrap of brown packing paper and a pencil they shared between them as they practiced their letters. The rest were absorbed in a game of jacks under the clothesline.

Lucy knelt beside the two studious boys. "May I have a corner of your paper and borrow your pencil for a moment?" They hesitated, so she offered, "I'll bring you a roll after the evening meal, and I promise to give the pencil right back." The bigger of the two boys tore a piece from their paper and held up their pencil.

In as few words as possible, Lucy begged Fletcher to go to Pete's Palace and do whatever it took to get Mama out of there. Without revealing details that could expose Fletcher to more peril than she was already placing him in with this request, she stressed the urgency of the situation and promised to explain soon. Though she had no idea when that would be.

She started to hand the pencil back to the boy who'd loaned it to her when she remembered to add that Fletcher must not tell the Davidsons about her plea because doing so would put them in danger. Finally, she signed her name and returned the pencil.

Lucy strode to where the tallest boy with the longest legs squatted beside the jacks game. "Could I convince you to run a note to Fletcher Johnson for me? It's very important, and he's bound to board a ferry for Sacramento at any moment. There's not a second to spare."

The lad rose and calmly appraised her. "What's in it for me?"

"I'll bring you my helping of tonight's meal." Her empty stomach protested the promise, but she didn't have much to barter with, and she refused to take any more of the Davidsons' money.

The boy sniffed, unimpressed.

Sweat beaded on Lucy's brow. "And I'll make sure Biddie saves you a slice of her next cake." Surely, Biddie wouldn't mind.

The boy's somber expression broke with triumph. "Done."

Lucy shoved the note toward him, and he took it before disappearing from the yard in a blur of gangly arms and legs.

Lord, please let him reach the Johnsons in time.

Only a moment's scanning was required to locate Lucy's dress on the laundry line. She pulled it free and hurried inside to change. Escaping the last of her maid's uniform felt as if she were one step closer to evading the Greens and the evil man working with them. She stepped out of the women's bedroom she'd borrowed and into a hallway that ran parallel with the back of the building. Following the sound of Mr. Davidson's voice, she made her way back to the kitchen.

He sat in a simple wooden chair, an empty plate on the table beside him and a babe in one arm as he kneaded dough with his free hand. The unoccupied infant sling hanging from the woman slicing onions nearby identified the mother. No doubt she relished the break from carrying the weight.

In any other home, the sight of a gentleman entering a kitchen would be surprising. For one to be caring for an infant and aiding with meal preparations? Downright shocking. But here, it was part of everyday life. Everyone gladly pitched in however they could to make life better for themselves and those around them.

Regardless of Mama's failure to appreciate the blessings offered within these walls, and despite the challenging circumstances the women here faced, this was a place that teemed with life and hope. A knot formed in Lucy's stomach. What would become of the people here once Mr. Green's true nature was revealed and his businesses collapsed as Junior had predicted?

Though of no blood relation, Henry and Cecilia Davidson had long treated Lucy as though she were their daughter. But could such a love withstand so much loss? Or would the only family she had left reject her as Mama had?

Lucy's steps faltered in the doorway. Of course, they'd reject her. How could they not, once she'd confessed how she'd betrayed them by sticking her foolish nose into business matters she didn't understand? And what would they do with the information that Mr. Green was a fraud and possibly a murderer? With what little she'd heard, she couldn't be sure who had actually killed Mrs. Prichard. None of the three men had shown any remorse for the loss of life.

Unlike Mr. Davidson, who'd held a funeral after a neighbor boy's dog had been struck by a racing wagon. Lucy's breath caught. If she revealed the secrets she carried, Mr. Davidson, in his quiet but firm manner, would confront Mr. Green with the accusations. Naturally, he would. He couldn't simply take her word on the matter. Even if he did, he'd no doubt try to reclaim his money. And then...

The room spun, and Lucy reached for the wall as Mrs. Prichard's lifeless body flashed in her mind again. Those evil men would go to any length to keep their secrets.

Mr. Davidson surged to his feet and rushed to place a

steadying hand on her shoulder. "Are you all right?" The babe in his other arm squirmed.

Lucy sucked in a deep breath and straightened. "Yes, thank you. Just a bit tired." She couldn't tell the Davidsons. No amount of money would save the charity home if Henry and Cecilia were dead. Besides, Lucy loved them too much to let them sacrifice their lives to save The Home.

Thoughts clearing, she realized she also couldn't stay here. The Greens would know to look for her at The Home. And again, the Davidsons would risk their lives to protect her. Had she placed them in danger simply by coming here? She needed to leave. Where could she go that might be safe? It didn't matter. Her only chance of evading the Greens and that dandy without endangering the Davidsons lay in fleeing the city and going somewhere they'd never expect to find her.

Her heart cracked as she paced toward the back door. How could she leave without saying goodbye to Biddie? Yet one look at Lucy would be all it took for her dearest friend to know something was wrong. And Biddie was nothing if not persuasive. She'd wheedle the truth out of Lucy before she knew what she was saying. She couldn't risk it. "I'm sorry. I forgot there was something I needed to do."

Mr. Davidson frowned as he returned the child to the woman with a sling. "Surely, whatever it is can wait until you've said hello to Biddie. She should have returned from her meeting with Mr. Green by now. I would think you'd be as eager as her mother and I are to learn how it went."

Lucy's knees wobbled. How could she have forgotten today was the day Biddie had arranged to meet with Mr. Green in hopes of securing his investment in her new bakery? Mr. Green knew she and Lucy were close friends. What if he'd kidnapped Biddie in an effort to catch Lucy, as he'd threatened to do to Mama?

Lucy dashed for the stairs and took them two at a time, Mr.

KATHLEEN DENLY

Davidson following. She sprinted toward the family's private upstairs sitting room and skidded to a halt in the doorway.

Inside, Cecilia Davidson sat in one of the four chairs flanking the embroidered screen that hid the empty fireplace. The older woman's hand rested on Biddie's shoulder, their matching sunshine curls glowing in the soft light filtering through two windows on the opposite wall.

Lucy exhaled. Biddie was safe.

Biddie must have heard Lucy's hasty entry because she looked up, revealing wet cheeks and blue eyes shimmering with tears.

Lucy rushed to her friend's side. "My goodness, what's wrong?" Possibilities too horrendous to contemplate tortured Lucy's mind.

From the doorway, Mr. Davidson looked to his wife. "What's happened?"

Mrs. Davidson took a sheet of paper from her daughter's trembling hands and passed it to him. "Virginia Baker has written."

Lucy gasped at the mention of Biddie's older sister who'd been missing for eighteen years. "Your big sister?" Lucy wrapped an arm around Biddie's shoulders, fighting back her own tears now that she understood her friend's distress had nothing to do with the Greens.

Biddie nodded, still silently crying.

Her response didn't make sense. "But that's good news, isn't it? Why are you crying?"

Mrs. Davidson answered for her. "Oliver has passed away."

"Oh." So Biddie's birth father, who'd left in the middle of the night when Biddie was four, taking her older brother and sister with him, was dead. Lucy looked from Cecilia to Biddie, waiting for someone to explain why this was bad news. From what little Biddie had shared, Oliver had been violent and cruel. As girls, she and Biddie had bonded over their evil pas

28

and agreed Henry Davidson was the only father figure they needed.

So why was Biddie crying? If Lucy had received news that her own vile father was dead, she'd be dancing a jig. She still didn't understand why God would allow such a man to go on with his life as if beating Mama and leaving her for dead while Lucy huddled in the corner didn't matter. Where was God's justice in that?

Biddie wiped the tears away and drew long breaths, obviously trying to calm herself.

"Campo..." Mr. Davidson adjusted his glasses. "That's that new settlement down by San Diego. The one they're calling Little Texas. Not much of a town yet. The Gaskill brothers have a blacksmith shop and a store that doubles as a post office. Other than a bunch of homesteads, that's about all there is, as I recall."

Mrs. Davidson nodded and returned to her usual *Bergère* chair. "I knew it sounded familiar. Can you believe she's in California? It could have been so much farther."

A meaningful look passed between husband and wife.

"That will make things easier." He handed the letter back to Biddie, then took the blue wingback chair beside Mrs. Davidson.

Biddie straightened. "Then you'll help her?"

Mrs. Davidson's eyes widened. "Well, of course. She's your sister."

"And beside that,"—Mr. Davidson covered his wife's hand with his—"we promised Poppy."

Of course, they'd made a promise to Biddie's mama before she died. It was precisely the sort of thing these generous people would do.

"That's right." Mrs. Davidson turned her hand over to twine her fingers with her husband's. "We promised your mama that if your siblings ever returned or ever needed anything, we'd do whatever we could to help them."

Biddie sagged against her chair. "Thank you."

Mr. Davidson ran the fingers of his free hand through his hair. "Of course, I'll need to verify this letter is actually from your sister before I can send any funds."

Lucy gave Biddie a quick squeeze before moving to the seat beside her. "How will you do that?"

"It's too bad Richard and Daniel are both back east." Father looked at Mother. "They're so well connected in the San Diego region, it would have been easy for them to ask around."

It took Lucy a moment to recall that Richard Stevens was a childhood friend of Daniel Clarke's and that the man now lived with his family on a ranch west of San Diego.

Mrs. Davidson tipped her head. "What about Mr. Thompson? He knows just about everyone in that county, doesn't he?"

Lucy recognized the name of the San Diego businessman who'd visited The Home on a handful of occasions during trips to check on his San Francisco investments.

Mr. Davidson chuckled. "He'd like to think so, but it's a pretty big county. He can't possibly know everyone. Still, he'd be a good person to ask." He nodded. "I'll send him a letter first thing in the morning."

Biddie shot to her feet. "But sending letters will take weeks! Ginny needs help now."

Mrs. Davidson's expression softened. "Now, I know you're worried, but it would be irresponsible of your father to send the money without looking into things first."

Biddie lifted the now-crumpled paper. "But I know this is Ginny." The earnestness in her tone tugged at Lucy's heart.

Mr. Davidson cleared his throat. "Even so, I—"

"I want to go. I want to see her." Biddie's sudden declaration didn't surprise Lucy. Not after so many nights spent imagining where her siblings might have gone and what adventures they might have had. Of course, Biddie wanted to see her sister and not just send money. No doubt, Lucy's big-hearted friend wanted to see for herself that Virginia was safe and healthy. Not to mention, ask a million and one questions about where the woman had been the last eighteen years. For that matter, how did she know where to find Biddie? And why had she waited so long to contact her? Indignation on behalf of her friend filled Lucy's chest.

Mrs. Davidson smirked at Mr. Davidson. "You see?"

He sighed. "Yes, you were right."

Biddie clasped her hands together, squeezing her fingers. "Right about what?"

Mr. Davidson smiled at his daughter. "Your mother predicted you'd want to visit your brother and sister if they ever contacted you." He patted his wife's hand. "And as usual, she was right."

Mrs. Davidson pressed a quick kiss to her husband's cheek as Lucy's mind began to buzz with a new thought. Traveling to the wild deserts that bordered Mexico was the sort of move the Greens would never expect Lucy to make. Could this be her chance to escape?

Biddie's gaze flittered from one parent to the other. "Does that mean I can go?"

Mr. Davidson sighed again. "Yes, but I'm coming with you."

Lucy hugged herself. Surely, Biddie would want Lucy's emotional support for such a momentous event. Before she could talk herself out of it, she forced out the words, "And me?"

Biddie's mouth fell open. Then she grinned. "Yes." She bounced on her toes. "Please, may Lucy come?"

Mrs. Davidson frowned. "What about your position?"

Biddie stilled. "Oh, right. What *are* you doing here on a Friday?"

Lucy's cheeks pinked, and she stared at the faded rug. "I um...lost my position today."

"What? Why?"

Lucy shook her head, unable to meet anyone's gaze. "I'd rather not talk about it, if that's all right." She peeked at Biddie. "But maybe…"

Biddie tipped her head. "What?"

"Maybe there's something of God's hand in the timing?" The words that had made sense in her heart sounded foolish once spoken. She shook her head. "But that's silly. I just—"

"No, it isn't silly." Biddie grasped Lucy's hand in a firm squeeze. "That's exactly right. Because now you're free to come with me." She turned back to her parents. "She can come, can't she?"

Mrs. Davidson's smile was wistful. "I agree. This does seem to be God's timing, because I'm afraid I can't go with you."

"Why not?" Biddie pressed a hand against her middle.

"Well, with everyone else gone, who will watch over things here at The Home?"

Lucy tensed. Ordinarily, the Davidsons timed their trips so that Biddie's cousins, Eliza and Daniel Clarke, were around to oversee The Home. But the Clarkes wouldn't return from the East for another month. Would Biddie delay the trip until her mother could join them? Waiting wasn't an option for Lucy. If Biddie delayed, she'd need to find another way out of the city and somewhere else to go.

Biddie bit her lip as she considered her father. "But you'll still come?"

Mr. Davidson's eyebrows rose. "You think I'd let you go without me?"

As the others began making plans for their immediate departure, Lucy slowly released the breath she'd been holding. This was going to work. By nightfall, she'd be out of the city. But would she be out of the Greens' reach? And what about Mama?

CHAPTER 4

NOVEMBER 1, 1873
SCRANTON, PENNSYLVANIA

Preston Baker strode across the makeshift wooden stage bathed in the warm glow of the setting sun. His boots echoed on the worn boards as he twirled his custom matching pistols, their barrels catching the last rays of sunlight. The traveling variety show's hanging backdrop, a tapestry of faded colors, rippled gently in the evening breeze. The scent of popcorn and sawdust wafted through the air, and a hum of anticipation swirled among the crowd as he stopped at the end of the stage and pivoted to face his targets—two playing cards. Each one was held between the forefingers and thumbs of the show's bravest stagehand so that the skinny sides of the cards faced Preston.

When Preston had first added this trick to his act, Harvey insisted that having a young woman holding the cards would draw a bigger crowd. Preston told him that if he wanted a woman to hold the cards, Harvey could do the shooting because Preston wouldn't. When Harvey, redder than a tomato, had threatened to do that, Preston nearly quit the show. Thankfully, Harvey backed down and agreed to let Alvin, a petite man of twenty-four whose baby face made him look twelve, hold the cards.

The man had a knack for acting, and each night, Alvin sat in the audience until Preston asked for a volunteer. Of course, Preston always chose Alvin from the few brave hands that rose. The man would act as if he hadn't meant to volunteer but merely scratch his head. Preston would pretend to persuade him to come on stage, anyway, and Alvin would convince the audience that a scared and trembling boy had accidentally found himself in a seemingly dangerous situation.

Now, the crowd hushed in collective awe as Preston raised his pistols, their metal twinkling like twin stars in the flickering light cast by the lanterns lining the front edge of the stage. Only the rustle of leaves in the nearby trees, the quiet snort of waiting horses, and the creak of wooden benches as people leaned forward in anticipation broke the near silence. Pretending to adjust his aim, Preston stretched their suspense a smidge longer.

He loved this moment—the pregnant pause before the shot, the collective held breath. Whatever troubles these people had at home, whatever sacrifice they'd made to buy tickets for the show, none of it mattered. For the people in the audience, the worries of the world were gone. With their eyes fixed on him, the crowd thought only of what he was about to do. They felt only curiosity, excitement, and hope. It was his gift and why he loved this job. He couldn't stop the evil in this world—heaven knew he'd tried—but at least for these few seconds, he could make this crowd of people forget the bad in their lives and feel hope again.

But that time was up.

Preston pulled both triggers at the same time. The sharp crack of the pistols shattered the stillness, echoing through the open air. The crowd gasped, and time suspended until the unmistakable sight of two card halves fluttering to the stage boards and Alvin staring at his hands as though stunned he hadn't been shot broke the spell. The audience erupted into cheers and exclamations of amazement. Several people jumped to their feet, still clapping. A few men tossed their hats into the air with loud whoops.

As the audience's delight washed over him, Preston's grin widened. He'd turned the skills honed by bringing death and horror with Berdan's regiment of sharpshooters into something that shone a bit of light into this dark world. He holstered his pistols and acknowledged the applause with a nod and a wink before grabbing his Sharps rifle and striding off stage to make room for the next act. The cheering continued as he crossed the encampment toward the performers' tent, until the master of ceremonies convinced the crowd to quiet down.

Scrapper, the nine-year-old boy responsible for passing out the performers' mail, stood in the tent's opening, waving something small and white. He grinned as Preston reached him. "You got a letter."

Preston's neck tightened as he accepted the envelope. It had to be from Ginny, Preston's big sister. She was the only one who knew or cared enough to write. He hadn't heard from her in months. He hoped nothing was wrong. Nothing more than the usual, anyway.

Seconds later, his shaking fingers made it impossible to read Ginny's hastily written words, and he fell onto the chair beside his cot in the performers' tent. The loud cheers of the audience faded to a distant hum. Could it be true? He ripped his thoughts from the letter's contents and focused inward.

Like settling into a well-worn saddle, he slid into the controlled breathing pattern he used before taking any long-range shot. The slow, steady cadence was at odds with the rhythm of his life, but it never failed to calm his nerves and hone his focus—two of the traits that had kept him alive through nearly four years of war. So why wasn't the habit helping now?

"Something wrong?" Scrapper crossed his arms.

Preston startled, having forgotten the kid was still there. He wasn't much taller than the steamer trunk that stood on end beside him. Had Preston been as small as Scrapper the day he'd last seen his mother and younger sister? Preston had been the same age.

What would the kid do if someone woke him in the middle of the night and ordered him to secretly abandon the troupe? Preston couldn't imagine the imp slinking off without a fight. Yet that was what Preston had done. He'd abandoned his mother and little sister without so much as crying out in protest. But that betrayal was nothing to what he'd done six years later.

Preston shoved down the memories and pulled a peppermint from his pocket. He unwrapped it and held it up, pinched between his thumb and forefinger, the way Alvin held the cards.

Scrapper grinned and stepped back with a nod.

Preston took another steadying breath, then tossed the candy high.

As the peppermint fell, the boy adjusted his position and caught the treat between his teeth. He flashed another grin at Preston, showing off his success before closing his lips over the sweet.

Instead of thanking Preston and leaving as usual, the kid lingered, his brows pinched over a frown as he sucked at the candy bulging his cheek. "Your sister ain't sick, is she?"

Preston grimaced. Few members of this ragtag group of misfits forming Harvey Arbuckle's Show of Wonders had anyone in the world to miss them, and even fewer who could afford the

SHOOT AT THE SUNSET

cost of postage. Still, most folks understood that sticking their nose into someone else's personal business was an invitation for the same to be done to them, so they kept their questions to themselves. Scrapper was different. Too young and kind-hearted to have anything to hide, he let his questions fly faster than the blades in their troupe's knife-throwing act. Which was why he was the only one who knew Preston had any family at all.

He scuffed his boot against the packed-dirt floor. "No, she ain't sick." But had Ginny been injured? He reread her letter. She'd written only that bandits had attacked the ranch, their father, Oliver Baker, was dead, and she needed Preston's help. Not a word about her own condition.

Scrapper's posture relaxed and he pulled out his greatest treasure—a bag of marbles. "Want to play?"

Preston shook his head as he read Ginny's missive a third time. Did he dare hope their pa, Oliver, was truly gone? Or was this another of the selfish man's cruel tricks? Preston rested his free hand on the pistol at his waist. Could Oliver have intercepted one of the letters that Preston had been secretly sending through Ginny's neighbor and forced her to write a false report?

Preston raked a hand through his hair.

No. Ginny was tougher than that. Smarter. If Oliver had tried such a thing, she'd have found a way to let Preston know. Yet he could find no hidden message in the few words on the page.

Still, he'd need to be careful. If it was a trap, he had no intention of being caught. Neither would he ignore Ginny's request. If the letter were true, writing it had cost his proud sister dearly. Things must be far worse than she was letting on. And the letter was dated almost six months ago. His belly churned. He should have given Ginny a better idea of how to reach him. But he didn't always know what town they were headed to next with the way Harvey was always changing their schedule.

He needed to go to her. Now. Even if the idea of facing her and all the memories that came with her left him feeling as if he'd downed a bucket of the slop Scrapper fed the dancing pig.

The thumping of the kid's marbles against the packed-dirt floor of their temporary living quarters brought Preston back to the present.

"Sorry, kid. I've got to see Harvey."

Without waiting for Scrapper's reply, Preston left the performers' tent and strode past the crowd that was now gasping as two jugglers tossed lit torches over a third juggler's head. The pungent scent of burning kerosene wafted toward him as he strode toward Harvey's private tents.

Two men near the back of the audience spotted Preston and shifted his way. Their hands twitched over the empty holsters at their hips. Thank goodness, the show had a strict policy against audience members bringing weapons past the ticket booth. Having to watch his back on the streets was bad enough. Too many men sought to impress their female companions by attempting to outdraw Preston or challenging him to a shooting contest. Thankfully, most weren't as rash as to demand a duel, but the confrontations often drew crowds too feather-headed to remain out of harm's way. And few would-be quick-draws or sharpshooters accepted no as an answer.

Preston kept his eyes locked on the show owner's office but pretended to adjust his coat—enough to flash a glimpse of his pistols, still in their holsters. The men turned back to the performance as Preston pushed through Harvey's tent flaps.

"I'm leaving."

Harvey didn't bother looking up from the stack of papers on his desk. He spoke around the cigar hanging from a corner of his mouth. "Fine, fine. Just stay out of trouble and be back by—"

"No. I mean, I'm *leaving*." Preston waited for his employer's eyes to meet his. "The show."

Harvey took the cigar from his mouth. "If this is about that man you punched for slugging his wife, I took care of that. You don't have to worry."

"I know, and I'm grateful, but I can't stay. I—"

"So, it's about top billing again. I thought you underst—"

"No, it ain't about that either. It's about my sister."

The man's bushy brows merged into one long gray caterpillar. "What sister? I haven't ever heard you talk about no sister."

"Don't matter. Fact is, I've got one and she needs me. So I'm going."

"Aren't you from California? That where your sister's at?"

"Yes."

"Then you'll be gone for weeks, maybe months." Harvey stabbed his cigar onto the scarred surface of his desk. "You leave now, I'll be in a bind. We've still got two weeks of shows here. Then we're on to Chicago. I've got posters up with you as our second act and tickets already sold."

"I know and I'm sorry." Preston hated everything about this conversation. He'd much rather stay with the show and people he trusted—or if not trusted, at least he understood them. He'd never understood his sister. But he loved her. And he owed her.

Since the war, Preston had been part of almost a dozen shows that had started and failed. This was the first to persist more than a handful of months. He'd finally found success, traveling with Harvey's show for the past three years. Last year, Harvey gave him second billing, and people began to recognize Preston if the troupe stayed more than a couple weeks in a town. Which was both good and bad. But the promotion meant Preston had begun making enough money to put some aside for his future. Returning to California would eat up every penny he'd saved. Still, he couldn't hesitate. His sister would come to his aid if he needed it. Truth was, she'd already done more for him than he could ever repay, even without the weight of his betrayal tipping the scales.

"I can't show up without a sharpshooter." Harvey jabbed a finger toward the ticket booth. "Folks pay for the whole show. I'll have to replace you."

"I know you'll try." Preston winked, then sobered. He opened his mouth to reassure Harvey that he'd be back as soon as he'd taken care of Ginny, but the truth was, he had no idea how long Ginny would need his help. If she was horribly injured, he may never be able to return. The thought clenched his gut. "I really am sorry. But I've still got to go."

He only hoped he wasn't too late.

CHAPTER 5

NOVEMBER 18, 1873
LUPINE VALLEY RANCH, CALIFORNIA

*P*reston rode up the southern side of the desert mountain following a narrow trail through rocks, cacti, and shrubs as the first light of dawn broke over the eastern horizon. He reined his mount to a stop just shy of the crest—suddenly trembling. How could the thought of seeing Oliver still make him shake worse than staring down an entire company of Rebels?

Preston clenched his teeth. He was being a coward.

Last night, he'd been asking the tight-lipped Campo store owner about the exact location of Ginny's ranch when Clyve Rowland—Ginny's neighbor and the man who'd been smuggling Preston's letters to his sister for years—stepped inside. He recognized Preston's custom engraved, matching holsters from the drawing Preston had included in one of his letters and guessed Preston's identity.

Since it was late, Clyve had invited Preston to stay the night at the Rowland Ranch rather than risk alarming Ginny by arriving after dark. The man then grimly confirmed the details of Ginny's letter—adding that the bandits had burned the entire place to the ground. He'd insisted Ginny was the only survivor.

Still, Preston couldn't stop the chill in his core.

He slid from his horse and left the animal tied to a large juniper bush. Silently calling himself every kind of weakling, he crept up a section of sloped rock spread like rumpled flooring on one side of the trail. He made his way toward a large cluster of boulders on the crest and peeked around the largest hunk of sandstone. In the valley below, pale streaks of early-morning sunlight washed over two buildings, a corral with horses, and a larger corral with milling cattle.

The fluttering skirts of a woman dashing toward the herd caught his attention. *Ginny?* With her back to him, he couldn't be sure.

Clyve had claimed that Preston's little sister, Biddie, and her friend, Lucy, were also at the ranch after arriving last June and refusing to leave Ginny until Preston arrived. The rancher had made a point of informing Preston that Lucy and Clyve were courting. He'd gone on at length about the woman's tireless work, deep loyalty, and quiet beauty. Not that Preston cared. With any luck, he'd help Ginny get back on her feet and be out of here in less than six months.

The woman below reached the corral and faced the herd for a few seconds. Then, as though she'd sensed his gaze, she spun south and searched the valley's rim.

Biddie. It had to be. Clyve had described Lucy as having dark hair, while the woman staring up at him had hair to match the morning sunshine. And she wasn't Ginny. Even in a hurry, this woman's movements were too graceful and feminine.

Last night, he'd dismissed Clyve's claim that Biddie had decided to live on the ranch. The notion hadn't made sense. Why would Biddie give up her fancy life in San Francisco? But, though the distance was too great to make out her features, his gut told him the fully grown woman in the valley below was, indeed, his little sister.

Preston shifted to stand behind the boulder, his heart pounding. Tears pricked at the backs of his eyes. She must be furious with the way he'd abandoned her and Mama all those years ago. What could he say when she confronted him?

He'd already been nervous to see Ginny after all these years and the way he'd left her. Facing Biddie as well was too much.

Preston charged down the rock-covered slope to his horse, mounted, and galloped away. He needed time to think.

~

*P*reston spent several hours riding in circles through the miserable desert before he accepted the truth—there were no good words to explain his actions. His choices were to turn around and return to the show as though he'd never received Ginny's letter, or he could behave like a man instead of a child and face the consequences of his decisions.

Preston refused to continue acting the coward.

He rode his horse back to the same bush he'd tied it to that morning and dismounted. He needed one more look to confirm Oliver hadn't still been asleep in the house that morning. If history proved true, their pa would have roused by now and should be making enough nuisance of himself to be heard miles away.

Preston reached the crest and surveyed the mountain valley. Near the barn, two women—one brunette, one blonde—spoke with a man. He must be the cook, Gideon, that Clyve had mentioned was helping the women rebuild. The man strode up the western slope to where another blond woman moved between the shrubs.

Preston took another look at the two still near the buildings. The blonde wore trousers. *Ginny.*

Preston grinned, his shoulders relaxing. Oliver would never allow his daughter to wear men's clothes. He must actually be dead.

Time to get his horse and make his presence known. He started to turn.

"Stop where you are, or I'll shoot." Ginny's shout, barely discernable at this distance, froze Preston in his tracks.

No time for his mount. Preston raised his hands well above his head and began inching his way down the slope toward his rifle-wielding sister. He adopted a playful tone that hopefully would help his sister recognize his voice. "Ah, Ginny, put the gun down. You know you ain't gonna shoot me."

In a blink, Ginny dropped her weapon and sprinted toward him with a joyous squeal.

Warmth filled his heart as he lunged down the hill to meet her. Wrapping his arms around his big sister, he lifted her off her feet and spun her in a circle. Her laughter echoed off the valley. Oh, how he had missed her.

When he set her back down, Ginny smacked him on the shoulder. "About time you showed up." Though her tone was teasing, even after all these years, he sensed the unspoken hurt his delay had caused.

He grimaced. "It took a while for your letter to find me. I came as soon as I received it. I'm sorry—"

"Never mind that." Ginny waved off his apology and gestured for him to follow her back toward the small cluster of buildings. "Tell me how you've been. Are you still with Harvey Arbuckle's show?" She rubbed her palm back and forth across his beard. "And what's with the scruff?"

Preston laughed. "It's part of my act."

"So the fur helps you shoot straighter?" Mirth sparked in Ginny's eyes.

"Harvey says people want to see a 'real western man,' and apparently, western men have beards." It was one of the more annoying aspects of his performance, but he put up with it.

Ginny smirked. "He has a point. Most men around these parts are too busy working to fuss with shaving." She tousled the fringe on the shoulder of his leather jacket. "I ain't seen none of them wearing such nonsense as this, though." She eyed the matching leather vest and pants, also trimmed with fringe. "You look more like one of them silly city women."

Preston flung his head back with a belly laugh. "You ain't changed one bit. Still shooting straight and fast."

"And why would I?" Ginny sniffed and lifted her chin. "Truth's truth no matter how you dress it up."

Preston opened his mouth to reply, but the sight of the scorched earth surrounding the new structures erased every thought from his head. Sobering, he noted the wide, flat-topped mound at the edge of the broad valley. A lopsided cross of twined-together branches marked it as a grave, though the raised dirt seemed bigger than any one man would require. Clearly, Clyve had been correct in the attack details—as few as he'd known. He'd said Ginny refused to talk about the event.

Preston stopped and studied his sister. "Ginny, what happened here? In your letter, you didn't say—"

"Because there wasn't anything worth saying." She kept walking, forcing him to catch up. "That storm's come and gone. Better to move on and be ready for the next one."

The swish of approaching skirts on his left drew Preston's attention from his stubborn big sister to his younger sister. While Ginny continued on, he stopped and swallowed hard. "Hey there, Biddie."

"It's good to see you." Her grin wavered. "How've you been?"

"Well enough." He should ask Biddie how she'd been. It was the polite thing to do. But what if her answer was less than happy? What if the seemingly wonderful family he'd seen her with in San Francisco had grown mean after he left?

He considered the man who'd trailed Biddie down the valley and waited several steps behind her. "You must be Gideon."

"I am." The man closed the distance between them and offered a hand to shake. "And you're Preston. Glad you could make it. Perfect timing, in fact. I was just preparing to leave and hated the thought of these three being on their own."

Preston's browse rose. "You're leaving?"

The man's expression hardened. "A long story, but trust me, it's for the best."

Preston caught the glance Gideon flickered at Biddie, laced with pain and longing. So the man had romantic feelings for Preston's little sister. A sentiment that must not have been returned if Gideon was leaving. Respect filled Preston for how the man was handling the situation. He held Gideon's gaze. "I understand."

Biddie huffed and her cheeks pinked. "I'm going to see what I have to make you a welcome home meal. I think I still have some dried apple slices." Her brows pinched as she asked, "Is apple pie still your favorite?"

Preston grinned. "Sounds great."

"Good." She hurried away, disappearing into the house a moment later.

Preston glanced to where the petite brunette poured water into a large pot hanging over a fire burning low in the center of the clearing between the house and what looked to be a barn. Ginny grabbed a thick branch and added it to the dying flames. Preston considered Gideon, whose gaze was still fixed on the closed front door of the house. "Should we go help them?"

With a jerk of his head, Gideon strode forward, and they continued to the yard together.

The woman, who must be the Lucy whom Clyve had

46

spoken so highly of, straightened from stirring the pot as they approached. Her wide brown eyes appeared to take him in from head to toe. He recognized the spark of interest in their depths as he offered his hand. "I'm Preston"—he winked as she accepted his hand—"and you can only be the famously beautiful Lucy." Her face reddened as a zing passed between their palms. His grip tightened a hair. She truly was breathtaking.

She tugged her hand free with a stiff smile. "Nice to meet you. Welcome to Lupine Valley Ranch." The formal welcome was barely complete before she pivoted and lifted a cutting board from a large nearby rock. She sat on the stone, placed the board on her lap, and began chopping carrots as though he weren't there.

Right. Lucy was also taken.

His gut sank. How long had Clyve said they'd been courting? Two weeks? Three? If only Preston had received Ginny's letter sooner. Perhaps...but no. What was he thinking? His unsettled life was no good for wives and families. Not to mention, he was far from husband material.

Best to ignore the strange sensation that had occurred with their touch. Though he'd never experienced quite the same thing with any other woman, that was likely because most women wore gloves in public. He'd had no reason to make skin-to-skin contact. This feeling, whatever it was, would fade away just as past moments of attraction had.

Gideon clapped him on the shoulder and murmured, "Don't take it personally. Lucy's a quiet one, especially around people she doesn't know. She'll warm up with time."

CHAPTER 6

*L*ucy pulled a clothespin from her lips and clamped it onto the laundry line, securing her spare work skirt against the strong winter winds. She peered up at the golden afternoon sun trying its best to warm her between the chilly gusts. Never would she have guessed the desert could be so cold. Then again, before fleeing San Francisco seven months ago and traveling with Biddie to this remote desert mountain valley, Lucy hadn't known a thing about deserts beyond their reputation for being hot. She could now add dirty, miserable, and dangerous to the list of words she'd use to describe this place.

Another gust pelted sand against her cheek, and she turned her back to the wind, her cheeks stinging as she pinned a bodice to the line. At least this storm wasn't as bad as the one last summer that had sent her, Biddie, and Ginny running for shelter within the boulder cave that Biddie's big sister had been calling home when Lucy and Biddie arrived last June. Though

Ginny's hair was barely a shade darker than Biddie's sunshine locks, the relentless sand had turned everyone's hair the color of brown sugar.

Frowning at the memories, Lucy bent to snatch a pair of Ginny's trousers from the basket at her feet. If this wind didn't relent, there'd be almost as much dirt stuck to the laundry after washing as there had been before she'd started at the break of dawn. She missed the cleanliness of the laundry rooms at the Green Hotel.

Ginny's letter to Biddie had failed to mention there was nothing left of the ranch buildings but ashes. Nor had the tight-lipped woman revealed that every man on the property had been murdered in an attack by bandits who'd also stolen the ranch's cattle.

Ginny had been the lone survivor. A miracle she'd yet to explain.

Biddie's original plan had been to deliver the requested loan money, spend a few days getting answers from her sister, and then return to San Francisco—a return trip Lucy hadn't planned on joining. But after Mr. Davidson's leg was broken in a terrible wagon accident before they reached Ginny, he was sent to recuperate at the home of dear family friends, Mr. and Mrs. Stevens. Meanwhile, Biddie and Lucy continued their journey in the company of the kind married man who'd rescued them. As soon as Lucy had seen the state of Ginny's Lupine Valley Ranch, her worries about explaining her refusal to return to San Francisco vanished. There was no chance that her dear, stubbornly generous friend would leave her big sister alone under such conditions.

True to form, Biddie insisted on remaining to help rebuild —against Ginny's protests. Just as Gideon Swift—Biddie's fiancé now—had chosen to stay.

The golden-haired, brown-eyed Texas rancher had come to Lupine Valley Ranch expecting to work as a cook for Oliver

Baker and the other ranch hands. He'd been as shocked as Biddie to find the place all but erased by the bandits' attack.

For reasons that Lucy could only assume came from Ginny's mysterious but clearly tragic past, the woman was adamant that men were unwelcome on her land. Nevertheless, Gideon had refused to leave three women alone in the desert. Which was a good thing since it turned out many parts of building a house, barn, troughs, and corrals from stone required more muscle than any of the women possessed.

Lucy had missed his muscular assistance in the nearly five weeks that had passed since she left the newly engaged Biddie and Gideon with Biddie's parents at the Stevenses' ranch which lay several miles west of Lupine Valley Ranch. While Gideon, Biddie, and her parents had continued to San Francisco to retrieve the rest of Biddie's belongings and prepare for their wedding, Lucy had chosen to return to the desert. Her excuse had been not wanting to leave Ginny and Preston alone to carry all the ranch duties. And of course, Lucy's courtship with Clyve Rowland. Though neither had been her true reasons.

Aside from Gideon, Preston and Clyve were the only exceptions to Ginny's no-men-on-the-ranch rule. Preston, because he was her beloved younger brother. Clyve, because he'd proven his trustworthiness by facilitating secret correspondence between Preston and Ginny in the years preceding Oliver's death.

Ginny's acceptance and trust of the two men was where their similarities ended, however. Clyve was a man of strong faith, steady, and responsible—some might say predictable. When he'd asked to court her during their cattle drive last November, she'd accepted.

Looking at him produced none of the butterflies she'd felt with Junior, and she counted that a good thing. The humiliating and terrifying events of last June were solid testimony that her attraction to and judgment of men were not to be trusted. With Clyve, she remained clear headed enough to know she was making a good decision, her thinking unmarred by the fog of foolish feelings. The strange pull she'd felt toward Preston from the moment of his arrival two weeks after the drive didn't change a thing.

Preston may not be a murderer like Junior, but the intensity in his gaze whenever he looked at her held an alluring mystery that both compelled her to explore and cautioned her not to delve too deep. It was the latter she intended to heed.

Besides, Preston had made it clear that he planned to return to a life of performing in traveling shows as soon as Ginny's ranch was on its feet. Preston lived for the limelight, while Lucy must remain in the shadows if she wanted to continue breathing. And she refused to play the doting, naïve wife waiting at home while he was off doing who knew what. That sort of blind trust in Lucy's father had destroyed Mama's life and shattered Lucy's childhood. She squeezed her eyes against the horrifying memories, shoving them back into her mental box and slamming the lid shut.

She pulled a pair of Ginny's trousers from the basket and shook the wrinkles out. If a woman as untrusting as Ginny found enough in Clyve's character to let him in without the bias of shared blood, that was good enough for Lucy. Add in that he planned to take over running his father's ranch one day —which happened to be located hundreds of miles from San Francisco—and Clyve had seemed to be the perfect catch. That he'd found something attractive in Lucy was a blessing. One she planned to repay with loyalty and hard work, if not love.

Biddie's glowing face as she gazed on her fiancé flashed in Lucy's mind. If only Lucy's heart would join in the plan her mind had settled on. Perhaps she could find a smidgen of the happiness Biddie exuded.

Lucy clenched her jaw against the childish longing as she lifted a pair of Preston's trousers from the basket. She slapped them over the line and jammed the pins in place. Then she wiped her hands on her skirts and eyed the garment as though it were a snake waiting to strike. As happy as she was for her dearest friend, love was a risk Lucy couldn't afford to take. Being practical was far safer. The breaking of Mama's body and soul had taught Lucy that.

Another gust of stinging sand cut through her painful thoughts. How she loathed the desert. Could she truly make it her home?

She pinned up the last piece of today's laundry. Tomorrow, when Clyve wasn't expected to stop by, Lucy would wash her and Ginny's unmentionables.

Lucy plucked the now-empty basket from the ground and set it against her hip before turning toward the house. At least the structure built of stone and mud mortar would protect her from flying debris, even if the wooden door and keyhole window covers couldn't keep all the wind out.

Located strategically, the windows that more closely resembled slots were barely big enough to allow a rifle's barrel to slide through. So they admitted less weather than the glassless windows she'd seen on the few homesteads she'd visited. Although, keeping dirt out wasn't a realistic goal with no real floor covering the packed earth beneath the furniture. Ginny had designed this building with practical self-defense in mind and little else. Biddie's insistence on a brick oven in addition to the fireplace was the sole concession Ginny had made to her original plans.

Lucy stepped inside and paused to admire the straight walls and built-in brick oven she'd helped to build herself. A soft chuckle escaped. Had anyone told her a year ago that she'd soon be engaged in such an endeavor, she'd have deemed them one shoe shy of a pair. Yet the lingering calluses on her hands proved the hard labor she'd put into splitting rock and digging clay from the creek bottom.

At least now that the worst bandits had moved farther north, according to newspaper reports, the ranch no longer needed around-the-clock guarding. Thoughts of bandits brought haunting memories of running miles through the desert desperate to beg the Rowlands' help in rescuing Biddie from the men who'd kidnapped her and stolen Ginny's cattle. Had it been less than two months ago? In some ways, it seemed like yesterday and in others, a lifetime ago.

Lucy shook off the painful recollections and set the basket on the floor. She shouldn't complain, even silently. God had been more than generous—first, by granting her escape and then through the miraculous discovery she'd made within this valley. Lucy's heart picked up speed as it always did when she recalled the hidden mine.

She set the basket on the floor and strode past the hanging curtain that separated her and Ginny's sleeping quarters from the main living area. Biddie's bed was there as well, though she wouldn't be using it for much longer. The thought of how Biddie's impending marriage would change their relationship caused a tiny pinch in Lucy's chest, but she ignored it. At least Biddie and Gideon planned to continue living and working on Lupine Valley Ranch. Once Lucy married Clyve, she'd be living on the Rowland Ranch. The Rowlands might be Ginny's closest neighbor, but their place was still several miles away.

Lucy shook off the melancholy thought. There was no point dwelling on what might never be. As dependable as Clyve's weekly courtship visits had been over the past three months, he'd not broached the topic of marriage. Not specifically. Though he had discussed their future as if their joined lives were a forgone conclusion. That had to mean something, didn't it?

Lucy slipped out of her dirty work dress and wiped the grime from her face and arms with a damp cloth. Then she pulled her best dress from a peg on the wall, a simple but beautiful creation of sky-blue cotton that Lucy had sewn from cloth Biddie gifted her last summer. With deft fingers, Lucy tied the skirt and fastened the buttons.

She wiped the dust from the small mirror hanging nearby and examined her reflection. For a moment, she wished for a lace collar and cuffs like Biddie had to spruce the outfit up a bit, then chided herself for being ungrateful.

She pulled her coffee-brown hair into a neat bun, leaving two wispy tendrils to frame her wind-chaffed face. She wrinkled her nose at the dry, reddened cheeks, then found the jar of salve Ginny had made with a recipe she'd learned from one of the Indian women she was friends with. Lucy spread a thin coating of the stuff across her cheeks and rubbed it in.

Satisfied that her appearance was the best she could manage, Lucy stepped outside and scanned the mountain valley's western slopes, searching for any sign of Clyve's approaching figure, but the valley remained undisturbed.

A distant clink of metal against metal reminded her she wasn't entirely alone. Although Ginny had ridden out shortly after breakfast, as usual, to check how the cattle were faring, Preston had remained to work on a metal pipe that ran from their tiny springhouse to the ranch's garden. Two weeks ago, that pipe had burst during the last snowfall of the season. Inspection of the disaster had revealed scratch marks in the pipe's straw-and-fabric insulation, which placed the blame on Biddie's cats. To say Ginny had been displeased would be an understatement.

As the temperatures warmed and the spring waters resumed flowing, they'd been forced to plug the pipe with clay to stop the flow of water until they could repair the break. Preston had made a trip to the mercantile in Campo to pick up their order of replacement pipe and a saw for cutting metal.

Lucy followed the sounds of Preston's efforts toward the garden, hidden from view by the stone barn.

Preston stood in the middle of the once-frozen puddle caused by the burst, now thawed into a mucky hazard. He had one boot propped on a large stone. The new pipe lay across his raised thigh as he worked at sawing it to the proper length. Despite the cool temperature, Preston's sleeves were rolled up, and his strong arms glistened with sweat and grime. The sun cast a warm glow on his chiseled cheekbones, stubbled jawline, slightly crooked nose, and unruly brown hair.

Preston's blade sliced through the bottom of the pipe, and the extra length fell into the mud. He appeared not to notice her as he leaned down to inspect the freshly cut edge still resting on his thigh.

What was he looking at? She eased closer until she stood almost shoulder to shoulder with him. Still, he stared at the rough metal circle. She tried to follow his gaze but couldn't determine what about the cut edge so fascinated him.

His head whipped around, a grin splitting his cheeks. "Made you look."

She jerked back, and her feet slid out from beneath her. She braced herself for impact with the hard, muddy earth, but the saw and pipe clattered to the ground as Preston's strong arms wrapped around her, saving her from injury.

Mirth danced in his velvety brown eyes as he gazed down at her. As she stared back, warmth spread from his touch, up her arms, and down to the tips of her toes. How could being held by this man feel like finally finding the home she'd always longed for?

"Careful, now." His shoulders shook with silent laughter. "It's slippery."

"Oh!" She pulled herself free. "Of all the...You are such a child." But that was a bold-faced lie. If there'd been any doubt before, the security of Preston's arms had erased any question of his being a full grown, well-defined man—even if his maturity was sometimes questionable.

Preston's gaze sobered as it lingered on hers, a question forming in the brown depths she couldn't answer—wouldn't answer. She took another step back. *Love makes a woman foolish, leaves her vulnerable.* Not that she felt anything like love for this man-child. Plain lust is all it was. And she'd learned enough from the women at The Home to know that was an emotion she wanted nothing to do with.

Preston shifted from one foot to the other, then reached for the saw he'd dropped when he caught her.

"I've got it." Lucy bent as she also extended her hand for the tool.

Their heads bumped, and she tipped her chin up. "Sorry." A soft gasp escaped her lips as they momentarily shared a space so close, his breath mingled with hers.

His gaze darted toward her lips, then he ducked lower to snatch the tool and straightened.

Lucy stepped back, her cheeks on fire. What was wrong with her? Why couldn't she shake this alluring magnetism?

He returned to the pipe, speaking over his shoulder. "Was there something you needed?"

Had there been? She couldn't recall. Shaking her head, she slogged through her muddied thoughts, trying to find the right path forward.

Lord, please take away these feelings. They aren't right. Especially considering Clyve's courtship. But I'm such a fool. Even after what happened with Junior, I can't rid myself of this dangerous desire. I need Your help.

The distant clip-clop of a horse's hooves drew her attention. *Clyve.*

Heart racing, Lucy spun toward the western side of the valley and spotted her beau's silhouette atop a horse ambling its way down the slope. Had he seen her entanglement with Preston? What had their position looked like from that distance? Hopefully, they'd appeared as innocent as the mishap had been. After all, she had no intention of nurturing her foolish attraction toward Preston. So Clyve had no reason to worry.

She glanced down and sighed. The hem of her beautiful dress was coated in mud, and splatters climbed toward her waist. She set a hand to her hair and nearly cried over its disheveled feel. So much for presenting her best self.

Lifting her chin and pasting a smile on her lips, she hurried to meet Clyve by the hitching post near the house.

He wore his usual pale hat atop his dark-brown hair, though it looked as though he'd given his mustache and full beard a fresh trim. When she reached his side, he grinned down at her and slid off his horse. "You look as pretty as a yucca plant in full bloom."

Ginny had taught Lucy about yucca plants. They were ugly things that looked and felt as though someone had managed to stick all their sewing needles into the same spot on a cushion—sharp ends out. The Indians used them to make everything from rope to soap. She hadn't been here long enough to see them bloom, but she struggled to imagine anything pretty could come from the plant. Still, Clyve clearly meant it as a compliment. "Thank you."

He tied his horse to the post, then removed something from his saddlebag. When he turned, he held a folded newspaper. "I thought you might want to read the news together before we take our walk. This came in three days ago, but I've been saving it to share with you. What do you say?"

A glance at the newspaper's heading revealed it was a two-week-old copy of the *Daily Alta California*, a San Francisco paper. A gentle refusal was on her tongue when the headline "Irene Prichard Found Dead" arrested her attention. She couldn't speak, couldn't breathe, couldn't look away from the bold-print words.

"Lucy? What's wrong?" Clyve adjusted the sheet so she

could no longer see the front page. "Oh. I'm sorry. I should've looked it over first. Of course, you wouldn't want to read about such gruesome things." He twisted and made as if to stuff the publication back in his satchel.

She caught his upper arm. "No, I want to read it. I was shocked, is all."

He tipped his head, studying her. "Are you sure? Your face went white as a ghost."

"I'm sure." She gestured to the upturned crates and large rocks that had been arranged in a circle around the cook fire. "Let's sit."

"Well, all right, but we'll skip over the grim stuff."

Lucy didn't protest, though she had no intention of leaving that article unread. Though a tremble shook her insides, she needed to know whether anyone else had discovered the truth about the wealthy socialite's tragic end. If the facts had come out without Lucy's speaking them, would that mean she and Mama were safe? Or would the Greens believe her responsible for unveiling their evil deeds?

Clyve tucked Lucy's hand in the crook of his arm and guided her to a seat on a rock before pulling a sturdy crate over to sit beside her. He shook out the paper and began reading aloud a commentary on the final sermon of the year given at the Howard Street M. E. Church by the Reverend Mr. Jewell. Lucy's attention, however, drifted down the page to the article on Mrs. Prichard.

The article shared that after months of searching for the missing gentlewoman, men working to fill in a section of the bay for the purposes of constructing a new block of buildings had discovered a woman's body in a barrel. Despite languishing at the bottom of the bay for who knew how long, her clothing was intact enough to aid in her identification. After examining the body, police had concluded she'd been robbed, stabbed, and stashed in the barrel before being dropped into the bay.

The article's author decried the police department's failure to bring justice for Mrs. Prichard's untimely death, though he begrudgingly acknowledged the lack of any evidence that might point toward the culprit.

So the Greens had gotten away with murder.

Lucy hid her trembling fingers in her skirt. But why did the article claim Mrs. Prichard was last seen leaving the Green Hotel and climbing into a hired hack? Surely, Mrs. Prichard's own driver and carriage had carried her to the hotel that fateful day. Why would she not return home in the same manner? More importantly, how had the corpse Lucy had seen on the floor of Junior's room walked out of the hotel?

The dandy's words echoed in her mind. *You managed to leave her clothing intact. That's something. I have a trusted resource about her size and coloring.* That was it. They'd dressed someone else in Mrs. Prichard's clothing and had the person pretend to be the wealthy socialite leaving the hotel. It was the only explanation.

The similarity to her own method of escape chilled her. Then she straightened. Whomever had impersonated Mrs. Prichard must also know the truth. Perhaps if Lucy could find her...but no. The dandy had said, *It'll be a shame to lose her, but there's nothing for it.* That woman, whoever she was, was surely dead now too.

"...don't you think so?" Clyve's words interrupted her thoughts.

She lifted her gaze to find him watching her with a look of anticipation. She squirmed on the rock. "I'm sorry. I'm afraid my mind drifted. Would you mind repeating the question?"

"Well, I was saying that I agree with this writer that it would be glorious if men refused to fight one another. But I'm not sure that's possible in this sinful, fallen world. Not until Christ's return, in any case. Until then, good men will continue to be called upon to stop evil wherever they see it and to protect the innocent."

She squeezed his arm with the hand still tucked into the crook of his elbow. "You're right, of course." If only there'd been good men around to save Mrs. Prichard. Then Lucy wouldn't be haunted with the fear that the Greens or the dandy would find and silence her.

CHAPTER 7

*T*wo days later, Lucy grabbed her canteen from the table in the house. A good shake confirmed it was still full. She bustled out the door and around the building toward the southern end of the valley. When she reached the large juniper bush concealing the entrance to the ranch's best-kept secret, she cast another look around. Then she slipped through the branches and into a dark, narrow tunnel, barely tall enough to stand in.

Lucy had learned her lesson last summer when Biddie had discovered Lucy's secret mining activities by noting that the candleholder usually stuck into the wall at the entrance was missing. Now, Lucy left the curled iron rod where it was whenever she came to dig.

Ginny's adamancy that the mine remain untouched was ridiculous. Why the stubborn, prideful woman had chosen to seek a loan from her estranged sister's adoptive parents instead of mining these gems and selling them to restart the ranch was another of those mysteries Ginny refused to explain. When Lucy questioned why she insisted no one was ever to enter the mine, her only words were, "Because I said so and this is my land. Break my rules and I will personally escort you off my ranch at gunpoint." Yet how could Lucy ignore her only hope of saving the Davidson Home for Women and Children from ruin at the hands of Mr. Green and his greedy accomplices?

Surely, once Lucy had completed the work of mining as much as the mountain would give, Ginny would see the right and good in gifting the treasure to the generous couple and the many they served. After all, if Ginny was refusing to mine the gems herself, she must not plan to use the money. And with the rough life Ginny seemed to have lived—the horrible father she'd survived—the woman ought to understand and sympathize with the plight of the women whom the Davidsons helped. At least, Lucy prayed this would be the case. There was always the possibility that Ginny would make good on her threat and evict Lucy from the property.

Lucy shuffled deeper into the mountain, running her right hand along the rough wall. Dust and the hint of smoke lingered in the air from yesterday's visit, tickling her nose. A gust of wind scratched the bush's branches against the mouth of the tunnel. The crunch of pebbles beneath her shoes seemed loud in the stillness that followed.

Her fingers stopped on the one-inch square she'd carved into the rock. She knelt and found her short, dipped tallow candle fixed to the center of a small tin plate. Further careful groping located the tinder box she kept beside it. She removed the lid and withdrew her flint and steel, leaving the char cloth in the open bottom of the tin.

Years of practice in lighting fires for her employers brought a spark on the first strike. She blew gently for several seconds to increase the pink glow of the embers. When they were hot enough, she held her candle so that the heat melted the tip, dripping tallow into the embers. A small flame appeared in the box, and she used it to light the wick before quickly replacing the lid on the tin, smothering the embers.

She lifted the plate and, with her free hand, dusted the spot in the tunnel wall she'd been working on yesterday. Candlelight glittered along the edges of the cinnamon-red gems waiting for her to chisel them free from their stone prison and add them to the box she'd buried at the back of the tunnel. Before Ginny discovered them in the mine last summer and ordered them all out, Gideon had declared the stones to be some kind of garnet. Though not as valuable as diamonds or gold, the precious treasure was her only hope of righting the wrongs done by Mr. Green. Wrongs yet concealed by her own cowardice.

Shame weighing on her, she again thanked the Lord that Fletcher Johnson had found Mama in time and secreted her to safety. At least, that was what she assumed had been meant by the addition to one of the letters Mrs. Davidson had written Biddie last summer.

Fletcher asks me to write that he was successful in retrieving the belongings Lucy forgot when she left her former employment and insists he will keep them until she returns. I see no reason he can't deliver her things to The Home, but then, he always has been an odd one.

How else was she to interpret those words? Mama wouldn't have liked being taken from the brothel—her only source of the opium she adored. How much trouble had Mama given Fletcher in return for his aid? If only she could see for herself that Mama was safe.

Ignoring the ache that refused to leave, Lucy snatched up her hammer and chisel and set to work. The soft whispers of her own breath mingled with the sharp chink of metal on stone, filling the tunnel.

Hours later, she paused to gulp water from her canteen.

A thunderous crack pierced the silence, causing her to choke on the last swallow. Gunfire.

A rapid succession of shots echoed with the thundering of horses' hooves. Bandits? She dropped her tools, the clang echoing loudly in the confined space. She blew out the candle and listened. There was something odd about the sounds, but she couldn't quite figure out what.

She scrambled to her feet and wiped her clammy palms across her dusty skirt as she crept toward the mine's entrance. The juniper bush concealed the source of the commotion. She reached for the branches, then paused, her heart racing. The shots were close. What if whoever was shooting noticed the bush moving and spotted her? She had no weapon to defend herself. The urge to smack her own forehead was almost irresistible. How could she have let the relative peace of the past few weeks lull her into such complacency?

The shooting stopped.

An abrupt silence filled the valley, broken only by the heavy breathing of a horse run hard. She took a bracing breath, separated the branches, and peered through the gap.

In the fading glow of twilight, a lone rider cantered gracefully between two rows of staggered columns formed by stacked rocks. The figure paused beside each one, dismounted, and lifted something from the ground before setting it atop the towers. Sunlight glinting off their pierced sides revealed they were empty tin cans.

Understanding dawned. They were shooting targets. Her gaze moved back to the man silhouetted by the setting sun, making him appear larger than life against the vast desert landscape. It must be Preston.

When the last can had been returned to its precarious

perch, Preston rode to the far end of the valley before kicking his horse into a gallop. His mount moved with fluid grace as Preston guided the beast between the rows of targets. Preston took aim with precision, firing his pistols in rapid succession. Left, right, left, right. The high pitch of metal meeting metal echoed off the surrounding slopes. Cans danced in the air, knocked off their rocky pedestals by the relentless barrage of well-aimed shots. The gunshots and thundering hooves melded into a thrilling symphony of sound and motion.

Lucy's heart pounded in her chest. Preston was magnificent. Considering that he'd claimed at dinner last night to have never performed his trick shots from horseback and thus, this must be his first attempt, his accuracy was astounding. He missed only two of the dozen targets he'd set up for himself. She couldn't tear her eyes away from the remarkable display of skill.

For a few precious moments, her worries faded away, replaced by the exhilarating sight of a man mastering his craft. It had taken her months to improve her aim with a rifle to something respectable. But she'd only ever stood in one place and aimed at a stationary target. How much more difficult would it be to shoot from the back of a moving animal? Her skin tingled with the desire to try—to fly over the ground, able to vanquish every enemy in her path.

~

*T*he next day, Lucy's mining was again interrupted by an unexpected commotion.

She checked the angle and intensity of daylight coming through the distant entrance. Many days of clandestine digging told her it couldn't be past four in the afternoon. Had Ginny and Preston returned from checking the cattle so early?

Lucy dropped her tools and snuffed the candle. With one

hand tracing the wall, she rushed to the entrance. Pausing behind the bush, she held her breath and assessed the clop of several horses' hooves on the hardpan desert echoing off the rocks and boulders that littered the landscape. The animals' panting breaths mixed with jingling bridles and riders' voices carrying on the wind, a distant murmur slowly growing louder. Ginny and Preston wouldn't create such a clamor.

Again, the worry of another bandit attack skittered through her mind and sent a shiver down her spine. She pressed her eyes closed.

"Ginny? Lucy? Preston? Is anyone here?" Biddie's cheerful call released the tension in Lucy's shoulders.

Thank You, Lord, for guiding them here safely at last.

Biddie and Gideon were meant to have returned from San Francisco last week. Lucy had worried when they'd not arrived on time but tried to assure herself that traveling with three additional women from the Women's and Children's Home was likely to slow them down—especially since two of the new women were bringing children with them.

Part of Lucy still struggled to believe Ginny had agreed to so many newcomers moving to Lupine Valley. Thankfully, Ginny's refusal to trust people hadn't prevented her from seeing the practicality in sending women from the Davidsons' overflowing charity home to work on a ranch where men weren't welcome. And the solution bought Lucy a bit more time to find the funds to prevent Mr. Green's actions from destroying everything the Davidsons had accomplished.

Lucy parted the branches enough to peek through. The swish of horses' tails and clouds of settling dust revealed that her friends and their companions had reached the ranch yard. Good. With the house between them, Lucy could sneak away from the mine entrance and pretend to be returning from her usual afternoon stroll.

She rounded the house and gasped with delight. "Carmen!"

Biddie's letter hadn't specified which of the charity house's occupants had agreed to come, but Lucy immediately recognized Carmen Davalos and her daughter, Josefina. "Josie! What a wonderful surprise!"

Two years ago, the twenty-eight-year-old Mexican widow and her daughter had taken shelter at The Home three days after Carmen's husband was killed by the men who attacked her. Thankfully, Josie had remained undiscovered and unharmed. At least physically. Lucy knew too well the toll of watching one's mother being beaten and left for dead—though in Mama's case, Lucy's own father had been the attacker. Thanks to Lucy's poor choices.

Josie slid from the horse and launched herself into Lucy's arms. "We've come to work the ranch with you."

"You have? But you're so young." The scrawny girl would be crushed by the large cattle.

Josie stepped back, lifting her chin. "I'm twelve. Plenty old enough to work."

Carmen dismounted with a shake of her head. "I keep telling her, *I'll* be working the ranch. *She'll* be helping at the house, where it's safe."

Safe? Could anywhere in this wild desert be considered safe?

Biddie hurried forward for her own hug. "Oh, it's so good to be home."

Lucy pulled back to give Biddie a questioning look. "Surely, you told them."

Biddie's wide eyes blinked at her. "Told them what?" She stepped back as Gideon joined her. His grimace and slight shake of his head told Lucy her dear friend had failed to share the full truth of the dangers that life in this valley presented.

Lucy glanced at the rest of the newcomers. Perhaps now wasn't the time to bring up the events of last fall. Better not to scare them right from the start.

Her gaze landed on a couple near the rear of the dismounted group. "Daniel! Eliza! I didn't know you were coming."

Biddie's older cousins grinned at her as they untied luggage from the packhorses.

Eliza Clarke's hat slipped sideways over her wavy brown hair as she set two large carpetbags on the ground. "It was a spur-of-the-moment decision. I *could* say we came along as chaperones for Gideon and Biddie—because they did need one." She sent a wink at the engaged couple. "But the truth is, it's been years since I had an adventure, and my boots were itching to join in the journey."

Daniel chuckled, merry wrinkles framing the corners of his brown eyes as he set a crate on the ground. "I think she was half packed before she bothered mentioning her plans to me." His muscles strained his dusty brown shirt as he slung an arm around his wife's shoulders.

"Pshaw!" Eliza playfully swatted his chest. "You wanted to come every bit as much as I did."

Daniel raised one brow. "Is that so?"

Eliza's cheeks pinked. "Well, almost." She turned from her husband. "It's too bad we can only stay two nights. There's too much waiting for us back home." She gestured toward the bunkhouse. "Is that where the women will be staying?"

Biddie answered for her. "Yes. There's a room for each of them. Carmen and Josie, you take the biggest room which is at the far end." She turned to a green-eyed, freckle-faced strawberry-blonde who appeared far too young to be the mother of the brunette toddler on her hip. "Esther, you and Deborah can have the middle room."

Esther? That was new. The last time Lucy had seen the sixteen-year-old redhead at The Home, she'd been going by *Red*, the name her owners and clients had called her in the brothels. She must have chosen a new one.

Lucy liked it. The biblical Esther was strong and brave, just as the redhead had been when she'd taken the risk of running away after discovering she was with child and knowing what would happen if she remained. She'd told Biddie, who'd shared with Lucy that two of the girl's friends had died after receiving the "cure" for their conditions. Lucy said another prayer of thanks that San Francisco's street children had directed the girl to the Davidsons.

Esther shifted Deborah to her opposite hip and took up a bag from the growing pile Daniel was making.

Daniel reached for it. "I can carry that for you."

Esther flinched away. "I've got it." She hurried toward the bunkhouse, offering a small smile to Lucy as she passed.

Lucy smiled back. "Welcome." She'd learned better than to offer to take Deborah. To Lucy's knowledge, Esther had never let anyone else care for her daughter.

Biddie interrupted her thoughts. "Lucy, I'd like you to meet Lei Yan. She arrived at The Home after we left last summer, so you wouldn't have had a chance to meet her before."

"Hello and welcome." Lucy waved.

The young Chinese girl's gaze was hard, her expression inscrutable. She nodded in response to Lucy's words, took a small satchel from the side of her horse, and made for the bunkhouse.

Lucy directed a questioning look at Biddie. "Why is she here?" The Davidsons didn't usually place the women out until they'd been at The Home for at least a year and had a chance to soften from the hard exteriors their difficult lives had forced on them.

Biddie's eyes grew sad, her expression worried. "Lei Yan's owner is furious that she's run away again. Twice, the tong has sent men to break into The Home and reclaim her. They've threatened my parents, as well, and some of the donors objected to having someone of her race at The Home." Biddie blew a loose strand of hair off her face. "Bringing her here seemed like the best solution. I'm praying she learns to trust us."

"Will she work?" Lucy quirked her brow. As big as Biddie's heart was, Ginny had only agreed to letting women come who were willing to work for their room and board. How would she react if Lei Yan refused to pitch in?

Biddie nodded confidently. "That's one thing Lei Yan excels at. In The Home, Mother could hardly convince Lei Yan to rest even on Sundays."

Rest and church on Sundays were a condition of remaining at the charity home. "What does Lei Yan think of Christ?" Lucy asked. The young woman wouldn't be the first to arrive without a faith in their Heavenly Father.

Biddie sighed. "I'm not sure. She attended service with everyone else, but she speaks very little." Biddie bumped Lucy's shoulder with her own. "Much like someone else I know."

Lucy rolled her eyes. "I'm not *that* quiet anymore."

"Not with me. But you still hardly speak with anyone else."

Lucy lifted her chin. "I say what is necessary."

"Uh-huh." Biddie's doubtful tone and teasing sparkle in her blue eyes said they'd have to agree to disagree.

Gideon walked past, leading two horses to the corral.

Lucy considered the pile of supplies. Several sacks of flour and other ingredients sat alongside crates that no doubt contained more necessary goods for the ranch. "I can start putting things away if you want to help Gideon with the horses." Nearly seven months of living on a ranch hadn't increased Lucy's fondness for large animals. Though she didn't particularly care for cooking, she was far more comfortable performing domestic duties than caring for four-legged creatures.

Biddie thanked her and led two more animals away. Daniel and Eliza followed with four more horses, leaving two hitched to a bush on the perimeter of the yard. Carmen's rich voice and Josie's boisterous laugh blended with the quiet conversation of those at the corral.

Lucy gaped at the mountain of food stuffs. They'd brought at least four times the amount of goods she'd been used to unloading from their trips to the nearest mercantile, twenty miles away. She reached for the nearest crate, then paused. Of course, there was so much more. There were that many more mouths to feed.

Would the valley ever regain the serene stillness Lucy had enjoyed each day when Ginny and Preston rode out to check the cattle? Would she still be able to slip away to do her mining? Or would watchful eyes now follow her wherever she went?

CHAPTER 8

*P*reston Baker drew his mount to a stop at the peak of the ridge surrounding the desert mountain valley that held the heart of Lupine Valley Ranch. The yard was crawling with people.

"I thought Biddie said they were only bringing three women." Preston turned to Ginny as she paused her horse beside his. Her work to help a birthing mama cow that afternoon had broken the strap on one of her twin braids, leaving half of her straw-colored hair to be tussled by the strong desert winds as they rode home. He bit back a laugh. Now she looked half schoolgirl and half scarecrow. Only the knowledge that the new arrivals would have Ginny on edge kept his humor in check.

A scowl marred her dirt-smudged, suntanned face. "Don't forget the two brats."

He followed her gaze to where a young girl with golden-honey skin played peek-a-boo with a pale-skinned toddler in the doorway of the barn. Both had thick, wavy brown hair. "Right." How could he have forgotten the fuss Ginny made about children being part of the deal? In his eyes, it was a small price to pay for help she could trust. And his big sister's bluster was just a shield for her soft heart. He pointed to an older couple seated in the shade of the barn on the bench he'd built for Ginny to use while she did maintenance work such as sharpening axes, cleaning guns, or oiling leather. "But who are they?"

Ginny's expression hardened. "I don't know." She urged her horse forward, no doubt eager to interrogate the unexpected guests.

Preston scanned the rest of the faces below. In addition to the two children and the couple, Gideon stood in the horse corral with a redheaded girl Preston assumed had come from the charity home. Weren't there supposed to be three women and two children? He checked the two girls still playing peek-a-boo. The redhead was definitely a few years older, but surely, she wasn't counted among the women. The wisp of a girl appeared to be chatting amicably with Gideon as they groomed the horses. Despite her tiny frame, she showed no fear of the large animals.

At the other end of the yard, two more new women stood with their backs to him, taking laundry from the line under Biddie's guidance. A job Lucy had been performing for as long as he'd been here. Where was she? He checked the yard again but saw no sign of her.

The door to the house opened and Lucy emerged, bowls of something in each hand and two more balanced on each arm. A model of beauty and grace. The wind tugged a lock of her dark-brown hair free of its bun and into her face. She tipped her head to clear her vision as she set the bowls on the table that had been moved into the yard. When she spotted the children playing, the warmth of her smile was evident even from this distance, causing his heart to flip.

Knock that off. She's taken. Had been before his arrival. As eager as he'd been to arrive, confirm their father's death, and aid Ginny, he'd never have guessed his main cause for regret over not arriving sooner would fall at the feet of such a quiet, hard-working, lovely woman.

Not that he'd change the situation now if he could. Neither he nor his lifestyle were right for Lucy—or any wife.

Traveling with the show was fine for a single man, but it took a toll on families. He'd seen it. Children and women alike were social creatures by nature. They yearned for lasting friendships made impossible by the constant move from one town to the next. The moment a performer took a bride, the clock started ticking down the weeks until she grew weary of the unsettled life and nagged her husband into leaving the show to put down roots and start a family. Those who stubbornly remained earned miserable wives in exchange.

Preston whipped his pistol from its holster, aimed at the tip of a rock across the valley, and imagined taking the shot. In his mind, the tip of the stone shattered, pieces flying in a million directions, and a crowd cheered, urging him on to his next trick. With a sigh, Preston replaced the weapon and nudged his horse down the slope.

As enticing as Lucy was, it was good she was being courted by a man with established roots and a community ready to come to his aid. Clyve Rowland might grind Preston's nerves with his predictability, but that was what would make him a good husband.

And that would make Preston's leaving easier once Ginny's ranch was financially stable. Or at least as stable as any ranch could be, as dependent on weather and good grass as they were. With the new women here to help, Preston was that much closer to being ready to leave. Now he needed to ensure the cattle were healthy and hale for when it came time to drive them to markets up north in three months. That should set Ginny up for the next year, allowing him to leave with the confidence that his sister and her beloved ranch were well situated to thrive. Hopefully, Harvey would let him back in the show when the time came.

Shoving thoughts of the future aside, he dismounted beside the horse corral and reached for the sack lunch he'd forgotten to eat. The crunch of hurried footsteps drew near.

"I can take your bag." Lucy's fingers collided with his over the strings tying the pouch to the saddle. "I—I'm sorry...I just..." Her cheeks pinked as she withdrew her hands.

His heart took to racing as he finished untying the sack, waiting for her to finish. Was it possible she'd been eager to see him?

When she finally spoke, it was with her gaze flittering around the yard. "With everyone arriving today, I worried that if I waited, I'd forget."

Of course. Preston resisted the urge to let his shoulders sag. She only wanted his sack to fill in the morning with tomorrow's midday meal, as she'd done every morning since she'd returned without Biddie and Gideon last month. That was good. It was good there was nothing more to it.

He straightened and gave the pouch a light toss. When the motion made her look up, he sent her a wink as he caught it. "No harm done. Only, I ain't finished with it quite yet."

Her coffee-brown eyes rounded. "You haven't eaten?"

He shuffled his feet. "There was a cow with its horns stuck in a bush. Plenty riled up. It took a while to get it free. Then one of the cows was having trouble with..." Preston's neck warmed, and he cleared his throat. "It was busy day."

She merely nodded in return. That was another thing he liked about her. She didn't prattle on the way some women did. And when she spoke, her words were gentle but to the point.

Thoughts like that weren't going to bring his heart rate back to a reasonable pace.

He led his horse into the corral. "Hey, Gideon. Glad to see you made it."

Gideon shook his hand and introduced the redhead before launching into the long tale of their journey east. Apparently, they'd stopped briefly at the Stevenses' ranch, and the Chinese woman, Lei Yan, had recognized the teacher there. Gideon said something about it being a miracle. But Preston's attention kept wandering to where Lucy had joined Biddie by the laundry lines.

Something Biddie said made Lucy laugh long and hearty, like a roaring waterfall filling the air with mirth. Laughing was the only time the woman could be accused of being loud. The refreshing sound had been absent since Biddie's departure. The way Lucy's guard came down for a moment was breathtaking.

He stepped in her direction.

"Preston?" Gideon's voice halted Preston's movement and brought his attention back to his little sister's fiancé. Gideon waited with an expectant expression.

Great. Preston turned his back to Lucy and fully faced Gideon. "Sorry. I missed that last part."

Gideon's gaze shot over Preston's shoulder, then back to him with a too-knowing grin. "I was saying, the new women will need to learn to defend themselves. I was hoping you and Lucy could see to that since Ginny and I will be teaching them to work the ranch, and Biddie will be busy baking and cooking for the lot of us."

"Not to mention, preparing for the wedding," the redhead chimed in. What was her name again? Esther? The girl ran a brush along a horse's side as she spoke. "She brought back bolts and bolts of fabric for that trousseau Mrs. Davidson wanted for her."

Gideon lifted the front leg of a horse, inspecting the hoof as he spoke. "Biddie's mother wanted to have the gowns made for her. Biddie insisted she had plenty of clothes. The bolts were their compromise."

What was he supposed to say about that? Growing up, most

of his and Ginny's clothes had come from charity bins. Pasting on a cocky grin, he whipped his matching pistols from their holsters and gave them a spin that ended with the barrels pointed at the sky. "You want me to teach the women to quick draw?"

Gideon laughed. "Sure. So long as you teach them to aim first. And if you could teach them some of those pugilist skills you mentioned, that couldn't hurt. What do you say?"

"Sure." Preston smirked. "But don't blame me for the broken hearts when it's time for me to head out." He spun his weapons back into their holsters with a wink. "My moves are known for charming the ladies."

The redhead's smile vanished, and she stopped grooming the horse. Her steely eyes looked him up and down. "Humph. You ain't nothin' special." She thrust the curry brush against Preston's chest, and his reflexes made him grab hold of it. She pivoted and strode from the corral.

Gideon guffawed and patted Preston's back as he left the corral. "I think the ladies will be just fine."

Preston scowled at the man's retreating back until Lucy's graceful movements drew his attention. As if sensing his gaze, she glanced over her shoulder, catching him staring. Again, his heart flipped, but he refused to look away—to give power to this fruitless attraction.

Still, when she turned back to Biddie and his chest pinched, he couldn't stop the worry that perhaps the women weren't the ones needing to guard their heart.

～

Three days after the newcomers' arrival, Lucy strolled with Clyve along the western rim of Lupine Valley as the sun neared the distant western horizon. He gestured toward the vast expanse of the dusty flatlands that began at the base of the mountain. "I think you've seen by now that raisin' cattle out here isn't for the faint of heart. It's a dance with the desert and the critters. It's all about knowing the land, knowing your cattle, and knowing the rhythm of life."

He pointed to a bush halfway down the hill that was mostly green but speckled with yellow. From this distance, she couldn't tell if the yellow was flowers or leaves.

"You've got to be patient and sturdy like those mesquite bushes, resilient in the face of hardships. They're slow growing but the stubbornest things I've ever seen. You can cut them down or burn them, but give them enough time, and they'll grow right back unless you pull the roots out." He surveyed the valley and the ranch yard filled with people going about their Saturday afternoon chores. "To my way of thinking, our roots are our hearts—the people we love." He slowed, took her hand, and held her gaze with a warm look. "So long as we have that, we'll be all right."

Lucy couldn't help returning his smile. No matter her foolish attraction to Preston. Clyve was a kind man, and she was blessed to have his affection.

A loud moo from the cattle corral interrupted the moment, and they both turned to where an expectant cow complained of being penned in. Ginny was concerned with the mama's lack of weight gain and had decided to bring her in for special care, but the cow was less than appreciative of being separated from the rest of the herd.

Clyve tucked Lucy's hand into the crook of his arm and continued walking. "Of course, keeping the cattle alive is key to keeping our loved ones well cared for. It's a delicate balance. Right food, right water, and keeping a watchful eye. Each critter has its own story, and you've got to learn to read them. Know when they're restless, when a storm's brewing, or when there's something ailing them. Not to mention, keeping predators away—the four- and two-legged kind."

Lucy tensed with the reminder of the ever-present threat bandits posed. Though the gang which had struck Lupine Valley Ranch twice in the past year was said to be hundreds of miles north, they were far from the only rustlers threatening this region. "Has there been more trouble?"

Clyve's lips pressed together and he nodded. "We lost a calf to a pack of coyotes three nights ago."

Lucy's heart pinched. Yes, nearly every cow on these ranches was bound for slaughter at the end of the season, but she tried not to think on it often. Especially when it came to the calves. Despite the mess of birthing, the miracle of the process was awe-inspiring, and the baby cows were so cute with their spindly little legs that wobbled for the first few hours. It was bad enough knowing that someday their lives would be cut short at the hand of a butcher. But to think of one dying by the teeth of a pack of coyotes...Tears sprang to her eyes.

Seeming not to notice her distress, Clyve scratched his beard. "Losing animals to coyotes or bobcats is part of life out here. But rustling—that's something else. Something we don't tolerate."

Blinking the tears away, Lucy glanced up.

A muscle ticked in Clyve's jaw. "Any man who don't respect a brand is asking for a short life."

Another part of this lifestyle she detested. Having witnessed the searing of symbols onto Ginny's new herd last fall, Lucy wanted nothing to do with the process. Again, she understood the necessity of it, but she couldn't stand the distressed crying the animals made while being shoved into the chute and held in place.

Oblivious to Lucy's thoughts, Clyve continued, "Branding's like marking your claim in this vast stretch of land. It's not just about ownership. It's a legacy, a symbol. Each brand tells a tale of the ranch and the folks who tend to it. It's our way of saying, 'This is our piece of the frontier.'"

She doubted Ginny's Indian friends would appreciate the sentiment. Growing up in San Francisco, it had been easy to buy into the stories frequently printed in the newspapers about vicious savages attacking innocent homesteaders. Since moving to the desert and tagging along with Ginny to visit some of the Indians scraping out a living in this desert, the seemingly clear picture had muddied.

Now she understood that many of these so-called savages had been defending their homes, families, and way of life. Not that violence was ever justified when there was another way. But what choice had been left them when strangers came in and, often violently, forced them off the land they'd lived on for hundreds of years? She'd learned from Biddie's cousin, Eliza, that Indians had even been arrested simply for not having an employer and forced into slavery. And it was all legal.

Yet, at the same time, families like the Rowlands and people like Ginny had come to this land to build a better life for themselves and their families. They were doing their best to live in peace with the Indians and treat them fairly. As she gazed across the wide-open expanse, she couldn't imagine there wasn't enough land for everyone to share and find a place to belong. Besides, it was hard to think of someone trying to provide for their loved ones as wrong.

The whole situation made Lucy's head hurt and was far too big for her to do anything about. She had her own, more immediate problems to worry about. So she shook the confusing thoughts away and realized that once again, she'd missed Clyve's words.

"...and that'd be a much bigger problem, of course. Pa's planning for the worst and building a special wagon for hauling water out to some of our drier pastures when the time comes. He thought up the plans last summer, but he's been waiting for the large barrels he ordered to come in, and they just arrived. So now he's got everything he needs, and..." Clyve went on to explain, step by step, how his father was building a new water-hauling wagon.

Lucy tried to stay focused on his words, but heavens above, what did she care about the exact measurements for something she'd never have a reason to build herself? Would he remain attentive if she were to go into the minute details of cleaning their linens? Not that he'd ever asked about her work here. Or what she'd done before coming to Lupine Valley. He seemed content with the little he knew of her past—that she'd worked as a maid in San Francisco and come to the desert to support her best friend, Biddie. Not that she wanted to share about her experience at the Green Hotel or the truth about her mother. Both were humiliating truths best left in the past.

Clyve had asked once about her parents and how they felt about her decision to come to the desert. She'd replied that they were both in Sacramento and had no concerns about her travel plans. Which was true as far as she knew.

The last she'd heard of her pa, he was living in Sacramento with his "real family," and Fletcher had taken Mama to his home in Sacramento. Lucy prayed the two never crossed paths. But neither parent could be concerned about travel plans they knew nothing about. Not that either would care if they did know.

As Clyve finished his description of the wagon build, he guided them toward the valley and the corral where he'd left his horse. After nearly three months of courtship, they'd established something of a routine. Clyve arrived each Saturday after completing the chores at his father's neighboring ranch, and when the sun touched the tops of the low-lying hills to the west, he began the return trip home.

She ought to invite him to stay for supper, as she'd done once or twice before, but the truth was, she was weary of his presence.

She cringed. What an awful thing to think about this kind,

hard-working, God-fearing man who would provide for and treat a wife well.

As they neared the yard, Ginny strode from the barn toward the bull's corral with an armload of hay. She was a walking testament to Clyve's goodness. Despite that woman's habit of trying to drive people away—especially men—Clyve had proven himself trustworthy and loyal in his behavior toward her. Lucy couldn't think of two more important qualities in a husband.

Careful not to turn her head, she studied Clyve's profile. He'd confessed to being a handful of years older than her, but she couldn't tell by looking at him. His skin was paler now than it had been over the summer and contrasted sharply with his dark, full beard and mustache. She'd never been particularly fond of men's facial hair, but somehow, Clyve's whiskers didn't detract from his handsomeness. Perhaps it was his strong build or the kind, and often flirtatious, sparkle in his dark-brown eyes that made the difference.

Whatever the cause, add good looks to the list of Clyve's husband qualities, and any woman would conclude he was a rare catch.

So why was she so eager for him to leave?

Yes, he tended to talk a bit much about ranch work and could go on for days about politics, but what was that compared to his other fine qualities?

Her gaze strayed to where Preston sat outside the barn, sharpening his blade with a whetstone. His dark hair bore a hat ring, and every inch of him was covered in dust from riding out to check on the cattle earlier in the day—including the stubble that had grown in since his last shave.

The day after his arrival, Preston had taken a straight-razor to his face, erasing the beard and mustache he'd arrived with. When Biddie expressed surprise, he'd explained the facial hair was part of his costume, and had remained generally clean-shaven since.

His current disheveled appearance was quite a change from the fancy leather-fringed costume he'd been wearing when he first showed up two months ago. She hadn't seen the strange outfit since Biddie gifted her brother with a set of plain work clothes shortly after his arrival. As he appeared now, one would never know he made his living as a trick-shooter in a traveling show, instead of working cattle like everyone else in the area.

Why did he pull at her attention whenever he was around? From the very first, there'd been something about him that both intrigued and repelled her. Which was highly inconvenient considering she'd already agreed to Clyve's courtship before Preston appeared in response to Ginny's letter asking for help.

Besides, Preston—though seemingly devoted to his sisters —had no home and no stable income. Everyone knew entertainers were constantly poor. They often drank in excess and caroused with women of ill repute. Though she'd not witnessed either of those qualities in Preston, it was possible he was on his best behavior around his sisters and lived an entirely different life while on the road. Preston was like the board her classmates had placed crosswise on a log at the school she'd attended before—

No. She cut the thought short and stuffed it back into the mental chest the memory had escaped from.

The point was, just like that board which the other kids had ridden up and down for hours before she worked up the nerve to try it and broke her arm, Preston was dangerous. He'd shared more than one tale of men eager to out-shoot one of Berdan's famous regiment of sharpshooters or challenge the trick-shooter in a quick draw.

Everywhere he went, Preston attracted attention. Even the Rowland *vaqueros* had ridden over and coerced Preston into

showing off his skills one day after their work was done. Ginny
had been less than happy having so many men on her ranch,
but since those same men had taken part in rescuing Biddie
from the bandits that tried to rustle Ginny's cattle, she'd let
them stay a few hours.

Lucy had been impressed by Preston's performance along
with everyone else. Which was precisely the problem. Preston
was a man who belonged at the center of everyone's attention,
while she'd lived in the shadows for years. And now, she
needed to disappear entirely—or as close to it as she could
manage.

And Preston might be here now, but as soon as he believed
Ginny no longer needed his help, he'd return to his traveling
show and posters that plastered his name and whereabouts all
over the country. Lucy wanted no part in such a life.

If only she could convince the magnet inside her to quit
turning Preston's way whenever he was near. When he'd
returned to the ranch shortly after Clyve's arrival, she'd felt his
presence before she'd spotted him strolling down the valley's
slopes with a jubilant Ginny at his side. Ever since, she'd
battled the urge to watch his lithe movements. There was something about the way he walked and handled his guns—even in
the way he stroked the blade he was sharpening against the
whetstone. His actions were graceful yet powerful, the same as
a golden eagle she'd once seen swoop down to capture a desert
mouse. Like Preston, the regal bird commanded attention and
she hadn't been able to look away.

As if sensing her scrutiny, he looked up and caught her
watching.

Her stomach jumped and she scowled. She jerked her
attention back to Clyve, who was still rambling about the
upcoming election, though it was months away. Beneath the
hand she'd placed on his arm, his gait felt sturdy and confident.
Reliable strength emanated from him like the glow of a gas

lamp. She mentally shook off her concerns. At Clyve's side was where she belonged.

He stepped away to saddle his horse, then took up the reins before turning to her. "May I call on you again next week?"

It was the same question he asked every week. She ignored the heavy sigh pressing against her chest and offered him a bright smile. "Of course. I look forward to it." Her traitorous eyes skipped to Preston before she pulled them back. "In fact, I'd be pleased if you'd stay for supper."

His grin widened and he started to release his reins.

She hastily stepped back. "Next week, I mean." She clasped her hands behind her. "I'll let Biddie know to prepare extra."

His smile flickered. Then he stuffed his hat on his head. "Until next week."

As he rode out of the valley, her gaze was drawn to the wide set of his shoulders—proof of his hard work and ability to protect a woman. At the ridge, he turned his horse and waved his hat in the air. She waved back. Clyve was the husband she needed, even if she didn't deserve him.

Turning toward the house, she tried to smother the guilt. Most folks in these parts kept their past to themselves. Keeping hers from Clyve wasn't wrong. Was it?

CHAPTER 9

*O*pal Arlidge wanted nothing more than to forget, but first, she needed to remember.

She stared at the bare wood ceiling of the tiny room located above the Johnsons' photography studio in Sacramento. Who had attacked her? Why? Would they seek her out to finish the job?

When she first awoke in this place, she'd assumed her injuries were the result of a drunken customer. However, Fletcher Johnson had claimed that as he was carrying Opal to the cart that brought her here, he'd seen Moira in the alley behind the brothel, whispering to Opal's attacker. After settling Opal in the cart, Fletcher attempted to confront them. Moira shoved a small pouch into the man's grasp, then disappeared into the brothel as Opal's attacker ran away. Unwilling to leave Opal unconscious and alone in the cart, Fletcher had let them go. Since then, he'd spoken with another of Pete's girls who'd confirmed that Moira had paid one of her regulars to hurt Opal. Or so Fletcher claimed.

She didn't believe a word of it.

Fletcher and Katie Johnson were kind, Christian people like their friends, the Davidsons. They probably wouldn't lie to her, but Fletcher was wrong. Moira was Opal's friend. Why would she want Opal hurt? Even if she did, Moira had no money. There had to be another explanation.

Opal shifted on the thin mattress and winced. Although the overwhelming pain of her first several weeks—months?—in the Johnson home had faded, the new ache in her jaw persisted. It was a tickle compared to the fire that had been burning in her right shoulder and neck for the past seventeen years, but if the Johnsons would give her the opium she needed, she could make it all go away. Their stubborn insistence that she could learn to live without her pipe was another thing they had in common with the Davidsons.

Despite her hosts' generous hospitality and encouraging words, Opal's time in this room had been something like she imagined hell would be. Shame warmed her cheeks as she recalled begging for her pipe in those first days. Retching into a bucket with two broken ribs and no opium to dull the pain had been nothing short of agony. If she'd been able to walk, she'd have left without a second's hesitation. But her ankle had been broken and her hip dislocated, making escape impossible.

Until today.

Voices downstairs announced the arrival of the Johnsons' first customers. An hour ago, Katie had brought Opal enough food and water to last until the evening meal, explaining that the studio would be unusually busy today. Neither she nor Fletcher would be back to check on Opal until twilight.

Opal rose from the bed and tugged her chemise and drawers into place. The pain in her shoulder increased as she pulled on her silk stockings and secured the garter ribbons. Her button hook made short work of closing her boots. She bit her lip to keep from crying out as she wrapped her corset around her torso and fastened the hooks.

Once done, she slumped onto the bed, exhausted. She'd nearly forgotten how draining the constant pain was. Which was why she needed to leave.

Her conscience—decidedly louder without her pipe— shouted that sneaking away was poor repayment for the care the Johnsons had given her these past months. But if they knew her plans, they'd try to stop her, and she couldn't take the pain a single day longer.

If she could manage to sneak aboard a ferry heading for San Francisco, a long walk and Pete's henchmen were all that lay between her and blissful, painless silence. If she were still speaking to God, she'd pray that Pete hadn't discovered the stash she'd hidden behind a loose board in her room at the brothel. As it was, she could only hope the trip wouldn't be in vain.

~

*H*ours later, Opal staggered away from Pete's Palace, her pain-fogged mind struggling to grasp everything Moira had told her, but it took all her concentration to keep placing one foot in front of the other.

Three blocks later, she blundered to a stop in a dark alley. Winded, she bent at the waist and rested her palms on her knees. Searing pain shot through her shoulders and neck. She jerked upright, lost her balance, and fell onto the muck.

Something sharp jabbed her left knee, and she sucked air through her teeth. She shifted onto her heels and lifted her skirts. A shard of glass was stuck in the rough blue wool of her stocking. Opal plucked the piece free and tossed it aside. All around her, broken bits of glass reflected the golden gaslight filtering through the yellowed cotton covering the upstairs windows of the saloon on her left.

It had been well past dark by the time she made it to the back of Pete's Palace. Before she could enter, Moira spotted her and came outside. She begged Opal to leave, but Opal's pain demanded she collect her hidden cache. Eventually, Moira admitted to stealing Opal's opium and using it to pay one of their regulars to damage Opal's face. She claimed to have done it so Pete would kick Opal out.

Apparently, Lucy had come to Pete's Palace and tried to convince Opal to leave—something she vaguely recalled now. Lucy had told Moira that dangerous men were searching for both Opal and Lucy. It seemed Lucy had heard or seen something she shouldn't. Now Mr. Green, his son, and a mysterious dandy were hunting her and Opal. Moira had assured Opal that Lucy had safely escaped the city, and had ordered Opal to do the same.

First, though, Opal needed relief from the relentless torment. She forced herself to her feet and shuffled another seven blocks before Frederick's Apothecary was finally within sight. The shop's windows beckoned her in the way Alcatraz Island's lighthouse guided ships safely through the bay.

Hopefully, the rumors that this druggist was willing to exchange medicine for discreet "favors" was true. Just a few more feet separated her from sweet relief. If only the single dose wouldn't cost her so dearly. Not that she hadn't paid such a price many times before. Her willingness to work for the medicine in place of cash was the main reason Pete had let her stay at the Palace as long as he had. But she hadn't been sober enough to fully appreciate the gravity of her choices in years.

She hesitated a few feet from the door. What if she didn't go in? What if she found another way to earn the money?

A derisive snort escaped her. She'd slammed the lid on respectable work the day she'd stolen from the Davidsons to pay for more opium—the day she'd turned her back on her precious daughter. Guilt heaped onto the pain radiating from her shoulders, propelling her feet forward.

Someone emerged from the alley beside the apothecary and plowed into her side.

Opal cried out and crumpled to her knees as lightning bolts shot through her body. Peering up, she opened her mouth to have a go at the oaf who'd knocked her down, but the angry words strangled in her throat. It was him. The owner of the fancy Green Hotel had found her. She was going to die.

He bent and reached for her.

She scrambled away, rose to her feet, and prepared to bolt.

He lowered his hand. "My sincerest apologies, miss. I'm afraid I didn't see you there. I do hope no harm is done."

He was apologizing? Why wasn't he grabbing her, tossing her into the alley beside the apothecary, and slitting her throat? Could Moira have been wrong? Or was he the sort who wouldn't dirty his hands and was just stalling until his henchmen arrived to do the job for him? She glanced around, but no one appeared to be paying them any attention.

He spoke again, causing her to jump. "Are you injured?"

She shook her head.

He smiled. "Good. And your clothes?" His smile dimmed a bit as he took in her plain clothing that'd clearly been dirty before he knocked her down. "Well, if no harm has been done, I must be on my way." He tipped his hat. "Good day." Without waiting for her response, he stepped around her and hurried down the road. A moment later, he turned the corner and was gone. Not once had he looked back.

Was it possible he'd not recognized her? She smacked her forehead. Of course, he hadn't recognized her. She'd never met the man before that moment. She only recognized *him* because Moira had one of his cabinet cards, forgotten by a client.

Knowing that Lucy worked at the Green Hotel, Moira had shown Opal the photograph.

She hadn't had her photograph taken in well over a decade, but her muddled reflection in the dusty apothecary window showed her the years had not been kind.

Another man she recognized emerged from the alley, his face illuminated by the faint glow emanating from the apothecary windows as he tucked something into his pocket.

She spun away, heart thudding in her chest. *Please don't notice me. I didn't see a thing. I swear, I didn't. I have no idea who you are. I know nothing. I'm a nobody, just another pile of trash.*

Chiv King's footsteps faded in the opposite direction.

Opal drew in a shuddery breath and heaved it out.

The apothecary's door swung open. A man wearing a long white apron eyed her. "I was about to lock up. You coming inside?"

She glanced over her shoulder. No sign of Chiv King. What had he been doing with Mr. Green in the alley? She shivered. Nothing good. That was certain. But did it have to do with her? Or Lucy? Mr. Green might not know what Opal looked like, but he certainly knew what Lucy looked like. What if he'd hired Chiv King to find and murder Lucy?

"Miss?" The druggist called to her. "If payment is your concern, I'm certain we can work something out." The look in his eyes left little doubt of his meaning.

She stared past him to the medicines lining the shelves that covered every wall of his store. There was no question he had what she needed. The bottles and jars called to her like the sirens' song in Homer's *Odyssey*, promising a pain-free night.

*T*he next day, Opal sat with her back against a piling on the wharf, as the ferry from Sacramento set anchor. She pulled her shawl tighter against the chilly gloom of the late morning. Just watching the men and women bustling to and fro added to her exhaustion after spending the night shivering on the back stoop of a fine house.

Without opium, pain and fear had kept her awake most of the night, but eventually, her body had given way to fitful sleep. She wasn't sure how long she'd slept, but she felt her eyes had barely closed before the housekeeper woke Opal with the whack of a broom and threats of calling the police.

Stiff and aching, Opal had taken nearly an hour to shuffle the few blocks to the wharf and another hour to find someone to help her.

She shifted in a vain attempt to find a more comfortable position on the hard wood planks. The overpowering stench of brine mingled with the foul odor of rotting fish while weary-looking sailors unloaded crates from large ships, passengers boarded ferries, and hired hacks rumbled up and down the boards. Somber seagull cries echoed in the thick fog hovering across the water.

What if the elderly woman who'd promised to deliver Opal's message to the Johnsons hadn't followed through? Of course, she hadn't. Relying on the kindness of a stranger had been a fool's notion. This was a waste of time. Even if Fletcher had received her message, he'd never come. Not after Opal had repaid his previous kindnesses with complaints and a rude departure.

Careful not to put any weight on her right shoulder, she gingerly rose to leave.

"Miss Arlidge!"

She pivoted. Fletcher waved at her from the disembarking crowd. Her mouth fell open.

He pressed between those lingering on the wharf and hurried toward her. Stopping a foot away, he studied her. "I can see you're hurting. Come"—he took her hand and placed it on his arm as if she were a lady—"I've brought something that will help." He attempted to lead her forward, but her feet wouldn't move.

"You came."

"Of course."

"Why?"

"You sent word that you needed help." His tone implied his answer ought to have been obvious.

"But I was so rude to you." The confession escaped without forethought as she drew back.

His brows rose, then he smiled. "I forgive you."

She gaped at him.

"Katie does too."

They forgave her? "But..."

"I caused you so much trouble." She sounded inane, but it was all she could think. "After all the kindness you paid me."

He nodded. "And we forgive you."

"Why?"

"Just as Christ has forgiven us much, Katie and I do our best to forgive others." He offered a gentle smile. "Besides, I can see how much you regret it."

He could? Tears pricked at the backs of her eyes. He meant it. She could see it in his gaze. "I do...I..." What was she to say? "Thank you."

"Now"—he replaced her hand on his arm—"let me take you somewhere we can eat, and I can give you the medicine I've brought." Her heart lifted with surprise until his next words dashed her hopes. "It isn't opium, but Katie assures me it will ease your pains without causing lethargy, itching, or nausea and—most importantly—it doesn't seem to gain the same grip on its users that opium does."

What could he possibly have brought her? Every doctor she'd spoken with had told her there was no other hope for her condition.

Fletcher must have read the skepticism on her face. "I doubt you've tried this medicine before. Katie's mother learned of it from an old Chinese man who gave her the treatment when Katie was young. I'm sorry we didn't have it for you sooner. Katie's mother is with God, and Katie hadn't spoken with the Chinese doctor in many years, so it took a long time to track him down. We received the medicine just this morning." He began leading her down the street. "I'd give it to you now, but Katie said the taste is unpleasant and it would be best to have food and water on hand to help wash it down."

Opal wasn't about to object. The last thing she'd eaten was a bit of stale bread she'd pinched from a baker's rubbish bin. What's more, the meal would give her a chance to work up the nerve she'd need to explain her plan. She'd never been much good at convincing a man to do anything but use her. Even so, if she couldn't convince Fletcher to help her, the Greens or their dandy friend might find and kill Lucy. Or worse, Chiv King might do the deed. If that happened, Opal may as well die too.

CHAPTER 10

JANUARY 12, 1874
LUPINE VALLEY RANCH, CALIFORNIA

*a*t the far northern end of the valley, Preston set three rifles on the makeshift table Lucy had helped him assemble from spare lumber and willow branches. They'd covered it with tent canvas to keep bullets from falling through the slats. Across from the table was a line of tin can targets set into the large dirt mound he'd created in the least rocky portion of the valley. Hopefully, the ten-foot-wide, six-foot-tall berm provided enough buffer. The last thing they needed was for a bullet to ricochet off a boulder.

The sound of small feet crunching dirt grew louder. He glanced right. Lucy was returning from the ranch yard with Esther and Lei Yan. Carmen was out with Ginny and Gideon, learning about the cattle, as she had been all week. Next week, the two younger women would head out to work the cattle and Carmen would learn to shoot. Josie's and Deborah's giggles floated on the breeze from inside the main house where Biddie was teaching them to make bread.

He offered what he hoped was a calming smile to the girls —he simply couldn't think of them as women, despite having learned the toddler belonged to Esther and that Lei Yan had recently passed her seventeenth birthday. Thinking of what these girls had been through made him want to punch every man who'd dared place a finger on them.

Esther's face lost its color, and she stepped back.

Preston followed her gaze and found his fists clenched. He swallowed a curse. Would he never overcome the habits of his father? He relaxed his fingers and glanced at Lucy. Her eyes had gone wide as well. And there was the truest reason he could never win her heart—he was his father's son.

Returning his attention to Esther, he slowly lifted his open hands to show he meant her no harm. "Sorry if I scared you." He tipped his hat back. Perhaps his earnest expression would set her at ease. "The thought of someone trying to hurt you made me mad. But I mean *you* no harm. I'm here to teach you to protect yourselves." With everything that was within him, he hoped they'd never need the skills he was about to teach them.

Esther's shoulders visibly relaxed, and she gave him a small nod.

Before he could make another blunder, he turned toward the prepared weapons. "You'll each be given a rifle today, and it'll be your job to maintain it and handle it safely." He hesitated, not wanting to scare them again, but they needed the truth of the situation they'd put themselves in. "No doubt you noticed the distance between here and the Rowlands' spread on your way in."

Both of the women nodded.

"The Rowlands are your closest neighbor, but even they are too far away to be much help in a true emergency. If you can make it to their place, they'll do anything they can to help you out. But if you're under attack here"—he gestured to the ranch yard and valley behind them—"it'll be up to you to defend yourselves. There are no policemen patrolling these vast desert lands. Your life may depend on the skills I'm going to teach you."

Lucy waved the two women closer to the table. "Come, I'll show you the different parts of the rifles."

Lucy was a natural teacher, patient and calm in her instructions. After expertly handling the rifles, pointing out the various parts and explaining their purposes, she demonstrated how to disassemble the weapons for cleaning and in the case of a jam. Then she showed how to put them back together again. Impressive. He knew from Gideon that Lucy had never handled a rifle prior to arriving at the ranch last summer, yet she spoke and handled the weapons with confidence.

"All right, now it's your turn." Lucy handed each of the women a rifle.

They carefully followed Lucy's instructions, their movements hesitant at first but growing more confident with each passing minute.

They disassembled and reassembled their weapons a handful of times before Preston demonstrated how to load, aim, and fire their rifles. He answered their questions, made sure they understood never to point their weapons at anything they didn't intend to shoot, then stepped back to let them practice.

He tried to remain focused on the task at hand, but his attention divided between the girls' progress and Lucy's calm words as she worked with the girls, giving them advice to improve their aim.

"You're flinching each time you fire." Lucy took Lei Yan's weapon. "Esther, you watch too. I know it's hard, but you need to keep your eyes open and fixed on what you want to shoot. Like this."

Lucy lifted the rifle, took aim, and shot a near bullseye on the target he'd drawn on an empty tin can. The daily practice she'd put in since Biddie's abduction last fall showed in her every move. It was as if the rifle was an extension of her body, as though it had always been there.

He stepped closer, placing himself behind her, and lifted her arm a fraction higher and to the right. "There." His voice came out rough, and he swallowed. The heat of her body so near his own stole his senses. He let his fingers trail up her sleeve to the lock of hair dangling against her shoulder. He tucked it behind her ear. "Try it now."

Clearing his throat, he forced himself to step back. He shouldn't have gotten so close. But the more he tried to suppress his feelings, the more persistent they became. The urge to pack his bags and return to Harvey Arbuckle's Show of Wonders became an ache at the base of his skull, but he couldn't leave the women of this ranch to fend for themselves. Not with what had happened days after his arrival in the fall. This was no place for defenseless women.

Lucy stared at him, a strange look in her eyes he couldn't decipher.

He gestured toward the target. "Go ahead."

Rather than take the shot, she lowered her weapon. "What—"

A shot rang out, shattering the moment and making the girls scream. Preston froze, his breaths slowing as he scanned the valley for the source of the shot. A settling poof of dirt less than six inches from Esther's skirt snagged his gaze. It took him a moment to realize that Esther had accidentally pulled the trigger.

Her face was nearly as red as her hair as she cringed. "Sorry."

He rushed over. Should he send Lucy for bandages? "Are

you hurt?" He grabbed the rifle from Esther's hand and set it on the table, barrel toward the targets.

She shook her head and stuck her feet past the hem of her skirts, one at a time, as if to prove she was unharmed.

He heaved a breath and began repeating the safety instructions. Before he could finish his sentence, another shot rang out, this time hitting the table.

Lucy and the girls screamed again.

Preston grabbed his rifle from where it leaned against the end of the table and scanned the horizon for the attacker. His heartbeat slowed as his thoughts sped.

"Get inside! Now!" He motioned for the girls to run for the house. He scanned the valley's ridge as they scrambled towards safety.

Raucous male laughter drew his gaze to the western rim. A lone man sat atop a horse, his rifle, now lowered, silhouetted against the late-afternoon sun.

Preston widened his stance and set his sights on the man, fury heating his veins. "You have ten seconds to vacate these lands, or I put a bullet through your skull."

Another rider galloped over the ridge, skidding to a stop beside the first. "Morly, you idiot. I told you to wait for me." Clyve scanned the valley as he spoke. "Ginny's as liable to shoot you as spea—" Clyve's gaze landed on Preston, and he lifted his hands wide to show they were empty. "Preston? What're you doing? Don't you recognize me?"

Preston kept his aim steady on the stranger. "You ain't the problem. It's whoever you're talking to that just took a shot at the women when our backs were turned."

Clyve swung toward his companion. "You did what?"

Morly sniggered.

"Are you out of your mind?" Clyve swung back toward Preston. "Was anyone hurt?"

Preston smirked. "Not yet."

Clyve yanked his hat from his head, whapped it against his thigh, and shouted at the man he'd called Morly. "You promised Father you'd be on your best behavior, or he'd send you packing again."

Father? Was this newcomer Clyve's brother?

"Oh yeah?" Morly made a show of looking around. "That's odd. I don't see him. Do you?"

"Of course not, but—"

The man's voice hardened. "And I know *you* ain't going to tell him."

"We aren't kids anymore, Mor. You can't scare me with your —" Clyve's words cut off as Morly raised his rifle toward him.

Preston sent a shot through the man's hat brim.

The horses skittered, forcing Morly to lower his aim as he struggled to calm his mount. Words unfit for ladies flew from his lips.

Preston levered another bullet into the chamber and recentered his aim. "Drop your weapon, Morly. Now."

"You put a hole in my hat, you..." Morly let fly more unsavory words as he turned his rifle on Preston, the movement reflecting a flash of sunlight.

"Don't be a fool." Clyve slapped his own hat back on his head and nodded toward Preston. "He was one of Berdan's sharpshooters. I've seen him shoot a tossed cigarette at two hundred feet off hand."

Morly's rifle didn't budge. "I ain't afraid of you."

A gust of wind blew through the valley, and Preston adjusted his aim. Waited.

Clyve lunged for Morly, knocking the rifle out of his hands as they plummeted to the hard-packed dirt. The two brothers grappled on the ground, their fists flying.

Preston sprinted up the hill and kicked Morly's weapon well out of reach. Not wanting to risk shooting Clyve, Preston set his own rifle aside and jumped into the fray. His first punch sent blood spurting from Morly's nose. The second was a solid right hook on the side of the low-life's jaw that knocked him back to the ground. He pulled back for a third strike, but Clyve caught his arm. Preston shot him a glare.

"Enough." Lucy's beau knelt on the ground with a split lip and a gash near his brow that would probably need stitches. Not to mention, what promised to be two ugly black eyes. "Look at him. He's done."

Preston studied Morly. Clyve was right. The man looked defeated, eyes closed as he groaned, his arms limp at his sides. Still, the desire to punish him for scaring the women and threatening Clyve pulsed through him. Was this what Oliver had felt when he would set into someone?

Preston took a step back. Then two more.

Clyve pulled his brother's hat from the dirt and placed it on Morly's chest. He moved to stand but swayed.

Preston lunged to catch his arm and helped him to his feet. "Feeling dizzy?"

Clyve grimaced. "I can't decide if my head or my hand hurts more." He lifted his right hand, knuckles swollen and bloodied from the fight. "I think I might've broken something."

Preston guided him toward the horses that had shied away from the ruckus. "We need to get you inside. But first..." He motioned to the rope tied to Clyve's saddle. "Can I borrow this?"

Clyve grimaced and glanced at Morly. "He'll be mad enough at losing the fight. If we tie him up, he's sure to want revenge."

"I don't trust him around the women."

"Smart man." Clyve nodded, then winced. "But let me convince him to go home instead of tying him up."

"He needs arresting."

"Are you going to haul him all the way to the sheriff? They won't even charge him over a fight with his brother."

"He shot at the women."

"You said none of them were hurt." Clyve sobered and turned to stare at the house as if he could see through stone walls. "Where's Lucy? And where's Ginny? I can't believe *she* didn't shoot Morly."

"Ginny's not here. She, Gideon, and Carmen are out checking the cattle."

"Is Carmen one of the new women?"

Preston retrieved his rifle and handed Morly's weapon to Clyve. "Never mind that." He pointed to where Morly was trying to sit up. "What are we going to do about him?"

Clyve's shoulders sagged and he lowered his voice. "Give me five minutes...ten, to get him back on his horse and headed home. If I can't, we'll do it your way."

~

*L*ucy held her rifle steady in the keyhole window as Clvye escorted the stranger to his horse. The man, still cursing up a storm, mounted up without his weapon and spun the animal away.

Lucy blew out a breath and leaned her rifle against the wall, then stepped back. "Everything's all right." Thanks to Preston's quick actions. Who *was* that stranger, and what was Clyve doing with someone like that?

Esther threw her hands up with a huff. "What's going on? Who shot at us?" With Biddie taking position at the only other window that afforded a view of the men, Esther and Lei Yan had been left comforting the little ones and waiting for answers.

Lucy pulled open the door. "I don't know, but I'm going to

find out." She strode through the yard and up the hill, meeting Preston partway up. "Who was that?"

Preston's tone matched his scowl. "Clyve's brother."

Lucy gaped at him. "His brother?" How could that be?

Toward the start of their courtship, Clyve had mentioned he had an older brother, but he'd said the man had taken off after an argument with their father more than a decade earlier and hadn't been heard from since. From Clyve's demeanor during the brief explanation, she'd gotten the impression the subject of his brother was a tender one. No wonder Clyve hadn't mentioned Morly again. How could the two of them have been raised by the same father?

The two riders nearing the western rim paused. Clyve turned his mount and rode back toward them, leaving Morly behind. He reigned to a stop beside her and tipped back his hat.

She gasped at the state of his face, her chest pinching. "You're hurt."

He shrugged. "I'll heal."

"You need stitches. Come to the house and I'll—"

"Thanks, but I need to get Morly home. I am so sorry for his behavior." He inspected her, head to toe, his brow creased. "Preston said you weren't injured." His tone held a question.

"I'm unharmed." So many questions danced on the tip of her tongue, but she pressed her lips together. Now was not the time.

His shoulders visibly relaxed. "Just the same, his actions were inexcusable. I'm sorry I let him follow me here. I'll be escorting him home now, which means you and I won't get the time together I'd hoped for." He paused, likely expecting her to express mutual remorse, but her thoughts were too jumbled to form the words. "I guess I'll see you next week?"

Keenly aware of Preston's presence, she nodded and forced a small smile.

Clyve hesitated another second, then turned his mount and rejoined his brother. The two disappeared over the valley's peak.

Preston faced her. "Are you all right?"

Lucy swallowed hard and took a deep breath. "I'm fine. But I can't believe Clyve's brother would do something like that. What kind of man takes a shot at women?"

Preston's expression hardened. "A coward, that's who. And a dangerous one at that. We need to make sure he doesn't come back."

"He's Clyve's brother. Can we really keep him out?"

"Being kin doesn't excuse what he did. And it doesn't mean he won't come back looking for revenge after the way he was just humiliated."

Lucy shuddered. "What are we going to do?"

"We'll keep an eye out. And we'll make sure the women are never alone."

A sense of unease settled over Lucy. Wrapping her arms about herself, she glanced toward their shooting range. "I'm not sure the women will be up for more shooting after that."

"Them learning to shoot is more important than ever." He kicked the dirt. "But you're probably right. Tell them we'll practice again tomorrow."

She returned to the yard, where both Lei Yan and Esther waited in front of the bunkhouse. Esther had Deborah in her arms and was stroking the girl's wavy brown hair.

Josie stood beside them, eyes as round as biscuits fixed on Lucy. "Was that a bandit?" Her whispered voice held a mix of awe and terror.

Lucy started to shake her head, then paused. So far as she knew, Clyve had no idea what Morly had been doing all these years, and his behavior just now didn't suggest he'd been leading a life of virtue. But it was best not to share such doubts with a young girl.

"He's gone now. You don't need to worry about him." Lucy faced Lei Yan and Esther. "It seems our shooting lessons are over for the day. Would you like me to teach you to sew?" Having been forced into immoral service at an abhorrently young age, neither of the women had been instructed in the domestic arts. Although Esther had begun learning at The Home, Lei Yan hadn't been there long enough.

The women glanced at each other, then to Lucy. Esther spoke first. "I think we'd both rather rest, if that's all right with you."

Finally. As she'd feared, Lucy hadn't had a moment to herself since the women's arrival. With Ginny, Gideon, and Carmen still away, perhaps she could sneak into the mine and extract more gems. She smiled at Esther. "Of course. I'll see if Biddie needs help getting supper started."

"Oh." Esther bit her lip, a torn expression on her face as she looked between Deborah and Lucy. "I can help with that."

"No need." She backed away. "I'm sure Biddie has it under control. You stay here and rest." Before the women could protest further, Lucy hurried back to the house.

A quick check assured her Biddie did, indeed, have supper well in hand.

Lucy snagged her canteen. "In that case, I'll go for a walk. Shake off the jitters and all." It wasn't a lie. Walking to the mine would help calm her nerves.

Hands covered in flour as she kneaded dough, Biddie paused to give Lucy an assessing look. "Just a walk?"

Lucy couldn't hold her best friend's gaze. "Of course." She yanked open the door, her heart heavy. Outside, she walked faster and faster. If she walked quickly enough, would the guilt blow off her shoulders and settle with the dust she was kicking up?

Minutes later, she crept into the tunnel. Cool air washed over her as she neared the back, calming her nerves. She made her way to the vein she'd been working on and began chipping away at the rock. It was tedious work, but she found the repetition soothing. The steady clinking of her hammer against the rock filled the silence, and her thoughts drifted to the problem that had plagued her since last summer, when Ginny had ordered her and Biddie never to enter the mine again. How was Lucy going to convince the stubborn woman to not only forgive her for disobeying that order, but to give the wealth to the Davidson's Home for Women and Children? Did the right words exist?

Lord, give me wisdom.

Sometime later, Lucy paused to wipe sweat from her gritty forehead with the back of her wrist. Her arms trembled with fatigue, and she let them hang limp as she sucked in a deep breath of dusty air. Amber candlelight flickered along the walls and ceiling, pushing back the pitch black.

A crunch near the entrance to the mine made her spin, hammer raised in defense. Had Morly returned and somehow found the mine? Heart pounding, Lucy straightened and held her breath. Another crunch. Then footsteps echoed in the mine. A figure emerged from the shadows.

"Preston." She lowered her hammer. "You scared me. What are you doing here?"

Brows furrowed, his nostrils flared as he strode toward her. "What am *I* doing here? What are *you* doing here?" He glanced at the piles of discarded rocks and scattered tools, then glared at her. "Ginny gave specific orders never to enter this mine."

"I know, but you don't understand. I need the money to—"

"And Ginny doesn't?" His gaze landed on something behind her. He pushed past her and stooped down.

Stones rattled in the wooden box, the sound bouncing around the walls as he pivoted with her gem collection. "Is this all of it? Or did you smuggle more with you when you went to

SHOOT AT THE SUNSET

Richard Stevens's ranch with Biddie and Gideon last December?"

Pain stabbed her heart. "What? No, of course not. I would never steal from Ginny."

He shoved the bucket toward her, its contents shifting. "What do you call this?"

"I..." She struggled to find the words to explain, but guilt squeezed her throat.

CHAPTER 11

*P*reston slammed the box of gems on the ground. "What other secrets have you been keeping?" Not waiting for her reply, he pivoted to leave. Ginny needed to know.

Lucy caught his arm, the zing of her touch halting him. "Wait. Please." She moved to stand in front of him, her grip sliding down to his wrist and lifting his hand to enclose his fingers with both of her hands. "Please, don't tell Ginny."

The pleading in Lucy's big brown eyes tugged at his heart, but he shook the sensation away. How could he have been so wrong about her character? "I won't keep secrets from my sister." Not anymore. Not after what had happened at Fort Colville fourteen years ago—the last place he'd seen his sister before coming to this ranch.

He'd not wanted to keep secrets from Ginny then either. But he'd believed his big sister was safer not knowing details about the errands Oliver had ordered Preston to run or anything about the ruses he was forced to learn and use on unsuspecting strangers. And Ginny *had* been safer, until the night their lives splintered.

That night, Preston had been ordered to keep quiet about another of Oliver's risky schemes to recover gambling losses. However, Oliver's pockets were empty. There had to be more to their pa's vile intentions than he was letting on. Still, Preston obeyed. As always.

When Oliver wagered Ginny in a game of Brag against Lieu-tenant Colonel Atkinson, Preston considered walking out, but Ginny would pay the price. What neither Preston nor Oliver anticipated was Atkinson's skill at stacking the deck. Despite Preston's card counting, Atkinson's stacked deck ensured their loss. Normally, Oliver would put a card cheat six feet under without blinking, but shooting a military officer would see Oliver hanged...

After the game, Preston stumbled out of the tent by the river and knelt in the dark, trying not to vomit. He tried to hide his furious trembling by petting his dog, Scruff.

The stench of sweat, whiskey, and smoke filled his nostrils as Oliver shook his lit cigarette in Preston's face. "Don't go blab-bing to your sister. You let *me* explain, if it comes to that." Oliver smirked. "But it won't."

"What do you mean, 'if it comes to that'? You lost. Gwen-dolyn needs to know." Preston hated the fake names, Gwen-dolyn and Peter, that Pa had been making them use since leaving Ma and Biddie in San Francisco. At the moment, though, he liked the idea that no one from this place would be able to follow them once they left and changed their names again.

Preston stood and signaled Scruff to follow him toward the log bridging the river. "We need to pack up and—"

Oliver grabbed the back of his collar, jerking him to a stop. "We ain't going nowhere until I get back what's mine."

Scruff growled, and Preston pulled free of his father's grip to give Scruff a reassuring pat on the head before Oliver could turn his anger on the loyal mutt.

He glared at his pa. "But Gwendolyn—"

"Atkinson won't lay a finger on your sister. I'll see to it."

Sure he would. Even as he spoke, Oliver's gaze drifted toward the saloon. Preston clamped his lips shut. He'd wait for Oliver to get drunk, as usual. Then Preston would sneak away with Ginny, just as he'd been trying to do for the last year. She couldn't refuse to leave this time. Not once she understood what Oliver had done.

Oliver leaned forward until his rancid breath feathered Preston's face. "I've got a plan, so you just keep your mouth shut, boy. You hear me?"

Preston jerked his head in a nod. He could hear Oliver, but at fourteen, Preston was already taller than half the soldiers— hardly a boy anymore. And he was through with obeying Oliver's commands.

Preston wasn't sure the few coins he'd managed to stuff into the soles of his shoes were enough to bribe someone to take them to Fort Vancouver, or even if anyone from Fort Colville was bound for that place soon. But he'd figure that out later. Worst case, he, Ginny, and Scruff would set out on foot, following the river until someone took them on board. It'd be a long, dangerous journey, but they were tough. They could make it. So long as they were together.

Oliver strode toward the saloon. Who knew how he'd pay for the booze. But he'd succeed somehow, just as surely as he had no plan at all to stop Atkinson from claiming Preston's big sister.

Five minutes later, Ginny gaped at him, her cheeks flushed from the heat of the cook fire outside their teetering shanty. "Have you lost your marbles? You know how dangerous—"

"I'd rather take our chances with wild animals and Indians than stay here, waiting for that scum to come claim you."

"I still don't believe you." She stirred the pot of soup hanging over the pink coals. "You must have misunderstood. Pa has his faults, but he would never—"

"He did." Preston resisted the urge to throw his stubborn sister over his shoulder. She may be a year older than him, but he was taller and stronger. "I was there. There's no misunderstanding. The lieutenant colonel made it clear he'd come for you first thing in the morning."

Ginny's face paled. "But you said Pa had a plan."

"Since when do you believe Oliver?" Preston held her gaze.

Her shoulders slumped. "All right. I'll go."

He thrust a flour sack at her. "You start packing. Make sure you add any food we've got left that'll keep."

"Where're you going?"

"To find out if anyone's heading to Vancouver in the morning." Preston strode back toward the river, Scruff at his heels.

An hour later, he'd learned of a small group planning to set off down the river at first light and located their waiting raft. Already loaded with empty crates and barrels to be refilled at Fort Vancouver, it would make the perfect escape. Preston jogged back toward their shack, set far back from the rest of the encampment that had grown up across the river from the fort. Ginny would be relieved they didn't have to walk through the woods.

As he neared, the scent of burned soup stung his nose. Smoke drifted from the pot still hanging over the coals. Preston's step faltered. Where was Ginny? A muffled cry came from inside the thin wood walls of their shanty. Scruff took off, barking ferociously. Preston sprinted after him.

A man yelled, "Get off me, you—"

Scruff yelped, then continued barking.

Preston jerked back the tattered sheet they used as a door

and took in the scene in a blink. Atkinson sat in the middle of Ginny's pallet, kicking at Scruff while jerking his trousers up from his ankles. Ginny hugged her knees in the corner behind Scruff, her hair mussed and tears streaming down her cheeks. Her lip was split.

With a roar, Preston grabbed fistfuls of the lieutenant colonel's shirt and yanked him onto his feet. He shoved the monster through the doorway and followed, fists flying. Blood spurted from Atkinson's nose and oozed from a cut on his cheek. The man tried to defend himself but stumbled over Scruff, who'd followed them out. Preston fisted the front of Atkinson's shirt and held him upright as he landed blow after blow, barely registering the pain it caused in his own hand.

"Peter, enough." Ginny's distressed cry interrupted his assault.

He glanced over his shoulder. She stood shaking in the shack's opening, red splotches on her face revealing where the brute had hit her.

Preston returned to punishing the man in his grip. Three blows to Atkinson's gut and another to his ribs.

"Stop! Please. He's an officer. They'll hang you if you kill him."

Preston didn't care. The man needed to die for what he'd done to Ginny.

Her fingers gripped his arm. "Please," she wept. "I need you."

Preston let her tug him back and released his grip on Atkinson. The man fell to the ground, groaning as blood leaked from his mouth, dribbling down his chin. Three of his teeth were missing.

Scruff stationed himself beside Atkinson, growling.

Preston turned away and pulled Ginny into his arms. "I'm so sorry. I never should have left you alone."

"You didn't know. You couldn't..." Sobbing swallowed the rest of her words.

A moment later, Scruff barked and Ginny shrieked, "Preston, look out!"

He spun as Atkinson reached for his pistol, which lay on the ground near the shack's opening.

Preston beat him to it and aimed the weapon at the lieutenant colonel. "I'm taking you to the colonel. The army won't let you get away with this, no matter what your rank."

The man laughed viciously. "You idiot. Don't you know who I am?"

The hairs on Preston's neck stood up. "I don't care. I'm turning you in."

Ginny set her hand on Preston's shoulder. "The colonel is his pa."

Preston tensed. He hadn't bothered learning too much about the soldiers in this place, figuring Oliver would have their little family moving on soon enough that it wouldn't matter.

Apparently, Preston had been wrong.

Atkinson laughed. "And my grandfather's a brigadier general. You try to take me in and they'll arrest *you* for assaulting a U.S. Army officer. And who knows what else they'll find to charge you with once they start asking around about a *Preston* Babbington?" He spit blood onto the ground. "Is that even your real last name, or is that a lie too? Not that it matters. My father will see you jailed for the rest of your life for what you've done to me."

"He's right," Ginny whispered.

Preston itched to pull the trigger. The scum didn't deserve to live, and if the army wouldn't punish him, then—

A glint near Atkinson's boot was all the warning Preston had before the man pulled a knife.

Preston squeezed the trigger.

Atkinson froze, then dropped the knife to press his hands over the hole in his chest. He stared at Preston. "You shot me." Retrieving the knife, Atkinson staggered to his feet and lunged for Preston.

Scruff sank his teeth into the man's calf.

Preston pulled the trigger three more times.

Atkinson fell again. This time, he didn't get up. A few seconds later, his chest stopped moving.

A chill passed over Preston and his fingers went limp. The pistol dropped to the dirt. He'd just taken a man's life. No matter that the man had left Preston no choice and deserved what he got. Preston's stomach threatened to upheave itself. He wrapped an arm around Ginny's shoulders. "Scruff, come."

The mutt released his grip on the dead man and followed them into the shack.

Preston turned Ginny to face him. "What do you nee—"

"What've you done?" Oliver's slurred words brought Preston's head around. Their pa glared at them from the opening. "I'll never get my money back now. You ungrateful..." Red-faced, he waved the lieutenant colonel's pistol at Ginny, too bleary-eyed to hold a steady aim.

Preston's chest burned and his fists clenched. "You ain't going to hurt me or Ginny no more." He leapt at Oliver, clamping a hand over the pistol in his pa's grip. They tumbled outside, wrestling for control.

Scruff joined the fray, sinking his teeth into Oliver's upper arm.

Oliver cried out just as his knee connected with Preston's crotch.

Preston gasped and adjusted his position to protect the tender region while still grappling for the pistol.

Oliver jerked the weapon free, aiming at the dog still clamped onto his arm.

Preston punched Oliver's face.

Bang!

Preston yanked the pistol out of Oliver's grip.

But it was too late.

Scruff lay unmoving, a hole in his neck and a pool of blood growing beneath him.

"No!" Ginny's cry mixed with Preston's.

He shoved Oliver away and knelt beside Scruff, running his free hand along the mutt's still body. Preston's chest ached as if *he'd* been the one shot.

Oliver made a clumsy grab for the weapon, but Preston spun away, jumping to his feet.

His entire being trembled as he raised the gun and aimed it at his pa.

"Preston, no!" Ginny leaped in front of the pistol, her eyes pleading with him for forgiveness. Despite everything, she still cared about Pa.

Preston forced his finger away from the trigger and lowered the weapon.

Shouts drew his attention to a group of soldiers in the distance, charging in their direction.

"Well, isn't this a pickle?" Oliver sneered over Ginny's head and looked pointedly from the approaching crowd to the lieutenant colonel's body. "Seems you're about to hang for murdering this man in cold blood."

Ginny clasped her hands over her mouth. "Pa, no. It wasn't...he didn't..."

"Sure, he did." Oliver's grin turned cold as steel. "And I saw the whole thing."

Ginny disappeared into the shack and reappeared a heartbeat later. "Run!" She thrust a lumpy flour sack at him, and he caught it with his free hand. A quick glance showed his clothes and a roll stuffed inside.

He looked from the soldiers, almost within shooting range, to his sister. "Where's your bag?"

"You'll be faster without me. Now, go!"

"Not without you."

She pulled Pa's rifle from where it leaned against an empty crate and aimed it at Preston. "I said, go!"

He backed up. "Ginny..." She couldn't mean it. Of course, she didn't mean it. She just wanted him to go. Ignoring the oncoming soldiers, he searched his sister's eyes. The stubborn girl had made up her mind. There'd be no changing it. And if he stayed, they'd hang him for sure.

Feeling as though his heart were being torn in two, Preston ran...

Like the coward who'd raised him, Preston had left his family behind. But in the years since, he'd promised himself that someday he'd make amends for his mistakes, and he'd never keep secrets from his sister again.

"Preston?" Lucy's voice brought him back to the present. She waved a hand across his vision. "Are you unwell?"

He pressed his eyes closed, shoving the memories back into the farthest corners of his mind. "I'm all right." He opened his eyes, picked up the box of gems, and stepped around Lucy. "And I'm telling Ginny."

Keeping secrets only led to haunting regrets.

～

*L*ucy's mind raced as she followed Preston out of the tunnel. Was there anything she could say to change his mind? Would her motives matter? She pushed through the juniper bush. The sky was already painted in pinks and oranges. Ginny would be home soon.

Preston stormed across the valley toward the house.

Lucy dogged his heels. "If you'd just listen to me, you'd understand. The Davidsons—"

Three riders, partially silhouetted against the setting sun, redirected Preston's steps toward the northern rim.

Gideon, Carmen, and Ginny rode down the valley slope. There was something odd about Gideon's posture. He appeared slumped to one side. As they drew closer, Lucy noted his squinted eyes and grimaced expression, all signs of one of the migraines he frequently battled—a souvenir from the war.

Ginny pulled ahead and met them at the edge of the ranch yard. "What's wrong?" She scanned the valley, then slid from her horse, Carmen a second behind her.

Preston thrust the box of gem ore forward for Ginny's inspection.

Her glare shot to Lucy. "You've been mining." There was no question in her tone. "After I ordered you to stay out." She gave a jerk of her head. "Pack your things. You're no longer welcome here."

"Now, hold on." Gideon reined to a stop beside them and slowly dismounted, misery evident in his every move. "Biddie won't be happy with you ordering her best friend to leave."

Ginny huffed. "Then she should pick her friends more carefully. I don't stand for anyone disobeying my orders here. Especially not thieves."

"I'm not a thief." Lucy's shout surprised her as much as anyone else.

Gideon flinched and pressed the heels of his palms to his eyes.

Lucy swallowed and took a deep breath before confronting Ginny's hard gaze. "I'd planned to convince you to give some of this to the Davidsons for The Home. You weren't doing anything with it, and they're always running low on funds." That much was true. No one needed to know the depths of the dire situation they'd soon find themselves in. Not if she could convince Ginny to share the wealth. It might be enough to minimize the impact of what was coming. "Leaving the gems in the ground seemed like such a waste when the money they'd bring could do so much good."

Ginny's glare flickered, but her scowl remained. "That wasn't your decision to make."

"Don't you want to help the people who helped you after the bandits stole your herd and burned the ranch to the ground, leaving you with nothing? Just like you, the women and children in The Home need help making a fresh start."

Ginny's tone turned defensive, and her chin raised. "I'm paying the Davidsons back—"

"And in the meantime, they're forced to turn away those in need for lack of the funds required to expand the way they'd planned to before receiving your letter."

"I took in these women, didn't I?" Ginny gestured toward the women's bunkhouse. "Besides, Biddie says that Green fellow should be paying them returns on their investment any day now."

If only Lucy could believe that. "But you could be doing more." She pointed to the bucket Preston still held. "This wealth would mean a world of difference to the Davidsons and the people they serve. Though you haven't said much, I know you understand what it's like for women at the mercy of bad men and bad circumstances. What would it have meant for someone to step in and help you when you needed it most?"

Ginny winced but said nothing. She stared into the gem ore with eyes that seemed to see right through the crystals, her expression softer, almost sad.

Biddie emerged from the house. "What's going on?" Her gaze skipped from one person to another before settling on the bucket in Preston's hand and jumping back to Lucy. "Oh, Lucy. Why?"

Lucy's shoulders drooped at the disappointment in her dearest friend's expression. "I'm sorry. I just wanted to help."

Gideon put his arm around Biddie—whether to brace her

from the news or seek his own physical support, Lucy couldn't tell. His pain-laced words came through gritted teeth. "Your sister has ordered Lucy off the ranch."

Biddie's eyes widened. "Gideon, I think you should go inside. I can handle this."

That the strong man left without a word was testament to how severe his pain had become.

Once the door had closed, Biddie rounded on her sister. "Lucy cannot leave. She's standing up with me at the wedding in two weeks. And besides, you agreed to let me keep a quarter of the ranch instead of paying Father back in full. That makes me part owner, which means I have a say in who stays and who goes. And I say, Lucy stays."

Lucy's heart warmed at her friend's defense.

Ginny's expression hardened again. "I still own three quarters of this ranch, and I say, she goes. I can't have anyone disobeying my orders and getting away with it."

Lucy's gaze caught on Preston's. His piercing look seemed to be searching her very soul for truth. After a moment, he rubbed the back of his neck, then looked at Ginny. "You're right. Obedience is important on a ranch. It keeps people safe."

Ginny nodded, and Lucy's heart fell to her stomach. Whatever he'd seen in her eyes hadn't been enough to convince him of her sincerity. She couldn't look at him as he continued.

"But I also know you have a good heart and don't want to turn away women and children in need—leave them suffering —when you could extend a helping hand."

Wait, what? Lucy tried to read his solemn expression. Was he changing his mind? Could he be on her side now?

He glanced at the box in his arms, then returned to studying Ginny. "What Lucy has found looks to be worth a lot of money. I don't understand why you don't want anyone mining these gems." He lifted one brow. "Are you afraid Lucy won't be honest about how much she finds, or are you worried others will find out and cause trouble?"

"Both. She's already deceived me. Clearly, I can't trust her."

"Then let me work with Lucy while she mines to make sure everything's done right. I remember enough from that time Oliver sent me into the mines to make sure nothing is wasted and no one gets hurt. And when we're ready to sell, I'll make sure we handle it in a way that no one knows where the ore came from." His serious expression split with an impish grin. "You trust me, don't you?"

Ginny's scowl cracked with the tiniest smile. "You know I do."

Lucy held her breath and waited for the rest of Ginny's response. It stung that Preston thought she needed watching to be kept honest, but at least he was willing to give her a chance to keep digging. He'd been so angry at first, she'd expected him to side with Ginny and escort her from the ranch's lands.

But would his offer be enough to sway the notoriously stubborn owner of Lupine Valley Ranch? Or would she be forced to leave, empty-handed—with little hope of her own survival and no hope for the survival of The Davidson's Home for Women and Children? Without those gems, there would be nothing Lucy could do to stop the destruction Mr. Green had planned for everything the Davidsons had devoted their lives to building.

Please Lord, let her be reasonable for once.

CHAPTER 12

November 28, 1873
San Francisco, California

*P*ain roused Opal from a restless slumber. Where was her pipe? Without opening her eyes, she fumbled for the small table beside the bed. Instead of rough, scarred wood, her fingers slid across a smooth, varnished surface. What in the world? She squinted at the table. It was simple, but far too fine for her room at Pete's. Where was she?

She examined her surroundings, but another surge of pain slammed her eyes shut with a sharp intake of breath. Her pipe. Where was her pipe? A small strip of folded paper sat on the table's surface where her pipe belonged. Bracing herself against the pain of movement, she took it up and unfolded it.

Your daughter needs you sober.

The events of the past few weeks came back in a rush. She'd written this note to herself at Fletcher's request and had been carrying it around, tucked inside her sleeve each day as she cleaned the rooms of the Green Hotel. At night, she set it on her table so she'd see it first thing in the morning. And resist temptation.

Oh, but the need for relief was strong this morning.

"Another bad morning, is it?" Cathryn's compassionate voice startled Opal.

She'd nearly forgotten about the other maid who shared the attic room Opal had been assigned the day she'd been hired. She still marveled that the manager had so readily accepted Fletcher's forged letters of character and recommendation. Did the man sincerely believe she'd just stepped off the train after serving at the Fifth Avenue Hotel for ten years? He must have, despite her complete lack of a New York accent. Why else would he have hired her?

"Here." A spoon, filled with dark liquid, came into Opal's view.

She opened her mouth and allowed Cathryn to pour in some of the medicine Fletcher had given her. How humbling it was to allow this girl, who was nearly the same age as Lucy, to tend to her, but Opal's agony silenced her pride. "Thank you."

After taking the bitter concoction for weeks now, she'd learned several minutes would pass before she felt the effect, and even then, the pain wouldn't entirely go away. But the medicine brought the misery down to a manageable level. That was all she needed for now.

"Will you be well enough on your own?" Cathryn hesitated at the door, two blond curls peeking from beneath her white mob cap.

Opal forced a stiff nod.

Her roommate seemed to relax. "I'll try to sneak a biscuit for you when Cook isn't looking, in case you don't make it to breakfast."

As the girl slipped out the door, Opal mumbled her thanks. Her mind, however, was already searching the pain-induced fog for memories of Mr. Green's schedule for the day. Had she heard Mr. Green planned to come to the hotel today or was it tomorrow? And what about Junior?

Opal drew in a long breath. *Be patient. Let the medicine work and your mind will clear.* The silent lecture did little to quiet the voice in her head shouting at her to hurry, her daughter's life was at stake. Chiv King could be out there hunting Lucy, even now. Or had he already found her? *No.* Opal battled the pain to concentrate on relaxing her muscles. Fletcher had confirmed Moira's claim that Lucy had left the city and was safely in the desert with her best friend, Biddie Davidson. If something had happened to her, Fletcher would have heard and told Opal. She needed to hold onto the hope that Lucy would remain undiscovered.

As the medicine took effect, her mental haze dissipated, and the events of the past three weeks pushed forward.

Ten days ago, she'd begun to despair of discovering what Lucy had accidentally uncovered. Opal's plan to find evidence of wrongdoings and turn it over to the police so the Greens and the dandy would be arrested and Lucy could return to San Francisco had begun to seem as foolish and improbable of success as Fletcher had warned.

Then Opal had overheard one of the maids whispering about a hidden passageway at the evening meal. A few careful questions had prompted the sharing of rumors that the secret hall had been designed to meet the needs of the wealthiest gentlemen guests who occasionally requested that entertainment be delivered to their room with discretion. The possibility that such a space might reveal secrets that could save Lucy had kept Opal searching long after tears had begun trickling down her face. For many nights, she'd not returned to her room until well past midnight.

But she'd found it. And the discovery had proven as useful as she'd hoped.

Mr. Green's office shared a wall with the secret passage.

However, because Junior was in charge of the hotel, Mr. Green spent less time on the premises than she imagined most hotel owners did. When he was around, he was usually busy with plans for the new, grander hotel he was having built across the street. From what she'd overheard, the place would rival some of the fanciest palaces in Europe—if he managed to complete it.

Over the past several days, Opal had managed to eavesdrop on four meetings between Mr. Green and his son. Unfortunately, a last-minute guest arrival had forced her to miss her employer's only meeting with the dandy. Today, she'd have another chance.

The mysterious man's real name, according to the porter she'd spoken to, was Senator Garfield Saville. Although, no one agreed on which big city from back east he represented. Regardless, the porter had learned from Mr. Green's valet that a meeting was scheduled between the powerful men for one o'clock this afternoon.

Opal pushed herself from bed and donned her maid's uniform. She'd need to work quickly if she hoped to have time to listen to their conversation.

Eight hours later, she rushed up the servant's stairs despite the fire in her back. She was late.

As best she could tell from the conversations she'd previously overheard, Mr. Green had secretly suffered tremendous losses in the recent economic panic that led to the closure of several banks across the country. What she couldn't figure out was precisely how he'd managed to conceal his dire financial situation. She'd gleaned enough to know it involved something shady, something he worried could ruin him, land him in jail, and possibly see him hung if brought to light.

And they believed Lucy had discovered this secret. No wonder they'd been desperate to silence her daughter.

Heart pounding, Opal slipped into the empty fifth-floor

corridor. She tugged the tapestry that released the hidden entrance and scurried to press her ear firmly against the wall in the secret hallway.

Male voices rumbled in Mr. Green's office. The meeting wasn't over. She'd made it in time.

"You're sure Lucy Arlidge hasn't told anyone?" Mr. Green's tense mention of Opal's daughter sent ice through her veins. This was the first time they'd mentioned Lucy. Opal had arrived just in time.

A deep voice that must belong to Senator Saville replied, "I've found no evidence that she has. Wherever she and her mother fled to, they haven't returned. Nor have the Davidsons received any mail from anyone by the name of Arlidge."

Opal blinked. They thought she'd left the city with Lucy? That answered the nagging, irrational fear that the men somehow knew Opal was posing as a maid and they were waiting for the right time to kill her.

Mr. Green's skeptical voice interrupted her thoughts. "How certain are you we can trust that spy of yours?"

"Completely." A chair creaked. "I think we scared Miss Arlidge enough, she'll keep her mouth shut. But I've got someone keeping tabs on the Davidson House and Pete's Palace, just in case."

"Fine. So long as she doesn't return to the city or write any letters, we'll let her go. For now."

The men exchanged farewells. Then footsteps followed by a muffled click signaled that Mr. Green had closed the door behind his departing guest.

She held her breath waiting for the sounds that had always come after Junior's departures. There it was. What *was* that quiet scraping? A drawer? A hidden cabinet door? More importantly, *where* was it coming from? If she could pinpoint from what part of the room the sound emanated, she'd have a better chance of finding whatever Mr. Green was hiding when she finally managed to sneak inside her employer's office.

At the far end of the secret hallway, a door quietly swooshed open. The dim light of a candle illuminated the secret entrance as a well-dressed man entered with a woman Opal didn't know but understood far better than any of her coworkers might guess. Opal straightened, her neck aching, and tiptoed in the opposite direction. Thank goodness, there were no fixed lights in this hall. If the couple noticed her at all, they'd never be able to recognize her at that distance in the dark.

Nevertheless, she held her breath as she eased open another door and slipped into an empty guest room. Once closed, the door disappeared behind a painting and cleverly cut decorative wood trim. If she hadn't just exited, she'd never guess the opening existed.

She crept across the room and cracked open the door to the public corridor. The space was unoccupied. Opal slipped out, closing the door behind her.

Less than three minutes later, Opal had completed a trip to the fourth-floor linen closet and strode, arms full of clean linens, toward the next room assigned to her for the afternoon cleaning.

The moment she stepped inside, a familiar smell tickled her nose. Tightness squeezed her chest. Pain blossomed in her cheek, and she cried out, closing her eyes. She thrust her hands up to ward off her husband's next blow. A burst of pain in her middle sent her to the muddy ground.

Her fingertips pressed into soft, woven fibers.

Wait...

Heart pounding, she forced her eyes open. Wiped away the tears.

She knelt on the carpeted floor of one of the Green Hotel's

guest suites. Not the hard wooden floor of the kitchen in their small cottage on the outskirts of San Francisco.

She pressed her fingers against the thick wool. Stroked it as she sucked in a slow, deep breath, held it, and then released it slowly.

You're not there. He's not here. You're safe. You're safe. It's over.

She forced herself to focus on her luxurious surroundings and continue breathing slowly. Her bedroom at the cottage had been decorated in blues and whites. This room was covered in greens and golds. Her headboard and footboard had been modest. This bed had tall, ornately carved posts at each corner.

With trembling hands, she gathered the dropped linens.

Echoes of her own screams mixed with his angry words in her mind. *"How dare you threaten me?"* Still kneeling on the carpet, her whimpered reply escaped as a whisper now. "I'm not. I'm sorry. I won't say a word."

It wasn't enough. He struck her again and again, until at last, he seemed to grow weary. He stomped out of the house without a backward glance. She lay still, no longer able to scream or even cry.

Opal blinked hard, shoving the memories away as she rubbed her palms against the silk linens in her hands. It was over.

She rose on shaking legs and faced the bed. He was gone.

No. He'd never been here. Not in this hotel, this room. She hadn't seen Lucy's father in years. He'd moved to New York. Or so Opal had heard. She'd never been brave enough to pass by his fancy mansion and check if it were true.

When she'd come to after the beating, she'd been told it was Lucy's screams that drew the attention of a neighbor. A doctor had been called.

Opal couldn't pay the bill. Somehow Henry and Cecilia Davidson had been alerted to her situation. They paid for the physician, and when men came to ensure that she and Lucy left her cottage, the Davidsons took them in.

Still reeling from the shock of the unexpected memory, Opal set the clean linens on a chair and bent to remove the soiled bedding. She froze. His cologne wafted from the pillowcase.

Her heart beating against her ribcage, she whirled and scanned the room. Again and again, her eyes sought out every possible hiding place. But her husband—or rather, the man who'd illegally married her while concealing the fact that he already had a wife—wasn't there.

Opal gripped the smooth cotton of her maid's uniform.

You're safe. You're safe. You're safe.

Still, she couldn't remain. Before she'd registered the decision to leave, she was in the hallway. Her gaze landed on Cathryn. Cathryn would help her. The room still needed tending, but there was no way Opal could force herself back inside. Not now. Not today. Maybe not ever.

Besides, she wasn't really here to clean rooms. She was here to save her daughter. Which meant she needed a plan for sneaking into Mr. Green's office.

CHAPTER 13

JANUARY 15, 1874
LUPINE VALLEY RANCH, CALIFORNIA

ucy tipped her chin toward the afternoon sunlight, enjoying its warmth and the relative silence as she refilled her canteen with frigid spring water. Ginny, Carmen, Lei Yan, and Gideon had ridden out early that morning to check on the cattle and hadn't returned yet. Near the cook fire in front of the house, Biddie used a spoon in one hand to stir a pot of something she must be fixing for the evening meal while she held up a slate with letters chalked across its surface. Sitting on crates and large rocks ringed around the fire were Esther, Deborah, and Josie. Their eyes were fixed on the slate, and their lips were moving, but what must be their alphabet recitation was little more than indistinguishable whispers from this distance.

She capped her canteen and started toward the barn just as Preston emerged from the tall stone structure.

He met her between the garden and the backside of the

barn with his own canteen in one hand and a blanket slung over his other arm. "Ready?"

"What's the blanket for?"

"I thought it would be more comfortable to sit on when we eat later." He jiggled the blanket to reveal a sack clenched in his other hand. "I know you've been working hard today, so I thought you'd appreciate a snack."

"How thoughtful."

He winked and gestured south. "After you."

Ignoring the unwelcome warmth his care and cheerfulness evoked, she turned toward the southern end of the valley and led the way to the hidden mine.

With the worry of being caught by Ginny a thing of the past, Lucy and Preston had brought more supplies to the mine, and the pattern of slowly chipping ore and timidly hammering it herself at the back of the tunnel had disappeared. Now, Preston and Lucy began their afternoons working side by side to free the raw material from the mountain. Once they had a decent-sized pile, Preston used their sledgehammer to break it into smaller chunks. Then they hauled it to where a half water barrel now sat against one side of the tunnel near enough to the entrance to get a decent amount of sunlight.

There had been some discussion of setting the wash station outside the tunnel, but there wasn't enough space between the bush and the opening. Setting it on the opposite side of the juniper, in plain sight of anyone who passed by, would draw too much attention. So the barrel had been set inside the tunnel.

They took turns using a mining pan to wash the ore, separating the rocks and dirt from the gems. Once the material was as separated and cleaned as possible, the raw gems were tucked away in the box buried at the back of the mine. As the mine extended into the mountain, the box's hiding place moved with it. At the end of each day, they set a lid on the box and covered the treasure with a pile of tailings. Just in case.

In place of her dim tallow candle, the light of two brightly flickering lanterns now cast shadows along the narrow tunnel as Preston chipped away at the hard rock wall beside her. Their pickaxe strikes echoed through the confined space and thickened the air with dust. She set her pickaxe aside and reached for her canteen.

A loud crack, followed by a rumble brought her head up just as the upper section of the mine wall she'd been working on gave way. Huge rocks tumbled down, bouncing off her head before she ducked, hands raised. Preston's arms came around her waist. He yanked her backward, and the two of them toppled to the ground. An avalanche of debris buried the spot where Lucy had been stooped a moment before.

"Are you all right?" Preston shifted out from beneath her to kneel at her side as the dust settled.

She couldn't take her gaze from the destruction.

Preston placed one hand on each side of her face and turned it toward his. Wincing, he lightly traced his thumb along her stinging, throbbing forehead. "You've got a scrape and probably a bruise, but I don't see anything serious here. How do you feel? Are you dizzy? Confused?"

She blinked, trying to rein in her thoughts. "I'm all right. I think. I have a headache, but I don't think it's serious."

Preston heaved a heavy sigh and reached for his canteen. He pulled a handkerchief from his pocket, dampened it with water, and pressed the fabric to her forehead. "I'm so sorry."

"It wasn't your fault. It was an accident."

"I should have seen it coming." He raked his free hand through his thick brown waves. "I'm the one with experience. I should have realized we were getting in too far. I should have seen the signs that the tunnel was unstable and insisted we stop. We need to install bracing beams. I should have—"

"Stop. It wasn't..." Lucy pressed her fingertips to his lips, intending to stop his self blame, but the moment she made contact, she knew her mistake. A pleasant dance of tingles erupted in her belly and sucked the air from her lungs. She jerked her hand away and backpedaled until she was against the opposite wall.

Surprise and then suspicion filled Preston's expression as he watched her retreat. He opened his mouth, clearly intending to question her behavior, but she spoke first.

"You saved me. That's what matters. If it weren't for you, I'd have been in here alone. So really, it could have been much worse. Thank you for saving my life."

Preston sucked in a breath and made a noise as if a word had tried to escape but he stopped it. His mouth closed, and he looked down before shaking his head. "No thanks necessary." He tucked his handkerchief back into his pocket and surveyed the pile of fallen debris. "I think we should call it a day, though. That was too close."

Lucy studied the place near the ceiling where the rocks had broken loose. "It looks stable to me. Do you really think more will come down?"

Preston stood and studied the area for several silent minutes, tapping on it now and then with his pickaxe. "No. It seems like what was going to come loose already has. Still, I want to get some bracing beams in here before we do any more digging. I don't want another scare like that." His eyes met hers with a deeper fright in their brown depths than she would have guessed.

She forced her gaze to the nearest flickering lantern and reluctantly agreed. "But what about this?" She shifted onto her knees and pointed at the new pile. "Shouldn't we check to see if any gems came loose?"

Preston lifted the sledgehammer. "Sure. Why don't you look through the pile?" With his free hand, he hefted a chunk bigger than her head and set it a few feet away. "I'll break up the larger pieces."

Lucy took a swallow of water from her canteen before carefully examining the loosened debris for glimmers of the cinnamon-red gems Preston called spessartine garnets.

Aside from the rhythmic strike of Preston's sledgehammer, an uncomfortable silence filled the tunnel—as though the lingering effect of her foolish touch to his lips still hung in the air between them. She searched her mind for a safe topic of conversation. Anything to strengthen the barrier around her heart.

"You know, I've never understood why neither you nor Ginny ever tried to find Biddie." What kind of heartless man abandoned his sister like that? Sure, their father made him leave initially, but Preston had been grown and on his own for years now. Why had he never contacted Biddie before coming to this valley? "She spent eighteen years wondering what had happened to you, Ginny, and Oliver."

Preston let the head of his sledgehammer drop to the ground, and he straightened. "The truth is, I did find her."

Lucy spun to fully face him. "You found Biddie? When? How? No, wait. Biddie would have told me if—"

"She never knew." Preston hesitated, then he released the tool handle, and his shoulders sagged. "After I ran away from Oliver, I went back to San Francisco hoping to find Biddie and our Mama. It had been six years since Oliver made us leave them behind, but I foolishly hoped they'd somehow made out all right and would still be in that miserable little house, waiting for me. Of course, they weren't. The house wasn't even there. It'd been replaced by a butcher shop. It took me almost two weeks to find someone who knew that Mama had died and Biddie had been taken by a wealthy couple who ran a charity home. I ran straight to the place, determined to rescue Biddie from what I thought would be a rundown orphanage with mean supervisors who beat her for no reason."

He shrugged sheepishly. "It was the only kind of orphanage

I'd heard of." He dusted his hands on his trousers before shoving them into his pockets. "Of course, the Davidsons' charity home is nothing like that. Right away, I could see it was well kept and the kids in the yard looked happy. I watched through the windows all day hoping to catch a glimpse of Biddie. The sun was almost set by the time a fancy carriage pulled up and out stepped Mr. Davidson, followed by my little sister, another little girl with brown hair"—Preston paused to shoot her a look that said he now suspected that brown-haired girl had been Lucy—"and Mrs. Davidson. Instead of being dressed in the cast-off rags I'd expected, Biddie was dressed like a miniature version of Mrs. Davidson with her hair done in fancy curls and everything. The two of you were grinning ear to ear as you skipped up the stairs, holding hands." He grinned himself. "Mrs. Davidson scolded you about proper behavior. You were eleven, after all, and far too grown to be skipping, she said. But I could tell she wasn't really mad. Her voice was so gentle...like Mama's was."

Were those tears in his eyes?

Preston blinked hard and cleared his throat. "That's when I knew I couldn't take her away from them...and you." Preston lifted the sledgehammer again and swung it hard onto what was left of the large chunk of debris he'd been working on. "I stayed a few more days, watching through the windows, just to be sure everything was as it seemed. Then I left."

"But why didn't you come inside? Why didn't you let Biddie know you were there?"

Preston took another large chunk from the pile and set it aside before thundering down on it with the sledgehammer. "I was afraid. Afraid that if I showed up, told them who I was, they might change their minds about taking care of her. My clothes were worse than what you find in charity bins, I hadn't a penny in my pocket, and I was running from the law."

Lucy opened her mouth to ask what he'd done to make him fear the law, but he continued before she could.

"Most well-to-do folks crossed the street when they saw me coming. I didn't know what the Davidsons knew about Biddie's past, but I figured it couldn't be the whole truth. I could tell she was happy and loved, not just by the Davidsons and you, but seemingly by everyone in that place. I didn't want my troubles ruining what seemed like a fine life for her."

"So you left without a word." Lucy's heart broke for the noble, lonely boy he must have been. Only a few years older than Biddie and having endured a harsh childhood at his father's hands, Preston had been alone in the world with no one to care for him. Lucy's father might be a monster, and her mother might have chosen opium over staying with Lucy, but at least Lucy had had the Davidsons' love and care to see her through. "Where did you go? How did you get on?"

Preston took another swing at the hunk of rock. "I found odd jobs here and there. Spent a lot of nights hungry, but that was nothing new." He continued pulling the biggest pieces of debris and smashing them down as he talked between swings. "Discovered I had a natural skill as a fighter and earned some money that way. Not my favorite experience, but it filled my belly. I made my way east to where I'd heard there were more factories looking for workers. It turned out I couldn't stand being stuck inside, doing the same thing day after day. So I found work in a small garnet mine in New York until it played out. Then got hired on to a nearby farm working for a man who was injured. By that time, the war was on, and I'd done some hunting for the family I worked for. My employer had seen my skills with a rifle and told me I ought to sign up for the new sharpshooter unit they were putting together. So I did."

"Weren't you too young?"

Preston smirked. "The man I was working for posed as my pa and signed the papers so I could join. The Union needed

135

men like a fish needs water. So no one was asking too many questions in any case."

Lucy frowned, thinking of the nightmares and injuries Gideon still struggled with as a result of the war. "Were you ever injured?"

"Sure. I was shot once." He pointed to his left shoulder. "But I got out better than most men I knew."

"Then what?" Lucy ought to be searching the pile for gems as she'd planned to do, but she couldn't take her mind from the miracle of all Preston had endured and lived to speak about.

"Then I learned of a traveling show looking for new acts. I showed them what I could do and was hired on the spot."

"And you've been with them ever since?"

Preston chuckled. "No, that was just the first show. The manager wasn't very savvy, and it didn't last long. After that, I joined a few more shows that didn't work out. Until I found Harvey's show. That's who I work for now. I've got second billing for Harvey Arbuckle's World of Wonders." His smile faded. "Or I did. Not sure what I'll get when I go back. If he has a spot for me at all."

Lucy pressed her lips tight against the thought of Preston leaving. "But you're still going back?"

Preston's gaze took on a distant, wistful look. "I've got to." Seeming to shake himself free of whatever memories had taken hold of him, he winked at her. "Trick shooting is the only thing I'm really good at." He took another swing with the sledgehammer.

Lucy wanted to protest his self-depreciation but swallowed the words. After their awkward moment before, she couldn't risk him misinterpreting her encouragement as romantic interest. Instead, she returned to her task and said, "You need to tell Biddie about finding her in San Francisco."

"Why? That was years ago. I don't see that it makes any difference now."

She felt Preston studying her but kept her gaze fixed on the rocks in front of her. "Trust me. Biddie will want to know. And I think it would be better coming from you."

There was a long silence in which he continued to stare at her. Then he said, "All right. If you think I should tell her, I'll tell her."

"Thank you." Lucy moved one of the lanterns closer and spotted a sparkle of red among the dust. She plucked it free and set it aside, biting her lower lip.

Why couldn't he be the cold-hearted, arrogant loner his profession suggested? It would've made keeping the walls around her heart so much easier. Instead, he'd proven himself as self-sacrificing as Clyve. Still, she refused to give in to the way he made her feel. The life of a traveling showman's wife wasn't a risk she could afford to take. More importantly, Clyve had placed his trust in her when she accepted his offer of courtship. That was a trust she wasn't willing to break.

~

Three days later, Preston strode through the chilly winter air to where Biddie was working on the new home she and Gideon would share after the wedding. Their house would be situated about a hundred yards southwest of the main house with a couple juniper bushes providing visual privacy between the two residences. At the moment, however, the place was little more than a square trench lined with large rocks that had been cut and placed to form a foundation.

Nearby, a pile of broken boulders waited to be added to the project. Preston's chest puffed a little as he eyed the large heap. Not a small accomplishment considering he'd had to split his time between harvesting the rocks and helping Ginny with the cattle during the nearly six weeks Gideon and Biddie had been gone.

As Preston drew nearer, the crisp breeze carried a strong earthy scent and the sun, now about halfway to its peak, cast long shadows over the landscape. Biddie stood near the foundation of her new house, sleeves rolled to her elbows and her hands deep in a wheelbarrow filled with a slurry of water, clay, and dried grasses.

He stopped at her side. "Is that more of the mud mortar Gideon used for the foundation?"

"It is." She continued mixing. "Thanks for offering to lend a hand while Gideon's out checking on the cattle."

"Of course. I'm here to help." He considered her labored movements for a moment. "Is there a reason you aren't using a shovel like Gideon did yesterday?"

"The muscles I use with shovels are cooked. I needed to try something different if I was going to keep working."

Preston rubbed the back of one ear. He should have gotten up earlier to finish his chores so he could've joined her sooner. He reached for the discarded shovel near her feet. "Here, let me take over."

"Thanks, but I'd rather you bring the rocks over, if you don't mind."

Leaving the shovel where it lay, Preston crossed to the mounded stones. He stacked two in his arms and returned to where Biddie continued blending. "Where do you want them?"

"Just line them up along the trench for now. Once this is ready, we'll slather a layer onto the rocks that are already there, then set the ones you bring on top of the mortar." She squinted at him. "Does that make sense?"

"I think so." Preston returned to the pile and continued lining stones along the edge of the foundation trench until Biddie announced the mortar was ready.

Adding new layers was a messy job. The mortar clung to their fingers and was soon smeared across the shins of his trousers.

Lucy appeared in the clearing near the barn and began stoking the cook fire. It must be close to time for their noon meal. As if sensing his observation, she pivoted and caught his gaze. Her brows lifted, and she tipped her head toward Biddie, clearly wondering if he'd spoken with his sister about finding her in San Francisco.

Preston gave a subtle shake of his head, then stole a glance at Biddie, who appeared oblivious to the exchange as she knelt beside the foundation.

Lucy's expression pinched in clear disapproval.

He discreetly waved his hand for her to relax and nodded to confirm that he planned to speak with Biddie soon.

Apparently mollified, Lucy returned to her task.

Preston drew in a long breath, held it, then let it slowly out. Lucy was right. What was he waiting for? This conversation wasn't going to get any easier.

He reached for the next rock and set it onto the bed of mud his sister had just made. "Biddie, there's something I need to tell you. Something I should've shared a long time ago."

Biddie paused in her work, glancing at him with a curiosity touched with dread. "Does it have to do with the night you left with Ginny and Pa all those years ago?"

"Yes, and no." He hesitated, and Biddie jumped in.

"I hope you know, I'm not angry with you. I know you were just a child then. Though, I have always wondered what happened."

Some of the tightness in Preston's gut eased. "I didn't want to go. One minute, I was sleeping on the floor by the fire. The next, Oliver shook me awake. It was still dark, but I saw Ginny was awake and getting dressed, so I reached over to wake you up, but he caught my hand. Squeezed it and said if I woke you up, he'd break it. That's when I noticed Mama was still asleep too." Preston rubbed the back of his neck. "At first, I thought he just had a job he wanted us to do. So I let him sneak us out like

139

thieves. But then he bought three tickets for a ship, and next thing I knew, we were heading for the newest gold strike." Preston kicked a rock. "It was days before I realized he never meant for us to go back and get you and Mama."

Biddie rose and scooped more mortar from the wheelbarrow. "I understand. As I said, you were just children." Straightening, she bit her lip and glanced away. "What I never understood—still don't understand—is why neither of you came looking for me before now. At first, I told myself you must not know where to find me. After all, Mama had died soon after you left, and I moved in with the Davidsons. It made sense. But then I received Ginny's letter. How did she know where to send it? How long had she known where I was and not made any contact?" She faced him again, her watery gaze holding his as mud dripped between the fingers of her cupped hands. "Did you know where I was too?"

Preston widened his stance. Time for the truth. "I'm the one who found you in San Francisco fourteen years ago. After I left Oliver and Ginny, I was intent on finding you and Mama. Then I discovered Mama was dead, and I saw that you were with a family who loved you. I was afraid if your new parents knew where you'd come from, maybe they'd kick you out. So I left."

Biddie's hands stilled, her gaze narrowing as the words settled around them. "You found me? In San Francisco? And you didn't let me know?"

Preston dropped his gaze to the ground. "I thought I was doing what was best for you, Biddie."

"That wasn't your decision to make." Biddie stalked toward the foundation.

Preston followed at her heels. "You have to understand."

She sank to the ground with a huff.

He knelt beside her. "I didn't have a penny to my name. I'd been sleeping in alleys and hadn't eaten in days. I had no way to care for you."

"Did it ever occur to you that I might have been able to help *you*?" She clenched her fists and flung the muddy concoction onto the next stone with enough force that huge globs bounced back at them. The spray caught Preston by surprise, his pale tan sleeves now smattered with dots of reddish-brown clay.

"Oh!" Biddie covered her rounded lips with her muddy hands, her eyes wide. "I didn't mean to do that. I just..." Her lips pinched. "You should've let me know you were there. My parents, the Davidsons—they would have taken you in." Tears spilled down her mud-splattered cheeks. "We might have grown up together."

The notion had never occurred to him. Preston's heart sank. So many years lost. How different his life might have been. "I don't know what to say, except that I'm sorry. And I'm here now."

She reached to pat his arm, then froze. "Oh dear, look at your sleeves. If we don't get them treated straight away, they'll have permanent reddish spots from the clay." Her nose wrinkled. "You don't want your shirt looking as though it's been spattered with blood." She stood. "Come on. You can change in the barn, then bring me your shirt, and I'll take care of it."

Preston hesitated. "Shouldn't I be doing things for you? After what I did—"

"You can't rewind time, can you?" Biddie's lips curved up, though her eyes remained sad.

He hunched his shoulders. "No."

"Then I think we'd better focus on the here and now, don't you?"

"I thought you were angry."

"I am. A little. Or...I was." Biddie peered up at him. "Something I've been learning lately is that God's timing, though occasionally mysterious and frustrating, is always best in the end. I wouldn't have chosen to be separated from you, but if you'd come to stay with me, you'd never have joined Berdan's sharpshooters and wouldn't have the career you love." She rubbed drying mortar from her fingers and face. "I have no idea how many other lives those choices have affected. But I trust that if God led you down that path instead of to me, He had good reasons for doing so."

Preston didn't know what to say. This wasn't the first time his sister had spoken of God with such complete trust. He'd also caught her singing hymns as she baked many times. Hers was a faith he envied. To have a loving "heavenly Father," as she called God, was something Preston couldn't relate to. So far as he could tell, God had washed His hands of Preston years ago.

Movement near the fire caught his attention. Lucy poured water into a large pot and hung it over the flames. He winced, thinking of the military preacher who'd urged soldiers to beg God's forgiveness or face the everlasting flames of hell. At the time, he'd brushed it off as superstitious nonsense, but reuniting with Biddie had reminded him of their mama's faith. Despite her lapse of judgement in marrying Oliver, Mama had been no fool. He remembered enough about the Ten Commandments to know he'd broken more than a few in his years. What if the preacher had been right? If hell really existed, there could be no doubt that was where Preston would go when he died

"Preston?" Biddie's soft voice broke through his musings. "Are you all right?"

He forced a casual tone. "Of course." He waved toward the barn. "Guess I'd better get changed." With a speed that belied his nonchalant words, he crossed the yard, passed Lucy at the fire, and disappeared into the shadows of the barn's interior.

CHAPTER 14

JANUARY 25, 1874

*L*ucy stood at the end of the loudly chattering throng of wedding guests buzzing around the long makeshift table holding the varied foods and drinks brought by Biddie's parents and their family friends, the Stevenses.

Biddie and Gideon's beautiful wedding ceremony had been held beneath an arbor that was erected for the occasion outside the small adobe schoolhouse located a little over three miles east of Campo and its hotel. Attended by families from as far as San Diego—not counting Biddie's family from San Francisco—the event was rumored to rival last year's Independence Day Celebration in size.

Lucy's heart had stopped beating for a moment when Biddie mentioned that she'd invited Mr. Green to the celebration. Thankfully, the scoundrel had declined the Davidsons' invitation on account of a previous commitment.

Each family had brought along their own chairs or blankets for the feast which now followed the ceremony. Unfortunately, there was scarcely enough room to fit them around the table. Most folks didn't seem to mind sitting elbow to elbow with their neighbor, but it reminded Lucy too much of her time in The Home with Mama. So she had gladly relinquished her seat to someone who'd brought only a blanket.

On blankets scattered nearby, the children eagerly awaited their turn to feast. Unlike at The Home where everyone ate at once, here the children were expected to eat only after the adults had their fill.

Lucy pretended to take another sip of the cream tea a well-intended woman had handed her twenty minutes prior. In truth, not a drop had passed Lucy's lips. Even the smell of the drink churned her stomach.

As a young girl, nothing had pleased her more than sitting down to afternoon tea with Mama in their garden, dressed in her fine silk dresses with lace trimmings. Mama had made her a pretty doll that served as their only guest for these occasions. No one else was invited since it was their special time together whenever Papa was away on one of his many business trips. She had loved the teas Mama served, but ever since—

Lucy slammed the lid on those memories as Biddie approached with Gideon at her side. The two held hands and wore matching elated expressions. "Congratulations to you both." Lucy returned their smiles, thrilled for her friends' happiness. She took her best friend's free hand and gave it a squeeze. "I'd ask how it feels to be a married woman, but I can see the joy written on your face."

Biddie giggled as Gideon wrapped an arm around her shoulders. "I am happy. Thank you again for your hard work in setting all this up." She gestured to the picnic table, arbor, and the freshly swept dirt where there'd be dancing later.

Lucy and Ginny had left the ranch early to prepare for the day's festivities. When they arrived at the school, Matthew

Roland, Clyve's father, already had Clyve and their vaqueros hard at work building the arbor and hauling wood for the table. Morly had been notably and thankfully absent—not arriving until the end of the ceremony, just in time to eat.

Lucy waved away Biddie's thanks. "It was nothing."

Someone called to Gideon, and he turned, his arm still around Biddie.

She slipped free and patted his hand. "You go on. I want to talk to Lucy for a moment."

Gideon looked between her and the man who'd called him. "I can wait."

"No, go." She gave him a pointed look. "This is women's talk."

"All right, but don't be long." Seconds later, he'd been swallowed by the mingling guests.

Biddie glanced around, then pulled Lucy farther from the crowd. "Earlier, I overheard Matthew telling Clyve that he needed to ask you something. He sounded pretty adamant." Biddie scooped both Lucy's hands into her own and squeezed with a quiet squeal. "I think he's going to propose to you today."

Lucy tensed. "Today? But it's your special day. I don't want to take away from—"

"Don't be silly. I'd love to share this moment with you." Biddie's grin dimmed. "If you're ready. Are you ready? Why don't you seem happy? I thought you'd be thrilled. The two of you have been courting for months."

Lucy shrugged. "Some people court for years before they marry."

"Years? Why would you want to wait so long?" Biddie's brow furrowed. "I knew it. I told Gideon something was wrong, but he told me I was looking for trouble where there isn't any. And I told him I knew my best friend. I should have listened to my gut." She tugged Lucy closer. "What is it, Lucy? What's wrong?"

Lucy forced a smile. "Nothing. It's just..." She searched for any reason beyond her unwanted attraction to Preston. "I still don't know Clyve very well, and we don't have much in common."

Biddie heaved a sigh. "Oh, is that all? Don't worry about that. You already know that he's a God-fearing man who'll protect and provide for you. And he'll treat you well. That seems like a solid enough foundation to me. As far as having things in common, look at me and Gideon. A baker and a rancher don't have much in common on the surface, but when you dig deeper, we share our faith and our values. Those are the things that really matter in keeping a marriage strong."

Over Biddie's shoulder, Lucy spotted Clyve assisting one of the elderly women with filling her plate. "I suppose you're right." But was a shared faith in God and love for friends and family enough to build a marriage on? Did she want to spend the rest of her life talking about cattle, local politics, and how to build wagons? Besides, how could she marry one man while she battled feelings for another? "But...what about...?" She couldn't bring herself to voice the worry.

Biddie placed a hand on Lucy's shoulder. "You're worried about your mother, aren't you?"

Lucy jerked. How could Biddie know of Lucy's lingering fear for Mama's safety?

Biddie pulled her in for a hug. "Just tell him. Clyve's a reasonable, compassionate man. I'm sure he'll be understanding of your mother's circumstances." She pulled back to look Lucy in the eyes. "You needn't be ashamed. You aren't responsible for the life she's chosen."

Oh. Biddie thought Lucy was worried about telling Clyve that Mama was a prostitute. Maybe she would be if Clyve weren't every bit as kind and compassionate as Biddie said. But Clyve hadn't expressed any interest in Lucy's parents beyond their whereabouts and her assurance that they weren't

SHOOT AT THE SUNSET

currently worried for her safety. The ugly truth of her parentage wasn't a topic Lucy enjoyed. So why bring it up?

Gideon called for Biddie to join him.

"Coming," Biddie replied over her shoulder before turning back to Lucy. "Just share some of your secrets, and I'm sure he'll share some of his. I mean, you've met his brother. His family isn't perfect either." She pulled her in for another quick squeeze. "Sharing the pains of our pasts was one of the things that drew Gideon and me closer. Trust me." Without waiting for a response—which was good since the idea of revealing her secrets to Clyve had stolen all thought from Lucy's head—Biddie hurried away to reunite with her groom.

Lucy remained at the edge of the crowd as children chased each other, and adults who'd finished eating bounced babies on their hips. Biddie and Gideon stood at the center, surrounded by their family, close friends, and new neighbors. It was a beautiful scene, but Lucy's mind kept drifting to the events of the past two weeks.

Mining gems was an exhausting and dirty job, but they'd managed to collect enough raw gems to nearly fill their wooden box. That Preston was able to convince Ginny to let Lucy keep mining still seemed a small miracle. Especially since the faster progress meant investing in a few bracing beams to stabilize the tunnel—something Lucy had expected Ginny to protest, but she hadn't. Lucy ought to be happy. Yet as the happy couples mingled and laughed, she couldn't help feeling like a fraud. She'd deceived Ginny and everyone else about her true motivations for mining the gems. Even Preston, who had kept his promise and watched over her while helping her, didn't know the full truth.

A tap on her shoulder interrupted Lucy's melancholy thoughts. Clyve stood at her side, holding a small plate of delicate pastries. "Here you go, Miss Lucy. Try one of these. I noticed you weren't eating, and these are delicious." The bruises on his face had turned greenish yellow, but the cut appeared to be healing well enough.

What had her own face looked like after the mining accident? Since Clyve wasn't allowed to know about the mine, when he and anyone not living on the ranch had asked about the injury, she said only that she'd taken a fall. Which was technically true. And yet the deception chafed.

She took a small bite of the pastry and forced a smile. It was sweet, flaky, and perfectly delicious as Biddie's baking always was, but Lucy couldn't bring herself to enjoy it. "Thank you, Clyve. You're very considerate."

He leaned in closer, his voice low. "I wanted to apologize again for my brother's behavior the other day. His actions were reckless, and his language was completely out of line. I think he was trying to prove something after his argument with Pa that morning, but it doesn't excuse his choices. I hope you know, I'd never let anything happen to you."

Lucy's heart lifted slightly at his words. "Of course. And thank you for your kind apology, but you aren't responsible for your brother." Something pinched in her chest. "We don't get to choose the family we're born into."

Clyve thanked her for understanding and switched the subject to the antics of his cattle over the past week, lingering at her side until men began to gather for the competitions that would take place before the dancing began at dark.

As he ambled away, Lucy spotted Morly and Preston amongst those readying for the first horse race. They were examining their horses' tack, expressions set with what appeared to be intense concentration. Morly's face looked as bad as Clyve's, even from a distance. Her focus was drawn to Preston, whose graceful movements stood out from the other men's.

As if sensing her attention, Preston looked up and caught

her eye. He gave her a wide grin and winked before turning his attention back to his mount.

Lucy's stomach fluttered, and she pressed her palms against her middle. She was being silly. He felt nothing special for her. The awkwardness in the mine the day it collapsed had been entirely in her head. His grins and winks were just part of his flirtatious, carefree nature.

She searched for Clyve and found him already mounted, ready to race. With her gaze fixed on his broad shoulders, she willed him to glance back and smile at her, but he seemed focused on the man shouting for all riders to take their places.

The starting gun shattered the dull rumble of conversation, and she held her breath as the horses thundered past her. A huge dust plume trailed in their wake.

Preston took the lead, his gelding's mane flying in the wind. But Morly was close behind. Lucy silently cheered Preston on as they barreled toward the finish line. At the last moment, Morly's steed nosed ahead.

The crowd erupted into cheers as Morly reined his panting mount in a circle. He stood in the stirrups and shot several rounds into the sky as the horse cantered.

Despite Morly's despicable first impression, Lucy couldn't help but smile at his boyish joy. It was contagious.

It wasn't long before the next round of riders—all youths, this time—were lined up and ready to race. Lucy was surprised to see Josie among the competitors, riding one of Ginny's geldings, and cheered as loudly as everyone else when the girl actually won.

Josie leapt from her horse into Carmen's tight hug. The proud mother's grin couldn't have been brighter.

"It's unseemly." An elderly woman's voice caught Lucy's ear. "Young girls ought to ride sidesaddle if they ride at all. And certainly, they have no business racing with the boys. But then, what do you expect from the Lupine Valley Ranch?"

"Indeed," another woman's voice responded. "Virginia Baker's the worst of them all. I heard she's taken up drinking like her pa. Sin's in the blood, you know."

Lucy pivoted and speared the gossipers with her sternest glare. If only she had the words to put them in their place, but as was usual in such cases, speech failed her.

The women merely sniffed, lifted their noses in the air, and sauntered away.

As the day wore on, the competitions continued with everything from a hilarious three-legged race to a cock-fighting event —something Lucy couldn't stomach and refused to watch. Despite her best efforts, time and again, she found her attention drawn to Preston as he participated in several events with skill, determination, and good sportsmanship.

The late-afternoon sky was awash in strokes of apricot and lavender when someone called for a halt so the dancing could begin.

Morly protested, "What about shooting? Ain't any of you men man enough to face me in a friendly shooting match?"

Once more, the jovial crowd roared with approval, and a hasty row of targets were set up. Several men made their way toward the line at the edge of the clearing. Lucy's heart skipped as Preston stepped forward to join them. She'd seen him shoot before but never in a competition like this. Did any of their neighbors hide skills strong enough to rival Preston's swift precision?

As the men took turns shooting at the targets, it quickly became clear that Preston and Morly were in a league of their own. As Morly repeatedly hit the bullseye with ease, she wondered how much he'd had to drink before arriving at Lupine Valley Ranch last week. How easy it would have been for his reckless shot to have struck one of the women or Preston instead of the table. A shudder passed through her.

In the end, Morly, visibly tired after a full day of competing, and not a little imbibing, finally missed a shot. This opened the door for Preston to take his turn, and the Baker brother not only made the shot Morly had missed—he went on to deliberately shoot the can off the board it'd been perched on, then shoot it twice more before it hit the ground.

Lucy winced for Morly. Being so handily defeated in front of everyone couldn't feel good. But she also couldn't deny the thrill of Preston's amazing talent.

Morly's face turned as red as the roses Mrs. Davidson grew behind The Home. "That weren't nothing but luck. I demand a rematch."

With the sun dipping toward the horizon, several couples had already wandered toward the area that had been cleared and swept for dancing. The men who'd been persuaded to lend their instruments to the merriment were strumming the first notes.

Clyve clapped his brother on the shoulder. "Leave it, brother. It's time for dancing with the beautiful ladies. I know you don't want to miss out on that."

Morly's jaw worked side to side as he glared from Clyve to Preston and then to the swiftly filling dance floor. "Fine. I haven't anything to prove to any of you. We all know who the best shot really is." He stalked toward a pair of blond sisters standing on the outskirts of the dancing area, his face morphing into a suave smile. The young ladies giggled at something he said, then the elder of the two stepped onto the dance floor with Morly as the fiddler announced a Virginia reel.

Clyve bumped Lucy's shoulder and offered his arm, his bruised face splitting into a grin. "May I have this dance?" A bit of green food stuck to one of his front teeth.

She licked her own teeth but said nothing. The messenger was never thanked and frequently blamed. Instead, she smiled, nodded, and let him lead her into line with the other dancers. The music was lively with a guitar, accordion, and fiddle working together to make a joyful noise. Arm in arm with Clyve as he spun her round, Lucy caught glimpses of Preston, dancing farther down the line with Carmen.

Lucy couldn't help a twinge of jealousy as the handsome couple twirled together. She pushed the feeling aside, reminding herself that she'd made her choice in Clyve. Besides, Carmen was a lovely woman who'd had a hard life. She certainly deserved happiness. Although, Lucy couldn't help thinking that Ginny would not appreciate Preston stealing away the woman meant to become foreman of Lupine Valley Ranch.

As the night wore on, Lucy danced with several other men, some young, some old, but none could keep her attention from Preston and his numerous partners. One might wonder whether the women of this region had ever seen a handsome man before, the way they flung themselves at him.

With aching feet, she cried off the next man who asked her to dance. "I'm sorry. I need to rest."

"Of course." The man accepted her declination graciously. "May I get you a drink?"

"I've got it." Preston appeared at her side, a glass of lemonade in hand.

She accepted the glass and savored a sip. "Mmmm. But how? I thought the lemonade was finished off." The pricey drink had been part of the Stevenses' contribution to the festivities. She'd been looking forward to the refreshment, but it had disappeared while she was busy dancing.

Preston grinned as her would-be dance partner shuffled off, likely in search of another lady to join him on the dance floor. "I noticed you hadn't enjoyed a glass. So I hid one for you until you seemed ready to rest."

"Thank you, Preston. That was very sweet of you." Despite her effort to savor the drink, she found the bottom of the glass staring up at her all too soon.

Preston remained at her side, a comfortable silence

enveloping them as they watched the dancers. The current song came to a close, and the musicians announced a waltz. Several people protested the controversial dancing style, but Mr. and Mrs. Davidson, Mr. and Mrs. Stevens, and Mr. and Mrs. Clarke all joined Biddie and Gideon on the dance floor.

Preston offered his arm. "May I have this dance?"

Her brows rose. "You know how to waltz?"

"It's quite common back east." He wiggled his arm. "What do you say?"

Her hand began to lift in acceptance, but she hesitated. Was it right to dance a waltz with a man other than her beau? She searched for Clyve among the crowd and spotted him chatting with a small group of men. He seemed completely unaware of the change in music.

Preston cleared his throat, drawing her gaze back to his sparkling brown eyes. "I promise not to bite."

She chuckled and allowed him to guide her onto the dance floor.

Though she tried to remain stiff, to keep her heart locked tight, the gentleness of his hand at her waist as they swayed to the music and the heat of his attention fully on her soon melted her resolve. She found herself relaxing in his arms.

As they twirled their way past the musicians for the second time, he spoke in a low voice. "I think that poor fellow you just sent away may be the only man here you haven't danced with."

Lucy stiffened. Was he criticizing her? "I could say the same about you and the women here."

"So you have been paying attention." He smirked, his thumb caressing the back of her hand. "Jealous?"

"Of course not. I..." As her cheeks warmed, she caught the teasing glint in his eye and ducked her chin.

It seemed they'd both been watching each other this evening. Did that mean he felt the connection growing between them as she did? More than once as they'd worked side by side in the tunnel, when they'd bumped shoulders or brushed hands, she'd felt a zing at the contact. Though she'd worked hard to ignore the sensation, she'd wondered if he'd felt it too.

She risked a glance at him, only to catch him studying her intently. And the look in his eyes...

Oh, no. He did feel it.

Joy and fear battled in her gut. *Lord, what should I do?* Preston was not a man she could afford to fall in love with. His nomadic life with the variety show drew too much attention—attention she couldn't risk being caught in if she hoped to keep her location a secret from Mr. Green. Neither could she tolerate being the naïve wife waiting at home while her husband toured the country doing heaven knew what. True, Preston appeared sincere and trustworthy, but he'd admitted to running from the law—a circumstance he'd never explained—and Mama had believed Father to be trustworthy as well. Yet that trust had resulted in being beaten and left for dead.

Not to mention, Lucy's commitment to Clyve. He'd not yet requested her hand in marriage, but surely, the question was forthcoming after all these months of courtship. What was she doing entertaining feelings for another man? Her stomach rolled. She refused to be anything like her adulterous father.

Her feet stalled, drawing them to a stop in the middle of the dance. Another couple barely missed colliding with them.

"I'm sorry," Lucy murmured as she hurried from the dance floor.

~

*P*reston followed Lucy through the crowd. These last days working with her in the mine had only fueled his regard for her. He should have let her explain her reasons for secretly mining the gems before allowing past betrayals to color her actions and flare his temper. Not that he regretted telling Ginny. But he should have handled the situation differently, shown Lucy the trust she'd earned in her many months of working at the ranch. And now...

He needed to convince her to stop letting Clyve court her when it was clear she felt the same pull Preston did and didn't share that magnetism with Clyve. At least, Preston hadn't seen evidence of attraction while watching the two of them walk and talk each Saturday. Respect? Absolutely. Affection? Perhaps. But her feelings appeared more that of a friend than a woman on the verge of falling in love. Clyve seemed a bit more attached, but even he didn't appear to be a man in love. At least, he didn't act the same as other men Preston had seen declare their love for a woman.

But was Preston judging fairly? Or did he only see what he wanted to see?

He could hardly call himself unbiased. From the moment Lucy had stepped from the house this morning in her fancy dark-pink dress trimmed with lace and bows, he'd struggled to take his eyes from her. Even during the horse race, a part of him had been aware of her exact position and picked out her cheers from the crowd. Had she been cheering for him? The distraction had caused him to miss Morly's last-second push and cost him the race. Thankfully, none of his fellow sharpshooters had been on hand to challenge him, or he might have lost the shooting match as well. Lucy was a strain on his focus, and that was a fact.

Dancing with the other women this evening had been a trial of his manners, but no woman enjoyed dancing with an inattentive partner. So he'd forced himself to make regular eye contact, smile, and nod at the appropriate moments, but no one had better quiz him on anything his dance partners said. He'd be revealed for the fraud he was.

Through every dance step, he'd been anxiously waiting for the time he could claim a dance with Lucy. Unfortunately, the other men seemed as aware of her appeal as he was, and every time he'd started in her direction, someone else had beaten him to it. Although her frequent, covert glances in his direction had been somewhat mollifying. Eventually, he'd settled on waiting for her to tire and hidden the last glass of lemonade to increase his wager on gaining her attention.

After the heat radiating between them during their waltz, he was convinced that not giving their feelings a chance to grow would be a disservice to them both—and Clyve too. If she felt half as strongly for him as he did for her, marrying Clyve couldn't be the right thing to do. Maybe Preston wouldn't be like his dad, after all. He hadn't pummeled Morly into oblivion as he'd been tempted to do after the fool shot their table. He'd listened to Clyve and shown restraint despite the urge to continue punishing the reckless scum. Restraint was something Pa could've never laid honest claim to. That had to count for something, didn't it?

Mrs. Davidson stepped into Preston's path just as Lucy disappeared around the corner of the schoolhouse. "There you are, Preston. I've been wanting to tell you how very impressed Henry and I were by your marksmanship earlier this evening. We both feel much safer knowing you're on hand to protect our girls at the ranch." She beamed up at him with startling blue eyes, crinkled at the corners. Lucy's brown eyes were much prettier, but they'd been sad, maybe even a touch fearful as she'd turned away from him. "And of course, I can never thank you enough for the role you played in bringing to justice those ruffians who kidnapped our dear Biddie."

Preston forced himself to pay attention to the kind woman's words. "Uh, my pleasure. She is my sister, after all."

"Yes, of course. And I know Biddie is so happy to be reunited with you after all these years. She's had so many questions that Henry and I had absolutely no way of answering for her. But now that you're here, perhaps—"

Preston quit listening as another figure sauntered toward the schoolhouse, disappearing around the same corner as Lucy. This one, male.

"I'm sorry, ma'am. But if you'll excuse me..." Preston stepped around the matriarch and bolted for the backside of the schoolhouse.

CHAPTER 15

*G*rateful for the relative privacy provided by keeping the adobe schoolhouse between her and the rest of the wedding guests, Lucy swatted the tears from her cheeks. What was wrong with her? How could she allow such a betrayal of Clyve's trust? No matter that he had no way of knowing the vileness of her treacherous feelings. Merely having them secreted in her heart was wrong. Clyve was a good man who deserved a woman wholly devoted to him. She sniffed and nodded. That was what she would be from now on. No more thoughts of Preston.

Even as she thought it, memories of their time mining together shoved their way through her mental wall. The way Preston had made her laugh and reminded her to drink enough water. His thoughtfulness in bringing a blanket for them to sit on while they ate the snack he'd packed. The time he'd plucked a twig of juniper from her hair. Just the memory of the intimate moment sent a shiver of pleasure through her.

She closed her eyes and clamped her hands on her head. "Stop it."

Morly's voice interrupted her mental war. "Stop what?"

She dropped her hands and straightened. Where had he come from?

He grinned and winked as he sauntered toward her. "I haven't even started yet." He seized her shoulders. "And I don't think you'll want me to stop."

Shuddering inwardly, she tried to step back but found herself pinned against the backside of the schoolhouse.

He leaned closer, his mouth aiming for hers.

She jerked her head to the side just in time to receive the scratch of his mustache against her cheek. "What about Clyve? Don't you think he'd be upset by what you're doing?"

"Don't worry. Clyve's busy dancing with that pretty new Mexican girl."

Did he mean Carmen? Lucy set her hands on Morly's chest and shoved. He didn't budge. Instead, he wrapped his arms around her, pressing their torsos together and trapping her hands between them. No amount of squirming set her free.

He pressed another rough kiss to her jaw. "I made sure Clyve was busy before following your signal. You're a clever girl. I don't think anyone else noticed you couldn't keep your eyes off me today."

"I don't know what you're talking about, but Clyve's your brother. He wouldn't appreciate the way you're treating the woman he's courting." She struggled to push him away, but he was too big, too strong.

Morly smirked. "What Little Brother doesn't know won't—"

In a blink, Morly was off her, stumbling backward.

Preston inserted himself between them. "Keep away from Lucy." His fist collided with Morly's jaw, and the louse staggered sideways. Preston followed. "Don't." Punch to the nose. "You." Punch to Morly's left eye. "Ever." Punch to his right eye. "Come near her." The punches came faster now. Too fast for her to track. "Again."

Morly attempted to defend himself, but it was clear Preston

had years of practice and knew how to block or dodge every blow Morly tried to land. Meanwhile, Preston's strikes continued hitting their marks like a swarm of angry bees defending its hive.

Morly fumbled for his pistol, but Preston was too fast. He seized Morly's arm and twisted it around. Preston wrenched the gun from his hand and tossed it aside before resuming the beating.

Blood oozed from so many wounds, Morly's face was a mask of red as he crumpled to his knees.

Still, Preston didn't let up. His eyes glazed with fury.

Alarm surged through her. "Stop! Preston, stop."

He didn't seem to hear her.

"You'll kill him." She tried to catch his arm, but his elbow caught her face, sending her tumbling to the ground. Her palms scraped across the dirt as tears filled her eyes, spilling onto her throbbing cheek.

The defeated man threw his arms over his head and still, Preston pummeled him, seemingly unaware that he'd struck her.

Terror squeezed her throat. If Preston killed Morly, they'd hang him.

"Help!" She scrambled to her feet and rounded the corner of the schoolhouse. "Someone stop him!"

Clyve was the first to hear her shouts above the music and revelry. He sprinted to her side. "What happened?" His gentle fingers grazed her cheek, and the muscles in his jaw visibly flexed as he spoke the next question through gritted teeth. "Who did this to you?"

By the time he'd finished his question, several more men, including Gideon, Mr. Clarke, Mr. Davidson, and Clyve's father had joined them.

"It's—"

Gideon must have heard the commotion from behind the

schoolhouse because he sprinted in that direction before she could explain. The rest of the men dashed after him, with several women on their heels.

As Lucy rounded the corner behind them, Gideon and Mr. Clarke had hold of Preston's shoulders and were pulling him away as Clyve knelt beside his brother.

"Morly?" Clyve wiped blood from his brother's eyes. "Can you hear me?"

The man's mangled face threatened to heave up the food Lucy had savored earlier in the day. How had a day of such joy turned into this?

Morly didn't answer Clyve's question, though his chest still rose and fell.

Thank You, Lord.

At least Preston hadn't killed him. Yet. Who knew what Preston's punishing blows had done to Morly's insides?

Please, Lord, let him live.

"Someone fetch a doctor." Mrs. Davidson wrapped her arm around Lucy's shoulders.

"There ain't one round here," a man Lucy didn't recognize answered. "Nearest doc is San Diego. I'll get Silas."

Lucy had forgotten the Campo store's co-owner was a hand with doctoring, though he'd never had real training. Would his skills be enough?

Ginny's somber assessment moved from Morly, to Lucy, to Preston. "He attacked her?"

Before Preston could answer, another man stepped forward. "I'm a doctor."

Lucy couldn't remember having seen him before, but then, most of those who'd come to the celebration were strangers to her. Living as far apart as people did in these parts made it difficult to get to know one's neighbors. That was why so many had come to witness the wedding of people they didn't know, despite the unending work they'd no doubt left at home. Any excuse to gather and socialize was accepted with excitement in these parts.

People made way, and the newcomer went forward to kneel at Morly's side. He didn't look like an educated doctor with his rough clothes, wild hair, and an unkempt beard covering most of his face. What if he was just a quack who liked pretending he knew medicine? His treatment could kill Morly instead of making him better. She'd known it to happen among the slums of San Francisco's Barbary Coast. But what choice did they have other than to trust him? Morly needed more help than any of them knew how to give.

The man pulled a surprisingly white handkerchief from his pocket and wiped the blood from Morly's face and ears. Though he appeared to be using a slight pressure, the ministration must have caused some pain since Morly moaned.

A collective sound of relief rippled through those watching.

"Morly?" Clyve leaned forward again, though he was careful not to get in the doctor's way. "Morly, wake up."

Morly's swollen eyes cracked open, though his gaze was unfocused.

The doctor held three fingers in front of Morly's face. "How many?"

Morly blinked twice and squinted before answering, "Three."

Murmurs passed through the gathered crowd.

Morly's swollen eyes caught on Preston. "You and that whore—"

Preston drew his pistols in a blink. "Say another word against Lucy and you're a dead man."

Clyve's pistol was drawn almost as fast. "He's addled, thanks to you, and not thinking right. Put your gun away."

Preston glared at Clyve, disgust written in his scrunched nose and slightly parted lips. "You're defending the man who attacked your woman."

SHOOT AT THE SUNSET

"I'm defending my brother." Clyve cast a concerned glance at Lucy, then turned back to Preston. "If what you say is true, it'll be dealt with once he's in a position to think clearly."

Lucy wrung her hands as Preston hesitated.

At last, he said, "Make sure he understands that if he comes anywhere near Lucy or any of the women at the Lupine Valley Ranch, he won't live to tell the tale."

Morly started cursing, but his father cut him off. "Shut up, you fool."

Clyve nodded solemnly at Preston.

Preston holstered his pistols, and Lucy sagged against Mrs. Davidson.

After several minutes of cleaning off blood and probing different parts of Morly's body, the doctor concluded Morly had a broken rib, a fractured nose, a possibly dislocated jaw, two broken fingers, and a concussion. He asked Morly several more questions that seemed aimed at assessing his mental state before declaring the patient was fit to be moved.

While Biddie found a damp rag to press against Lucy's cheek, a wagon was fetched and Morly carefully loaded onto it. Seconds later, Clyve drove the wagon away, his father at his side and the doc in the back to tend Morly through the long, bumpy journey home.

Several families began packing their chairs and other belongings for their own ride home.

Mr. Davidson turned from watching the Rowland wagon leave to pin Preston with a grave look. "You'd better have a good explanation for what you did to that man."

Someone must have brought Preston a damp rag as well, since he appeared almost as he had before the attack, save the spattered blood stains on his shirt—especially his sleeves—and a few bruises on his knuckles. He looked at her, no doubt expecting her to explain Morly's unwelcome advances, but her thoughts were stuck in a loop, playing the grizzly details of

Preston's assault over and over in her mind. She dropped her gaze to her skirts. They too had drops of dried blood on them. She closed her eyes and felt Biddie's arm come around her waist, tugging her into a comforting hug.

"Morly was behaving in an ungentlemanly fashion toward Miss Arlidge." Preston's voice boomed in the quiet anticipation of those still gathered. "I stopped him."

"You did more than stop him." Gideon's hard voice was just as loud. "You nearly killed him."

Lucy couldn't resist peeking to see Preston's response. His hard expression hadn't changed. "What would you have me do? That man was trying to force himself on Lucy. Any man that tries to harm a woman in such a way deserves to die." His gaze seemed to dare anyone to argue. "I hope the rest of you are as willing to protect your wives, daughters, and sisters." He'd hesitated over that last word, his eyes flicking to Ginny before returning to the men around them.

Murmurs of agreement sounded from several of the men.

"You can be sure he won't be trying that again," one man declared.

Still frowning, Gideon faced Lucy. "Did Morly...did he hurt you?"

Heat filled her face with the thought of having so many people privy to something so personal. But denying Morly's actions would see Preston arrested for sure. And as much as she wished he had stopped his assault on Morly sooner, Preston had been defending her. At least, that was how it started.

She couldn't lift her eyes above Gideon's collar. "I was seeking a moment alone, but Morly followed me behind the schoolhouse and...and..." She couldn't bring herself to explain the details. "Preston saved me." She tried to force herself to meet Preston's gaze and fake a smile, but the bump on her cheek was too painful. And the memory of the raw power and primal rage he'd demonstrated sent shivers down her spine.

After these many months living and working together, she would have declared to anyone that she knew Preston and understood the selfless heart hidden beneath his flirtatious manner. If she was honest with herself, a small part of her had even worried she might be falling in love with him in spite of her efforts to remain loyal to Clyve. But never had she suspected Preston was hiding such a dark truth.

She turned away, unable to look at him. He was just like her father.

~

*P*reston saddled his horse as the dancing resumed. Though the celebration seemed ready to continue through the night, it was clear he was no longer welcome. Not that Biddie or Gideon had asked him to leave. No one had outright asked him to leave. But the sidelong, wary looks of those around him seared him as surely as a branding iron, marking him a monster.

He'd been a fool to think he could be any different.

Despite his bold words to the others, defeat slumped his shoulders. He couldn't regret defending Lucy, but the way his fury had taken hold, blocking out all rational thought, sent a chill down his back. He hadn't felt that white-hot rage in so long, he'd convinced himself he'd overcome it. But as usual, reality had snuffed out his foolish spark of hope.

Ginny came over. "I'll head back with you."

"No." Preston mounted up. "You stay and enjoy the celebration. Biddie needs at least one of us not to ruin her wedding day." He turned his mount east.

Ginny grabbed his reins. "You didn't ruin her day. You protected her best friend. Some of the others may not see that, but I know she does."

His jaw clenched as he stared into the darkness, unable to

meet Ginny's gaze. "Gideon's right, and you know it. I did more than protect Lucy." The image of Morly's bloodied body being loaded onto the wagon flashed in his mind. "I lost control." He almost couldn't say the next words out loud but managed to force the truth through his teeth. "I'm just like Pa."

Ginny punched his leg.

"Ow!"

She scowled up at him. "Quit talking nonsense. You aren't anything like him. Pa was a no-account drunk and a gambler that cared for nothing and no one but himself. If he'd seen what Morly was doing, he'd have kept on walking and pretended he didn't."

A sliver of truth ran through her words, lightening the darkness within. "Maybe." But she didn't know how completely he'd lost control. If the others hadn't stopped him...

Preston shuddered. Morly might be dead.

Preston fiddled with the horse's dusty mane. "I think you should let Lucy keep on mining by herself." The fearful way she'd regarded him as Morly was being examined had sliced Preston to the core. He'd never hurt any woman—especially not her. But it was clear she no longer trusted him. "With the rain still holding off, you're going to need to move the cattle to higher ground soon. You'll need my help with that."

"If it comes to that, we'll need everyone's help. Including Lucy's. But I know a few more patches of grass we can try before giving up. I'm still holding out hope. Rain this time of year can be unpredictable. Moving the herd so far will be a pain and a half. It's too far to ride every day. Someone'll have to stay with them to keep an eye out for thieves and coyotes."

"Staying with the herd would suit me fine. So long as you let Lucy keep mining. I don't know why it's so important to her, but she's as determined and passionate about chipping at those rock walls as Biddie is about baking." Except Lucy's work in the tunnel had an edge to it, as though something was chasing her, driving her on. He'd tried asking her about it, but she always managed to evade the question and change the subject. Sensing there was pain in the answer, he hadn't pushed.

It was Ginny's turn to look away, but not before he caught a haunted look in her eye that made him want to retract his request. He glanced around to be sure they were still alone, then leaned down and spoke in a low voice. "What is it? Something about that mine has you rattled."

Ginny's frightened profile turned hard. "Nothing. I'm all right. Just tired." She faced the dancers, her back to him. "I'm glad you trust Lucy, but either you work with her, or the mining stops." Without waiting for his response, she marched away.

CHAPTER 16

JANUARY 26, 1874

Standing behind the spindly kitchen chair, Lucy's little legs shook uncontrollably as she squeezed the stuffing from her favorite doll. Mama's whimpered pleas had no effect on Father's rage. The wooden spoon he'd snatched from the bowl on the table snapped under the force of his blows. He cast it aside, continuing his punishing beating with his fists. Then he reached for the fireplace poker.

Tears trickled down Lucy's cheeks as she screamed, begging Father to stop. "Please. I'm sorry. I won't tell! I won't tell!" But Father wouldn't listen. It was too late. Lucy had told Mama the secret. She couldn't take it back. Now Mama was going to die. And it was all Lucy's fault.

She pressed her hands over her face and screamed until her throat was raw and her voice stopped working. Mama made a loud thump when she fell down. Father kicked her. Again and again.

Lucy clapped her hands over her ears and sobbed, though she could make no sound.

Eventually, it seemed too quiet. Lucy peeked between her lashes. Father was moving funny. Was he getting tired?

Father kicked Mama's head.

Lucy squeezed her eyes shut.

His heavy steps stumbled away. She peeked again. He grasped the edge of the washtub on the side table, pumped fresh water into it, and washed his hands, then his face.

He turned and Lucy flinched. Closing her eyes, she curled into the smallest ball she could in the corner behind the chair. Maybe he wouldn't see her.

Thump. Thump. Thump. Thump. His steps came closer.

She bit her tongue, every muscle squeezed tight. She needed to be smaller.

Thump. Thump. Thump. He passed her by. The front door opened. *Thump, thump.* The door closed.

Lucy's eyes drifted open, her whole body stiff as she stared through the pitch black toward the backside of the curtain separating the sleeping quarters from the front of the stone house. Tears trickled from the corners of her eyes. She hadn't dreamed of that day in years, but that it came now was little wonder. Not after what Preston had done to Morly.

She pressed her eyes closed, wiped away the tears, and shoved the memories back into the box she'd kept them in for so long. Then she locked it tight. Thoughts of that day would do her no good now.

Slowly, she stretched one leg and then the other, followed by her arms and back. Last, she circled her neck and wiggled her shoulders, shaking off the last of the tension left by the nightmare. Then she stood.

In addition to her usual chore of milking the cows, she had a morning meal to fix. Biddie and Gideon had spent the night in a private tent protected by the half-built walls of their new house. This morning, they'd be busy packing for their week-long wedding trip.

Once dressed, Lucy crossed the room to stoke the cook fire. Odd. Small flames flickered in the fireplace as brightly as they had last night when she'd drifted off to sleep. Ginny must have gotten cold and replenished the wood while Lucy slept. Thankfully, it didn't take much to warm the one-room cabin.

Lucy hung a new pot of coffee near the edge of the fire and hurried out to the barn to milk Patty and the two new milk cows that had been delivered a few days ago as wedding presents. As far as she knew, they'd not been named yet, but names or not, they needed milking before she could start cooking.

Lucy stepped into the dim interior as Biddie exited Patty's stall, a full bucket in one hand and lantern in the other. Lucy jumped clean out of her skin—or so it felt. She placed a hand over her pounding chest. "Biddie, are you trying to scare me to death? What are you doing here?"

Biddie wrinkled her nose. "Sorry, I thought Ginny told you."

Lucy straightened. "Told me what?"

"Gideon and I decided to forgo our wedding trip."

Lucy took the bucket from her friend as she passed. "But why?"

"Mother let slip that Father had decided to delay withdrawing any money from his investment in Mr. Green's railroad venture. Which means they're short the money urgently needed to make repairs on The Home after this winter's unusually strong storms." Biddie frowned as she continued toward the door. "With all the recent bank troubles causing supply delays, construction on the railroad is almost a year behind now. However, Mr. Green has assured everyone that the project will be complete and profits realized within the month. Which is good since Mother and Father need the money more than ever now."

Confession clawed at Lucy's throat as Biddie held the door

for her and they stepped outside. Yet saying anything now would do no good. The Davidsons' investment was gone. The only hope was in Ginny's agreement to let them have the money from the gems.

"So Gideon and I told them to take the money they were going to give us for the trip and use it for repairs on The Home's roof instead."

The first rays of dawn broke over the valley's ridge as they continued toward the house. "Couldn't Mr. Clarke fix the roof?" As a carpenter, a roof leak would surely be manageable for him.

"He could, but they couldn't afford the materials needed. Most of the donors my parents rely on haven't been able to spare the money or supplies they'd normally donate."

"Is that because of the bank troubles you mentioned?"

"First, the problem was increased competition from the East putting pressure on local companies after the transcontinental railroad was completed. Now, with all the bank closures that have happened in recent months, even the businesses that survived the added competition are struggling to pay their expenses. Some have collapsed completely, leaving my parents with almost no donors to turn to." Biddie's usually cheerful expression was grim. "Meanwhile, Mother and Father had to move three of the children into their personal parlor due to a leak that started in one of the children's rooms the day before my parents left to come here." She paused outside the house, likely not wanting to wake Ginny, who was enjoying a rare late morning. "They'd planned to scavenge for discarded materials in the slums when they returned from this trip. I told them to use our wedding trip money to purchase proper supplies."

"And they agreed to that?" The Mr. and Mrs. Davidson Lucy knew would be appalled by such a suggestion. Then again, she couldn't remember The Home ever going without prompt repairs.

Biddie's grin held a hint of mischief. "Gideon and I didn't

give them a choice. They can't pay for a trip that we refuse to take, now, can they?" She slung her free arm around Lucy's waist and tugged her into a side-hug. "Thank you again for telling them about Mr. Green's railroad plans. I admit, I was nervous when they first told me they'd invested everything they had into the venture, but now I'm so grateful they have Mr. Green to rely on. The project may be behind schedule, but it's the only hope of funding Mother and Father have in these troubled times, and more than the roof needs fixing." Biddie released her, eased open the door, and crept inside.

Lucy didn't move, the weight of an anvil holding her in place. This was all her fault. If she hadn't convinced Mr. Davidson to invest with Mr. Green, they'd have the money to make those repairs and pay for Biddie's wedding trip.

Lucy rushed toward the springhouse and poured the bucket of milk into the jug they kept in cool waters flowing inside. She must hurry through her chores and get back to the mine. When the Greens' scheme finally collapsed, she needed to be ready with the money to save the Davidsons and everyone who depended on them.

She scurried with the bucket back to the barn. There were two more cows to milk, chickens to feed, the morning meal to complete—unless Biddie was working on that since she wasn't leaving today—and three bread loaves to start before she could break away for a few hours of mining.

With the empty pail clanging against her leg, she rounded the front corner of the barn. Biddie was bent over the outside cook fire, adding sticks to a tiny flame.

Lucy paused. "Are you making the morning meal, after all?"

Biddie nodded. "I can get the bread started, as well, before I start helping Gideon with our house."

Lucy thanked her, her steps lighter as she hastened into the barn. The loft boards creaked overhead as she approached the stalls, letting her know Preston was awake and preparing for the day. She ignored the sounds and focused on her task.

Half an hour later, she dashed past Ginny in the house doorway. Lucy cut a hunk of cheese and wrapped it in a cloth before tucking it in her pocket. Then she snatched her canteen from its peg on the wall and dashed outside, mind fixed on fetching water from the spring before heading to the mine.

Across the yard, Ginny was in the horse corral, leading her mare toward the gate.

Biddie called out as Lucy passed, "Where are you headed? The food will be ready in five minutes."

"I've got some cheese." Lucy patted her pocket without missing a step. "I want to get some mining in before I come back to prepare our midday meal."

"What about Preston?" Biddie's question caused Lucy to slow and turn around.

With a glance at the quiet barn, Lucy closed the distance to Biddie and whispered. "After what happened yesterday, I was hoping it would be all right if I mined on my own. I haven't seen a man lose his temper like that since..." She swallowed the words, but Biddie's expression softened with understanding. She was the only person who knew the full extent of what Lucy had witnessed as a child. "I don't feel safe—"

"Preston would never hurt you." Biddie's soft gaze turned admonishing. "He was protecting you."

"He lost control. I couldn't get him to stop. If the men hadn't come, he—"

"Preston is *not* your father. I can't believe you would think that." With her spatula, Biddie scooped the sizzling beef strips, flipped them, and slapped them onto the pan beside the eggs. Her tone was as sharp as her movements. "He was defending you. I would think you'd be grateful."

Hurt sliced Lucy's heart. Biddie hadn't spoken to her this way since an argument when they were children. "I am grateful. Truly. I just..." Lucy's throat tightened as Biddie, eyes fixed on the eggs she was flipping, shifted so her back was mostly toward Lucy. "I don't trust him anymore. How can I after—"

"Enough." Biddie spun toward her, her arms crossed with the spatula sticking out one side. "You're wrong. Preston is the last man on earth who would ever hurt a woman. He's selfless and kind, and he saved my life. I can't believe you're insisting on comparing him to your horrible father. I won't listen to any more." She pivoted and strode into the house, slamming the door behind her.

Lucy jumped as though it had struck her.

"She's right." Ginny's voice came from behind.

Lucy pivoted, bracing herself for Ginny's anger. Instead, tears in Ginny's gaze stole the defensive words from Lucy's tongue.

"Preston is the best man I know." She blinked, and the moisture was replaced with an ice-cold steel. She walked forward, still leading her horse, until less than half a foot separated her from Lucy. "If you hurt him, you're gone. I don't care whose friend you are. My family comes first. Understand?"

Throat too tight to speak, Lucy nodded. Preston was at least four inches taller and far stronger. How could she possibly hurt him even if she wanted to? All she wanted was to work alone without the worry of whether something might set off his shocking temper.

Ginny held her gaze a moment longer, then led the horse toward the barn.

Movement near the door drew Lucy's attention. Preston stood in the opening. How long had he been standing there? His pained expression as Ginny and her horse passed him said he'd heard enough. He looked away the second Lucy's gaze collided with his. "I'll be ready in two minutes." Not waiting for her reply, he disappeared into the shadows of the barn's interior.

Before she'd finished filling her canteen, Preston had joined her at the spring, though he was careful to wait for her to leave the springhouse before stepping inside with his own container. When he exited, his somber gaze finally met hers. "I promise, you have nothing to fear from me, Lucy. I would never hurt you."

"I...I know that." And she did. So why couldn't she stop the trembling that shook her head to toe? She stepped back and turned south.

Preston took the cue and led the way.

For the next three hours, they worked together in silence, with Preston choosing whatever task kept him farthest from where she was working. Though she appreciated his attempt to set her at ease, her mind remained cluttered with flashes of terrifying memories. A mixture of yesterday's brutality and the events of her childhood, keeping her from bridging the chasm that had formed between them.

As they gathered their things to return to the ranch yard, he let her know that he'd be helping with the cattle the next day, so they'd need to wait until dark to work in the mine. She'd nodded her understanding, and they returned to the ranch in silence.

After she'd gotten the midday meal started, Lucy walked to where Biddie and Giddeon were unloading a barrel of rocks to be used in the home's walls. "Need any help?"

Gideon glanced up as he lifted one of the larger rocks. "If you think you can—"

"No, thank you." Biddie's voice was cold, and she kept her back to Lucy. "I know you have better things to do."

Lucy opened her mouth to protest, but Gideon caught her eye and shook his head with a sorrowful expression. It was clear he thought Biddie needed time to cool down.

Chest aching, Lucy returned to the cook fire.

Though everyone else behaved as usual, Ginny and Biddie

remained polite but cold the rest of the day. Preston kept his distance—something that left her both grateful and deeply remorseful.

By the time she fell into bed that night, Lucy couldn't hold back the tears. The next morning, she awoke exhausted from a night spent running from her father, Junior, and even Preston.

Though her nightmares were an exaggerated, distorted version of real memories, at the morning meal, when Preston reached past her to accept the cup of coffee Biddie held out by the cook fire, Lucy couldn't help jumping.

He immediately stepped away and positioned himself on the other side of the fire.

Lucy accepted her own coffee and turned to go.

Biddie's hand on her shoulder stopped her. "Wait."

The gentleness of Biddie's voice brought hope as Lucy faced her.

Biddie glanced at her brother, then back to Lucy. "I may not understand why you think as you do, nor do I agree with what you said, but I know you're not trying to be hurtful. I'm sorry for the way I've been treating you."

Lucy burst into tears and fell into her best friend's open arms. "I'm sorry too." Lucy couldn't help how Preston's actions made her feel, but she hated that her mistrust had caused her dearest friend so much pain.

When Lucy finally wiped her tears and looked across the cook fire, Preston was gone. She glanced around and spotted him at the corral with Ginny, preparing to ride out and check the cows with Carmen and Lei Yan. Despite his promise and considerate behavior yesterday, fear was still mixed with the feelings she experienced when she looked at him. Would that ever go away?

CHAPTER 17

JANUARY 17, 1873
SAN FRANCISCO, CALIFORNIA

*A*fter another quick look that confirmed Opal was alone in the fifth floor hallway, she knelt in front of Mr. Green's office door and plucked two hairpins from her bun. She bent one into a lopsided *Z* shape and the other into an *L* shape. She inserted the *Z*-shaped pin into the lock and carefully turned until she heard a soft click. Keeping the tension with the first pin, she inserted the *L*-shaped pin and lifted until another click confirmed the door was unlocked.

Thank you, Moira.

The woman had taught Opal more than a few shady tricks in their time together at the brothel. This skill had come in particularly handy when Pete got angry and locked one of the girls in their room without food. Being able to sneak food while Pete snored downstairs had prevented many a miserable day.

Opal jabbed her pins into her hair and checked up and down the hall once more, then turned the knob and slipped inside. She paused, holding her breath and willing her heart to slow. She needed to be calm, to think clearly. But the voice screaming at her to run from this foolish, dangerous plan before it was too late would not be silenced.

She ignored it, anyway. Just as she had ignored Fletcher's insistence that she leave the city after San Francisco's *The Daily Chronicle* had burned down within hours of Fletcher submitting his anonymous article about Saville. The report had been based on a sheet of incriminating notes she'd stolen the last time she broke into Mr. Green's office. Unfortunately, the evidence had burned to ashes along with the newspaper office.

At their meeting this morning, Fletcher had insisted the timing made it clear the Greens and Saville had spies at the newspaper, and if they'd seen the account he'd written, they must be suspicious of someone spying inside the hotel. He'd argued that the risk was too great.

Opal had told him that any risk was worth a chance to save her daughter. And now that Opal fully understood what her daughter had uncovered, there remained no doubt Lucy wouldn't be safe until Mr. Green, his son, and the senator were behind bars.

Opal crept toward the back right corner of her employer's office. The scraping sounds she'd heard after each of the men's meetings were definitely coming from somewhere in this area. They had to be. She'd already searched the rest of the room during previous visits.

She checked the timepiece all hotel staff were required to wear. Payment for the watch and her two uniforms had swallowed her first three weeks' wages. Only fifteen minutes before Mr. Green was scheduled to arrive at the hotel for another meeting with the architect who'd designed his new hotel.

She crossed to the oil painting of a steam engine emerging from a mountain tunnel and peeked behind the large frame. No signs of a hidden safe or cabinet met her eyes.

She eased the frame back and scanned the rest of the wall,

the joints at the corner and ceiling. Nothing appeared suspicious.

The carpet ran from edge to edge with no signs of tampering. Still, she knelt and ran her fingers through the plush fibers, searching for hidden cuts that might be pulled back to reveal loose floorboards beneath.

Several minutes later, she sighed and sat back on her heels. The carpet was unaltered, and every part of her body burned with pain.

She wiped the tears from her cheeks, closed her eyes, and sucked in a deep breath. Thinking with her pain this severe was as difficult as threading a needle in the dark. But she must for Lucy's sake. *Think, Opal. What are you missing?*

She forced her eyes open and studied the room. The only places she hadn't searched were the dainty chair and matching round table that occupied the corner. But the table's top was bare, and a thorough search of its underside revealed no hidden compartments.

She checked her timepiece again. Only eight minutes until Mr. Green's meeting. She should leave now to ensure she was out of sight before the men entered the hallway.

Defeat weighted her to the spot. She couldn't leave again without the evidence she needed to protect Lucy. This was her only chance to make any sort of amends for the terrible mother she'd been for the past decade.

Her gaze returned to the dainty wooden chair with its round floral cushion. A rather feminine piece for an otherwise very masculine room. Did Mr. Green bring women to his office? She'd never witnessed any, nor heard rumors that he'd ever entertained mistresses at the hotel.

Suspicion nudged her forward.

She ran her fingers along the thin wooden arms, not really sure what she was expecting to find. The piece was so slight, it seemed impossible anything could be hidden inside. She pressed her palms against the fabric but felt no odd bumps or lumps that might indicate hidden contents. The legs proved as smooth as the arms.

She ignored the lightning heat in her neck and lowered her head until her cheek brushed the carpet, then turned her gaze to the bottom of the chair. Nothing but a smooth wooden chair base.

Wait.

She lifted her head and eyed the depth of the wood trim surrounding the base of the cushion. It was almost three inches tall, yet the wood base under the seat was flush with its bottom. She pressed her hand down on the cushion. Her fingers sank only a half inch before pressing against what had to be a second wooden base beneath the thin padding. That meant there was a gap between the top and bottom of the seat base. It had to be the hidden compartment she'd been seeking, but how was it opened?

She felt around the edges of the fabric but found nothing. Pressing against the trim at the front of the chair proved equally fruitless. She grasped the top of the chair and rotated it so she was looking at the back.

There. A tiny scratch near the top of one engraved grapevine. If she hadn't been searching so carefully, she'd never have noticed it. She pressed down on the grape leaf, and the bottom of the cushion base swung down, dropping a thick leather journal onto the carpet.

She snatched the book up and pressed the hidden door upward until a click sounded. The grape leaf returned to its previous position, and the chair appeared exactly as it had before.

She checked her timepiece. Three minutes until Mr. Green's meeting. He could be in the hallway even now. She'd stayed too long.

CHAPTER 18

*T*he hard edges of the upturned crate pressed into Lucy's backside as she sat in the cold cellar. Her arms ached after many long minutes of thrusting the dasher into the butter barrel, yanking it up and thrusting it down again with a twist. Still, the work was far easier than washing laundry on this unusually warm day—a miserable task she'd need to see to tomorrow.

Pausing, she pulled the dasher from the barrel to check the cream's progress. Whipped, but not yet butter. Biddie needed plenty of butter to keep up with not only the ranch's needs, but also for the many baked goods she sold to the Gaskills' store in Campo. Which was why the Stevens family had gifted Biddie and Gideon with two new milk cows. Three cows were more than enough for Lucy who was usually responsible for milking them all while Biddie prepared the morning meal for everyone.

Of course, now that Biddie and Gideon were married, their

attention and energy were focused on finishing their new house. And that meant Lucy was responsible for most of Biddie's chores as well as her own. Not that she minded except for how it impacted the time she could spend in the mine. She'd do just about anything for the only person who knew everything about her and loved her, anyway. Well, almost everything.

Lucy shoved the dasher back down with a bit more force than necessary, and it thumped hard on the bottom. She winced and sucked in a deep breath, calming her strokes. There was no point in telling Biddie about Mr. Green. There wasn't anything either of them could do about him, and Lucy was already doing what she could to mitigate the harm his evil deeds would cause. All the more reason she needed to finish making this butter and get back to the mine.

She shook her shoulders loose of the burning tension and continued the song she and Biddie had learned from one of the cooks at the home. Each time she made butter, the simple chant came as naturally as breathing.

> "Come, butter, come!
> Come, butter, come!
> Peter stands at the gate
> Waiting for a butter cake;
> Come, butter, come!"

Despite the chill of the deep cellar beneath the stone house, a cool sweat formed on her brow as she forced the dasher through the thickening cream. After a while, pressing the dasher down became so difficult, the butter must be ready. She withdrew the dasher and used the wooden butter pat to scrape the yellowish chunks into a bowl before pouring and scraping out what was left in the barrel.

She washed the butter with cold spring water and squeezed the buttermilk out. Several repetitions later, the water remained clear, indicating the butter was ready for the mold. She pulled the rectangular wooden mold from the cool water it had been soaking in and shook off the clinging water drops. Using the butter pat, she pressed chunks of butter into the mold until it was crammed full and scraped flat. She flipped it upside down onto a platter and pressed the top of the mold down until the butter came free in a neat block.

Lucy repeated the process of filling and emptying the mold until all the butter had been used up. After covering the butter platter with a cloth, she placed it on a high shelf, then covered it with an upside-down box to keep the dust and cats away. The furry cuties Gideon had gifted Biddie last summer did a wonderful job of hunting mice, but they occasionally caused their own mischief, making the box covering necessary.

All that was left to do was clean the things she'd used to make the butter and put everything away. Then she'd be free to start digging in the mine. Assuming Preston was finished with repairing the fraying ropes he'd planned to work on that morning.

Working with him in the days since the wedding had been mostly silent and awkward. Though he was as solicitous as ever, their easy conversation had vanished, along with Preston's usual smile and casual flirtations. It was clear he was doing his best to set her at ease, yet his newly somber demeanor unsettled her almost as much as the violence he'd displayed at the wedding.

She plucked up the butter mold, then tucked the churn barrel under one arm before snagging the wooden pat with her free hand. Getting up the steep cellar stairs was awkward, but she made it.

If she gave Preston notice that she was nearly done, maybe

that would encourage him to work faster. Otherwise, she'd have to find something else to do while she waited for him to finish. She set everything on the table before closing the cellar door and hurrying to the open front door.

Although several large juniper bushes and a pile of boulders partially obscured the site of Biddie's new house, the sounds of boots crunching dirt and the *thwap* of stone onto mud came from where Biddie, Gideon, Josie, and even little Deborah worked to finish the structure. Josie and Deborah had been given the task of slapping mud mortar onto the stone walls. Judging by the size of their smiles despite—or perhaps because of—the amount of mud they'd been covered in yesterday, both girls reveled in the job.

Ginny, Carmen, Lei Yan, and Esther were away checking on the herd, so Preston sat alone in the shade outside the barn, twisting a new section of strands into an old rope.

Lucy stepped into the yard, and Preston's head lifted. Her shoulders tensed. She shielded her eyes to get a better view of his expression. A welcoming smile warmed his eyes. She exhaled. Although he'd shown no signs of fury since the wedding, a small voice inside kept her wary, bracing for its return. She infused a bit of cheer into her voice as she spoke. "All I have left is washing the churn, pat, and butter mold. Then I'll be ready. How about you?"

Preston lifted the rope in his hands. "Last one."

"Wonderful." Lucy offered her own smile before returning to the house. The churn took the longest to wash thanks to the nooks and crannies in the dasher and the barrel's tight inside corners, but eventually, everything was clean and in its place.

Preston appeared in the doorway. "Are you about ready?"

She plucked her canteen from the table. "I just need to fill this."

Minutes later, they reached the mine. Lucy plucked a lantern from a hook in the wall near the entrance and lifted its glass while Preston lit the wick. Thankfully, her nerves around him had slowly faded as they worked together over these last weeks. They'd even regained some of the friendship they'd previously had as they added several more feet to the tunnel's depth, installed more bracing, and discovered a second vein of the cinnamon-colored gems.

Lucy poured another scoop of raw gems into the box at the back of the tunnel. On impulse, she retrieved a palm-sized hunk of the ore and lifted it toward the lantern light. "You're sure these are garnets? They're browner than any I've seen before."

Preston landed another blow on the chunk he was breaking with his sledgehammer before coming to kneel beside her, his gaze fixed on the rock in her hands. "I'm sure. They are browner than the ones I mined before, but they're still garnets."

"Gideon thought they were garnets too. What if you're both wrong? Or what if no one wants them because of their color?"

Preston took the piece from her hand and stood. "Come on." He strode down the tunnel, and she hurried to keep up.

He pushed past the juniper and held the branches back for her. When she was through, he stepped to her side and lifted the gem-embedded stone in front of her eyes, tilting it this way and that to catch the light. "What do you see?"

"They're catching the sunlight."

"And?"

"And it's beautiful."

He grinned at her. "Exactly. Trust me, women are going to want these gems in their jewelry collection."

"Even though they're different?" She squinted at the shimmering dark-red gems.

"That's what makes them so special. They're rare. That makes them more valuable."

"You think so?"

"I know so."

She pursed her lips. So much was depending on these gems. "Maybe we should talk to Ginny again about taking them to the assayer."

Preston lowered the rock as he shook his head. "She won't agree. Declaring a find draws too much attention."

Lucy heaved a sigh. He was right. Once Ginny made up her mind, she rarely budged. If Lucy pressed for an assessment, Ginny might order them to stop mining altogether. It wasn't worth the risk. Lucy would have to continue trusting in Preston's experience.

Several hours later, they decided to stop for the day. Well, Preston had decided they should stop. If the decision had been left to Lucy, they would keep working through the night.

As they emerged from the bush, the sun hung low in the sky. A blazing ball of oranges and reds, its rays stretched out to bathe the landscape in a warm golden light that belied the dropping temperatures which confirmed winter had yet to release its grip on the desert valley.

Despite the lateness of the hour and the burn of fatigue in her muscles, Lucy fought the urge to turn back and continue digging. Ever since the wedding, she'd had this terrible sense of urgency that wouldn't leave her alone. Not that she hadn't felt the pressure to replace the Davidsons' lost investment before, but this feeling was different—like a executioner's ax was about to fall. A shiver ran through her with the thought.

Preston studied her as they neared the house. "Cold?" He started to remove his jacket.

She lifted a staying hand. "No, I'm fine, thank you. Besides, I'm sure fixing our evening meal will warm me."

"I can give you a hand, if you like." His eyes held a silent plea for trust. He must sense her continued hesitation around him.

Relenting, she sighed. "Can you slice onions?" It was her

least favorite part of cooking, but the root vegetable added so much flavor to many dishes, cutting it was almost unavoidable.

Preston grinned. "Of course, and cook them as well. Who do you think makes my meals when I'm traveling with the show?"

In truth, she hadn't given the subject much thought.

He opened the front door and held it for her. "What are we cooking tonight?"

"Scots Collops. It's a recipe I've made many times, so I've no fear of ruining our meal. It'll be edible, at least." She stepped inside, heading for the Dutch oven waiting on the side table, but Preston's hand on her shoulder caused her to pause.

He stepped around to face her, his expression serious. "I won't lie and say you're as grand a baker as Biddie. But you shouldn't speak so poorly of your skills in the kitchen. I've enjoyed many fine meals by your hand." His gaze shifted to the top of her head, and he brushed his fingers across her hair, sending unwanted tingles along her scalp. His warm gaze returned to hers, his lips tipped to one side. "You had a bit of dirt."

"Oh." Her voice came out breathless and she blinked. What was wrong with her? Shaking her head, she stepped around him, but the ground wasn't there. A cry had barely left her lips before he caught and lifted her. His strong arms wrapped around her, steady and safe. Pressed against his chest, she stared into his deep brown eyes.

"Are you hurt?" His breath feathered across her cheek, muddling her thoughts and warming her middle.

Her gaze shifted to his lips, words evading her. What would it be like to kiss him? She closed her eyes and shook her head again. What was happening? What was she thinking? This was Preston. The nomad with no home, no steady income, and worst of all, no control over his temper. Just like Father. Feeling safe with a man who could do what he did to Morly made no sense. She pressed her palms against his chest.

"Lucy?" Clyve's confused voice startled her, and she jumped back.

Preston's arms fell away as she whirled to face Clyve. "Clyve? What are you doing here?" That didn't sound polite. "I...I mean, what a welcome surprise. I wasn't expecting you today." She stepped toward him, but he shuffled back.

"Evidently." His frown darted between her and Preston, his poor hat brim crushed by one hand. "Morly's been insisting there was something going on between the two of you, and I refused to believe it. But now—"

"No, you don't understand. I fell and..." Wait. Why had she fallen? She spun to look at the ground beside Preston. "The cellar door." It lay wide open. If Preston hadn't caught her...

Preston shifted his stance, drawing her gaze, though his serious expression was fixed on Clyve. "I kept her from falling down the stairs."

The memory of how swiftly his arms had caught her, how safe she'd felt in his embrace, threatened to scramble her thoughts again.

Clyve's indignant voice broke in. "Who could have been so careless? Leaving that door open is dangerous. Not only for you, but what if Josie or Deborah had come in here?"

Lucy remembered closing the door. Or was she remembering a different day when she'd closed it? No, she'd closed it right after bringing up the butter-making things that needed to be washed. And there they sat on the table where she'd left them to dry. She looked back to the gaping square hole. Could her memory be so wrong? That seemed to be the only logical explanation. She cringed. "I suppose I was too eager to—"

Preston's sharp look cut off her near blunder in revealing the mine's existence. Ginny had insisted no one outside the ranch could know of the mine, and that made sense to Lucy even if she did think Clyve was trustworthy.

"I guess I was in too big of a hurry to escape on my afternoon stroll. I'll be more careful from now on." The excuse sounded pathetic, but what else could she say? She stooped and swung the door closed. The thought of one of the girls falling down those steep steps churned Lucy's stomach. She needed to focus on something else. Straightening, she faced Clyve. "How is your brother? Recovering well, I hope?"

"That's why I've come. Or part of the reason." Clyve brushed his hat against his thigh. The doc's been staying with us since the wedding to care for Morly's wounds. He says he needs more honey for a poultice, but we're plumb out. Pa thought Biddie might have some she could spare." Clyve shifted his feet, still glancing between Preston and Lucy. "The doc intended to come, but I told him I'd fetch the honey since I..." His gaze finally fixed on Lucy. "I wanted to see how you were faring after everything that happened. I'm sorry I haven't been by sooner, but with Morly injured and no rain, there's been more work and—"

"I understand," Lucy hurried to assure him.

Clyve's shoulders relaxed as he released a loud breath. "I wondered if perhaps you might spare a few minutes to speak with me." He cast Preston another frown. "Alone."

"Of course." Lucy handed Preston a knife and pointed at the onions in the crate she'd brought up earlier that day. "If you don't mind getting started, I'll be back shortly." Without waiting for his reply, she plucked the water bucket from the floor and slipped her hand onto Clyve's arm. "You can walk me to the spring."

~

*L*ater that evening, Lucy tugged her shawl tighter against the lowering temperatures and shifted in her chair across from Biddie at the table they'd moved into the yard. Small tables and chairs from the bunkhouse had been brought outside as well. Everything had been lined up to create one long table with enough room for all of the ranch's residents, plus Clvye, who sat to her right.

He leaned back in his chair as Biddie continued the story of how she and Lucy had first met in The Home when Lucy was nine and Biddie was ten.

"It was well before dawn. I had come down to bake pastries for donors Mother had invited to tea that afternoon when I heard this strange noise. It took me a moment to figure out what it was."

Lucy chuckled. "I thought I'd found someplace quiet to hide, but then you came into the kitchen. I tried so hard not to make any noise and hoped you'd leave."

Biddie sliced her collops into bite-size pieces. "As if I could leave you there, crying under the kitchen table." Her soft smile was a mere glimmer of the vastness of her big heart. "Your sniffles weren't very quiet."

"Why were you crying?" Clyve set his fork down.

Her smile dimmed as other parts of that long-ago day tried to invade her thoughts.

"At first, I pretended I hadn't seen her." Biddie saved her from answering. "I went about gathering my ingredients as if it were any other Saturday."

Lucy's chest warmed with the memory. "You were singing too. One of the hymns from church."

"'Amazing Grace.'" Biddie nodded as she sipped from her cup.

"But then you started talking to yourself about what you were making, and I got curious."

"I remember being so excited when I saw your eyes peek over the table."

Lucy chuckled. "Too bad I decided to look just as you clapped your floured hands together."

"The whole top of your face was ghost-white, like a mask." Biddie's tinkling laughter seemed to brighten what was left of the sun's rays. "I couldn't help it. I laughed so hard..." Her words trailed off as they both gave in to hearty laughter.

The rest of the group joined in their amusement for a minute or two before settling into an easy quiet.

Lucy smiled across the table at her dear friend. "But you also helped me clean up and fed me a slice of the strawberry cake you'd been saving for Sunday." She shared knowing glances with the others. "Even when she was that young, Biddie's baking was worthy of winning contests."

Biddie's blue eyes twinkled. "Or at least the heart of a treasured new friend."

Clyve twisted sideways so that he was facing Lucy. "I'm still curious why you'd wanted to hide in the first place."

Lucy's smile fell, the warm feelings dissolving like suds in a washtub. "It was my third day at The Home." Painful memories she worked hard to ignore came rushing in like a sandstorm, grating and stinging everything in its path.

After Father had left, Lucy tried and failed to wake Mama. Desperate, she beat on their neighbor's door, screaming for help until the old woman opened it. Then she snatched the woman's hand and dragged her to where Mama lay. What happened after that was a blur, but somehow, she and Mama had wound up at The Davidsons' Home for Women and Children.

On the day she met Biddie, Lucy had just overheard the doctor say Mama would be lucky to pull through after the beating Father had given her. The doctor wasn't sure if Mama would ever regain full use of her right arm, but for the moment, at least she was alive.

Guilt had chased Lucy from the room and under that kitchen table. She never should have opened her mouth, never told Mama about the fancy lady and two little boys she'd seen with Papa on the ferry. Then Mama wouldn't have been upset with Father and shouted at him.

Even after learning, years later, that the woman had been Father's legal bride and the boys his legal heirs, while Mama and Lucy were his second—and therefore illegitimate—family, regret haunted her. Mama had been so happy before Lucy revealed the truth. Not that she'd had any idea the news would upset Mama. She'd merely been curious. Just as she'd been curious the day she'd heard an unfamiliar voice coming from Junior's bedroom.

She squeezed her eyes shut. When would she learn to ignore that pull of curiosity? She sucked in a deep breath and let it out slowly. At least she'd learned to keep her mouth shut. Too bad Mrs. Prichard hadn't been given a second chance to learn.

Biddie's voice broke into Lucy's thoughts. "Lucy's mama had been gravely injured, and Lucy was worried about her."

Clyve cleared his throat. "I'm sorry. I didn't mean to bring up a painful subject."

Lucy wanted to tell him it was all right, but her stomach was still too queasy from the memories.

"It is a bittersweet memory." Biddie reached across the table and grabbed Lucy's hand. "But in the end, I gained the dearest friend anyone could ask for."

Preston lifted his tin cup as if in toast. "And we all gained a cook for this delicious meal."

Words of agreement and gratitude spattered across the table as Preston's gaze caught and held hers with a look of understanding he couldn't have. Or could he? Perhaps he did understand what it was not to wish to speak of a painful past. He certainly hadn't shared much of his time before running away from Oliver.

Biddie released Lucy's hand to join in toasting her, then stood. "Help me bring out dessert?"

Lucy followed Biddie inside as the evening meal spoiled in her clenched gut. Would Biddie understand when the truth finally came out? Or would Lucy lose the only real family she'd ever known?

CHAPTER 19

JANUARY 18, 1874
SAN FRANCISCO, CALIFORNIA

*O*pal's heart pounded in her chest as she stuffed her spare dress into the already bulging carpetbag. This was it. She had everything she needed to see Green, his son, and Senator Saville thrown in jail. Or hung. If she'd read the cryptic notes right, there was enough evidence in those pages to tie the men to at least three murders in addition to their overly complicated and definitely suspicious accounting. She set the carpetbag in the bottom of the laundry basket, beside the paper-wrapped package, and covered them both with the soiled linens she'd hauled up from the fourth floor.

The trek to the ground floor was agonizingly slow with her body forcing several stops to rest. Why had she thought hiding her bag in a heavy laundry basket a good idea? Finally, she stumble out the servant's back entrance and into the alley.

As Fletcher had promised, a boy waited there. What was the secret phrase she was supposed to say? "Umm. Change can

SHOOT AT THE SUNSET

be hard, don't you think? It, um, reveals a person's trustworthiness, though."

The boy cocked his head as though she hadn't quite gotten the signal right. Oh dear. She held her breath as he seemed to deliberate answering. This *was* the boy Fletcher had sent, wasn't it? She searched the alley, but no other child appeared. He must be the right one.

At last he said, "Trust is true when what's hidden is safe from whispers."

Her shoulders sagged at hearing the code Fletcher had given her to verify she trusted the right person. She pulled the carpetbag from beneath the laundry and handed it over.

The boy took off without a backward glance.

She retrieved the paper-wrapped package and left the laundry beside the back door. She had her own delivery to make.

An hour later, the crisp morning air bit at Opal's cheeks as she sat on the park bench. She glanced over her shoulder, unable to shake the feeling of being watched. A finely dressed man standing in the shade of a nearby tree turned and walked away. Opal froze. Was that Senator Saville? His height and build appeared the same. Even his hair color matched. But where was his cane? The senator was never without his cane. Besides, the senator was supposed to be meeting with the mayor on the other side of the city this afternoon. The departing man crossed the road and disappeared down another street.

Opal gave herself a shake and searched the others mingling beneath the trees and among the newly planted shrubs. There were no familiar faces, nor did anyone appear to be paying her a lick of attention.

She shifted on the bench. A passing carriage caught her attention, but it did not stop. Hopefully, the Davidsons would arrive soon. Waiting was beginning to tie her thoughts in knots.

She had not seen the couple since she was evicted from their charity home many years before.

As she tossed and turned through the long night, Opal's mind had raced with thoughts of what she would say to them. Would they be forgiving?

Opal smoothed the skirt of her plain dress. *You're not the same woman they knew. The Bible says you're born again.*

Thanks to the Johnsons, she was no longer a slave to the opium that had taken over her life after Lucy's father had left her for dead. She'd been sober for months now and had no intention of going back. On days when her pain was at its worst or the memories tried to take over her mind, a yearning for oblivion still tugged at her. When that happened, she reminded herself that oblivion had left her daughter afraid for her life with no mother to turn to. The harsh truth held firm her resolve. Her new knowledge of their heavenly Father's love brought her comfort.

Despite the limited time they'd been able to speak, each time they'd met, Fletcher had shared a little more about his faith. At first, Opal had dismissed his words the same as she'd ignored other preachers who'd dared to enter the Barbary Coast with their Bibles in hand. But his gentleness, forgiveness, and persistence had sparked a curiosity in her.

Perhaps, once this was all over, she'd attend the church he'd been urging her to visit.

For now, the new medicine and words of truth Fletcher had shared with her at each of their covert meetings had made her a new person. She could finally make things right with the Davidsons. She owed them so much more than an apology. Perhaps her efforts to save Lucy would aid the Davidsons as well—only time would tell. For now, her sincere words of regret and promises to make better choices moving forward would have to do.

The Davidsons' carriage pulled to a stop at the edge of the

park. The couple immediately spotted her on the bench but were forced to pause when a bearded man in tattered clothes crossed their path. He mumbled something incoherent before shuffling past Opal and into the park.

The Davidsons offered kind smiles as they approached.

Opal exhaled and rose to greet them.

Mrs. Davidson drew her into a hug, and Opal gasped, tears pricking at her eyes.

After a brief squeeze, Mrs. Davidson stepped back to hold Opal at arm's length. "My goodness, but you do appear so much better—just as Fletcher assured us. I couldn't believe it when he told us you'd given up opium and had been holding a respectable job for months." She released Opal and lowered to the bench, waving for Opal to join her. "Tell us everything that's brought about this magnificent change."

If only she *could* tell the kind family the whole story. But she and Fletcher had agreed it would be safer to keep the details secret until the truth was revealed in the newspapers and the men responsible were behind bars—unable to threaten or harm anyone else.

Opal settled for the abridged version Fletcher had helped her create. "I can't fully explain my change in circumstances. One day, I woke up and realized that despite being grown now, my daughter still needed me, and I didn't want to keep letting her down." She wrung her hands in her lap. "With the Johnsons' help, I've quit using opium and gained proper employment."

They didn't need to know she'd just snuck away from that employment with no intention of returning. The important part was that she would never go back to the life she'd been living—or rather, enduring—before Fletcher rescued her.

She swallowed the lump clogging her throat. "I wanted you to know that I am deeply sorry for the trouble I caused you. I hope someday you can find a way to forgive me."

Mr. Davidson adjusted to fully face her from the other side of his wife. "You're already forgiven."

Opal searched his earnest gaze before turning to Mrs. Davidson, who smiled and patted Opal's hand. "We forgave you years ago and have been praying God would turn your heart toward Him."

Opal's face warmed. "Fletcher *has* been telling me about God."

Mr. Davidson beamed at her. "Lucy will be so happy." He shared a look with his wife, who nodded. "Would you consider traveling with us to celebrate our daughter's wedding? We're leaving this afternoon, and I believe it would mean a lot to Lucy to have you there. You could stay at the ranch, or I'm told there's a hotel in Campo if you prefer. That's the nearest town, of sorts, though it takes most of the day to reach it from the ranch. We'd pay for your fare, of course."

Opal ached to accept. "You're so generous to invite me. I wish I could join your celebration, but I'm afraid there are a few more things I must tend to before I'm ready to reunite with Lucy."

Opal lifted the paper-wrapped package from where it had been waiting at her feet. "This is for Lucy. It's a small birthday present for her." She held it toward Mrs. Davidson. "Would you take it and ask Biddie to keep it secret until Lucy's birthday? I'd like it to be a surprise."

With Lucy's birthday still two months away, Opal hoped the truth would be revealed and the three rotten men locked away in time for her to safely join Lucy to celebrate. But in case things didn't go as planned, it seemed wise to send the package with the Davidsons.

Mrs. Davidson patted a gloved hand on the package. "I'll take good care of this. I promise."

After everything she'd heard from Lucy about her daughter's dearest friend, Opal was confident she could trust the girl to keep the package safe. Opal pressed her lips together before adding, "If you could also ask Biddie to keep my news a secret... I'd like to tell her myself. I have much to apologize for."

Was it selfish to want to see Lucy's response to Opal's changes? Her daughter wasn't likely to believe the report, in any case. Not that Opal could blame her. Were she in Lucy's shoes, she would need proof of such a miraculous turnaround.

Mr. and Mrs. Davidson shared a look before reluctantly agreeing.

A few more pleasantries were exchanged before Mr. Davidson announced it was time for them to meet the Clarkes and board the ship taking them to San Diego. He invited Opal to see them off at the wharf so that their driver could return her to her place of employment afterward.

She hesitated. Was it wrong to accept his kind offer when she wouldn't be going back to the Green Hotel? She buried her hands in her skirts. She hadn't experienced the warm feeling of being with people who cared about her in years. Riding with them to the wharf would mean a few more minutes in the presence of this kind couple.

Finally, Opal accepted the offer. Once the Davidsons were gone, she could tell their driver to leave her at the store where Fletcher had told her to speak with the storekeeper's wife named Janie. Not having to worry about being caught walking the many blocks east when she was meant to be working would be a relief. She didn't think the Davidsons would mind once they learned the full truth.

Less than an hour later, Opal waved goodbye as their ship left the dock, a sense of peace washing over her. She had apologized, and the Davidsons had forgiven her. Opal had been given the chance to start anew. Assuming the Greens and Senator Saville didn't catch her before she revealed their crimes to the world.

CHAPTER 20

JANUARY 31, 1874
LUPINE VALLEY RANCH, CALIFORNIA

he next afternoon, the scent of simmering stew wafted through the air as Lucy stirred the pot and poured chopped vegetables into the savory broth. The sun hung high in the sky, bathing the desert landscape in warm hues. Across the yard, Preston sat on the bench outside the barn sharpening a shovel blade. Nearby, Deborah and Josie explored a cluster of boulders. Thankfully, it was too cold for snakes to be much of a worry. Biddie and Gideon had gone to town for supplies, and the rest of the women were off the ranch, working the cattle with Ginny.

Josie's gleeful laughter echoed as she leaped from one boulder to the next, her youthful energy a stark contrast to the quiet expanse.

Deborah whined Josie's name from the ground near the smallest boulder. "Wait for me."

Lucy checked to be sure Deborah's attempts to climb were, indeed, futile. The last thing Lucy wanted to worry about was

Esther's precious daughter getting injured. Thankfully, the girl's legs were far too short to get her onto the three-foot rock.

Lucy glanced toward Josie and dropped the spoon. Josie was attempting to conquer the tallest boulder. Somehow in the few seconds Lucy had been distracted, the girl had removed her shoes, managed to find finger and toe holds, and was halfway up the rock's fifteen-foot vertical face. "Josie, stop! That's too high!" Lucy shouted as she dashed across the yard.

Preston jumped up and was at her side in a flash.

"I'm fine. I can do this." Josie continued her ascent, fingers searching for a secure hold.

"Josie!" Preston shouted as they reached the base of the rock pile. "Lucy's right. It's too dangerous." He began scrambling his way through the maze of rocks in an attempt to intercept the girl.

"Josie, please come down." Lucy scurried after Preston, though she couldn't climb as fast in her skirts.

Before Preston could get to Josie, a sharp gasp cut through the desert air. Lucy's breathing stopped as Josie lost her grip and plummeted to the ground with a sickening thud. "No, no, no!" Lucy cried as she reached the foot of the biggest boulder.

Preston was already lifting the unconscious girl into his arms. Blood oozed from a nasty gash on her forehead. He cradled her close, his voice somehow both firm and gentle. "Josie, honey, wake up. You've gotta wake up now." When she didn't respond, he jiggled her. "Come on."

Lucy wrung her hands. "What do we do?"

"Josie?" Deborah's warbled cry tugged Lucy back to the base of the rocks, where she scooped the frightened girl into her arms.

Preston followed more slowly, his balance encumbered by his burden. The entire way down, he spoke to Josie, urging her to wake up.

Finally, as he stepped down from the last boulder, a moan slipped between the girl's lips.

Preston stroked her hair, still striding toward the bunkhouse with Josie held tight against his chest. "That's right. Now, open those beautiful brown eyes for me."

Lucy rushed beside him with a silently crying Deborah in her arms.

Preston stepped into the room Josie had been sharing with her mother and lowered the girl to the bed.

Her lashes began to flutter.

Lucy sagged as Deborah began to kick and squirm to be let down. Lucy set the toddler on the floor, and she lurched for her playmate.

Preston raised his arm to block her. "Not right now, sweetie. Josie isn't feeling good. You need to give her some space."

Josie's eyes still hadn't fully opened.

Trembling, Lucy met Preston's gaze. "She needs a doctor. Clyve said Doctor Smith agreed to stay on with them a while since there's such a need in the area, but I'm not sure how much longer he was supposed to stay. What if he's already moved on?"

The corners of Preston's lips turned down. "If he's there, I'll fetch him. If not, I'll go on to Campo and bring back Silas." He nudged Deborah back toward Lucy, who crouched down and wrapped her arm around the child. Then he strode from the room.

Seconds later, Lucy heard hoof beats thunder out of the valley.

She took Deborah by the shoulders and looked into her watery eyes. "I need you to be a big girl now so we can help Josie. Can you do that for me?"

The child's lower lip quavered but she nodded.

"Good. What I need you to do is stand right here and watch Josie for me while I run and get some supplies to help her. If she opens her eyes or makes any sound, I need you to call for me. But you can't touch her because it might hurt her. Do you understand?"

Again, the child nodded.

Praying Deborah would do as told, Lucy sprinted from the bunkhouse to the main house where she grabbed a handful of rags, a bowl, and the bucket of fresh water they kept for drinking. Then she hurried back as fast as she could without sloshing all the water out of the bucket.

As she neared the door, Deborah's little voice called out. "She's waking up."

Lucy stepped inside the bunkhouse and sure enough, Josie's eyes were open.

"What happened?" The girl started to lift her head, then winced and laid down again.

"Don't move. You fell off that rock I told you not to climb and hit your head. Preston's gone for the doctor."

"What? Who're you? *Donde esta mi mamá?*"

Lucy's skin ran cold at the girl's unfocused gaze and terrifying questions. Had she damaged her brain? *Please God, let her be all right.* "My name's Lucy. I'm a friend. Your mamá asked me to take care of you while she's away. You were climbing some rocks and fell down."

"Ooooh." The girl moaned and her cheeks bulged.

Lucy just managed to get her rolled onto her side so the vomit spilled onto the floor and not the bed.

"Eeew." Deborah backed against the opposite wall.

As Lucy held her shoulders, Josie vomited again.

When she was finished, she shoved weakly at Lucy's chest. "I don't want you. I want mi mamá."

"I know, sweetheart, but she's not here right now. She'll be back soon." Lucy dampened one of the rags and began washing the blood from Josie's forehead.

"No." The girl batted feebly at Lucy's hands.

"I'm sure it hurts, and I'm sorry, but I need to stop the bleeding." With one hand, she caught Josie's wrists and held them out of the way. With her other hand, Lucy washed the blood from the girl's face until the size of the wound was clear. Thankfully, the bleeding was slowing, but Lucy applied pressure with the cloth to be sure it stopped.

The girl screamed her protest and thrashed her head.

"Please, Josie, be still. I'm trying to help."

The girl refused to obey until she'd worn herself out. By then, the bleeding had stopped on its own.

Lucy sagged to her knees.

Josie's eyes drifted shut.

Lucy's breath caught. What if the girl didn't wake again? "No, no, no." Lucy gave Josie's shoulders a gentle shake, and her eyes popped open again. "You've got to stay awake until Preston gets back with the doctor."

For what seemed an interminable amount of time, Lucy prayed for Preston to hurry while she did everything she could think of to keep Josie's eyes open. Finally, the sound of horses galloping into the valley brought sweet relief.

Minutes later, Doctor Smith preceded Preston into the bunkhouse, brushing past Lucy as though she weren't there. Though cleaner than when she'd seen him at the wedding, his clothes still bore several worn patches and strings hanging from the cuffs. His face was also still covered by a thick brown beard and bushy mustache. He moved directly to the bed and knelt beside it with his brown leather satchel. "Glad to see you're awake, little girl."

Preston met Lucy's eyes. "How long have her eyes been open?"

"I'm not sure. She woke up not long after you left, but she keeps trying to go to sleep. I was afraid she wouldn't wake up again, so I haven't let her sleep." Lucy looked at the doctor whose full attention was on Josie, his back to the rest of them. "Was that the right thing to do?"

He replied without turning to look at her. "It does help with the examination if the patient is responsive."

Thank goodness, she hadn't made things worse. Lucy scooped up Deborah, who had her first two fingers in her mouth, and settled the child on one hip. "She doesn't remember me."

The doctor hummed thoughtfully as he used his fingers to pry Josie's eyelids wider, one at a time, peering into each eye. Though clearly agitated by the doctor's examination, the girl seemed too tired to fight him. He probed her head and asked her name. Thankfully, Josie knew her own name. However, when asked a few more questions, it was clear Josie's mind was still rather confused.

Tears pricked at Lucy's eyes.

Preston stepped close and wrapped his arm around her, then addressed the still-kneeling doctor. "Will she be all right?"

"She's suffered a severe blow to the head." The doctor reached into his satchel and removed a small bottle along with a piece of paper. "Let her sleep when she wants to and eat when she's up for it. Keep her still and quiet for the first day or so. After that, she should be right as rain, though it does sometimes take a week or more to fully recover from injuries such as these. You'll know by how she's acting." As he spoke, he removed the cork and tapped a small pile of white powder onto the center of the paper. After resealing the glass container, he folded the paper so that it encased what Lucy presumed to be medicine. He returned the bottle to his satchel before rising. Then he offered the packet to Preston with one hand as he slung his satchel over his shoulder. "Add this to a cup of tea for the girl every handful of hours or so. It'll help with the headache."

Lucy tried to catch the doctor's eye to thank him, but he

stepped outside before she could catch his attention. "I'll be back tomorrow to check on her, but I doubt I'll be needed. Of course, if anything changes overnight, you can always send for me."

Lucy followed him. "Won't you stay for a meal? It's the least we can do to thank you."

"No, thank you. I'm sure the Rowlands' cook has a plate waiting for me." The doctor didn't pause in his seeming haste to return to his mount, which had been left hitched to the post near the main house. "Keep your focus on that girl, as it should be." In one smooth motion, the man was back on his horse and cantering out of the valley.

The sound of Josie's moan spurred Lucy to action, and she called back to Preston. "I'll get water on to boil if you'll keep an eye on Josie."

Preston agreed, and Lucy carried Deborah to the main house, praying the whole time for Josie's full recovery. How were they going to explain what had happened to Carmen?

February 2, 1874

Two days later, Lucy's backside was sore after riding for three hours through the desert mountains to find the herd. She shifted in her saddle as Ginny and Carmen counted the cattle meandering across the western slope. Ginny had been right. Not a single clump of grass remained taller than the cattle's reach. Desperate for forage after clearing out the last place, the herd had eaten it all in less than a day.

Ginny finished counting. "We're short ten heads."

Lucy scanned the herd again, her heart sinking at the realization that the missing cattle might have been stolen. Indians were known to steal cattle for eating, but they usually only took one or two, and from the larger outfits. Ginny was friends with some of them and had already promised to give them three of her cattle when it came time for market. So she hadn't had any trouble in that regard. Which meant if the cattle were stolen, rustlers were likely to blame.

Lucy fisted the reins, her breath coming quick as memories of last fall's trouble flashed through her mind. She thought of Biddie and Gideon back on the ranch with Deborah and Josie. Gideon was suffering another of his migraines, so Biddie had chosen to stay behind to keep an eye on him and the girls.

Thankfully, Carmen, though upset by her daughter's injury, hadn't blamed Lucy or Preston for the accident. More importantly, Josie had recovered miraculously well. By the time the doctor arrived to check on her the evening after her fall, Josie had been up and playing jacks with Deborah. Her complete return to normal behavior had so reassured everyone that today Carmen had agreed to leave the girl in Biddie and Gideon's care on the promise that Josie wouldn't be climbing rocks for a very long time.

Lord, please keep them safe.

Lucy took a slow breath, exhaled, and turned her attention to where Preston was recounting the herd. They hadn't had an issue with bandits in this region for a few months, and all the newspaper reports indicated the gang that had attacked Lupine Valley Ranch in the fall had moved northward.

At last, Preston sighed. "My count matches."

Ginny rode her horse slowly around the edges of the gorge, her intent gaze fixed on the ground. Eventually, she released a growl of frustration and surveyed the surrounding desert slopes again. "The ground is too churned up here to get a read on which way they went. We need to comb the area, try and spot any tracks or signs of where they might have got to. Let's hope they went searching for more food or joined in with another herd. But I don't want anyone riding alone. Lei Yan and

I will head east, see if they somehow made it to the eastern slopes." She steered her horse over to Carmen. "I want you and Esther to search south as you drive this bunch toward that canyon I showed you yesterday."

"I know the one you mean. We'll see to it." Carmen rode off with Esther right behind her.

That left Lucy and Preston. She glanced over to find him studying her with a raised brow. She smiled and nodded to let him know she was fine with being paired with him.

He moved his horse closer to hers. "Lucy and I can head north."

Ginny agreed and everyone parted ways.

Lucy and Preston picked their way north for what seemed like hours, scanning the ground for any signs of the missing cattle. The sun blazed down, searing the earth and making it impossible to make out any impressions in the hardened dirt. Lucy's throat was dry and coated with dust. She tried to swallow, but her tongue stuck to the roof of her mouth. Her vision grew unfocused. She squeezed her eyes shut for a moment, and when she reopened them, her vision was a bit clearer.

She reached for her canteen and took a long drink of warm water. The tightness in her throat eased, but her eyes ached and her head began to throb. Even her stomach was uneasy.

Preston glanced over at her. "You don't look so good. Let's take a break."

Lucy followed him to a cluster of boulders. Carefully, she dismounted and leaned against the nearest rock, grateful for the shade it provided.

Preston joined her. "Are you feeling sick?"

Lucy wiped sweat from her forehead. "I think the heat is getting to me." Unbidden, her thoughts drifted to the past, as they'd been doing more often since Biddie had reminisced over dinner last week.

Where was Mama? Was Fletcher still keeping her safe? Or had Mama returned to her opium?

Please Lord, don't let her have returned to San Francisco. Wherever she is, keep her safe.

In the shade of a tall boulder, weary to the bone, Lucy sank to the ground.

Preston sat beside her and held out her uncapped canteen. "You need to drink more."

Her stomach protested his suggestion. She shook her head and immediately regretted it. Every muscle, every bone, every part of her ached unbearably, like when she'd suffered an ague as a child. Was she getting sick? She'd felt fine this morning. She rested her head against the rock and let her eyes drift shut. If only she could sleep. Oblivion seemed the only hope for relief.

The weight of her hat vanished and was replaced by warm water that soaked her hair before trickling down her neck and into her collar. She gasped, her eyes flying open with a yelp of surprise.

Preston put the cap back on his canteen with a grin. "You can't go to sleep."

"I wasn't," she lied. "I was just resting. There was no need for—"

"You're heat sick." He lifted the canteen as though he was giving a toast at a fancy party. "The water will help you cool off."

Lucy scowled at him. A part of her knew he was right, but the bigger part of her was silently raging against the increased pain the water caused. Every muscle, even her skin, seized in protest. Then, to her horror, a tear slipped out. "It hurts."

His amusement vanished. "I know. I'm sorry."

She squinted at him. "How?"

His head tipped. "How, what?"

"How do you know it hurts?"

He looked away. "I had plenty of experience with heat sickness during the war."

"Oh." She swallowed against the persistent nausea. "I'm sorry."

They sat in silence for several minutes as she sipped water, breathed slowly, and willed her body to cool itself. She finished her first canteen, and Preston fetched her second. Eventually, her stomach settled and the ache in her head eased.

She peeked at him from the corner of her eye. Somehow she'd forgotten that he fought in the war. Could his battle experiences explain the primal rage he'd displayed at the wedding? She'd heard some men had been permanently changed by going to war.

He caught her looking. "What?"

Her cheeks warmed. "I was just wondering..." She hesitated. Was there any point to asking about his behavior at the wedding? No explanation could change what he'd done.

Preston straightened and looked away, a muscle flexing over his clenched jaw. "Go ahead. Ask what's on your mind." Still as a statue, he waited for her words like he'd wait for a blow.

"Never mind. It's none of my business." She forced another sip of water.

"No, go on." He turned back to hold her gaze. "I'll tell you anything you want to know." Something deeper flickered in his eyes, beneath his words.

She closed her eyes. She was being silly. The heat sickness was making her see things that weren't really there.

His hand slid beneath hers, his fingers slipping through to clasp hers tight.

She looked at him as confusion swirled.

"I mean it. Ask me anything."

She couldn't look away. "It's about the war."

He stiffened but didn't turn away or withdraw his hand. A curt nod encouraged her to continue.

"Did it... Is that why you...at the wedding, with Morly. Why didn't you stop?"

His grip tightened as his head fell.

"I'm sorry. I shouldn't have—"

"No." He lifted his head again. "I'm glad you did. I've wanted to apologize, but it never seemed like the right time. You were right to call the others. I should have stopped, and I'm so sorry that I hurt you. I never meant to—"

"I know." She squeezed his hand. "It was an accident. You would never intentionally hurt me." Despite the nervousness her roused memories had caused in recent weeks, deep inside, she'd known Preston would always protect her, never hurt her. "I forgive you."

He exhaled and seemed to study his boots. "I told myself I'd never be like him, but when I saw Morly with his hands on you...it was like a match lit inside me, and before I knew what was happening...all I could see, all I could think about was what happened to Ginny. I wasn't there for her. I didn't get back in time, but this time—"

Huh? "What happened to Ginny?"

"Nothing." Preston pulled away, leaving her hand empty. "Sorry. I shouldn't have said anything. I just..." He shook his head again and plucked a blade of dry grass with his free hand. He quickly shredded it, then met her gaze. "I couldn't bear for anything to happen to you."

The desperation in his tone and passion in his eyes made Lucy's heart pound faster than a galloping horse. What was he saying? His words, his look...they implied more than friendship. Didn't they?

His gaze dropped to her lips as he leaned toward her. "Lucy, I—"

Her chest tightened. Was he about to kiss her? She couldn't do this. "So it was because of the war?"

Preston froze, blinking up at her. "What?"

"Why you couldn't stop. Was it because of the war?" No, wait. He'd said something about Ginny. She opened her mouth to change her question, but he beat her to it.

"No." He leaned back, frowning. Whatever emotion she'd seen in his gaze vanished. "At least, I don't think so."

She hated herself for forcing him to explain what he'd already apologized for, but her senses were still reeling from the near kiss, and she couldn't think of any other safe topic. One that kept him at a distance. "Then why?"

"Pa." He yanked a clump of grass from the dry, hard earth and twisted the blades between his fists. "I swore I'd never be like him, but I can't escape the blood running through my veins." He hurled the mangled mass away, muttering his next words so quietly, she almost missed them. "You're right to reject me."

Tears pricked the corners of Lucy's eyes. What she'd gathered about Oliver Baker through conversations with Biddie and the few things Ginny had mentioned was that he'd been a selfish, violent gambler with no regard for the wants or needs of his family. Frequently drunk, he'd vented every frustration on those who loved and depended on him.

Preston had dropped everything to come help Ginny, and he hadn't hesitated to risk his life by going after the bandits that had kidnapped Biddie. With Gideon and the other women here to help, he could have left by now, returned to pursuing his own dreams. Instead, he continued to work hard every day to ensure Ginny succeeded in her first year as head of Lupine Valley Ranch.

She shifted to face him fully. "You are nothing like your father. You work hard, you're loyal to your family, and you're one of the kindest, most selfless men I've ever met." She chewed her lower lip. "I won't pretend that I understand or approve of what happened at the wedding, but that was one day, one storm of weakness, in a vast sea of goodness. You can't judge who you are by one mistake. I—" She stopped herself from confessing that she felt nothing resembling a rejection of him. In truth, that was the problem. The more time she spent with Preston, the more her traitorous heart wanted to be around him, flaws and all.

"Maybe." He glanced at her, but then scowled at the empty desert surrounding them. "But bad blood will out. Haven't you heard that? A man in my regiment was always saying it. And I think he was right."

She stiffened. She *had* heard that phrase—more times than she'd dusted the sconces at the Green Hotel—and it never failed to ire her. "Then you think I'll become a prostitute someday?"

Preston jerked and gaped at her. "What?"

"My mother's a prostitute." She held his gaze, daring him to repeat that horrid phrase. Daring him to reject her for her mother's choices. "She wasn't always, though. She started out the darling only child of an upper-class couple. But she fell in love with the wrong man, and one day, he beat her." She swallowed down the bile that rose in her throat any time she recounted the tale. "He left her for dead, but she survived. The doctor prescribed a small amount of opium for her pain, but she grew greedy. When we had nowhere to go, the Davidsons took us in, and she repaid them by stealing from them to buy more opium. When I found out, I told the Davidsons. They gave her the choice to give up opium or leave their charity home." Lucy couldn't hold Preston's gaze any longer. Chin lowered, she whispered the awful truth to her lap. "She chose to leave. And she left me behind. She became a prostitute to pay for the opium."

CHAPTER 21

*P*reston couldn't believe what he was hearing. He'd had no idea about Lucy's past. He'd suspected it wasn't easy considering she'd wound up living in a charity home, but he'd figured she and her ma had run into a bit of bad luck. He'd never suspected a violent pa was something they had in common. He wanted to reach out and hug her, to tell her that he understood, but he didn't want to make things worse by overstepping. Especially after his foolishness in almost kissing her. Instead, he kept his eyes trained on the horizon, fighting to push away his anger at Lucy's ma and the man who'd hurt her.

"Lucy." He cleared his throat, trying to dislodge the lump that had formed as she shared her story. "I'm so sorry. That's...that's a terrible thing to go through."

She shrugged. "It's in my blood, too, right? Bad blood." She gave a mirthless laugh. "From both my parents."

"No." He turned to face her, his voice firm. "That's not true. You are not your ma or your pa. You are your own person, and you get to decide who you want to be. And the Lucy I know is kind and brave and smart. You have a good heart."

She looked up at him, her eyes shining. "So do you." Her pink lips curled in a smile.

He couldn't help himself. He cupped her shoulders and leaned forward.

Moo!

They both jumped and spun. A cow meandered into the clearing, followed by four more.

Preston and Lucy's eyes met and they both laughed.

He released her and stood, ignoring the pang of disappointment. The interruption was for the best. "I guess the cattle found *us*."

"Looks like it." She accepted his hand up, and they both remounted their horses.

Five more trailed up to join the others, all bearing the Lupine Valley Ranch brand. She frowned. "Do they look extra skinny to you?"

He considered the cattle, his expression matching hers. "Now that you mention it, they do look as though they've lost more weight than the rest of the herd." Quite a bit more. "That must be why they wandered off looking for more feed." It seemed they were moving the cattle to a greener pasture just in time.

As they rounded up the small group, Preston watched Lucy to be sure she was still feeling well, but she appeared fully recovered from her bout with heat sickness. Which was good. Because if they had to stop again, he wasn't sure he'd be able to keep himself from trying to kiss her. Again. And wouldn't that be a foolish thing to try? Because if he kissed her, there was no doubt in his mind that he'd lose his heart in the process. But no woman as wonderful and smart as Lucy would ever choose a hotheaded nomad with nothing to offer a wife over a steady, kind, future ranch-owner like Clyve. Which was how it should be. No matter what his stubborn heart wanted.

~

*a*fter delivering the cattle to the new pasture, Lucy rode alongside Preston back to the ranch. She searched her mind for something to say, anything to break the awkwardness that had hung between them since the cow's timely interruption. But maybe it was better this way. As wonderful as Preston was, she couldn't be the wife of a traveling showman. Not that he ever mentioned an interest in marriage. For all she knew, he was planning to remain a bachelor the rest of his livelong days.

Keeping a better distance from Preston and sticking with her plans to marry Clyve was the wise thing to do. Assuming he ever asked. Clyve may be a bit predictable...all right, he was downright boring. But there were worse things to have in a husband. Clyve was good and loyal, steady and dependable. He had a strong faith in God and a secure future on his father's ranch. He was the type of husband she wanted. Lucy nodded as if sealing the deal with herself.

As she and Preston crested the rim of the mountain, the sun hung low in the sky, casting a red-orange hue over the empty clearing below.

She reined her horse to a halt and glanced at Preston. "Where is everyone?"

Movement at the south end of the valley drew her eye. Four figures, two tall and two short, were making their way toward Biddie's new house. They were pushing two wheelbarrows.

Preston followed her gaze. "That must be Biddie, Gideon, and the girls. I guess Gideon's feeling better now." He shaded his eyes with one hand. "What are they doing? I thought they'd planned to keep working on their home today."

"Looks as though they're hauling clay," Lucy replied, her curiosity piqued. "At least, that's what I assume they're pushing in those barrels since they seem to be coming from the creek."

"Didn't they say they'd collected enough?"

"I thought so." Lucy nudged her horse forward again. "Let's go see what changed."

The little group had just reached Biddie and Gideon's nearly finished house when Lucy and Preston reached the ranch yard.

Biddie smiled up at them. "Welcome back." She wiped sweat from her brow. "We're just finishing up for the day." She shielded her eyes against the sun with one hand and scanned the slope behind Lucy. "Where's everyone else?"

Preston adjusted his grip on the reins to keep his anxious horse in place rather than heading toward the corral. "There were a few head missing when we got there today. Lucy and I brought in a handful from the north while Carmen and Esther drove the bulk of the herd to the new pasture. When we joined our group with those at the new pasture, they said they'd stay until Ginny and Lei Yan returned. Those two were supposed to be scouting east." He glanced back toward the valley rim as if expecting his big sister to appear there. "If they're not all back in an hour or so, I'll head out to check on them."

Lucy took in the clay-filled barrels. Well, Gideon's was full. Biddie's was half full, since that was the most she could push up the steep incline between the creek and the valley. "I thought you were almost finished and had enough."

Biddie's expression turned sheepish. "We decided on an addition. It'll mean a bigger roof, but I think we'll be more comfortable this way."

Lucy's stomach flipped and she examined Biddie's middle, then studied her friend's expression. "Are you...?"

Biddie's brow furrowed. "What?"

Lucy glanced at Preston, then slid from the horse to whisper in her friend's ear. "Are you expecting?"

Biddie gasped. "Goodness, no." Her face flushed. "What made you think...? Oh! No, we're adding an entry room over the front door to help keep the sand and dirt out." She giggled.

"Oh." Lucy joined in Biddie's laughter. "Sorry. I just thought..." Better not to finish the sentence. "Forget it. An entry room makes a lot of sense."

Biddie was forever muttering about the difficulty of keeping the desert sands out of her baking. With the new oven her parents had promised to have delivered soon and the entryway to keep the dirt out, Biddie's baking would be much easier.

Deborah and Josie, both covered head to toe in clay dust, began to chatter excitedly about the fun of digging for clay.

Preston dismounted and reached for Lucy's reins. "I'll take care of the horses."

Lucy sobered. "Thank you. I'd better get the evening meal started."

"I'll help you, and so can the girls." Biddie frowned at her dust-covered skirts. "But I think we'd better wash up and change first." She directed the girls toward the bunkhouse, and she and Lucy walked toward the main house. "Mother would have a fit if she knew I let the girls get as dirty as they do so often. But I can't resist their smiles."

Lucy chuckled. "They do seem to love playing with the clay and mud. Josie, especially. I don't think I ever saw her behaving like a child before she came here." She reached the front door and froze. It stood three inches open. She frowned at Biddie. "Did you—"

Josie's scream from the bunkhouse sliced through Lucy's words.

Lucy and Biddie raced toward the building even as the sound cut off as abruptly as it had begun.

"Stop!" Preston shouted, steps behind them.

She hesitated and he flew past, pistol in hand.

He burst through the bunkhouse door, Gideon and Biddie on his heels.

Lucy entered last. Morly had one arm around Josie and the

other hand clamped over her mouth. The stench of whiskey and foul sweat assaulted her nose.

"Let her go." Preston's voice was as hard as the boulders scattered across the valley, his gun aimed squarely at Morly's head.

"Now." Gideon echoed Preston's warning, his own gun in hand, though pointed at the ground. No doubt, he worried about hitting Josie by mistake.

Morly flinched. "Quit your yelling and make these two"—his bloodshot eyes narrowed on Josie and the wailing Deborah, who'd latched onto Josie's legs—"promise to quit their cater-wauling, and I'm happy to let her go."

Biddie inched forward, careful not to get between Preston's gun and Morly. She pried Deborah from Josie's legs, carried her back to Gideon's side, and bounced the girl on one hip. "There now, honey, everything's all right. You're all right now. I've got you. Everything's going to be just fine."

Deborah hid her face against Biddie's neck as her loud cries softened to quiet whimpers.

Lucy caught Josie's terrified gaze. "You're going to be quiet, too, aren't you, sweetheart?"

Josie nodded as much as she could within Morly's grip.

With a grunt, the brute thrust Josie away from him. The movement seemed to send him off kilter because he staggered sideways, then backward before falling to his rear on the stone floor.

As the dust settled around Morly, Josie's arms squeezed the air from Lucy's lungs. She pried her own arms free to pat the girl's back. "Can you loosen up just a"—she fought to suck in air—"bit?"

The vice-like grip eased. "Sorry."

Lucy drew a grateful breath and rubbed Josie's back. "It's all right. You've grown stronger than you realized from helping with the ranch."

"What were you doing in here?" Preston's demand brought Lucy's attention back to Morly, and she realized the bunkhouse was a mess around him. Every mattress was upturned. Clothes and the women's few belongings were scattered everywhere. Even pillows had had their chicken feathers removed. It looked as though a wild animal had been set loose inside.

Josie's shaky voice offered, "He was sleeping on the ground, right there." She pointed to a spot beside her bed.

Morly scratched his arm, appearing genuinely confused. "It was like this when I come in, but—"

"Tell the truth." Gideon lifted his gun just enough to catch Morly's attention. "Why'd you come in here? What were you looking for?"

Morly started to shake his head but flinched again and jammed the heel of his palm into one eye. "I was just trying to find out if anybody was home. There wasn't nobody in the yard or the main house, so I thought maybe you was all in here." His mouth quirked to the side. "Least, that's what I think I remember." He glared at the chaos. "But I didn't do this. That I know for sure. This is the way it was when I come in."

"And I'm the governor." Preston's sarcasm could have tanned a cow hide.

Gideon stepped forward. "Come on, get up. I want you out of this building and off our property."

Morly tried to stand but fell back down when he was halfway up.

With a low growl, Preston sheathed his weapon and jerked Morly to his feet. Not waiting for the man to find his balance, Preston propelled him outside. "Where's your horse?"

Morly looked toward the spring, and Lucy followed his gaze. Sure enough, a strange horse stood munching on the small patch of grass that grew around the ranch's lifeblood.

"I'll get it." Gideon strode toward the spring while Preston kept his hold on Morly.

A few minutes later, and after some heated whispering between Preston and Gideon, they had their unwelcome visitor mounted and pointed toward the trail out of the valley.

"Let me be completely clear." Preston kept hold of Morly's reins as he looked up at the drunkard. "If you *ever* set foot on this ranch again, I'll shoot first and ask questions later. Understand?"

Morly scowled. "Can't a man pay his neighbor a friendly visit without threats against his life?"

"Your first visit started with reckless shooting, and now you've wrecked the bunkhouse." Gideon glared at him. "Those actions aren't 'friendly' by anyone's definition."

"Now hold on," Morly whined. "I said I didn't have anything to do with—"

"And I said I don't believe you." Preston released the reins and slapped the rump of Morly's mount. "Now get out of here and don't ever come back."

They all watched until Morly's mount disappeared over the mountain's peak. Then Preston turned to Gideon. "I still think we should have arrested him."

Gideon waved dismissively. "He didn't actually break anything or hurt anyone, just made a mess. A dumb drunk wouldn't spend more time in jail than it took to sober him up. That would happen before we could even make it to San Diego. And it'd take two of us to bring him in if we wanted to sleep at night without worrying he'd get loose somehow." He lifted a brow at Preston. "Do you want to be gone that long?"

"We could've taken him to Campo and left him there for the sheriff to fetch."

Gideon set his hands on his hips. "The sheriff isn't going to ride this far east for a man that tossed a few things about in a drunken stupor."

Preston's frown didn't budge but he quit arguing and stomped toward the barn.

Biddie looked at Deborah still clinging to her. "How about I help you put things to rights before we change and wash up?"

The girl's curls bounced as she nodded vigorously.

"All right." Biddie held a hand out for Josie, who accepted it. "Let's get going, then. Your mamas will be home soon, and they'll be hungry."

Lucy started for the main house, calling over her shoulder, "I'll get the evening meal started." She paused again at the slightly open door, then shook herself free of the nerves it caused. Morly had mentioned looking for them in the house. He must have forgotten to shut the door. She only hoped he hadn't left it in the same state as the bunkhouse. Bracing herself for a disaster, she pushed open the door and stepped inside.

Not a thing appeared out of place.

She strode across the room and pulled back the curtain hiding their sleeping quarters. A quick glance revealed no mess. She stepped toward her apron hanging from a peg on the wall near her bed, then froze. A paring knife had been stabbed into the post of her bed. It held a scrap of paper.

A chill swept through her and she made another quick scan of the one-room structure. No one lurked in the shadows. Even the cellar door was shut.

Hesitantly, she shuffled forward and pried the knife free from the bed. The paper fluttered toward the ground, but she caught it and lifted the slip toward the amber sunlight filtering through the nearest keyhole window. Elegant script covered the bit of parchment.

Words not meant for your ears must remain unspoken. Consider your actions, for your choices shape the destiny of all. Return what was taken, for the shadows hold more than they reveal and the sand in the glass runs low.

There was no possibility Morly had written such a note.

Hands shaking, she read it again. *Words not meant for your ears must remain unspoken.* That had to be a reference to what she'd overheard in Junior's suite. What else could it be? Her stomach churned. They'd found her.

But what did the writer mean by *return what was taken*? She hadn't taken anything. No, wait. The dress she'd donned to sneak out of the building and the bag she'd carried her maid's clothes in. But why would they care about those things? And in any case, she didn't have them. She'd left the fancy clothes and bag in an alley all those months ago.

She threw her arms up in exasperation, the note waving with the movement. Something on the back caught her eye. She looked closer. It was a hand-drawn map leading to what looked like an unusual stack of boulders in the shape of a letter *T*.

Flipping the paper over again, she read the note a third time, different words popping out at her. *Your choices shape the destiny of all...the shadows hold more than they reveal...sand in the glass runs low.* What did it all mean? Was it another threat against Mama or the others here on the ranch?

An image of the ravaged bunkhouse flashed in her mind. Had Morly been telling the truth? Was the mess caused by whoever wrote this note as they were searching for...whatever they thought she had? If so, what could she do?

The paper crinkled in her tightening grip. She couldn't return what she didn't have.

CHAPTER 22

*L*ucy strolled with Clyve along the southern rim of Lupine Valley, her hand resting in the crook of his arm, the sun slowly sinking through the pink and orange clouds. A cold breeze swept over them, and she shivered. The mountaintop seemed especially vast and empty today with most of the others—including Preston—off checking on the cattle. Biddie, Gideon, and the girls were down at the creek collecting more sand for their house and would return soon. But at the moment, Lucy and Clyve were enjoying the most privacy they'd ever had. The only sounds were the crunch of their steps and the occasional rustling of wind through a nearby juniper bush.

More wind played with the hairs that had come loose from Lucy's bun, blowing a lock across her eyes. She used her free hand to tuck the hair behind her ear as Clyve resumed talking about the calves he and his father had found with the herd that morning.

"We knew a few of the mamas were getting close, but it was still a surprise to count four new heads in the herd this morning. We watched them a while. They and their mamas seem to be doing just fine."

"Is that why you seem so happy this afternoon?" From the moment he'd arrived, there'd seemed to be an extra bounce in his step.

Clyve's gaze shifted toward the buildings and corrals in the distance. "Partly. But those calves got me to thinking about other kinds of babies."

Lucy's steps faltered when his sparkling gaze turned on her. Surely, he didn't mean...

"Since we started courting, I've been thinking more and more about the future of Rowland Ranch and the kind of legacy I want to create."

Lucy's heart sped, and her breath came in short gasps she struggled to conceal. She wasn't ready for this. He hadn't even proposed. What was he thinking, bringing up such an intimate—

"Do you remember the mare I rode in on when I first came to visit last summer, the one with the grace of a dancer?"

Wait. What did a horse have to do with babies? Numbly, she nodded that she remembered the dark-brown beauty with a full set of white stockings and a white star above her eyes. It'd been one of the most beautiful horses she'd ever seen.

"Well, about this time last year, I bred her with the stallion we got from Old Man Turner—the fastest one in the county," Clyve said, his grin wide enough to reflect the sun. "She's due to foal any day now."

"Oh." He'd been talking about horse babies. Of course. Lucy swallowed a laugh at her foolishness. "That is very exciting." At least, *he* appeared delighted by the prospect.

Clyve's voice grew dreamy as he gazed in the direction of the Rowlands' land. "I see our ranch becoming more than just a cattle operation. I want it to be known for having the finest horses around. Imagine horses that can traverse vast ranges without tiring, agile enough to turn on a nailhead, and swift as the wind. Not to mention beautiful. Horses that'll make our place stand out."

Lucy tried to imagine what he described—tried to catch his enthusiasm—but all she pictured was a heaping load of more work. Raising cattle in this arid land was difficult enough. Why add a whole other animal that would compete for grazing and probably require even more daily care than the cattle? "But why horses?"

Clyve pointed to the few horses mingling in the horse corral at the center of the valley. "Horses are the heart of our work. So I started thinking about how I wanted ours to be the best they can be. Then I realized what a blessing that kind of horse would be for our neighbors, and the idea grew from there."

Not knowing what else to say, Lucy asked, "Is that why you stopped riding her? She's expecting?"

Clyve nodded. "And I have this feeling it'll happen soon, so I've been sleeping in the corral the last few nights, just in case. Not that it's any hardship." He looked up at the now-golden clouds drifting overhead. "Even on these cold winter nights, breathing in the fresh air and watching the stars play peekaboo with the clouds is a great way to fall asleep." His attention shifted to the flatlands below. "Those people up north can keep their crowded forests and mountains that make you feel hemmed in on every side. There's a beauty in this wide-open desert the rest of the world can't hold a candle to."

Lucy forced herself to smile and nod as they continued walking. Though she'd become accustomed to life on a desert ranch, there was nothing about living in this dry, muted-color landscape that particularly appealed to her.

How Clyve could speak of sleeping exposed on the hard dirt as though it were enjoyable was beyond her comprehension. As beautiful as the stars were, she much preferred a comfortable bed inside a snug tent. A sturdy house would be even better, but at least with a tent, one was protected from the elements. She had endured the long cattle drive that brought the new herd to the ranch last fall because she cared for Biddie and because she had nowhere else to go that was safe.

Was Lucy still safe here?

Who had left that mysterious note? How had they sneaked into the house without being seen? What did they think she had? Was anyone other than herself in danger? The questions chafed at her mind as if asking them enough times would produce answers she didn't have.

Clyve paused for a moment, and she opened her mouth, wanting someone else's advice. But he didn't seem to notice and continued speaking before she could form the words. She closed her mouth.

Was there any way to ask without confessing the full truth? Not that she could think of. And until she knew the note's meaning, what was the point in alarming everyone? They wouldn't know any better than she what to be on guard for. Sharing this new secret would be causing worry for worry's sake.

Clyve stopped and faced her, taking both her hands in his. "Lucy," he said softly, his voice husky with emotion. "We've been courting for months now. I was wondering...that is...would it be all right if I kissed you?"

Lucy sucked in her breath, holding it. She'd known the request would come eventually. Why hadn't she seen it coming today? She shook her head. It didn't matter. What mattered was that he was asking and she should say yes. Kissing is what courting couples did.

His expression fell. "I see. Is it that you're not ready, or—"

She shook her head again. "You misunderstand. I didn't shake my head because...I mean, I wasn't saying no."

His eyes lit. "Then...are you saying yes?"

Was she? Of course, she was. One shouldn't court a man for months if she wasn't interested in being kissed by him. And she certainly couldn't expect to be happily married to a man she was averse to kissing. So where was the ache of yearning she'd felt when Preston had almost kissed her? Why wouldn't words of permission form on her tongue? Rather than wait for the lump in her throat to give way and allow speech, she lifted her chin and closed her eyes. Waiting.

Then his lips pressed gently against hers and...nothing. She felt nothing. No warmth. No spark. Where were the butterflies filling her stomach and the brush of desire heating her skin the way she'd heard women at The Home describe kissing?

Clyve began to pull away, but she lifted onto her toes, pressing her lips firmly against his, desperate to feel something, anything like the pleasure she enjoyed at the merest accidental brush of Preston's hand across her skin.

But there was nothing.

Lucy lowered to her heels and looked away. Why weren't her emotions cooperating with what her head knew was best?

Clyve squeezed her hands. "Thank you." Happiness was evident in his tone.

Lucy hoped the curve of her lips formed a smile. Had she just made a huge mistake? Clyve seemed to believe their kiss meant more than she felt. She hadn't meant to mislead him. Should she end their courtship now that she knew his kiss brought none of the feelings she'd both dreaded and secretly hoped for? Entering into a marriage based on friendship and mutual trust was one thing. If Clyve was falling in love with her and she didn't return those feelings, it wouldn't be fair to accept his proposal.

She needed to know where he stood—if he felt more than friendship for her and wanted more from a marriage than loyalty and companionship. If so, she would end things now.

Whatever the cost to her future, she wouldn't deceive him into believing she harbored more than friendly feelings for him. She tugged her hands free and clasped them behind her back. "Clyve, I—"

Thundering hooves interrupted her fumbling words. A rider charged toward them from the direction of Rowland Ranch.

Clyve stiffened. "That's our man, Jorge." Clyve sprinted toward the oncoming rider and shouted, "What's wrong?"

"Your mare. She's in labor."

"Is everything all right?"

"*Sí*, but your pa said you wanted to be there for the birth. You'd better hurry."

Clyve let out a whoop and raced to where he'd left his gelding in their horse corral. Less than ten minutes later, he was galloping past her. "See you next week!"

Lucy lifted her hand in farewell, but he never looked back. She sank her fingers into her hair. What should she do now?

~

FEBRUARY 4, 1874

*L*ucy adjusted the canteen slung across her body and pushed back her bonnet to feel the bright morning sun casting its long, warm rays over the rugged mountainside. With Ginny leading the way and Preston following Lucy, they tromped up the steep slope and deep into a thick woodland.

Ginny stopped and turned to face her and Preston. "Watch out for the cactus." She pointed to a cluster of prickly looking balls near a small boulder, then to a branching, fuzzy looking thing that was as tall as Lucy's knee, and finally, to a cactus that reminded Lucy of her butter pat—if her butter pat was covered in clusters of needles. "That one's a called Prickly Pear because after it blooms, it'll produce a delicious fruit."

She gestured to the larger shrubs around them, most as tall as or taller than Lucy's shoulders. "There's also sage and pinyon pine here. Both useful plants. But today we want the juniper." She pointed to a large bush-like tree beside her. "Junipers are the ones with that twisted, gnarled bark, and their branches tend to sprawl out from the base of the trunk as though they're arms reaching for the sky. The leaves are similar to scales, pressed tight against the stems. Pinyon pines, on the other hand"—she pivoted to point to a tree on her other side—"have shorter needles grouped in pairs, and their bark is smoother, almost as though it's been brushed. They stand tall and straight. They produce seeds we can eat, but they won't be ready for harvest until at least the end of summer, most likely in the fall."

Ginny sure knew a lot about these plants, but then the woman had been foraging to survive when Biddie and Lucy arrived last summer.

"Now, the juniper berries," Ginny continued, gesturing towards the clusters of bluish-purple orbs.

Lucy and Preston stepped forward for a closer look, their shoulders nearly touching. She worked hard to focus on Ginny's continued instructions instead of the sizzling awareness Preston's closeness caused.

"They're ready when they're plump and soft. If they squish between your fingers without much resistance, you've got a ripe one. The green ones still need some time. They take years to ripen, so be careful not to pick ones that aren't ready."

They each pulled out the small cloth pouches they'd brought along and spread out. Lucy scanned the bushes for clusters of berries. When she found one, she used her fingers to gently press and roll each berry, testing for ripeness before plucking it free and dropping the tiny fruit in her bag.

Engrossed in their task, they moved through the desert flora, quiet as the birds scuttling through the brush.

Ginny's sudden yelp and a loud crash shattered the stillness, making Lucy jump.

Preston rushed past Lucy toward the sound of Ginny's angry mutters. Lucy followed him.

Ginny sat on the ground beside a cluster of those ball-like cacti she'd pointed out earlier. Palm raised, she was plucking at what looked to be a hundred needles stuck in her hand.

Lucy knelt in front of her. "What happened?"

Ginny shoved a rock the size of a cow pie with the heel of her boot. "I tripped over that stupid thing."

Preston's eyes crinkled with a mix of sympathy and amusement. "Well, ain't that a sight? Reminds me of the time we were kids and you got splinters in your hand trying to jump over a fence."

Ginny scowled up at him, but there was a humorous twinkle in her eye. "Which was your fault."

Preston feigned exaggerated offense. "Excuse me? You're the one who was chasing me."

"Only because you'd stolen the last cookie when you knew Ma had saved it for me."

Preston shrugged. "I didn't see no name on it."

Ginny stuck her tongue at her little brother, then laughed. "I still don't know how you managed to get over it without getting splinters yourself."

Ginny had a playful side? Lucy snapped her gaping mouth shut as the normally stone-faced woman resumed plucking the needles out of her hand.

"Hey, wait." Preston held up a hand. Then he used his knife to scrape some sap from the trunk of a nearby pinyon pine. He turned back with a grin. "Remember how we got the splinters out?"

Ginny lifted her palm, and Preston smeared a layer of resin over the lodged cactus needles. "Just let it dry and peel it off."

"Thanks." Ginny's usually hard expression filled with as much warmth as Lucy had ever seen. "I'm glad you came."

Preston reached down, and Ginny took his hand with her good one, letting him pull her to her feet. Then he winked at her. "Someone's got to be around to save your stubborn hide."

Lucy looked between brother and sister, a new hope growing in her heart. Was it possible Preston had changed his mind about returning to the traveling show? Lucy nibbled her lip as they returned to berry picking. If he chose to remain on Lupine Valley Ranch, could he and Lucy have a future together? The urgency to clarify things with Clyve churned in her gut, but he wouldn't be back for another six days.

Five hours later, Ginny, Preston, and Lucy returned to the ranch, their sacks filled to the brim with ripe berries. Meeting them in the yard, Biddie accepted the bounty gleefully and left to stash them in the cellar.

"Better go work on that bridle." Ginny strolled toward the barn.

Preston stopped his sister with a hand on her shoulder. "Actually, I was hoping I could show you something."

Lucy swallowed her disappointment as she glanced south. She hadn't had time to mine in two days and had been hoping Preston would agree to work with her this afternoon.

Then he turned an excited expression on her. "You too. I was hoping to show everyone."

She couldn't say no to the eager-little-boy look he wore. "All right."

With a skip, Preston dashed toward the bunkhouse, and less than five minutes later, he'd directed everyone to the clearing in the southern end of the valley where she'd seen him practicing his riding and shooting act.

Lucy's hopes fell to her boots as she realized what it was he wanted to show everyone.

A second later, he charged past them on his gelding, shooting the target off the top of each column as he'd done before. Only this time, he didn't miss a single one.

Reaching the end of the clearing, Preston holstered his pistols and turned his mount around. He cantered over to them, beaming and breathing hard as everyone cheered.

Once they'd quieted, he asked, "What do you think? Will it be enough to convince Harvey to let me back into the show?"

His words snuffed the tiny spark of hope she'd foolishly allowed to grow. While everyone else voiced their agreement that the new act was sure to win him his spot back, Lucy turned away. Brushing at the tears she couldn't stop, she walked briskly through the trees until she reached their outhouse.

Opening the door, she stepped inside and huddled in the dark interior, praying no one would ask later why she'd left in such a rush. What a fool she was. Of course, he hadn't changed his mind. Performing was part of who he was. The joy on his face when people cheered ran almost as deep as the joy Biddie and Gideon had found together. Hoping he'd decided to give up his passion had been a selfish dream. She ripped a page out of the catalogue hanging on a nail in the wall and blew her nose. She couldn't take that from him, even if by some miracle he offered. She'd been right in the beginning. Love made women foolish, and there was no future for her and Preston.

Sniffing once more, she wiped the last of her tears away. Clyve was her best chance at a safe and happy future. *If* he would accept the type of marriage she could offer. Six long days stood between her and his answer.

FEBRUARY 5, 1874

he next day, Lucy moved both reins to one hand as the midday wind blew hot and gritty across the dry grass pasture, stirring up a haze of sand that scoured Lucy's face and seeped into every nook and cranny. The gust brought with it a foul odor worse than the cattle's usual manure.

She shielded her eyes from the sun and surveyed the herd.

The cattle were even skinnier and more lethargic than they'd been the day she and Preston had helped drive them to this new pasture. Although there was still plenty of grass, they weren't eating or walking around. Eyes dull and unfocused, most just stood in place, and a handful were laying down. None of them made a sound. Her heart sank. "It's been three days. Shouldn't they be getting fatter and moving around more?"

Ginny scowled at the herd. "Something's not right. Look at all the grass they haven't touched and look at their backsides." She groaned. "They've got diarrhea." She slid off her horse and strode toward the nearest cow, touching and examining it in the way Lucy imagined a veterinarian might. "Fever." She crouched and pressed her ear to the cow's side, just behind its front, left leg. "Heart's beating too fast."

Eyes wide, Ginny straightened and surveyed the rest of the herd. She lifted her hat and ran a shaky hand over her braids. "It's Texas Fever."

She marched from cow to cow, performing the same checks. When she reached a cow on the ground, she tried to make it stand, but the creature was either unwilling or unable to move. "Get me a rope," she shouted to no one in particular.

Preston brought a rope, and they looped it around the cow, working together to coax the animal onto its feet. The skinny beast didn't budge.

Preston let go, but Ginny kept tugging. "Ginny." Lucy strained to hear his soft voice. "It's no use. She's too far gone. Let her go."

"No. We've got to get her up. This pasture's infected. We've got to move them all before it's too late."

Carmen's expression was grim. "It's already too late."

It was the first time Lucy had seen Ginny look scared. Even the day Biddie had been kidnapped, Ginny had appeared calm and determined. Now, though, her expression was frantic, desperate. "No, it ain't. We just need to get them up and move them to the mountain pastures. It's what we should have done before, but it ain't too late. Once they get that good green grass in them, they'll recover." She gave the sluggish cow another tug, then glared at Carmen. "Don't just sit there. Come and help me."

Carmen crossed her arms over the pommel. "They'll never survive the drive. Even if we can get them moving, there's not enough grass."

"Then we'll buy hay. The cost will set us back, but if we lose the herd, we lose the ranch." Ginny gave up the rope and moved to push the cow from behind.

Lucy gagged at the sight. She was *not* doing that.

Ginny seemed unfazed by the manure coating her hands and shoulder. "The drive will be hard, and some of them will die. But this land is infected, and if we don't get them to new pastures soon, they ain't going to make it to market."

Preston and Carmen slid from their horses and began prodding cattle to their feet. Lucy joined them, though she was careful to stay clear of their soiled backsides. Some cows responded to their efforts while others proved as far gone as the one Ginny was still trying to help.

Ginny paused in her efforts and looked around. "This is taking too long. We need the others." Her gaze connected with Lucy's.

"I'll get them." Lucy remounted and rode back to the ranch to fetch Esther, Lei Yan, Biddie, Gideon, and the girls. It would take all of them to get the sickly herd to the distant Laguna Mountains.

Lucy's unexpected early return brought everyone to the ranch yard. She quickly explained the situation and Ginny's plan.

Gideon strode toward the horse corral. "I'll ride to the McClains' ranch. Last time I was in town, I heard they had hay to sell. I'll see if there's enough left to get us to the mountains."

Biddie wiped dried mortar from her hands. "We'll need to gather supplies for a trip like that. The rest of you head back to help with the cattle. I'll load our packhorses and catch up with you."

Gideon stopped with his hand on the corral fence to frown back at Biddie. "I don't like you being alone."

Lucy's chest squeezed. Would whoever had written the threatening note harm Biddie if he caught her alone?

"The newspaper says the bandits are still somewhere up north." Biddie waved a dismissive hand. "I'll be fine. Besides, Lucy said Ginny wants all the help she can get."

Gideon opened his mouth to argue, but Esther cut him off. "I'll stay with Biddie. We can stop by the Rowlands' on the way and see if their cook is willing to look after Deborah and Josie while we're gone."

Appearing mollified, Gideon entered the corral.

Biddie's brow furrowed. "I almost forgot. I intended to make a trip to Campo tomorrow. I have that batch of rolls in the oven that I planned to sell to Luman for the store."

Esther set her hands on her hips. "Then we'll stop at Campo before joining everyone else. It shouldn't take us more than a day to catch up."

Biddie pointed at Lucy. "Don't leave until I give you enough food for today and tomorrow." Without waiting for a response, she disappeared into the house.

By the time Lucy had watered her horse and refilled her

canteens, Biddie had loaded satchels of food onto a packhorse, and the others had readied their mounts. Lucy tied the packhorse to her horse's saddle, and they set off for the infected pasture at a brisk pace, but the sun was nearing the horizon by the time they rejoined Preston, Ginny, and Carmen.

Getting the herd moving was a grueling task, and by the end of the day, they were exhausted. But Lucy's weary shoulders straightened as the cattle slowly made their way across the dusty desert floor, headed for the distant mountains. Her perseverance had paid off.

Hours later, she laid out her bedroll beneath the stars and begged God to bolster the herd's strength. Because if the cattle didn't survive, Lucy was certain Ginny would change her mind about sharing the gems with the Davidsons.

CHAPTER 23

*T*wo hours after leaving the Davidsons, Opal was back at the bay. She clutched the strap of her small bag as Fletcher guided her along the Broadway wharf. The late-afternoon sun did nothing to warm the cold, salty air. And the nervous glances Fletcher kept casting over his shoulder added to the chill covering her skin. "What is it?"

"It's probably nothing, but I've got the feeling we're being watched. I'm starting to doubt I lost the man who was following me this morning."

When she'd arrived at the store, Janie, the store owner's wife, had escorted Opal to a back room where Fletcher had been waiting. He'd assured her that the man who'd been trailing him all morning had disappeared somewhere near the south end of the city after Fletcher had led him on a meandering, twisting path through more than a half-dozen neighborhoods.

Opal shivered, and her steps slowed as she searched the crowd around them.

Fletcher tucked her arm in his. "Let's keep moving."

They were almost to the dock holding the ferry headed for Oakland Long Wharf when Fletcher stiffened.

"Do you see someone?" she whispered.

"Don't look around, but I've just spotted Chiv King near a stack of crates behind us."

Opal stiffened, expecting a knife to her back, but she heeded Fletcher's warning. "You think he's here for us?"

After a few moments of hesitation, Fletcher said, "We need to take the Stockton Steamer instead." Not waiting for her agreement, he steered them in the direction of the ticket counter. They had just enough time to purchase tickets and board the ferry.

Fletcher guided them to where a small group loitered near the railing.

As they left the dock, Opal leaned toward Fletcher and whispered, "Do you think we lost him?"

Fletcher shook his head. "He's about ten feet behind us, but don't worry. I have a plan."

Opal's heart beat in her throat the entire ride across the bay. The boat pulled in at Vallejo, but Fletcher kept them with the crowd onboard. When it pulled into Benicia, though, he led her off and hurried through the streets, turning one corner after another.

Despite the dose of medication she'd taken at the mercantile, her shoulders screamed. Unaccustomed to such a rapid pace, Opal's lungs soon burned. She stumbled as they dodged across another street.

Fletcher tugged her along a narrow dirt lane. "I'm sorry. I know this is hard for you, but we're almost there."

Another turn, then he pulled her through a thinned section of large, scratchy hedge.

Gasping for air, she considered the immense manicured garden they stood in. "Where...are we?"

Fletcher placed a finger over his lips as running steps pounded nearer.

Opal struggled to quiet her breathing.

The steps continued down the dirt lane they'd just abandoned.

Fletcher visibly relaxed and guided Opal to a nearby bench, which she nearly toppled onto.

His brow furrowed. "I'm sorry. This was the only way I could think of to lose him."

She lifted her hand. "I...understand." Beyond the garden, a two-story building stood with rows of curtained windows. Thankfully, no curious faces peeked out at them. "What is this place?"

"My cousin attended school here years ago. I'm grateful they never patched that hole in the hedge."

She silently agreed with him. Her trembling legs shouted that she'd have been unable to maintain their rushed speed much longer, even with Fletcher's assistance. She let her lungs rest a few more seconds before daring to ask, "Now what?"

Fletcher checked the watch pinned to his vest. "We can wait here another ten minutes. Then we'll make our way back to the wharf and catch the last ferry to Martinez. From there, we can head toward Oakland and take the train to Chicago as planned." He sat beside her. "In the meantime, would you pray with me?"

Opal nodded. A small voice inside whispered that Fletcher was wrong about God listening to the prayers of someone as soiled as her, but she squashed the fear. Fletcher had shared many stories from the Bible of the Lord's forgiveness. She would hold on to those promises and not let her past take His peace from her.

Fletcher took her hands and spoke a prayer for wisdom and

safety. Then, as if he'd heard Opal's inner struggle, he thanked the Lord for His unconditional love and forgiveness.

When he was finished, she lifted her head and caught his gaze. "Thank you." She checked the thinned section of hedge for signs of movement. "What if Chiv King sees us heading back to the wharf?"

Fletcher pushed aside his coat and patted the pistols holstered at his waist. "Then I'll do what I must."

CHAPTER 24

FEBRUARY 6, 1874
SOMEWHERE IN THE ANZA BORREGO DESERT

*R*iding at the rear of the herd, Lucy adjusted the cloth that covered the lower half of her face, protecting her from the choking dust the cows kicked up. Ahead, Preston and Carmen rode along the right side of the line of cattle weaving its way through the desert shrubs and cactus. Esther and Lei Yan rode the left side. Way at the front, Ginny and Gideon kept the herd on course.

Lucy smiled as Biddie returned from prodding a straggler and brought her mount alongside Lucy's at the rear of the herd. "How are you doing?"

"Honestly? I'm worried." Biddie adjusted the angle of her hat to block more of the late-morning sun. "When Esther and I were in Campo, I received a letter from my parents."

A chill ran down Lucy's spine, though she tried not to let the fear show. Had Green's scheming finally crumbled? From what she'd overheard before fleeing San Francisco, it seemed a miracle the truth of his actions hadn't yet come to light. Part of

SHOOT AT THE SUNSET

her wished for the waiting to be over, but a greater part of her pleaded with God for more time to earn as much as possible so the impact of Green's deceptions wouldn't be enough to close The Home. Allowing only a mild sense of worry in her tone, she asked, "What did it say?"

"Mother shared that the bank where Father keeps most of their money has failed due to the panic in the East last September. I knew that tumult had already caused their businesses to suffer, but I didn't realize how great the impact had been. She admitted that if it weren't for the payment they received from Mr. Green last week—late and smaller than expected, though it was—they wouldn't have been able to fulfill their obligations this month."

How had the Greens found the money to make any payment at all? Had Junior been exaggerating the direness of their situation? Surely not, if he believed killing Irene Prichard was necessary to keep the truth a secret. Lucy maneuvered her mount around the left side of a large juniper bush while Biddie went around the right.

When they rejoined on the other side, Biddie continued. "Mother says Mr. Green's company is one of fewer than five companies still making payments to their investors, while so many others and even some banks have closed their doors."

Was this the beginning of the end, or had Mr. Green found a way to prop up his failing scheme—whatever it was? "But you said they had enough to make good their obligations, right?"

"For this month, yes, but Mother admitted to being worried about next month. And Mother never tells me when she's worried."

Preston steered his gelding closer to Carmen. A moment later, she threw her head back in a hearty laugh.

A sour taste filled Lucy's mouth, and she swallowed, forcing her attention back to what Biddie was saying. "Did your mother explain why she's worried?"

"She heard a rumor that even though Mr. Green paid Father, no one else has received a payment in months. She confessed to having a bad feeling and asked me to pray."

Then the Greens' machinations were still coming apart. How much longer could they hold out? Lucy glanced at Biddie's furrowed brow. "And have you prayed?" Prayer was Biddie's usual response to troubling situations.

Biddie visibly relaxed. "Yes, and you're right. I need to remember to trust God with our future."

That wasn't precisely what Lucy had been thinking, but of course, it was the right thing, and Biddie seemed less worried now. There wasn't much else Lucy could do until they returned to the ranch and she could mine more gems. From the sound of things, the money from that treasure would be needed very soon.

Ahead of them, a cow broke free of the pack, and Preston rode after it, disappearing into the thick forest of juniper and mesquite bushes.

Biddie was quiet for several minutes before giving herself a shake and turning her focus on Lucy. "But I didn't come back here to share my worries. I came because I noticed you've been frowning a lot today and thought I'd better check on you." Biddie tipped her head. "What's going on? Is the heat getting to you?"

Lucy shifted in her saddle. "No, I'm fine. I was just thinking about Clyve. It was nice of him to agree to watch the girls while we're away. This would be a difficult trip for them." If only she'd gotten a chance to speak with him about his views on their future.

She glanced at Biddie, who frowned back. "But why would that make you frown?"

"It's not that. It's..." Lucy fiddled with her reins. Would Biddie scorn Lucy's plans for a loveless marriage? "He still doesn't know about Mama."

Biddie's eyes widened in surprise, and understanding dawned on her face. "You haven't told him yet? About any of it? I thought at my wedding, we'd agreed you would."

"The timing never seemed right." How did one interrupt a lecture on how to read the weather with the announcement, *By the way, you might want to know my mama is a prostitute*? "But, obviously, after the story you shared at dinner a while ago, he at least knows that we lived at the charity house. I just...haven't told him anything about why we left or what Mama's been doing since." Lucy shrugged in an effort to loosen the tension in her shoulders. She'd told Preston the truth. Why hadn't she told Clyve? "It's not that I think he'll blame me. I just worry that it might change how he feels about marrying me. He wouldn't just be getting me. He'd be accepting a prostitute as his mother-in-law. I can't imagine many men would be willing to do that."

"You may be right. But putting off telling him isn't going to change how he responds. Wouldn't you rather know sooner than later?"

"I suppose." Lucy scanned the shrubs to the right of the meandering herd. Where had Preston gotten to? Was he in trouble? It didn't normally take this long to coax the cattle back in line.

Biddie's thoughtful tone interrupted Lucy's worrying. "What you said earlier...does that mean, until I told the story of how we met, Clyve didn't know you'd lived at The Home?"

Lucy guided her mount around a cholla cactus. "Yes. Clyve had no idea before that."

"Hadn't you told him anything about your childhood?"

"He never asked."

Sounding exasperated, Biddie demanded, "What in the world have the two of you been talking about during all those walks?"

"Ranching."

Biddie gaped at her. "Ranching? You've been talking about ranching every Saturday for more than three months?"

"And politics. Sometimes he brings a newspaper for us to read together."

"Haven't the two of you discussed anything personal?"

"He told me about Morly when we first started courting and how their mother died giving birth to Clyve. He also said Morly had gotten into a fight with Matthew and taken off about ten years ago."

Biddie studied her. "And?"

"And what? That's all the personal things he's shared."

There was an even longer silence through which Lucy avoided Biddie's gaze. Was it her fault if Clyve didn't seem interested in personal discussions? Was it the woman's responsibility to broach such topics? If it was, no one had told her.

Finally, Biddie spoke again. "How do *you* feel about *him?* I know you were having some doubts during my wedding. Are you still uncertain?"

Lucy squirmed in her saddle. Biddie's love for Gideon made her so happy, Lucy was certain her friend hoped for that kind of relationship for Lucy as well. She hated the thought of disappointing her. "Clyve is a wonderful man and a dear friend." Did it matter if he couldn't make her heart race with a look or her skin tingle at the slightest contact the way Preston could?

Biddie wrinkled her nose. "That's all? Still? With all the time you've spent together, no deeper feelings have grown between you?"

Lucy shook her head, then nodded, then shrugged. "He did kiss me the last time he came to visit."

Biddie squealed, startling the cows directly in front of them and drawing glances from the other riders. She waved a dismissive hand. "Sorry, we're fine."

Carmen's gaze seemed to search Lucy's, and she turned away, her face warming. Where was Preston? What would he

SHOOT AT THE SUNSET

think if he knew she'd let Clyve kiss her? Did Preston still think about their almost-kiss with longing and curiosity the way she did?

Biddie waited for everyone to return their attention forward before spearing Lucy with a hard look. "Why don't you seem happy about that?"

"I am." Lucy's protest was as much an argument with her own heart as with Biddie. "Of course, I'm happy Clyve kissed me. He's my beau." Or she would be if she could be certain what she had to offer would be enough for Clyve.

"Uh-huh." Biddie shifted her reins to one hand and plopped her other onto her hip. "You're about as convincing as a pocket watch that's quit ticking."

Lucy gave up pretending. Biddie could always see through her. "I'm trying. Really, I am."

"But when he kissed you, there weren't ...sparks, or warm tingles, or...anything?"

Lucy cringed. She couldn't lie to her best friend. "Nothing."

"Wow." Biddie's shoulders sagged.

"It's not as though I hated it." Lucy hurried to reassure her. "It was...nice."

Biddie squared her shoulders. "Well, if your feelings really aren't any deeper than friendship, that isn't the end of the world. As I said before, many successful marriages start with less. Look at my parents. Mother married Father for his money and only fell in love with him years later."

Lucy gaped at her. "You've never told me that." It didn't seem possible that the loving, doting couple she'd always known the Davidsons to be hadn't begun their marriage already deeply in love with one another.

"It's true, and there's a long story behind it. Mother told me all about their relationship while Gideon and I were in San Francisco this winter." Biddie steered her mount to guide a wandering cow back toward the herd, then returned. "She said

247

that marrying for money is starting your life out on a purely selfish foundation."

Lucy flinched. Was that what she was doing by marrying Clyve to gain a stable life away from Mr. Green, Junior, and the dandy? Was hoping to make Clyve happy through friendship and companionship enough to acquit her of selfish motivations?

Biddie continued, "But I think that if you care about Clyve as a friend, then you'll want what's best for him just as you would if you were in love with him."

Lucy's heart lifted. That was true. She did want what was best for Clyve, and she had every intention of being the best wife that she could be. How could that be selfish? So long as Clyve knew how she felt and agreed to such a marriage.

"So friendship isn't a bad place to start, but..."

When Biddie didn't continue, Lucy turned to face her friend and found Biddie's intense gaze fixed on her. "Don't rush into marriage. Just because Clyve is the first man to show you attention, and just because you agreed to let him court you, doesn't mean you have to marry him if he asks." A warm glow filled Biddie's face. "Being in love is incredible, and I so want you to have this experience. Please don't settle."

Lucy forced a small smile as her stomach sank with the confirmation of her suspicions and the guilt of never having told Biddie about her secret relationship with Junior. Unfortunately, Clyve was not the first man to show Lucy attention. He was just the first *good* man to express interest in her. Besides, Biddie was beautiful, kind, talented, and from an upstanding family. Any man would have been blessed to claim her as his wife. Lucy was glad Gideon recognized that. But Lucy's father was a monster and her mother a prostitute. Lucy had no money to her name and no unique skills. What enticement could she offer a groom besides a tidy home and decent meals?

As kind as Biddie's words were, a marriage of companionship to a good Christian man was the best Lucy could hope for.

But what if Clyve wasn't willing to settle for friendship? His
reaction to their kiss seemed to hint that his feelings ran deeper
than hers. What would she do if he wanted more than she
could offer? Would Ginny let her continue living at Lupine
Valley Ranch?

Lucy tried to imagine living out her days as the grumpy
Ginny's spinster housekeeper. It wasn't a future that made her
smile.

~

*W*hen Biddie and Lucy's conversation faded into
silence, Preston steered his horse so that the
stray cow he'd been driving moved far right before returning to
the herd. Yes, it had been unfair of him to slow his mount and
listen when the two women believed their conversation was
private, but overhearing Lucy's confession of feeling only
friendship toward Clyve had snared Preston's attention as
firmly as a fishhook in his mouth. Yet, from her silence after
Biddie's caution not to settle, it seemed clear Lucy planned to
marry him despite her lack of romantic attachment.

Preston had gotten to know Clyve well enough to understand that while he was immensely kind and generous, Clyve
was looking for true love. Would he still marry Lucy if he knew
of the inescapable stain on her family *and* that Lucy's feelings
ran no deeper than friendship? Preston couldn't imagine
marrying someone he thought loved him only to discover they
had married him for the sake of a stable home and security. A
deception like that was so unlike Lucy. Was she that desperate
to be married? Why? Did it have something to do with Biddie
getting married? Did she feel left behind?

Whatever the reason, the idea of Lucy settling for anything

less than whole-hearted romantic love rubbed at him like a burr under his chaps. She deserved the kind of glowing happiness that Gideon and Biddie's love had brought his little sister. But what could he do? Should he reveal the truth to Clyve?

Lucy would be furious. And hurt. She'd see it as a betrayal of her trust, without a doubt. Perhaps it was, but he'd learned long ago that some secrets weren't meant to be kept. And if he were in Clyve's boots, Preston would want to know.

CHAPTER 25

*L*ucy knelt beside the swiftly flowing stream. After hours of scrubbing laundry, her fingers ached from the icy chill of the water. She'd been told by the man who owned the land that the creek ran with runoff from snow that still blanketed acres of land farther up the Laguna Mountains. However, the pasture behind her, blocked from view by a stand of trees, was filled with lush green grass. Above her, birds fluttered through the mostly bare branches, twittering as they passed. Though it was almost noon, the winter chill which had long left their home at Lupine Valley Ranch lingered here, allowing the land to retain the moisture needed to keep the grasslands growing. The place was everything they'd hoped for and had cost less than they'd anticipated to lease for the season.

Unfortunately, more than a quarter of Ginny's herd had died on the journey.

After securing the land yesterday, it had been agreed that

everyone would stay for two days to rest and keep an eye on the cattle. If all went well, they'd head back to Lupine Valley tomorrow morning. Everyone but Ginny and Lei Yan who would stick around to guard the cattle for the first month. Then Esther and Carmen would take a turn watching the stock.

For now, they all waited with bated breath to see which of the cattle would survive. Already, another quarter of the poor creatures had died despite rest and good feed, leaving Ginny with half the herd they'd started with.

The moos of happy cows and the quiet murmurs of everyone else busy at their various tasks around camp filtered through the line of trees behind Lucy as she rubbed more soap into Lei Yan's chemise and resumed scrubbing the garment against the washboard Biddie had packed for their drive.

Please, Lord, don't let any more cattle die.

Movement near the edge of the beautiful mountain creek drew Lucy's attention. She paused her scrubbing and lifted her hand to shield her eyes from the bright afternoon sun that filtered through a gap in the surrounding trees. Ginny and Preston strode toward her, matching grim expressions on their faces.

Lucy dropped the chemise in the bucket and stood. "How many more?"

"Twenty since sunrise." Ginny looked as though she was going to be sick. "We're down to a quarter of the herd. And we'll be lucky if they make it."

Face averted, Ginny yanked the hat from her head and dunked it into the chilly creek water before slapping it back onto her hair. She didn't fool Lucy. There were as many tears as there were rivulets of creek water streaming down Ginny's face. "All that money and work for nothing." She picked up a river stone and hurled it down stream. "I never should have taken out that loan for more cattle just because Gideon said he'd stay and help. I'm such a fool." She kicked at the rocks lining the creek. "I knew better, but I didn't listen to my gut. I let myself dream, and now I'm going to lose the ranch."

Preston's glance toward Lucy set her nerves on edge. What was he thinking? Why did his eyes seem to be pleading with her for...what?

He turned back to Ginny. "You're not going to lose the ranch."

Ginny glared at the creek bank as she gave a harsh, humorless laugh. "Sure, I'm not."

"You're forgetting about the gems."

Ginny's head whipped up, hope sparking in her eyes.

Lucy gasped, "No!" As soon as the word left her mouth, she clamped a hand over it. What was she saying? The ranch wasn't hers, which meant the mine wasn't hers, which meant the gems weren't hers. No matter how hard or long she'd worked to extract that treasure from the earth, in the end, it all belonged to Ginny. Still, Lucy couldn't hold back her protest. "But you promised to give that money to The Davidsons' Home for Women and Children."

Ginny's gleam dimmed, then hardened. "Yes, I did, but I didn't expect to lose so much. If I give that money to them now, it'll be the last act of good I'll ever be able to do. But if I use it to save my ranch, my home—if I can make a success of Lupine Valley Ranch—I'll be in a position to give them a little something next year and even more the next year and so on for the rest of my life. Not to mention that if I lose my ranch, Carmen, Lei Yan, Esther, the girls, Biddie, Gideon, and you will be out of a home. Maybe that doesn't mean much to you since you're fixing to marry Clyve. But everyone else is counting on me." She kicked a rock into the creek. "I don't aim to let them down."

"But..." If the Davidsons didn't get the money they needed this month, let alone this year, there wouldn't be a home for Ginny to give to next year or the year after that. Short of a miracle, The Home would be gone, closed. And every woman and child sheltering within its walls would be cast back onto the streets they'd come from. Which was why—or so she'd thought —God had revealed the mine to Lucy.

But she couldn't explain all that. Not without confessing the terrible secret she'd been keeping for months. Not without confessing that the Davidsons' impending destruction would be all her fault.

And even if she could, Ginny was right. The others were all counting on Lupine Valley Ranch to succeed. She absently resumed scrubbing the chemise. Was there any hope left for saving The Home?

～

FEBRUARY 15, 1874
LUPINE VALLEY RANCH

*S*enator Garfield Saville—aka Dr. Smith—stood in the shadow of a large juniper on the ridge of the valley holding Lupine Valley Ranch. His back to the midmorning sun, he looked out over the desert and released a curse. The inhabitants of the ranch were nearly back. Judging by their casual pace and distance, he'd be lucky to have an hour to search the barn before they entered the mountain valley.

He ground his teeth. The task of retrieving Green's missing ledger had been filled with one obstacle after another, beginning with Opal Arlidge's conversation with the Davidsons. Garfield had listened from his position behind a nearby bush to the entire exchange. It didn't take a genius to deduce the brown paper package she'd asked them to deliver to Lucy must be the stolen evidence. Unfortunately, he'd been unsuccessful in his attempts to intercept the couple.

By the time he'd arrived in the desert, the wedding ceremony was over and the package nowhere to be found. He'd considered gaining residence on Lupine Valley Ranch itself, but concerns that Lucy might recognize him if placed in such close quarters combined with Ginny Baker's reputed aversion to men on her ranch had persuaded him the nearby Rowland Ranch was his best option. Thankfully, Morly's injuries had given Garfield the excuse he needed to move in.

Since then, he'd been kept busy both as a doctor—apparently, the single women in this area figured a single doctor was a fine catch—and as the part-time ranch hand he'd signed on to be in order to justify his extended stay.

So far, he'd managed to search Ginny Baker's main house and bunkhouse, to no avail. Even the note he'd left Lucy during his last attempt had proved fruitless. He'd waited hours at the odd stack of boulders he'd indicated on the map he'd drawn, but she'd never shown. The maddening woman must have completely missed his message.

Morly's unexpected appearance had forced him to improvise. After knocking out the fool from behind, Garfield had poured alcohol on Morly's head. Then he'd posed the man's body amid the chaos Garfield had created in the bunkhouse. By the time that was done, he'd had seconds left to arrange the note and ride out of the valley without getting caught.

Perhaps he hadn't jammed the knife deep enough into the bedpost and the blade had fallen after he left. The note might have been kicked beneath the bed, unseen. Maybe.

Or maybe the woman was tougher and more foolish than she seemed.

Either way, Josie and Deborah's arrival at Rowland Ranch had been the break Garfield had been waiting for. With everyone from Lupine Valley Ranch busy driving cattle to the mountains, the place was deserted.

Garfield had tried volunteering to care for the milk cows and chickens their neighbors left behind, but Clyve insisted on seeing to the tasks himself. So Garfield set his mind on sneaking off to search at night.

Before he could, though, a man came thundering to the Rowlands' front door shouting about his wife having trouble with her labor. As if Garfield knew the first thing about birthing a child.

He'd expected disguising himself as a doctor to get him inside homes he otherwise wouldn't be welcome in. It was a ruse he'd successfully used before. Generally, his experience as a nurse during the war—a position that had kept him off the battlefields—was enough to convince those he encountered. Unfortunately, nothing from the war had prepared him for enduring the wails and complaints of a laboring woman. Nor had he any idea the process could take so long. Nearly three days passed before the woman finally birthed a son.

As the babe finished his first cry, another man arrived in hopes that Garfield could help him tend a backside filled with cactus needles. The tedious chore had taken all day.

Now, with the residents of the Lupine Valley Ranch almost home, Garfield needed to work swiftly. What went wrong before didn't matter now. He needed to find that cursed ledger and get out of this hellish place.

Dust coated his tongue, and he spit into a nearby bush where the spittle would go unnoticed. He wasn't cut out for the rough life of a ranch hand. He'd been made for greater things. He should be at home enjoying the opulence of his plush mansion, not toiling in this God-forsaken place. Even a trip to the continent—the lie he'd spread to cover his absence—would be better than this.

Careful to remain hidden in the shadows, Garfield retreated below the valley's ridge. He remounted his horse and galloped through the ranch yard. He tied his horse behind another set of boulders, well out of sight from the main trail into the valley, to account for the slim chance the group picked up their pace and surprised him.

Garfield broke off a juniper branch and made his way to the ranch yard. A few hurried strokes obscured his horse's hooves as well as his own boot prints. He stopped at the entrance to the barn and strained his ears for any sign of activity. With the horse corral empty, only the quiet scuttle and chirp of birds in the nearby chicken coop and the scrape of hooves across the packed-dirt floor of the barn interrupted the relative silence. He carefully pushed the door open.

The pungent scent of hay and animals permeated the musty air inside the hot barn. A cow lowed quietly as he took in the stalls lining either side of the center aisle. A ladder led to a loft and what looked to be a tack room in the back corner. The door stood ajar. Clyve must have left it open when he'd come by to milk the cows and feed the chickens that morning.

Garfield set the juniper branch to one side and shut the door behind him. He searched the tack room first but found no hidden compartments or wrapped packages. After riffling through the piles of hay on the ground floor, Garfield climbed the ladder to the loft.

At the back, there was a cot, an upturned crate being used as a side table, and three pegs in the wall. This must be where Preston lived. Bypassing the mounds of hay on either side of the loft, Garfield bee-lined for the makeshift sleeping quarters.

The top of the upturned crate held nothing more than a few grooming items, a small lantern, some stationary, and a stack of three letters.

A quick scan of the opened letters revealed one from Ginny asking him to come to the ranch, another from someone named Harvey Arbuckle insisting that Preston return to his show, and the last appeared to be Preston's unfinished response. Garfield carefully returned the papers to the exact position they'd been in.

The bottom of the crate held a box of ammunition and a partially mended rope, while the underside of the cot concealed a spare blanket and a folded, fringed leather outfit. Garfield lifted the pillow and grinned. Two custom-made, matching pistols lay on the rough canvas.

Garfield surveyed the space again, confirming the man's rifle wasn't present. Preston must have assumed his rifle would be sufficient for a cattle drive. Garfield set the pillow aside and lifted the beautiful pair, testing their weight and balance. Picking a knot on the opposite wall of the barn, he sighted down each barrel, then let out a whistle. These weapons were a masterpiece of workmanship, no doubt. Too bad they were too recognizable to take with him. Garfield returned the pistols to their place and checked his watch. Slightly more than half an hour had passed. He needed to stay focused.

He stepped toward the nearest hay mound just as the door below burst open.

"Who's in here?" Morly's slurred voice shattered the quiet of the ranch.

Garfield swallowed a curse. What was the drunken fool doing here? And how did he always manage to show up in the middle of Garfield's searching? It didn't seem possible a man as hapless as Morly could be stealthy enough to follow Garfield without him knowing it. The first time had seemed a coincidence, but twice? Then again, if Morly *had* followed Garfield, why would he be asking who was in the barn? He'd already know.

Barely visible through the slats of the loft, Morly swung his gun from one side of the barn to the other, clearly looking for an intruder. "Come on out now, before I start shooting."

Garfield crouched slowly to avoid creaking the boards beneath his feet. He slipped one hand beneath the pillow and quietly scooped ammunition from the box with his other.

Morly's head jerked up, and he squinted at the loft. "I hear you up there, and if'n you don't show yourself by the count of three, I'm going to start shooting. One, two—"

"It's me." Garfield interrupted the simpleton's counting to cover the sound of loading Preston's pistols. "Don't shoot. It's Dr. Smith. I'm just looking for medical supplies."

"In a barn loft?" The hard edge in Morly's voice had changed to confusion. He scratched his temple with the thumb of the hand holding his pistol.

"Well..." Garfield cocked the hammer. "I know Preston sleeps up here and"—he crept toward the top of the ladder—"I thought he might..." Garfield took aim and pulled the trigger.

The box Morly had been holding in his other hand crashed to the ground, spilling something that caught the light pouring in from the open door. Sparkles of reddish-brown light bounced around the barn.

~

FEBRUARY 15, 1874

*D*espite the early hour, sweat dribbled down Preston's back as he brought up the rear of their small group headed east. Lucy, Biddie, and Esther rode immediately in front of him while Gideon and Carmen took the lead. The soft slap of leather and steady rhythm of hoof beats drowned out the otherwise peaceful sounds of the desert.

They'd set out at dawn, and near as he could tell, they were passing through the northern stretch of the Rowland Ranch. That meant they had a couple more hours before they'd reach Lupine Valley Ranch.

Of course, I'm happy Clyve kissed me. He's my beau.

Lucy's unconvincing words echoed in his mind and churned his gut, reigniting his silent war of indecision. Did he respect Lucy's right to make her own decisions, or did he warn a good man of impending heartbreak?

Movement to the south drew his eye toward two riders approaching their group. He whistled to gain everyone's attention, then pointed toward the silhouettes. The newcomers weren't coming on fast, so Preston felt comfortable waiting to see if they were friend or foe. But he readied his rifle just in case.

After a few minutes, he recognized Clyve Rowland trotting his horse beside Josie and Deborah. The girls rode double with huge grins.

Preston retied the leather string securing his rifle to the saddle, but the tension in his shoulders remained.

Esther and Carmen cantered out to greet their daughters with warm hugs. The girls' excited chatter added to the din of the troop.

Clyve pulled alongside Gideon and assured him their livestock and everything else on the ranch was just as they'd left it. "Aside from the stream of folks still coming to see the doc, things were quiet while you were gone. Even Morly seemed on his best behavior."

Gideon thanked him and filled him in on the losses they'd sustained. Clyve whistled and expressed his sympathy. Then he fixed his gaze on Lucy.

Preston straightened and called out, "Clyve." When the man looked Preston's way, he waved for Clyve to join him at the back of the group.

After a reluctant glance at Lucy whose curious gaze was bouncing between the two of them, Clyve steered his horse to join Preston.

Clyve touched the brim of his hat in greeting. "Glad to see you made it back safely. It's a real shame about the cattle."

"Thanks." Preston discreetly slowed his horse. "Have you heard anything about other herds being affected?"

Clyve grimaced. "Yeah, I asked around while you were gone and found out another herd had passed through that same pasture from Mexico. They all died before making it to market up north." Clyve shared more stories of how similar situations had occurred many times over the years, going into detail about the tragic losses that had forced dozens of ranchers to walk away from their land.

As they rode up the trail leading to Lupine Valley, Preston's grip tightened on the reins. If they had known about the infected herd before moving their cattle to that pasture...but it didn't matter now. What was done was done. He needed to focus on preventing future mistakes.

Clyve had kept pace with Preston so they now rode several yards behind the others. With the wind blowing from the east, their conversation should be private. Preston shifted in his saddle as they crested the ridge into the valley. It was now or never. "There's something I think you should know."

Clyve's brows lifted, but he said nothing, patiently waiting for Preston to continue.

"It's about Lucy." Preston hesitated. Was there any easy way to share such an awful circumstance? He couldn't think of one. The plain truth would have to do. "You know she doesn't speak much about her parents, but if you're serious about marrying her, I think you have a right to know." If the truth changed how Clyve felt about Lucy, then his feelings weren't what they should be to begin with. "Lucy's mother uses opium habitually and works in a brothel in San Francisco."

Clyve's mouth fell open and his eyes widened. "That's..." His expression changed to confusion. "Wait. How do *you* know about Lucy's mother?"

"Lucy told me herself."

Clyve scowled. "She confided in you?"

Preston nodded, his gut twisting with the knowledge that

he was betraying her trust. But it was for her own good, so he forged ahead. "And there's more you should know."

If Preston were a steak, he'd be burnt clean through by the heat of Clyve's glare. "So tell me."

"I overheard Lucy telling Biddie that her feelings for you are no more than that of a friend." There. He'd told the truth. What Clyve did with the information was up to him.

Clyve reined his horse to a halt. "You're lying."

Preston stopped his horse as well, hoping his expression revealed how deeply sorry he was to be hurting this kind man. "I wish I were."

"I'm sure." Clyve's voice was thick with sarcasm. His focus turned to where the rest were dismounting in the ranch yard. "We'll see." He spurred his horse to catch up with the others.

Preston urged his mount after Clyve's, his gut clenching. Preston had expected Clyve to be upset, even angry. But he'd also expected the usually measured man to take the time to calm down and think things over before deciding how to confront Lucy. It appeared Preston had misjudged him.

CHAPTER 26

*P*reston galloped into the ranch yard as Clyve slid from his horse and said something to Lucy that caused the color to drain from her features. Then she nodded.

Preston dismounted as Clyve's face grew red.

The rancher yanked his hat from his head and crushed it in his hands. "Then it's true, what Morly said. You and Preston—"

"No." Lucy's horrified gasp cut Preston like a knife. "There's nothing—"

"There must be, or you wouldn't have trusted him with something so personal. Something you never told me." Hurt was etched in every inch of Clyve's expression. "I'm done." He mounted his horse in one fluid motion. "We're through."

Tears streamed down Lucy's cheeks. "Clyve, wait."

The angry man ignored her, urging his horse up the slope, out of the valley.

Lucy's tear-filled eyes turned on Preston. "How could you?"

Every part of Preston wanted to cross the yard, take Lucy in his arms, and hold her until the pain passed. But he couldn't do that. Because he'd caused this pain. It didn't matter that he'd done it for her own good and to make sure Clyve knew what he

was getting into. She deserved a marriage filled with unconditional love—the kind of love he'd rarely seen but knew existed.
Both she and Clyve deserved a life filled with the kind of happiness Biddie and Gideon had. But Lucy wouldn't see Preston's
sincere intentions now. Maybe not ever.

Lucy stormed across the yard toward him, fire in her eyes. "I
trusted you. What right did you have to tell him what you did?
How dare you eavesdrop on our private conversation?'

Preston gritted his teeth against the unjustness of being the
target of her anger when it was Clyve who'd truly betrayed her
trust by reacting rashly. Yet there was no satisfactory answer he
could give to her question. Instead, he stepped around her and
jerked his belongings from his horse before storming toward
the barn. With his rifle in one hand, he was forced to tuck his
bedroll under one arm to open the door. He took one step into
the dark interior and slammed the door behind him. Why was
he always getting into trouble for doing the right thing?

With his eyes still adjusting from the bright sunshine, he
hurled his bedroll toward the loft and stomped toward the
ladder.

Preston's boot collided with something on the ground, and
he looked down. A man lay sprawled in the dirt. It took Preston
a moment to recognize Clyve's brother. "Morly?" The man
didn't stir. Great. He must have passed out. What had possessed
the fool to get drunk in their barn? Preston leaned his rifle
against the ladder and fetched his lantern from its hook near
the door.

Back at Morly's side, Preston lit the lamp and set it on the
ground. "What on earth are you—" He froze at the glint of red
liquid seeping from a gaping hole in the man's shirt and
pooling in the dirt around him. He shook Morly's blood-spat-
tered shoulder. "Morly, wake up."

A rattling breath escaped the man, then nothing. Preston
knew that sound. He'd heard it too many times during the war.

Bang!

Preston shrank into a ball, searching the shadows for the source of the shot. No figure moved in the dark, but something shiny winked at him from the nearest haystack. He reached for it and discovered one of his pistols. How had it—

The barn door burst open.

Instinctively, Preston spun, his pistol aimed at the intruder.

Gideon stood in the doorway, his own pistol drawn as his gaze jumped from Preston to Morly's body and back. Quietly, he shifted his aim to Preston and ordered, "Put the gun down."

Preston lowered his weapon. "Where are the women?" Where had that shot come from? Where was Lucy? He stepped toward the door.

Gideon cocked his pistol. "I said, put it down."

Preston stared at him. "What are you talking about? We've got to get out there. Someone's shooting. We've got to make sure the women are safe."

"The shot came from in here." Gideon jerked his chin toward Morly's body. "There's the proof."

Preston shuffled back. "No, I didn't shoot. There's some—"

"Put your pistol down first. Then we can talk."

Preston's jaw clenched. "Stop being a fool. We've got to get out there and protect the women." He lunged for the door, but Gideon shifted to block him.

His expression was stricken, yet determined. "Please don't make me shoot my wife's brother."

"Gideon?" Biddie's voice called from somewhere that sounded like the main house. "What's going on?"

Gideon responded without taking his eyes or his weapon off Preston. "I'll explain later. Just stay inside."

Why was Gideon behaving so strangely? Any moment now, his brother-in-law was going to receive a bullet to his back. They needed to get outside and find the shooter.

Desperation made him search the barn for another exit, but

of course, there wasn't one. There was nothing but cows lowing in their stalls and a dead body leaking blood onto the dirt floor. No one else was in here when the shot went off and echoed strangely in this boulder-strewn valley. But with the body in here...a chill sped through Preston's veins. Gideon thought Preston was the murderer. Finally, he dropped his pistol in the dirt and raised his hands. "I didn't shoot him. He was already shot when I came in. Almost dead."

Gideon grimaced. "We all heard the shot. There's no one else here."

"What about the stalls? Someone could be hiding in there. Although, to me, the shot sounded as though it was outside."

Gideon's focus flickered to the stalls and back. "Kick your pistol toward me and step away from the rifle. Then I'll search the barn, and if no one's in here, I'll search outside."

Preston did as he was told, his heart racing. "You can't seriously believe I did this."

Gideon toed the pistol behind himself. "Now, sit. Over there." He gestured toward the opposite corner with his free hand.

Preston shuffled to the place indicated and sat.

"Turn and face the wall."

Preston ground his teeth. "You're wasting time worrying about me while the real culprit is probably sneaking away as we speak."

Gideon just glared at him.

With a huff, Preston turned to stare at the wall.

His brother-in-law's voice shifted, and stall doors creaked as Gideon presumably searched the rest of the barn. Seconds later, he growled and loosed a word Preston hadn't known was in the man's vocabulary. "Preston, what am I supposed to do? There's no one else here. You're the only one I couldn't see when the shot went off." His stomps came to a stop behind Preston. "And you've threatened to kill Morly twice."

He twisted to stare up at Gideon.

"Do you have any idea what this is going to do to your sisters?"

Preston's head hung.

Hoof beats pounded into the yard. Gideon dashed outside and Preston leapt up. He looked for his rifle, but it wasn't by the ladder. Nor was his pistol anywhere to be seen. Gideon must have hidden them.

Growling, Preston charged outside.

Clyve's mount skidded to a halt as the man flung himself from the saddle, rifle in hand. He strode toward Gideon. "What happened? I heard a gunshot just as I was leaving the valley. I searched but didn't see anyone lurking. Who was shooting?" His attention landed on the smeared blood drying on Preston's hands, and he froze. "Who's been shot?"

Gideon lowered his weapon and stepped toward Clyve. "It's Morly. He's dead."

Clyve shook his head. "Where? How? Who did it?"

"He's in the barn." Preston lifted his hands thinking to calm Clyve, then realized the blood on his fingers would likely have the opposite effect. "We don't know who—"

Clyve pushed past Preston into the barn and a moment later, his wail filled the yard. Preston followed Gideon back into the darkened interior.

Clyve knelt at his brother's side, hands fisted as tears streamed down his face. It was several moments before he spoke through gritted teeth. "Who did this?"

Gideon spoke at the same time as Preston.

"I don't know."

"I'm still figuring that out. Preston was the only one in the barn at the time."

Clyve roared to his feet and raised his rifle to Preston's chest.

"No!" Gideon tackled Preston as a blast filled the barn. With them both on the ground, Gideon flipped over, keeping his body between Preston and Clyve. "Clyve, put the gun down. You're not thinking right."

Biddie appeared in the doorway. She took in the scene, emitted a warrior's cry as terrifying as any rebel yell Preston had heard in the war, and launched herself at Clyve.

Exactly as Preston had taught her, she wrapped her arm around the rifle and twisted her body, moving its sights away from herself and her loved ones. With her other hand, she clawed at Clyve's face, pushing him backward.

Caught off guard, Clyve released the weapon and staggered.

Gideon leapt to his feet and took the weapon from Biddie, placing himself between his wife and Clyve.

Preston slowly rose to his feet as Carmen, Lucy, and Esther appeared in the doorway, weapons in hand. A stream of relief flooded through Preston at seeing Lucy unharmed.

"Everyone calm down," Gideon ordered.

Clyve touched his face and winced, his fingers coming away with blood from the scratches Biddie had inflicted.

"What is going on?" Biddie demanded from behind Gideon. Her horrified gaze seemed fixed on Morly's body.

Clyve jammed a finger at Preston. "He killed my brother."

All four women gasped and stared at him.

"I did not." Preston lifted his empty hands. "He was already shot when I came in."

Esther's face took on the cold mask he'd only ever seen her wear when speaking of her former life. "Then how do you explain the shot we heard coming from the barn?"

"And the blood all over your hands," Carmen added, pointing at the drying blood coating his raised hands.

Lucy searched his gaze. "Did he threaten you when you came in?"

"No." Preston shook his head vigorously. "I'm telling you, he was already shot when I found him."

Gideon shifted his grip on Clyve's rifle, though, thankfully, he didn't raise it. He looked over his shoulder at his wife. "He was holding his pistol when I came into the barn after the shot, and no one else was in here. Except Morly, who was dead."

Preston looked desperately from face to face. This couldn't be happening. How could the people he'd lived and worked with for months believe he could shoot a man in cold blood? If Ginny were here, she'd believe him and put a stop to this madness. "I didn't do it." He found Biddie's confused gaze. "You believe me, don't you?"

She blinked, and her expression cleared with a nod. "Of course, I do." She faced the others. "I don't know what happened here, but if Preston says he didn't do it, then he didn't do it."

Lucy stepped fully into the barn. "I believe him too. Preston may have his faults, but he wouldn't lie about something like this."

"Any man faced with a noose would lie to save his own skin." Clyve sneered. "You all know Preston has a reckless temper, and you've heard him threaten to kill my brother. He's a danger to society. He needs to hang for what he's done."

"No!" Biddie and Lucy shouted as one and moved to stand in front of Preston.

"No one is hanging today." Gideon shook his head. "We don't know for sure what he's done."

Preston's chest lifted. Was it possible Gideon believed him despite the suspicious circumstances?

But his brother-in-law wasn't finished. "In the very least, he deserves a fair trial."

Biddie turned on her husband. "You can't mean to turn him over to the law?"

"What choice do we have? Look at the evidence." Gideon looked so remorseful, Preston almost felt sorry for him. Almost. The man was willing to leave it up to strangers to decide whether Preston lived or died for a crime he hadn't committed.

~

FEBRUARY 15, 1874
CAMPO, CALIFORNIA

*P*reston sat in the nearly pitch-dark, leaning against the rough wood wall of the small shed behind the Gaskills' blacksmith shop. To say Luman Gaskill, who served as the local justice of the peace, had been surprised when Clyve, Biddie, and Gideon had ridden in with Preston's wrists bound would be an understatement. The man fell out of his chair when he heard the story of what had happened to Morly Rowland and repeatedly expressed his disbelief that Preston, who'd aided local posses alongside Luman no less than three times, would commit such a heinous crime. Still, he reluctantly did his duty as Clyve demanded and locked Preston away for the night. In the morning, Preston would be escorted to San Diego where he'd await trial.

He'd come to California to help his sister. How had he wound up in jail with a noose over his head? It didn't seem real. And yet, some of what Clyve had said was true. Preston did have a reckless temper and had threatened Morly's life more than once. Could he really blame Clyve for believing the worst?

If only Preston had learned to control his temper sooner. Vile or not, every man deserved a chance to change, to be better. Even Morly. Preston had meant what he said to Lucy when he apologized. He was glad she'd stopped him from ending Morly's life. Teaching a man to respect a woman was far different than trying to take on God's role in deciding who lived and who died.

God's role. Preston closed his eyes, trying to remember how

Biddie began her prayers before each meal. *Dear Heavenly Father*. Preston winced. If God was anything like Preston's earthly father—

The grind of a key turning in the metal lock interrupted Preston's thoughts. The orange rays of the setting sun pierced the shadows as the door swung open to reveal his little sister holding a plate. Clyve stood behind her, a scowl on his face and his pistol on his hip.

Biddie smiled despite the sadness in her eyes. "I've brought you food."

Preston started to stand, but she waved him back down and sat on the ground beside him.

Clyve's scowl darkened. "I said you could bring him food, not stay for a visit."

Biddie raised her chin. "You're going to take my brother away tomorrow on accusation of murder. This may be the last time I ever see him. Are you really going to deny me this time to talk?"

Clyve grunted. "I don't have all day to stand here."

Preston resisted the urge to roll his eyes. Because Clyve obviously had so much to do waiting around to take Preston to his doom.

Biddie sniffed. "So lock me in with him and come back in an hour."

Clyve ran a hand down his face. "I'm not locking you in with a murderer."

"That's right. You're locking me in with my innocent brother."

Shaking his head, Clyve shut the door, and a moment later, the key turned in the lock. "I'll be back in an hour."

They sat in silence as the crunch of his steps grew so faint Preston could no longer hear them. The smell of roast chicken and some other vegetables he hadn't paid enough attention to when there was light to identify them wafted toward his nose. "You didn't have to do this."

"I couldn't let you go hungry."

His stomach clenched. "I'm not sure I can eat."

In the slivers of light filtering between the boards, he saw her set the plate aside. "Then why don't we pray?"

A bitter taste filled his mouth. "You go ahead."

"You won't pray with me?"

"God doesn't want to hear from me."

"Why not?"

"Why not? Do you have any idea how many times I've screwed up? Look where I am. I may not have actually killed Morly, but I wanted to. And it isn't as though I haven't killed before."

"You mean during the war? That's different."

He'd always thought so, but with how things had played out since coming to California, he was beginning to think there had always been evil in his blood, passed down from Pa. "Maybe Clyve's right. Maybe I'm too dangerous." Not that he wanted to die. He just wanted to stop hurting the people he cared about. He wanted to know that there was enough good inside him to pull back and do what was right, even when it was hard.

"You are not dangerous." The vehemence in Biddie's voice left him speechless. "You are a man with faults, and you are working on them. I don't know exactly what you and Ginny went through after our paths divided, but I know enough to be certain it was something no one, especially not children, should ever have to endure. Especially not at the hands of the man who was supposed to love and protect them."

"But that's just it. I'm like him, unable to control my temper."

"You are *not* like him. You've made some mistakes, I'll agree, but I have seen you control yourself in many situations where Oliver never would have." She scooted onto her knees and grabbed his shoulders, leaning close enough that he could just make out her eyes. "Preston Baker, you have a beautiful heart. You are kind and selfless. You risked your neck to protect me, and you've done the same to protect our neighbors—people you don't even really know. Making mistakes does not make you evil. It makes you human. And that's why God sent his only Son to earth to live a sinless life and be crucified on a cross in our place. God has already forgiven your sins. All you have to do is accept His precious gift."

Tears stung Preston's eyes. He ached to believe her. "It can't be that easy."

"I didn't say it was easy. Christ dying on the cross wasn't easy. And giving your life over to God, accepting Jesus as your Lord and Savior isn't easy either. We all want to think we're in control of our lives, but the truth is we never were. So place your hope and your trust in the one who loves you more than you can ever imagine. Let Him wash your sins away with His love and forgiveness."

He couldn't hold back the tears any longer, but hopefully, she couldn't see them in the dark. "How?"

"Just pray. Ask Him to be your Lord and thank Him for the gift of Christ's sacrifice that paid the price for your sins."

"Just pray?"

She nodded. "Just pray."

Preston closed his eyes and reached out to God.

CHAPTER 27

FEBRUARY 15
LUPINE VALLEY RANCH, CALIFORNIA

CW ith the afternoon sun lowering toward the west, Lucy stood in the center of the ranch yard, watching Matthew Rowland ride out of the valley. The broken-hearted man had wrapped his son's body in a bedsheet and draped him over a packhorse for the ride back to Rowland Ranch.

Lucy waited for tears to come. Morly may have been a hard, troubled man, but his life still mattered. Yet her heart seemed locked in an icebox, out of reach after everything that had happened over the past hour. She'd barely had a moment to comprehend Clyve's abrupt ending of their courtship before a shot rang out and Preston was hauled away on accusation of murder.

She lifted her head toward the sky. *Did I do something wrong?*

A voice inside whispered the secrets she carried, threatening to drown her with the weight of guilt. But she wasn't the one who'd killed Mrs. Prichard. Why should she feel guilty?

Because she should have told the Davidsons the truth months ago, as soon as she knew Mama was safe.

No, that wasn't true. No good came of revealing unpleasant truths meant to be hidden. Look what had happened to Mama when Lucy told her about Father's first family. And what had happened when she confessed to the Davidsons that Mama had stolen some of their money to pay for more opium? Mama had chosen the opium over staying at The Home with Lucy.

Time and again, she'd seen the truth played out—no one thanked the bearer of bad news. Besides, it wasn't as though the Davidsons could have done anything about Mr. Green's schemes. Though they would have tried. And probably ended up just like Mrs. Prichard.

Lucy squared her shoulders. She'd done the right thing. She just needed to mine enough gems to save Lupine Valley Ranch and pay for the Davidsons' losses so that The Davidsons' Home for Women and Children could remain open.

Mind made up, Lucy filled her canteen and marched toward the mine. Weary to the bone, she wanted nothing more than to curl into a ball and go to sleep, but there was no time for rest. There was nothing she could do to save Preston. But she could work the mine and help everyone else in the process.

Please, God, let the truth prevail and bring him safely back to us.

Preston's betrayal of her trust still stung, but he'd wrongly believed telling Clyve was the right thing to do. Because despite his flaws, Preston had proven himself a good man who tried to make good choices. Even if he sometimes missed that goal completely.

Pushing through the juniper bush that had grown thin from the almost daily passage of her and Preston over recent weeks, she lifted the lantern sitting near the entrance and lit it. She carried the light to the back of the tunnel and froze. The pile of tailings they used to disguise the buried box was spread across the floor, and the box was gone. She scoured the tunnel, searching for their treasure, but it wasn't there.

The candlelight caught on a dull slip of white near the tailings. She knelt and lifted the scrap of paper.

Return what's taken by midnight, and come alone, or your mama and Fletcher will die.

A cry ripped from her lips. Fingers trembling, she flipped the note over to reveal the same map leading to the *T*-shaped boulder pile.

There could be no doubt. Mr. Green or whoever he'd hired knew where Mama and Fletcher were—in fact, may already have them imprisoned somewhere—and were planning to murder them both if Lucy didn't return what they thought she'd stolen. But she hadn't stolen anything they could possibly care so much about. What in the world was she to do? Problems kept crashing down on her as though an unending rockslide. It was too much. Her thoughts tangled and knotted, resembling a ball of yarn the cats had gotten hold of.

Shaking head to toe, she stumbled from the mine.

Carmen spotted her entering the ranch yard. "What's wrong, *mija?* You look as though you've seen a ghost."

Before she could hide the note, Carmen snatched and read it. "I don't understand. Who is Fletcher, and what does your mama have to do with Morly?"

Lucy blinked at her. "What are you talking about?"

"This note. It is from whoever really killed Morly, isn't it?"

She was right. The timing was too much of a coincidence. Morly must have run into whoever was after Lucy, and the note-writer had killed him to keep him quiet.

But why make it look as though Preston had killed Morly? And how? They'd all heard the shot. She shook her head to try to rid herself of the confusing thoughts. It didn't matter how. It only mattered that this was the evidence she needed to convince Clyve that Preston was innocent. She'd been wrong.

Despite the experiences of her past. Silence hadn't kept her or the ones she cared about safe. It was time to tell the truth. Even if it cost her the only family she had left.

She wrapped her arms around Carmen. "You're a genius." Then she plucked the note from Carmen's hands and dashed for the horses. She had to reach Campo before sunrise.

$\sim$

FEBRUARY 16, 1874
CAMPO, CALIFORNIA

*P*reston looked up as the door opened the next morning. Biddie stood in the doorway again, but this time, Gideon was at her side.

Preston ignored his brother-in-law. "Hey, sis. Is that for me?" He tipped his chin toward the bowl in her hand. The new peace he'd found with God hadn't erased his troubles, but at least the smell of food didn't turn his stomach anymore.

"Of course it is." She slipped inside to sit beside him the same as she had the night before. She handed him the bowl of scrambled eggs and waited until he'd finished eating to speak. "How are you doing?"

He couldn't help the snort that escaped. "How do you think I'm doing? I'm accused of murder, and my own brother-in-law is the key witness that will probably see me hanged."

Gideon lowered to a crouch. Unlike Clyve, he'd hung around, leaving the door open while Preston ate. "That's not what I want."

"Then why am I here?"

Gideon ran a hand through his hair. "I didn't know what else to do. I heard a shot that sounded as though it came from the barn. I opened the door, and there you stood with your pistol in your hand and Morly's body at your feet. No one else

KATHLEEN DENLY

was in the barn, and when we searched the yard, it was empty. If the boots were on the other feet, what would you have done?"

"I'd have believed you when you said you didn't do it." Maybe he was being unfair, but he couldn't help it. He'd spent a miserable night on the filthy floor of a disused shed with who knew what crawling over him. An incredible weight had left him the night before when he'd prayed as Biddie suggested, but today he was facing a long ride with a man who hated him and most likely a hangman's noose as a reward for reaching his destination.

Biddie squeezed his arm. "Have you thought of anything else that might help? Anything at all that might prove someone else was there?"

He shook his head. "I've told you everything I can remember. I bumped into Morly's body but didn't realize he was dead. I heard the shot, same as everyone else, but it didn't come from inside the barn."

"Then where'd it come from?" Gideon interrupted. "We all heard it go off seconds after you entered the barn."

"Maybe from behind it?" Preston had been wracking his memory the entire ride into Campo and most of the night for any detail he'd overlooked. He was almost certain the sound had come from behind the barn, but with the way sound bounced off walls and boulders, it was impossible to be certain.

Biddie gasped. "That's right. The shot happened too fast."

Gideon's brow furrowed. "What do you mean?"

"Preston didn't have his pistols on him when he entered the barn. He'd left them in the loft when we left to drive the cattle. There wasn't enough time between when he entered the barn and when we heard the shot for him to have climbed all the way up the ladder and come back down again to shoot Morly."

Gideon's expression lightened. "You're right. I knew it didn't make sense that we didn't hear them yelling before the shot."

He considered Preston. "So what *did* happen when you went inside?"

"As I told you before. I bumped into something, lit the lantern, realized Morly was dead, and heard the shot. While I was looking for the shooter, I found my pistol in the hay, covered in blood, and—"

"Wait, that's it." Biddie clasped her hands together and shot to her feet. "Wait here. I'll be right back."

Preston looked at Gideon, who just shook his head, clearly as confused as Preston.

A minute later, Clyve and Luman trailed Biddie back to the shed. She stopped to one side of the entry and pointed at Preston's chest. "Look, see, there's no blood on his shirt."

Preston looked down. She was right. The only blood had been on his hands, and he'd rubbed most of the dried substance off during their long ride to town. He looked back up at his sister. "So?"

"So there's dried blood splattered on your pistol but none on your sleeves. Remember the time I accidentally sprayed you with mud?" She faced Clyve, Luman, and Gideon. "Think about how his shirt looked after he beat Morly at our wedding."

Preston grimaced. "Not sure how bringing that up is helping." Clyve was mad enough already.

"*Think* about it." She insisted. "If you'd been close enough to get blood spatter on your gun, it stands to reason it would have at least spattered your sleeves like the mud, or when you beat Morly before, but look at them. The only blood is on the hem of the cuff, which fits with how you said you tried to shake him awake." She narrowed her eyes at Gideon. "Think hard. Do you remember what the barn looked like when you first went in? Did you notice blood anywhere other than on Morly?"

"I assume you're not talking about the blood on Preston and his pistol." Gideon scratched his head. "Actually, there was a lot of blood just inside the door." His eyes widened. "The door-frame had new dark spots too."

She grinned at the stunned men surrounding her. "Add to that what I already told you about there not being enough time for Preston to get his pistol before the shot was fired, and I think you have to agree that my brother is innocent."

Gideon and Luman exchanged a look Preston couldn't read while Clyve glared hard at him for long, excruciating seconds. Finally, he nodded. "She's right." His fists clenched at his sides, he opened his mouth to continue, but Lucy's voice caused the other four to turn.

"Who's right?" Sweat dripped down Lucy's face, and she was breathing hard.

Preston jumped to his feet. "Lucy, what's wrong? What are you doing here?" He searched the area behind her but saw no sign of Esther or Carmen. "Did you ride all this way by yourself?"

"I had to show you all this." She thrust a slip of paper toward the group.

Clyve was the first to shake off his surprise and take it. He read the note aloud.

"And this isn't the first note I've received." She pulled another paper from her pocket. "This one was attached to my bedpost with a knife the day we found Morly drunk in the bunkhouse."

Biddie set a hand on Lucy's shoulder. "What does the note mean about returning something that was stolen? This doesn't sound like Morly."

Clyve snorted. "It's not." He scowled at Lucy. "Do you know who wrote this?"

She returned the message to her pocket. "I don't know who wrote it, or what they think I have, but I think it has something to do with the murder I witnessed before leaving San Francisco."

Biddie gasped. "You what?"

With a shaky voice, Lucy explained everything that had happened to drive her from San Francisco, why she'd been so desperate to give the mine's gems to the Davidsons' charity home, and how she now thought the Greens must be tied to the strange things that had been happening recently on the ranch. At the end of her tale, Lucy clasped Biddie's hands. "I'm so sorry. I thought if I told you, it would put you in danger and that you might reject me for ruining everything your parents had worked for. But keeping quiet didn't make things any better. Instead, I put you all in danger. I should have told you long ago. Can you forgive me?"

"Of course, I forgive you." Tears dripped from Biddie's eyes. "I only wish you hadn't tried to carry this burden alone."

As the two women embraced, the hairs on Preston's neck rose. "You've got to get back to the ranch. Carmen, Esther, and the girls shouldn't be there alone."

"They're aware of the danger and on guard," Lucy assured them.

Clyve clamped a hand on Preston's shoulder. "You're coming with us."

Preston ground his teeth. "Look, I promise I won't try to make an escape while you're gone. Just get going. Dragging me along under guard will only slow things down, and there's no time to waste. You can't afford distractions."

Clyve shook his head. "Between these notes, everything Lucy just shared, and what Biddie pointed out, I know I almost made a grave mistake." He held out his hand. "If you can forgive me for almost killing you, I would appreciate your help keeping everyone safe."

*T*he heat of the rising sun warmed Lucy's skin as she pressed her tired mount faster, flanked by Biddie, Gideon, Clyve, and Preston on their horses. She prayed the brief rest, food, and water her animal had received in Campo was enough to get them home. Their horses' hooves thundered against the ground, kicking up clouds of dust.

Lucy tightened her trembling fingers around the reins, still unable to believe she'd managed to free Preston and how easily Biddie had forgiven her. Revealing the truth had lifted the weight of ten barrels of stones from Lucy's chest. Months of fear and guilt had washed away with Biddie's warm embrace.

Would the Davidsons be as understanding? They stood to lose everything they'd spent a lifetime building. Not to mention, what would become of the women and children the Davidsons cared for? With the gems gone, there was no possibility Lucy could help ease the blow.

She mentally shook away the thought. There'd be time to figure all that out later. Right now, she needed to focus on returning to Lupine Valley Ranch and ensuring Carmen and the others were safe. Then they needed to work together to determine who had left the threatening note and how they could be stopped.

Lucy glanced at the others riding beside her, and a different fear grew inside like a poisonous vine snaking up her throat. Grateful as she was not to be facing this danger alone, if harm came to any of them, it would be entirely her fault.

FEBRUARY 16, 1874
LUPINE VALLEY RANCH

*E*very muscle in Garfield's body ached as he carefully adjusted his position in the pitch-black boulder cave. Waiting.

Nearly a full twenty-four hours had passed since he'd shot Morly, staged his body, and poorly covered Preston's pistol with hay.

The reddish-brown gems Garfield had scooped into the box Morly had dropped reminded Garfield of garnets. Thankfully, the nosy man had been conscious enough to answer Garfield's demands to know where the treasure had come from. Morly had confessed to overhearing Deborah and Josie talking about a whole box of sparkling red stones that Lucy kept in a secret mine. Unfortunately, interrogating the dying man had taken so long, Garfield had almost gotten himself caught by the group riding into the valley. A smug smile curved his lips. Almost.

The timing had been close, but he made it to the backside of the barn in time to avoid being seen. He'd waited until light peeked through the barn slats, letting him know Preston had discovered the body. Then Garfield fired his own pistol, causing the exact effect he'd hoped for.

Once everyone was inside the barn, Garfield had dashed for the mine. Now that he knew what to look for, he easily spotted the worn path that appeared to end at a large juniper.

Seeing no other sign of loose gems in the mine and very few still captive in the walls of the tunnel, Garfield had left his note in the square hole surrounded by tailings, indicating where Morly must have found the box.

While the commotion over Morly's death continued in the distant ranch yard, Garfield had sneaked to the boulder cave.

His plan had been to wait for the cover of darkness, then creep to his horse and ride out of the valley. As empty as the mine was, there was no possibility Lucy would miss seeing his note this time. And with her weakness for people she cared about, there was no doubt she'd finally retrieve the package from wherever she'd hidden it and meet him at the *T*-shaped boulders.

What Garfield hadn't anticipated was Lucy galloping from the valley. Watching her go, he'd wanted nothing more than to shoot her from that horse and torture the truth of the ledger's location from her dying lips. But there were still too many witnesses on the ranch.

Not that he couldn't handle three women and two girls. However, these women wouldn't go down without a fight. A shootout would create enough noise that Matthew Rowland— who hadn't seemed in any rush as he rode out—might still be close enough to hear. Even if he weren't, Garfield didn't like the idea of killing children, and one of the girls was definitely old enough to tell tales if he left her alive.

Plus, Lucy's horse had borne no satchels. Which meant she was almost certainly coming back. Perhaps she'd even ridden off to fetch the ledger from a hiding place that wasn't on the ranch. That would explain why he'd never found it. So instead of giving in to his killing urge, he had waited.

Now, everyone had returned to the ranch and gone to bed except Gideon and Clyve. The two men prowled opposite ends of the valley. Thankfully, their attention was focused outward, clearly expecting an intruder from outside the valley.

Garfield grinned as he slipped from the boulder cave. Only a sliver of moon hung in the sky, creating wide pockets of shadows almost as dark as the cave had been, making it easier to creep through the valley to the main house. Still, stealth was required to avoid his movements being heard on the valley's rim or inside one of the structures. He reached the side wall of the main house and paused. Both Biddie and Lucy would be asleep within. Catching Lucy and keeping her quiet would be much easier if he didn't alert Biddie to his presence. But how to lure her out?

CHAPTER 28

*L*ucy lay in her bed, unable to sleep while Biddie's soft, steady breathing confirmed she had fallen asleep long ago. Tension held Lucy's shoulders in a vice, knowing Gideon and Clyve were out there somewhere, standing guard over their mountain valley.

Lord, please keep them safe.

Maybe she should leave. She was the one Green and his accomplices were after. If she left, maybe no one on the ranch would get hurt.

But what about Mama and Fletcher?

The men had convinced Lucy that keeping the midnight appointment was a suicide mission. Once whomever had written the note had what they wanted, they'd kill Lucy for sure. If she arrived without what they wanted? There was no telling what they would do. Even if she managed to convince them that she *had* nothing they could want, there was, again, no reason to leave her alive. Yet lying here doing nothing felt infinitely wrong, and no matter how hard she tried, sleep refused to come.

If she had told the truth on the day she'd witnessed Mrs. Prichard's corpse lying at Junior's feet, might all of this have been avoided? She couldn't be sure. But one thing was certain —Preston would never have been arrested for a murder he didn't commit. She'd wanted to apologize to him, but there'd been no time in Campo, and when they returned to the ranch, the men had been too focused on creating a plan to keep everyone safe.

In the end, they'd agreed to take turns guarding in pairs. Gideon and Clyve were first. Biddie and Preston were next. Then Gideon and Clyve would take another turn. Lucy, Carmen, and Esther had protested being left out, but the men insisted that Carmen and Esther remain with their children to keep them safe and that having Lucy stand guard would be like waving a red flag in front of a bull. Or in Preston's words, "Just plain foolish."

Still, she couldn't lie here any longer. The need to move, to do something, pushed her out of bed. As quietly as she could, so as not to wake Biddie, Lucy dressed and slipped her shoes on before tiptoeing toward the door.

Preston might not want her standing guard, but hopefully, he'd give her a moment to apologize. She wouldn't wake him. She'd just sit outside the barn door and wait for him to come out to take his turn guarding the ranch.

She stepped into the darkened ranch yard, lit only by a sliver of moon that hung in the air above the ranch, and inched the door closed behind her. The soft click of the clasp seemed loud in the stillness of a desert night.

Lucy crept across the yard until something cold and hard pressed against her back. She froze.

A low voice whispered in her ear. "Make a sound and I'll kill everyone here."

The odd scent of rosemary mixed with licorice almost made her gag. Then she stiffened as ice trailed down her spine. It was him. The stranger that had been in the room with Junior that day. A scream surged up her throat, but she swallowed it down as her entire body began to tremble.

*P*reston awoke with a start, his heart hammering against his ribs. He'd been dreaming that he was running through the night, his feet pounding across the hard earth, desperate to catch up to someone he couldn't see. He shook off the lingering tension and rubbed his eyes. What had woken him?

"Preston?" Biddie's concerned call had Preston stumbling from his bed toward the loft's ladder.

He peered down.

His sister's worried face gazed up at him, illuminated by the gas lamp in her hand.

"What's wrong?"

She held the lantern high. "Is Lucy up there?"

Preston reared back. Why would Lucy be in the loft with him in the middle of the night? "Are you saying you don't know where she is?"

Biddie shook her head. "Coyotes woke me, and I realized it was past time for Gideon to have called me for our turn guarding the ranch. Then I noticed Lucy's bed was empty."

"Maybe she went to the bunkhouse or the outhouse."

Again, Biddie shook her head. "I've already checked. Carmen and Esther are getting dressed and..." Her voice cracked. "I can't see Gideon or Clyve."

Preston's stomach turned to lead. "I'm coming." He strode

back toward the box beside his bed. He snatched up his holster and strapped the pistols to his waist, checking that they were loaded before hurrying down to the tack room and grabbing a bridle. No time for a saddle.

Biddie dashed from the barn, and a moment later, she fired one shot in the air. The signal for trouble.

By the time he reached the yard, Biddie had mounted a horse, bareback, and was guiding it out of the corral. Her rifle sat balanced across her lap. She caught his gaze. "I still don't see them." Without another word, she spurred the horse toward the south where Gideon was meant to be guarding the valley's main entrance.

Preston looked north, searching for any sign that Clyve had heard the shot and was headed for the ranch, but all was still. He dashed for the corral and his own horse.

Carmen passed him, her own rifle in hand. "I'll catch up with Biddie." In one graceful leap that paid testament to a life-time spent on the back of a horse, Carmen mounted the nearest gelding and galloped out of the yard.

He glanced back at the bunkhouse door, which remained a few inches open. Esther must be watching from the deep shadows within, guarding the children.

Wishing he had half the experience the women had demonstrated, Preston approached the horse he usually rode and slid the bit between the animal's teeth. Tightening the straps seemed to take forever, but it was probably less than a minute before he was ready to mount and ride north. The coming dawn had begun changing the sky from black to gray, but Clyve's figure refused to emerge from the lingering shadows. Preston called for the man but received no response.

His sister's distant cry of distress pierced the relative quiet, whipping Preston's head around. He turned his mount and rode hard south.

A few minutes later, he found Carmen standing guard

beside Biddie, who knelt on the ground, cradling Gideon's head in her lap. He appeared unconscious, though thank the Lord, his brother-in-law's chest still rose and fell. "What happened?"

Carmen scanned the slopes around them. "I don't know. She found him on the ground like this."

Biddie looked up, dawn's early light reflecting off her damp cheeks. "There's a nasty lump on the back of his head. It looks like it bled a lot but has stopped now. We need to get him back to the house so I can clean the wound."

"What about Clyve?" Carmen asked Preston as she reached for Gideon's legs.

Preston nudged Biddie out of the way and helped Carmen lift Gideon onto Biddie's horse. "I was still looking for him when I heard Biddie's shout."

Gideon moaned as they raised him and blinked as Biddie mounted behind him. "What's... What happened?" He squinted down at Carmen and Preston, his expression dazed.

"You're awake!" Biddie's arms squeezed Gideon's middle, and when he twisted to look at her, she pressed kisses to his cheek. "Thank You, Lord."

All at once, Gideon's expression cleared. "Someone attacked me. Lucy!" His gaze searched their little group. "Where's Lucy?"

Preston nodded even as the truth of the situation solidified like a block of ice in his gut. "She's gone, and we're not sure about Clyve. I was looking for him when Biddie found you." Preston fetched Gideon's hat from the ground and held it up.

Gideon accepted the hat and ran a hand over his hair, wincing before he gingerly set the hat on his head. "Someone attacked me from behind. No doubt, they got Clyve too."

Carmen mounted her horse. "I'll find him." She took off toward the north.

Preston hesitated. Everything within screamed for him to find Lucy. At the same time, Carmen shouldn't be searching for

Clyve alone. Then again, he didn't want to leave Biddie alone to care for and possibly defend her injured husband.

"I'm fine. Go help Carmen." Gideon waved him away. "I'll drop Biddie at the main house and be right behind you."

Biddie reined her horse toward the ranch yard and nudged her mount forward. "You will do no such thing. You've a wound on your head that needs tending."

"That can wait. Lucy and Clyve—"

"Will not be helped at all if you get another one of your migraines or the wound gets—"

"It's just a bump. I can—"

"It won't take five minutes for me to—"

Preston used a nearby boulder to remount and rode past the arguing couple. By the time he reached Carmen, she was on the ground between two large juniper bushes, cradling Clyve's head much as Biddie had cradled Gideon's. With her free hand, she held her canteen to Clyve's lips.

She looked up at Preston's approach. "He was knocked out too."

"What are you doing here?" Clyve glared up at Preston. "Why aren't you out looking for Lucy?"

Preston resisted the urge to snap back that he'd been busy making sure no one else was harmed and he couldn't very well search for prints in the near-dark. It was obvious Clyve was hurting and worried. So Preston blew out a long breath before catching Carmen's gaze. "Do you need any help with him?"

Carmen shook her head.

Preston rode back to the ranch yard, searching the lightening landscape for any sign of movement. Nothing, not even a breeze, disturbed the utter stillness on the wide, gentle slopes of the valley's bowl and along its rim. Biddie's horse stood riderless in front of the main house, its tail flicking.

Preston slid from his mount and crouched just outside the main house. In the light spilling from the open door, he tried to pick out Lucy's small shoeprints in the dirt. It was no use. Too many other prints marred the area. He stood and glared at the sun rays just beginning to streak up from the horizon, the light too faint to be of any help. He stomped to the barn, fetched another lantern, lit it, and returned to the yard.

Beginning near the main house, he fanned out in arcs, searching for any clear indication of the way she might have gone...or been carried. How could someone kidnap Lucy from the bed directly beside Biddie and carry her away without anyone being the wiser? Even with Gideon and Clyve unconscious, the rest of them should have heard something. Lucy would never have gone without a fight.

Reaching the edge of the clearing, Preston was about to give up when he spotted an unfamiliar boot print in the dirt. One corner of the heel appeared to be missing. None of the men on the ranch owned such a shoddy pair of boots.

Could it be Morly's? Preston strained to remember if he'd seen the bottom of Morly's boots. No helpful memory popped into his mind.

Preston stooped to get a closer look at the tracks leading into the brush northeast of the yard. Careful not to step on them, he held the lantern out in front of him and followed the tracks until they reached a spot behind a cluster of boulders. There, the boot prints ended in a smattering of horseshoe prints. The horse tracks continued northeast.

Preston's grip on the lantern tightened, and he stormed toward the barn.

Carmen and Clyve were just entering the yard. "What'd you find?"

"Horse tracks heading north." He threw open the barn door. "I'm going to follow them."

Clyve slid from Carmen's horse. "I'm coming with you."

"So am I." Biddie's voice spun Preston around. She marched toward him from the main house.

"No, you need to stay here and take care of Gideon."

Gideon emerged from the house behind his wife. "I'm fine and I'm coming too."

He didn't have time for this. Preston rubbed the back of his neck as he glared at his brother-in-law. "You and Clyve have barely recovered from being knocked out, and I don't want Biddie getting hurt. It's best if you let me go alone."

Without a word, Gideon, Clyve and Biddie strode past him into the barn. Preston followed them to the tack room where they were busy gathering their riding gear. Bunch of stubborn fools.

He grabbed his own tack and trailed them back out of the barn. "What about Carmen, Esther, and the girls? Shouldn't someone stay to help protect them?"

Carmen answered from where she was speaking with Esther in front of the bunkhouse. "We'll take the girls and ride to Rowland Ranch. If whoever took Lucy has friends, you'll need help, and we can stay with their cook until you get back."

"Fine." Preston stomped toward the horse corral. He was surrounded by mules disguised as people. "Tell them we're headed to the badlands."

~

Something foul assaulted Lucy's senses, and she moaned, trying to open her eyes, but her eyelids were so heavy. And her head. What had happened to her head? It felt like a cracked eggshell.

The smell came again, and Lucy's stomach heaved. She rolled onto her side, vomiting.

With great effort, she pried one eyelid open. A dark figure moved in her blurry vision. Said something she couldn't understand. The darkness spun, then swallowed her.

~

*P*reston clenched his jaw searching the ground for more tracks. They'd been clear as the freckles on Esther's nose until they'd entered the badlands. But when they'd reached the point where two canyons converged and crossed with a wash, the tracks suddenly vanished. As if God had reached down and plucked both horse and rider from the face of the earth. For at least an hour, he, Clyve, Gideon, and Biddie had been searching for where the tracks picked up again to no avail.

Gideon returned from his exploration down the wash. "Nothing."

Biddie's frantic gaze caught Preston's. "She can't have simply vanished."

Preston's gaze landed on a patch of bright white among the branches of a juniper bush. "What's that?" He dismounted and thrust his hand into the bush, dislodging a broken branch that had been caught among the other branches, its splintered end glaringly pale among the dark, scaly juniper leaves. Preston lifted it from the ground, the truth snapping into place like the click of a bullet in the chamber. "They covered their tracks." He studied the ground again.

Gideon tipped his hat back. "If they used that to cover their tracks, wouldn't they leave the branch at the end of wherever they went?"

Preston scowled. Gideon was right. But..."There." He pointed to suspiciously smooth dirt trailing the side of the canyon they'd just emerged from. "Look." He turned the branch upside down and walked toward the narrow pathway he could suddenly see clear as day, and demonstrated what the criminal must have done to cover his tracks. Tracks that led *back* to the ranch. "It's a trick. A false trail." Preston tossed the branch aside and flung himself onto his horse. "We've got to get back."

Please, don't let us be too late.

∾

*L*ucy's head swam, and her entire body shook as she stumbled toward the ranch yard, hands bound. Her heartbeat pounded in the lump on her skull. Her stomach threatened to heave again, though it had no more contents to evict.

Lord, help me.

Judging by the setting sun, she'd spent hours moving in and out of consciousness in the boulder cave. When she'd finally fully woken, her hands were bound and Dr. Smith loomed over her, livid.

The situation made no sense. Why was the doctor who'd tended Morly's injuries and had been working on the Rowland Ranch all these weeks holding her captive? What did he have to do with Mr. Green and Junior? Despite the lingering smell of rosemary and licorice, the unkempt man behind her looked nothing like the finely dressed man she'd seen that day in the hotel. Except those eyes...

She half turned to get another look at their earthy hue, resembling chestnuts darkened by flame. They held a cold calculation that seemed to absorb light rather than reflect it. Just as the dandy's gaze had. Lucy's legs wobbled. She'd been right. It *was* him.

"Move." The 'doctor' jabbed Lucy's side with the muzzle of his pistol, forcing her to continue staggering forward. "Show me where you've hidden your mother's 'gift' before your friends come back, or I'll make you watch as I kill them all."

What was she going to do? She still had no idea what this stranger thought she had, and Dr. Smith had assured her

SHOOT AT THE SUNSET

everyone who might have helped her was long gone, following a false trail he'd laid for them. She scanned the yard and buildings as though the 'gift' the vile man referred to might magically appear. Her gaze caught on Biddie's new home. Biddie and Gideon hid their money in a hole beneath their bed. Along with a loaded pistol.

Lucy cast a look over her shoulder.

He waved the pistol at her. "Eyes forward. Keep moving. Time's ticking."

She scanned the valley's rim. Did she want her friends to return or not? On the one hand, she wanted them nowhere near this madman. On the other, with no idea what the man thought she was hiding from him, her only hope seemed to be in their returning to rescue her. Unless she could get that gun. If she could manage to get Biddie and Gideon's hidden pistol, maybe she could turn it on her captor fast enough to avoid being killed. Maybe.

Still shaking, she shuffled toward Biddie's new house.

Please, Lord. Let the pistol be in there. Let me be fast enough. And...

She couldn't form the words to pray that her aim would be quick and true. It didn't seem right asking God to help her kill a man. A part of her knew the choice was her life or the doctor's. But the idea of actually killing someone churned her stomach. Was this really happening?

"Hurry up." Another jab in her back. She'd be bruised for weeks. If she lived beyond today.

Please, God, don't let me die, and keep my loved ones safe.

Lucy hastened her steps, and soon they were moving from the partially finished entry room into the main room of the new house. Except for the missing roof, an empty space where the stove should be, and the lack of interior walls blocking off what would become two bedrooms at the back, the home appeared almost complete. Unlike the ranch's main house with the keyhole windows Ginny had insisted on, Biddie's house had six regular-sized windows—two on the front and back and one on each side of the house. Amber light filtered through oiled window paper onto the bed tucked into the back left corner of the large space.

Lucy shuffled toward it. "I...it's under here." She started to kneel, but the doctor grabbed her collar and jerked her back up.

"Just a minute." Keeping his gun aimed at her, he used his boot to flip the tick mattress off the ropes, letting it sink to a heap against the wall. Nothing but bare floorboards stared up through the taut ropes, and he glared at her. "Where is it?"

She nodded at the floor. "Under the boards."

With a grunt, he grabbed one post of the bedframe and dragged it away from the wall.

Her heart raced. He was going to lift the board himself. He'd find the hidden pistol first. While he tugged at the bed, she searched the room for a new idea. A sledgehammer sat propped against the wall not five feet away.

"Uh-uh. Don't get any ideas." The doctor's voice brought her attention back to where he stood and eyed her knowingly. He waved the pistol toward the space he'd just cleared. "Go on. Get it."

The world spun as Lucy lowered herself to the floor. She struggled to breathe. Her fingers shook so badly, it took three tries to pry the loose board from the floor. Inside sat a small flour sack holding Biddie and Gideon's savings, and on top lay the pistol, just as she'd hoped. She fumbled for the handle, her shaking and bound wrists making the weapon difficult to grasp. Finally, her fingers closed around the smooth wood.

The cold barrel of the doctor's gun pressed into her temple. "Drop it."

Lucy froze. If she released the weapon, she lost her only hope of escape. But there was no way she could turn and shoot faster than the doctor could pull the trigger. She let the pistol drop back into the hole. "Please don't shoot me."

"You lied to me." The pistol's barrel shook against the side of her face as the doctor shouted. "There's no ledger in that hole."

She flinched, praying he didn't accidentally pull the trigger. "I'm sorry. I didn't know what else to do. I don't know what you want." Wait, did he say, 'ledger'?

"Liar." He shoved her away from the opening and began shifting from foot to foot, almost pacing in place, his fury making his movements jerky. Still, he kept his gun pointed at her face. "I saw your mother give the package to Mrs. Davidson. I know she brought it to you. Tell me where it is, or I'll shoot you and burn this whole ranch to the ground." He cocked the hammer and steadied his aim. "You have until the count of three. One..."

"No, wait." He would never accept the truth. Lucy scrambled for a plausible lie.

"Two..."

She had to buy time. Surely, the others would figure out they were following a false trail and return soon. "You're right! I know where it is, and I'll show you."

The doctor's eyes narrowed. His aim didn't waver. "Where?"

"I buried it in the desert. The location is too difficult to describe." She sucked in a breath. "Let me show you."

A long, agonizing second passed as he seemed to deliberate. At last, he waved the gun toward the door. "No more tricks. If it isn't wherever you're taking me, I'll shoot you and leave you for the buzzards. Then I'll kill your friends and burn the ranch down."

She staggered to her feet and hurried toward the door. Once outside, she turned west.

It was likely someone had gone to the Rowland Ranch for help as she'd done when Biddie went missing. But they'd have left at least one man to guard the Rowland Ranch, wouldn't they? Could she possibly guide Dr. Smith close enough that whoever was on guard might spot them and come to her aid? As unlikely as it seemed that the doctor's patience would last that long, it was the only plan she could come up with.

Lord, help me.

CHAPTER 29

*P*reston shook off the shock of seeing the doctor from Rowland Ranch holding Lucy at gun point. Sweat trickled down Preston's back as he crouched in the shadow of a tall boulder and scooped a handful of fine dirt. Lucy and Dr. Smith were nearing the western rim of the valley, opposite Preston's position. He stood, widened his stance, and steadied the long barrel of his Sharps on the chest-high boulder in front of him. With the butt of the gun nestled against his shoulder, Preston released the sand, noting how the gentle northerly breeze affected its fall. He adjusted his sights and took aim at the doctor's chest.

The man had a gun to Lucy's back. Preston's blood burned. How dare the vermin threaten Lucy? He needed to die.

Preston's finger twitched, but he caught himself. He wasn't God and this wasn't war. It wasn't his place to decide whether this man lived or died. Not while there still existed another choice. Everyone deserved a second chance to make better choices. He took a long, deep breath, then let it out slowly.

Lord, help me be a better man, and help me save Lucy.

He checked the wind again and adjusted his aim, searching

for a target that would disarm but not kill. Lucy and the doctor had reached the rim of the valley. Despite his racing heart, Preston forced himself into the controlled breathing pattern he used before taking any long-range shot. If he didn't make his move in the next few seconds, Lucy and the doctor would descend the other side of the mountain, out of sight. But the setting sun was flashing in Preston's eyes, making it difficult to see. If he missed this shot, he could hit Lucy.

He wiped his watering eyes across his shoulder and tried again to find his mark. *There.* He pulled the trigger.

$\sim$

a shot rang out and Lucy's whole body flinched. She waited for the agony of a gunshot. It didn't come. She'd heard of victims going numb for a few seconds after being wounded. She looked down, patting her torso, her shoulders. Nothing. No blood, no pain, aside from the aching in her head that had been there since she'd regained consciousness.

The sharp intake of breath drawn through clenched teeth drew Lucy around. The doctor writhed on the ground, blood streaming from a hole in his thigh. His right arm reached for the gun that had fallen near Lucy's feet.

A second shot rang out, and a hole appeared in the doctor's right hand.

The man howled and curled into a ball. Enough foul words spewed from his mouth to fill an outhouse pit.

Wrists chafing against the rope binding them, Lucy snatched the pistol from the dirt and took several steps back.

Thundering hooves drew her gaze to the northern rim. Gideon, Clyve, and Biddie galloped toward her. Where were Preston, Carmen, Esther, and the girls? Another rider, this one racing down the eastern slope of the valley, caught Lucy's eye. Preston. Her heart surged. Those had been his shots. Of course, they were. Warmth filled her. Preston had saved her. He flew through the ranch yard, headed straight for her.

The doctor, still cursing, began trying to drag himself across the ground with his good hand, away from the oncoming riders. She lifted his pistol and aimed it at his chest. "Don't move, or I'll put another bullet in you."

Dr. Smith ignored her.

She shifted her aim to about a foot in front of his outstretched good hand and pulled the trigger.

He returned to his balled-up position.

"I said, 'don't move.'"

His glare could melt steel.

She glared right back. "Where are my mother and Fletcher?"

He clamped his lips shut, an arrogant gleam returning to his gaze as he pushed himself up onto his good leg.

She shuffled back, leveling the gun at his chest and cocking the trigger.

Before he could take a step, a lasso whipped passed her head, snagging the man and dragging him face first into the dirt.

Gideon raced past her, rope in hand. In a blink, the doctor was trussed up like a calf. Clyve stood over him, rifle ready.

Biddie barreled into Lucy, squeezing her tight. "I was so worried."

Preston's horse skidded to a stop beside her, and he leapt down. "Are you all right?"

Biddie released her and moved aside as Preston approached.

He took Lucy by the shoulders and inspected her head to toe. Jerking a knife from his belt, Preston sliced through her bindings, setting her hands free. His gaze narrowed at the raw skin, then he paced around her, no doubt spotting the blood caked in her hair. His face redder than the sun setting behind him, he took two steps away and punched the doctor in the face. Just once. Then he was back, drawing her into his arms. "I thought I'd lost you."

"Lost me?" The look in his eyes released a battalion of butterflies in her stomach and fogged her thoughts.

Tenderly, he caressed the loose hairs from her face. "Did he...are you hurt anywhere else?"

She started to shake her head, but the lingering pain stopped her. "No."

His gaze dropped to her lips. "Lucy, I—"

Clyve cleared his throat. Loudly. "Here comes my father and the rest of our men." He tipped his chin to indicate a small band of riders galloping across the desert toward the mountain. "I don't see Esther, Carmen, and the girls. They must have stayed at our ranch."

Lucy reluctantly backed out of Preston's embrace and palmed her burning cheeks. She was so addled, she'd nearly kissed Preston right in front of Clyve. At least, she thought Preston had been about to kiss her. She pulled in a long, deep breath, desperately trying to slow her racing heart and mind.

Clyve waved his hat in the air, signaling to the approaching reinforcements that the threat had passed. They must have understood because their pace slowed.

The doctor wriggled against his restraints, his furious gaze fixed on Lucy. "You have no idea who you're dealing with. I'll be free in a week. Less. Then you're going to regret ever crossing me, you little—"

Gideon gave him a none-too-gentle kick to his wounded thigh, leaving him too busy gasping for air to continue making threats. "It's too late to set out for Campo tonight. We'd better figure out what we're doing with him until morning."

Lucy groaned. "I'll need to come with you."

Preston hooked a thumb in his belt. "What do you mean?"

"I need to send a telegram to the Davidsons telling them the truth about Mr. Green, Junior, and"—she gestured to the trussed-up man—"whoever he is. They need to know so they can inform the authorities. Although, I'm not sure which policemen they can trust."

Biddie set a hand on her shoulder. "We'll tell them that too. Father is smart. He'll know what to do."

Lucy nibbled her lip. "Maybe I should go back. They'll probably need my testimony, and I need to find out what happened to Mama and Fletcher."

Biddie shook her head. "You've been through a lot. Let's wait and see what my parents say. Besides, we can send a telegram to Sacramento as easily as San Francisco. Who knows? Maybe Fletcher will respond that he and your mama are safe and sound." She cocked her head toward the doctor. "For all we know, he's been lying to get you to cooperate."

Preston widened his stance. "Biddie's right. You need to rest. We can figure what comes next when we know more."

CHAPTER 30

*P*reston stood guard beneath the star-filled sky, eyes fixed on the silhouette of the "doctor" who drooped on the ground. Hands and feet still bound, the imposter had been tied at the waist to a fencepost for the night. Gideon had washed and bandaged the man's wounds. Preston couldn't bring himself to perform the task.

Despite his promise to God, it still took every ounce of will to refrain from venting his anger against the man who'd hurt the woman he loved. The man was vile and didn't deserve the second chance Preston had given him. But then, neither did Preston deserve the second chance he'd been given. Nor did he deserve the look he'd seen in Lucy's eyes before Clyve's interruption. So warm and trusting. But more than that. Her gaze almost seemed to convey—

The crunch of nearing footsteps interrupted his thoughts. Clyve crossed the distance from the ranch yard. Behind him,

Lucy and Biddie stepped into the main house, closing the door behind them.

Once Clyve's father and the men who'd come with him had confirmed everything was secure at Lupine Valley Ranch, they'd returned to Rowland Ranch, where Esther, Carmen, and the girls waited with two men guarding them. Matthew promised to keep everyone safe for the night and escort the women and children back in the morning. Clyve had insisted on remaining to help guard his brother's true killer.

Now, his eyes were fixed on the doctor as he shook his head in disbelief. "What you did—how you shot him—was incredible."

Preston waved off the compliment. "I've had years to hone my skill."

"That's not what I mean." Clyve stopped in front of him. "Your shots were precise. You didn't miss. You could have killed him if you wanted. Most men would have." He ran a hand down his face. "*I* would have killed him. But you didn't. Why?"

"I wanted him brought to justice." Preston shifted his stance, his gaze drifting to the canopy of stars. "It wasn't my place to end his life. Besides, with what Lucy said, he may have her mother and Fletcher Johnson locked up somewhere. If I'd killed him—"

"Not that he's told us anything." Clyve kicked the prisoner's leg. "You ready to talk yet? Tell us where they are. Or how about your real name?"

The man's dark eyes glittered up at them in silent defiance.

Clyve gave Preston a long look. "You've changed."

Preston stared at the ground, scuffing his boot across the dirt. "I'm trying to do better. To show mercy, as I've been shown." He risked a glance at Clyve and found him nodding knowingly.

"You've had a talk with God."

Preston blinked. "How'd you know?"

Clyve's smile caught the faint moonlight. "The only times I've seen a man changed like that, God's been involved." He studied the prisoner, discreetly wriggling in his bonds. "You think he can be redeemed?"

Preston shrugged. "Only God knows."

"You're right." Clyve was quiet for a long time before he heaved a loud sigh and clapped Preston on the shoulder. "Knowing you've given your heart over to God takes some of the sting out of Lucy's choice."

Preston eyed him. "What do you mean?"

Clyve grimaced. "I don't think anyone missed the way she was looking at you tonight."

Hope rose in Preston's chest, but he quickly stuffed it down. "It doesn't matter. I don't deserve her. Especially after the way I stepped in to tell you something she had the right to say or not." He rubbed his neck. "I told myself I was doing it for your sake and hers, but I should have kept my mouth shut. She deserves someone steady and dependable like you."

"True. But her heart chose you." Clyve stepped to within inches of Preston's face, his voice turning hard as stone. "And you'd better not break it."

~

That night, Lucy stepped into the large round tub filled with warm, soapy water and hissed.

"What's wrong?" Biddie frowned at her, another warm pot in her grip.

"The water stings the raw skin on my wrists." She lifted them from the tub.

Biddie's gaze turned soft. "I'm sorry, but you know it's important to clean wounds."

Lucy nodded and leaned back against the wooden sides of the tub that barely reached her shoulders. "The warmth feels good on my muscles, at least. Thank you for preparing this for me." She cast a guilty look at the dust-coated dress Biddie still wore. "You must be exhausted after riding all day."

Biddie waved off her concern. "I'm all right. Now, lean forward so I can pour this over your hair. We've got to get the blood out."

Lucy did as told, holding her breath against the pain still beating on the back of her head, and watched the bath water turn pink. When her hair had been thoroughly rinsed, Biddie moved a chair behind her and began soaping Lucy's long brown strands. "Do you think he has Mama and Fletcher locked up somewhere? Or do you think he already...already—"

"We can't know what he's done or where they are. He hasn't said a thing since we tied him up, and I don't think he intends to. We'll just have to pray and wait to see what reply comes to the telegram you send tomorrow. Maybe he's lying and they're perfectly safe at Mr. Johnson's home in Sacramento."

"Maybe." But Lucy couldn't stand not knowing.

"I think I've got all the blood out," Biddie announced as she moved toward the fireplace where another pot of water waited in the embers. On her return, her steps faltered. "Lucy, I..." Her mouth hung open a moment before she pressed her lips tightly and shook her head. "I think we should pray right now for everyone we love, including your mama and Mr. Johnson."

Lucy bent forward again, and as Biddie slowly poured more clean water over her head, she prayed for the safety of those they cared about, both here and up north.

Lucy murmured her amen of agreement.

When the pot was empty, Biddie set it aside and dried her hands, her gaze fixed on the dish towel. "Why didn't you tell me about Preston?"

"Tell you what about Preston?" Lucy gripped her hands together under the water.

Had Biddie noticed their near-kiss? Lucy couldn't help

wishing Clyve hadn't interrupted when he did, but then, it wouldn't have been fair to him to kiss Preston in front of everyone like that. But she did want to kiss him. The confession, even to herself, brought added heat to her already warm cheeks.

"Oh, come on. Look at you. It's obvious you have feelings for him. The way the two of you were staring at each other before Clyve interrupted—"

"What do you mean?" Preston obviously wanted to kiss her. They'd come too close too many times for the attraction to be completely in her head. But what did it mean? Was she just a pretty face to him, or did his feelings run deeper?

Biddie rolled her eyes. "By the expression on your face, you'd think Preston painted the sunset for you."

Lucy ducked her head, splashing water on her face. "He *had* just saved my life."

Biddie continued as if Lucy hadn't spoken. "And my brother was regarding you in the way Gideon looks at me."

Lucy blinked the water away and studied her friend's face. "Are you saying...?"

Biddie's eyes sparkled, though her grin was tempered. "My brother's in love with you."

Lucy covered her mouth with her hand. Could Biddie be right?

Her voice grew serious. "Before yesterday, I'd have been concerned, but now that Preston's given his heart to God—"

"He did?" Lucy had wondered where his faith stood and realized it was a question she should have asked him long ago. Not that she'd had reason to make such a personal inquiry before now. "How do you know?"

"I had a long talk with him the night we arrived in Campo. I was there when he asked for God's forgiveness."

Tears of joy pricked the corners of Lucy's eyes, and her

throat tightened. She barely squeezed out the words, "That's wonderful." *Lord, thank You for opening his heart to Yours.*

"How long have you been feeling like this about my brother?" Biddie tipped her head. "And what about Clyve?"

"You heard him. He doesn't want to court me anymore." Lucy shot from the tub and wrapped herself in the towel waiting on a nearby chair. "Besides, nothing's happened. I'm not even sure Preston cares for me as you say."

Biddie laughed. "Well, I am certain. It was written all over his face. Trust me." She sobered. "But you still haven't said what you are going to do about Clyve. He was pretty hurt by what Preston shared earlier."

Lucy tucked the towel under her arm and flopped backward onto her bed. "Apologize, I guess. And tell him the truth of my feelings. It's the least I owe him." She threw one arm over her face. "Oh, Biddie. I can't marry anyone else knowing I'm in love with Preston. But what if you're wrong? Where would that leave me?"

Biddie's squeal preceded her pouncing onto the bed beside Lucy. "I knew it. We're going to be sisters."

Lucy chuckled even as her gut twisted. "You don't know that. You might be wrong. I could end up an old maid."

Biddie pried Lucy's arm from her face and leaned over her. "You won't. But first, you need to tell Clyve." She waved for Lucy to get up. "Which means, we need to get you dressed."

Less than ten minutes later, Biddie nudged Lucy out the front door with a whispered, "I'll be praying."

Gideon strode toward her from the barn. "All finished?"

She nodded, and he passed her to enter the house. The door closed behind her as her gaze found Clyve sitting beside the smoldering firepit in the middle of the yard. His back was to her as he peeled slivers of wood from a short branch with his knife.

She glanced to where Preston sat, pistols at his waist,

KATHLEEN DENLY

roughly ten feet from where they'd tied the doctor to the fence more than a hundred yards away. Preston's sober gaze revealed nothing of his feelings. Had she only imagined the passion that had burned in his eyes as he held her less than two hours ago?

She returned her attention to Clyve, noticing the dark patch on the back of his head. No doubt it was blood from the blow he'd also received. As she prepared Lucy's bath, Biddie had explained how she'd been woken by coyotes, then found Lucy gone and both Clyve and Gideon unconscious. Lucy fought the urge to turn around and hide in the house. Clyve had done so much for her, and she was preparing to break his heart. She squared her shoulders. The least she owed him was the truth.

She marched across the distance and paused at his side.

He glanced up, sadness in his eyes. "Hello." Then he turned back to his whittling.

Could he already know? Of course, he did. Biddie had insisted Lucy's feelings were obvious today. Surely, she wasn't the only one to have noticed. Lucy wrung her hands, hating herself for hurting such a good man. "May I join you?"

He shrugged.

She cast another glance at Preston, who was still watching her, then sat beside Clyve.

He continued slicing thin strips of wood and letting them fall to the ground. If he was aiming for any particular shape with his carving, she couldn't tell.

She cleared her throat. "I owe you an apology."

Still, he didn't look at her. "I know. I—" His voice caught. "I'm sorry too. For the way I reacted when Preston told me what he did. I lost my temper." He gave a rueful chuckle. "I guess I'm not so different from him, after all."

"You were speaking out of hurt. I'm so sorry. My head was so sure you were the right person for me that I was ignoring my heart. I should have admitted the truth sooner, to myself and to you. I—"

310

"It's all right." He placed a stilling hand over hers. "I forgive you."

She blinked back the tears forming in the corners of her eyes. "You do?"

He tossed the wood into the fire, put his knife away, and met her gaze. "Of course, I do. You can't help who you love."

There was so much pain in his look, she couldn't restrain her tears. "I'm so sorry. I tried. Really, I did. You're such a good man. A wonderful man. You'll make someone a marvelous husband."

He nodded. "Just not you." His eyes shimmered in the faint light of the fire's embers.

She forced the word past the regret clogging her throat. "No."

He reached up and tucked a strand of hair behind her ear. "Just promise me you'll be happy." His jaw clenched. "And if he breaks your heart, you let me know, and I'll break his nose."

A sob broke free, and she covered her mouth, trying to smother more. She had no right to act as though it were her heart being broken.

Clyve pulled her into his arms, rubbing her back. "Shh. Everything'll be all right." Clearing his throat, he took her shoulders and set her back. Then he stood and strode off into the dark past the barn.

Lord, please bring him a woman worthy of his goodness.

When he'd rounded the corner and was out of sight, she wiped away her tears, stood, and pivoted toward Preston. Rather than watching her as before, he'd turned away, facing his prisoner.

If You could also lend me a little courage now, I'd appreciate it.

CHAPTER 31

*P*reston turned from the sight of Clyve holding Lucy in his arms. Clearly, Clyve had changed his mind about conceding Lucy's heart to Preston. Which was as it should be. Preston might have decided to live a better life from now on, but Clyve had always been the better man. Clyve's path was sure, safe. What if Preston failed in his new mission to show mercy? What if he lost control? He'd come so close, looking down his sights at the imposter doctor this evening.

Preston checked that the man's restraints were secure and received spit in his face for the effort. Preston fisted his hands, but he didn't swing. He stepped back and wiped the spittle from his cheek. The vermin wasn't worth breaking his promise to God.

A calm Preston couldn't explain eased his muscles. He looked to the sky.

Thank You, Lord, for giving me the second chance I didn't deserve. Thank You for loving me even if I fail. Help me to be a better man. With or without Lucy.

"Preston?"

He spun and found Lucy standing not six feet away. How

had she snuck up on him? He glanced past her, but Clyve was nowhere in sight. Foolish hope stirred within. He clenched his teeth against it, waiting for her to explain why she'd come.

She shifted from foot to foot, her gaze skipping around him but never settling on his. "I...um...I was wondering if we could talk." She glanced at the prisoner. "In private."

Preston crossed his arms to keep from reaching for her. "I shouldn't leave him unguarded."

She nodded and turned to go, then paused and glanced back at him. "I could ask Gideon to watch him."

He couldn't resist the quiet hope in her voice. And he hadn't yet apologized to her for how he'd interfered in her relationship with Clyve. So he dipped his head.

She hurried back to the main house, tapping on the door. After a moment, Biddie opened it a crack, and the two spoke in words too quiet for Preston to hear.

He ran his palms against his thighs. What could she want to talk about? And why in private? Would she forgive him for betraying her trust? He searched the dark again. Where was Clyve?

A few minutes later, Gideon emerged from the house and approached Preston with a wide grin. "Biddie said to tell you that you'd better not break her best friend's heart, or she'll put salt instead of sugar in all your favorite treats."

Preston stared at him, stunned. Did that mean...?

He looked past his brother-in-law to where Lucy waited outside the house. She offered a hesitant smile that drew him forward. He barely registered Gideon's clap on his shoulder as he passed.

As Preston approached, Lucy's cheeks pinked, and her gaze darted from the ground to him and back again. He stopped just out of reach. Maybe he should let her speak first. "You wanted to talk?"

She nodded and searched the yard before meeting his gaze. "Should we walk?"

Preston glanced at the house behind her, imagining Biddie with her ear pressed to the closed door. "That's probably a good idea."

They walked past the barn, toward the sounds of the spring on the other side of the garden. She stopped and lowered herself to one of the small boulders clustered near the very small pond that provided the ranch's source of life. A frog croaked and crickets chirped as she patted the space beside her. "Would you like to sit?"

He sat and whipped the hat from his head, suddenly unable to wait. "Actually, would you mind if I said something before... before whatever it was you wanted to talk about?"

She faced him, her expression wary as she nodded.

"I'm sorry for eavesdropping on your conversation with Biddie. When I heard her squeal, I rode over to make sure everything was all right. When I realized it was, I should have ridden away instead of sticking around to listen. More than that, I shouldn't have made the decision to tell Clyve what I did on your behalf. You're a smart woman with a good heart. I should have trusted you to do the right thing." He swapped his hat from one hand to the other and ran his damp palms across his trousers. "I hope you can forgive me."

She smiled softly. "Of course, I forgive you."

Thank You, Lord. He waited for her to go on and say whatever it was she'd wanted to talk about. Instead, she turned back to the reed-filled water.

He spun the brim in his fingers, figuring she'd speak when she was ready. In the moonlight, he could just make out the small current of water that followed the rock-lined channel they'd created. It flowed through an opening at the base of the tiny springhouse wall, disappearing inside. When several minutes passed in silence, he dropped his hat on his thigh and asked, "What did you want to talk about?"

Her gaze seemed fixed on the moonlight shimmering across the pond's surface. "I wanted to thank you. For saving my life, of course."

His heart sank. "Oh." He was a fool. What had he expected —a declaration of love? Lucy was too smart to fall for a man like him.

"And to let you know that I've ended my courtship with Clyve."

"Oh?" He sounded like a dolt, but shock had stolen all other thoughts from his mind. Sure, Clyve had declared their courtship over earlier, but he'd been hurt and angry. He might have given Lucy another chance. But had she just said *she'd* ended her courtship with Clyve?

She lifted her chin and faced Preston. "And to ask if you would finally kiss me."

He stared at her dumbfounded. He couldn't have heard her right. "Finally?"

She wilted slightly. "Yes, you...you did seem to—"

Taking her in his arms, he pressed his lips to hers. Though he intended only a gentle caress, the eagerness of her response ripped a groan from his throat, and he moved his lips across hers with all the passion he'd kept trapped inside for as long as he'd known her. Her fingers dug into his hair, holding him close and he thrilled at her clear enjoyment.

After an eternity and not long enough, the need for air forced him to pull away. He pressed his forehead to hers. "I love you. I know I don't deserve you, but I can't seem to stop myself. You're kind and brave and beautiful and the hardest-working woman I've ever known, except maybe my big sister."

She chuckled, her arms still circling his neck. "No one works harder than Ginny." Then she sobered. "And you do deserve me.

You're loyal and funny and the most selfless man I know. You gave up everything to come care for your sister, and you haven't complained once, even though I know this isn't the life you want."

He shook his head. "That isn't anything any other man wouldn't do."

"You're wrong. Don't underestimate yourself. I wish you could see what I see when I look at you."

He sucked in a breath. "What do you see?"

"The most handsome man I've ever seen." Eyes sparkling, she stroked his cheek. "The man I love and want to spend the rest of my life with."

His heart stopped as he searched her gaze for any hint of doubt. "Are you sure? But I thought you wanted someone steady like Clyve with a ranch and roots and a good family. I don't have any of those things. I can't offer you a house or even a steady income. Sometimes the show gets rained out and—"

She pressed a kiss to his lips. "I'm sure."

Preston let the last of his protests whither on his tongue and kissed her back. Lucy's love was a miracle—a gift from God. One he planned to cherish for the rest of his life

~

*L*ucy walked hand in hand with Preston through the moonlight to the door of the main house, a grin she couldn't smother making her cheeks ache. They came to a stop and Preston leaned toward her.

From across the yard, Gideon cleared his throat.

With a mischievous twinkle in his eye, Preston pressed a quick kiss to her lips before stepping back. He lifted her hand and pressed another kiss to her knuckles. "Until tomorrow."

"Goodnight," she whispered. Were her feet even touching the ground?

He sauntered to where Gideon still stood guarding the doctor.

Lucy dragged her eyes from him and entered the house.

"So?" Biddie's hopeful expression turned knowing as Lucy's cheeks warmed. "Aha! I was right. He loves you, and you love him, and we're going to be sisters." She squealed again and wrapped Lucy in a warm embrace. Then, without letting go, Biddie began dancing them around the room. "We're going to be sisters. We're going to be sisters."

Never in her life had Lucy felt so loved and accepted. For all of her. Even knowing that Lucy's actions would cause Biddie's parents to lose their home and charity, and knowing that Lucy had kept that secret for months, Biddie still forgave her and loved her enough to want her as a sister. And Preston, knowing all the shameful secrets of Lucy's past, loved her just the same and wanted her as his wife. It seemed too good to be true, and yet it was.

If only Mama had loved her as much. Maybe then she'd have chosen Lucy over the opium. Because, for the first time, Lucy realized it wasn't keeping or sharing a secret that protected her. It was the love of those she trusted that made the biggest difference. And after her long talk with Preston, she knew both he and Biddie were passing on the love and forgiveness they'd found in the Lord.

In all the years she'd spent trying to convince Mama to give up the opium and leave the brothel, why hadn't Lucy considered telling her about God's love? Yes, Mama had attended the required Sunday services during her time living at The Home, but had she ever truly listened? What if the one thing Mama truly needed was Christ and Lucy had never shared Him with her?

Biddie must have picked up on Lucy's dipping mood because she stopped dancing them around and stepped back, still holding Lucy loosely in her arms. "What's wrong? I thought you were happy."

"I am." It wasn't difficult to resurrect her smile, remembering Preston's declaration of love and his new faith in the Lord. "Truly, I am. It's just...I was thinking of Mama."

Biddie squeezed her tight again. "What a confusing time this must be for you." She leaned back to peer into Lucy's eyes. "But God is watching over your mama just as He watched over you today. Everything will be all right. You'll see."

Biddie couldn't actually promise that Mama would be safe, but Lucy appreciated her friend's attempt to reassure her.

"Oh, for goodness sake. This is silly." Biddie seemed to be talking to herself more than Lucy. "You need to know." Biddie released her and spun toward the door. "Stay here. I'll be right back."

The door swung shut behind Biddie before Lucy could reply.

Lucy busied herself slicing a piece of bread and a hunk of cheese to nibble on. She'd still been too nauseous to share the evening meal with everyone else, but now that her stomach was settling, she was famished.

A few minutes later, Biddie returned bearing a large rectangular package wrapped in brown paper. There were bits of dirt caught in the creases. "Surprise!" She set the package on the table in front of Lucy. "Happy Birthday! Of course, I know your birthday isn't for another few days, but I figured your mama wouldn't mind me giving you her gift a few days early, considering the circumstances."

"What?" Lucy couldn't have heard her correctly. "You bought me a birthday gift?"

"Not me. Your mama." Biddie waved at the package. "Go on. Open it."

A sinking sensation settled in Lucy's stomach. "How long have you had this?"

"Mother and Father brought it with them from San Francisco. They gave it to me at the wedding." Biddie's smile dimmed, but only slightly. "They said your mama *insisted* that you not receive the package or know anything about her changed circumstances until your birthday. So I buried the box in the garden, far enough from the plants that the package wouldn't get wet, of course. But keeping quiet has been harder than waiting for a soufflé to finish baking."

"Wait. Are you saying your parents spoke with Mama?" So far as she knew, Mama hadn't spoken with the Davidsons since she'd chosen to leave The Home.

Biddie nodded vigorously. "And Lucy..." She held Lucy's gaze. "She was sober. Fletcher told them she hadn't used opium for months. Can you believe it? Apparently, he'd helped her find respectable employment."

Dazed, Lucy tried to picture her mother without opium and couldn't. "Are you sure?"

"Yes, and she told them she's hoping to come here for your birthday, but she had some things to do that might delay her. So she asked them to ask me to keep this safe, just in case."

Lucy stared at the package. A gift. From Mama. Just as the doctor had claimed. A chill ran over her.

Biddie huffed. "Lucy, what's wrong now? Aren't you happy? It's what you've wanted for so long." She plunked into the chair across from Lucy. "In all our years of friendship, you have never been so confusing. I—"

"It's the *doctor*." Lucy reached trembling hands toward the package. "This is what he wanted. The gift Mama sent me. But I didn't know I had a gift."

"I thought you said he thought you had a ledger."

"He did. But at first, he called it a 'gift' and said Mama sent it to me." Lucy slowly tore the paper away, revealing a plain box. She cast a glance at Biddie, then lifted the lid.

Shredded newspaper covered something lumpy. Lucy

brushed it aside, uncovering carefully stitched brown eyes, pink lips, and a sculpted nose at the center of a cloth face wreathed with long strands of brown yarn. The ends of the doll's arms had been stitched and sculpted to resemble hands, and feet peeked out from beneath a blue-and-white polka dot dress. It was exactly like the doll she'd propped into a third seat at the table whenever she and Mama had their afternoon tea.

Lucy tugged the gift from the box and held it to her chest, unable to speak as tears rolled down her cheeks. She'd thought Mama had long forgotten about their special times together.

"Aw," Biddie cooed. "What a sweet doll. It must have taken your mother a long time to make her." She ran her fingers through the remaining newspaper shreds. "Hey, what's this?" She withdrew a folded piece of paper and held it out to Lucy.

Lucy shook her head. "You read it, please."

Biddie cast her another odd look, then began reading. "'My darling Lucy, I cannot begin to make amends for the many ways I've hurt you, but I hope this gift brings you the joy of fond memories. If you can find it in your heart to forgive me, I'm planning to come for your birthday and hope you'll consider having tea with me. I'll understand, of course, if you cannot forgive me and promise not to make a nuisance of myself. But I have missed you greatly and have much to share. Love, Mama.'"

Lucy buried her face against the fabric doll and sobbed.

Please, Lord, let Mama be all right.

CHAPTER 32

FEBRUARY 19, 1874

*L*ucy sat on a bench outside the barn, darning a hole in Preston's sock. Beside her, Preston sharpened one of Biddie's kitchen knives with a whetstone. The rhythmic scrape of the stone against the blade broke the peace of the sunny day, but like a giddy schoolgirl, she secretly enjoyed the brush of his arm against hers as he worked.

She sneaked a peek at him and caught him looking back with a grin. A light breeze blew through the valley, rustling the sparse desert scrub and carrying the distant sound of coyotes yipping. A loose lock of hair tumbled across her forehead, and Preston set his whetstone down to tuck it behind her ear. He pressed his lips to her cheek quicker and lighter than a hummingbird's wings before resuming his work.

She flushed and checked whether anyone else had noticed. Biddie grinned at her from beside the fire where she was checking on their midday meal. However, Esther seemed too focused on stitching a new dress for the quickly growing Deborah to have noticed, and Carmen and Josie were out of sight, working in the garden. Gideon was hunting rabbits for their evening meal.

How were Ginny and Lei Yan getting along in the mountain pasture? Would Ginny object or approve of Lucy's engagement to Preston? Despite their conflict over the mine, she believed Ginny viewed her as a friend after all these months working together. But did that friendship extend to accepting Lucy as a sister? Only time would tell.

At least the gems had been recovered from where the doctor had hidden them under some rocks in the back room of the boulder cave. Ginny would be able to save her ranch. Lucy tried not to dwell on what would happen to the Davidsons when Mr. Green's fraudulent businesses collapsed.

Considering what she'd overheard that last awful day in the hotel, it seemed a miracle the scheme still continued. Though, it didn't seem right to credit God with perpetuating something so evil. She said a silent prayer that God would bring justice and restitution. It was all she could do now.

Her gaze returned to the sock, but her thoughts shifted to the man beside her. It still seemed like a dream that he loved and wanted to marry her. Yet each time she doubted it, all she needed to do was look at him. Since announcing their engagement yesterday morning, on return from delivering the doctor into Luman Gaskill's care, Preston had made no secret of his affections.

They'd not spoken of future plans. How long did Preston intend to remain on the ranch before returning to his life with the traveling show? His original plans involved leaving as soon as this year's cattle were driven north and sold. Was that still his plan? While things remained so uncertain regarding Mama and Fletcher, he'd probably not press her to leave California.

With a sigh, she tipped her face toward the sky and said another prayer for their safety and asked that God might speed word of it, if He didn't mind.

As her gaze lowered, movement on the trail entering the far side of the valley caught her eye.

Preston shot to his feet as a horse and rider crested the horizon. His hands went to the handles of his pistols, which he hadn't gone without since rescuing Lucy. Esther scooped up Deborah and ran toward the garden, no doubt to warn Carmen. Biddie retrieved the rifle she'd propped on a rock nearby and turned to face the rider.

Lucy reached for her own rifle, leaning against the barn, but Preston shifted to stand in front of her.

"Go into the barn," he ordered.

Lucy lifted her rifle with a huff. "I am not about to hide while my friends risk their lives to protect me." She stepped to the side so she'd have a clear shot and caught sight of two more riders entering the valley behind the first. The brown skirts of the lead intruder billowed in the wind. "The first one's a woman."

Preston didn't budge, but Lucy's heart pounded with suspicion. She squinted, trying to make out the rider's face, shadowed by an unfashionably wide-brimmed bonnet.

"Stop," Preston called out when the rider was within shouting distance. "State your name and purpose."

The rider drew to a halt. "My name's Opal Arlidge. I'm looking for my daughter. I was told—"

"Mama!" Lucy dropped her rifle and sprinted forward.

Mama was slower lowering from her horse and had just touched the ground when Lucy reached her. She remembered Mama's pains at the last moment and slowed herself to gently wrap Mama in her arms. "You're here. You're safe."

For the first time in years, Mama's arms returned Lucy's hug. "Oh, my darling girl. I'm so sorry for everything I've put you through. Can you ever forgive me?"

Lucy leaned back to study her. Tears glistened on Mama's cheeks, but gone were the persistently bloodshot eyes and sickly pale skin. Gone, too, was the nauseatingly sweet smell of opium. "Then it's true? You've given up opium?"

Mama nodded. "I haven't had a bit of it since Fletcher took me from the brothel." She cupped Lucy's face in her hands. "And I have you to thank for that. If you hadn't sent him to rescue me..." Her words trailed off, and she pressed her lips together, shaking her head. "You saved my life. You and God."

Lucy gaped at her. Since when did Mama speak of God? Before she could voice that or any of the dozens of questions swirling in her head, the other two riders joined them.

Lucy gasped as Fletcher swung down from his horse with a grin. "Your mother's a new woman from when we first met."

Lucy wanted to hug him, too, but restrained herself. "How can I ever thank you?"

He waved away her gratitude. "No need. I'm only passing on the good God has given me." He glanced at the petite red-haired woman still atop the other horse. "Right, dear?"

The woman laid a hand atop her bulging middle. "Aye. We are blessed beyond measure, 'tis true."

"Is that you, Katie?" Biddie called from the ranch yard.

"Aye." The redhead called back. "And I've brought the sneaky one with me too."

Fletcher laughed and looked to Lucy. "Shall we join the others? We have much to tell."

She took Mama's horse reins in one hand and clasped Mama's fingers with her other before nodding. "You go ahead. We'll be along."

Fletcher remounted, and he and Katie rode ahead to a warm welcome from Biddie, who called for Carmen, Esther, and the girls to come out. But Preston stood to the side, watching as Lucy and Mama strolled along.

She let Mama set the pace. "How are you feeling? You must be in agony after such a long journey." Yet Mama appeared nowhere near as pained as Lucy would have expected.

The wrinkles around Mama's eyes crinkled. "Mrs. Johnson knew of a new medicine. One from China. It isn't as strong as the opium, but almost so. And it doesn't fog my thinking or make me crave more and more."

Lucy squeezed their joined hands. "I'm so happy for you."

Mama peered at her. "Then you're glad I've come?"

"Of course. I wanted you to come with me when I left San Francisco."

Mama's gaze dropped. "I know. I...I mean, I didn't remember at first, but then Moira said..." Her gaze met Lucy's again, full of pain and regret, but most of all, full of love. "I'm so sorry. Daughters aren't supposed to care for their mothers. It's supposed to be the other way around, but for years, it was you who looked after me. Despite my stubborn ingratitude. And then, when you needed me most, I failed you."

"I won't lie." Lucy stopped. "It hurt—no, it crushed me—when you chose the opium rather than stay with me at The Home. It took a long time for me to believe it wasn't because I was unworthy of love. I thought you rejected me because I told the truth, about the stealing and about Pa."

Mama covered her gasp with her free hand as tears poured down her wrinkled cheeks. "Oh, my precious girl. No, it was never you. *I* was the broken one. The one unworthy of love."

Lucy swallowed a sob. "But when I visited you, every week I begged you to leave with me, and you refused." She couldn't keep the tears from streaming down her own face. "There were days you didn't even know who I was. My own mama..." Lucy's sobs finally broke loose.

Mama pulled her hand from Lucy's and wrapped her arms around her. "I know. I know." She rocked Lucy side to side as they cried. "And I'm so sorry. I would give anything to take back the pain I've caused you."

Lucy let her cheek fall to Mama's shoulder. "Why now? What changed?"

"At first, I told myself I could quit the opium whenever I wanted. Then I grew angry with the people who wanted to take away the one thing that made the pain stop. I told myself they, and you"—regret laced Mama's tone—"didn't really care about me or they wouldn't ask me to give it up. But one day, I looked in the mirror and realized what I'd become. The shame pushed me to drink in addition to the opium. Sometime after that, you came and begged me to leave as you always did, and I told myself that eventually, I'd find the strength to go with you."

"Is that why you kept saying, 'next week'?"

Mama nodded. "When Fletcher forced me to give up the opium, I was in so much pain, I couldn't think beyond finding relief. Until I saw Mr. Green leaving a meeting with Chiv King."

Lucy gasped and straightened. "What?"

"That's when I knew. If I went back to the opium, I'd lose you forever." She stroked Lucy's hair. "I finally decided I'd rather live through agony than leave my previous girl to fight for her life alone."

Lucy crossed her arms over her stomach, the forgotten reins pulling tight across her body. Could everything Mama was saying be true? She held Mama's watery gaze. "Promise me."

Mama nodded vigorously. "Anything."

"Promise me, you'll never go back to the opium."

"I—"

"Only, don't say it if you can't keep it." She couldn't take another broken promise.

Mama's eyes filled with a grave determination. "I promise. Fletcher and his wife have offered me a position helping in their photography studio. I'll get to live in their spare room, and they've promised to help me stay strong." She stroked Lucy's hair. "For you."

Lucy sniffed, unsure what to say.

Mama cupped her cheek. "I...I know it's too soon to ask. But

I need to tell you that I've been praying that someday, you'll find a way to forgive me."

"Mama, I—" The words caught in her throat. After all these years and all the hurting, Mama was really here, saying she was sorry. She wasn't making excuses. She was asking for forgiveness. The deepest, widest wound in Lucy's heart finally began to shrink. Damage wrought by years of betrayal would take time to fully heal. But for now, she took a deep breath and said the only thing she could. "I forgive you." And she meant it. Rebuilding trust would be a gradual journey, but for the first time in her life, Lucy felt hope for their future. She released the reins and wrapped her arms around Mama. Then she whispered, "I love you."

Mama rubbed Lucy's back, then shifted to catch Lucy's gaze. Remorse and gratitude mixed in her warm brown eyes. "And I love you."

Lucy's fragile control broke again, and she wept, soaking Mama's shoulder. When had she last heard those words from Mama? Lucy couldn't remember. *Oh Lord, You are so good. Thank You for giving Mama back to me.*

"Oh, my darling girl." Mama's shoulders shook beneath Lucy's cheek as her thin arms held Lucy tight, one hand still stroking Lucy's hair. "I love you so much."

Unable to speak, Lucy sobbed and held onto Mama. When the torrent of emotions eased, she stepped back, wiped her tears, and glanced behind her. Preston was still watching them, though the others appeared to be purposely looking away. "We should join the others."

Mama pulled a kerchief from her sleeve, patted her face, and blew her nose. Then she tucked the fabric away and nodded.

When they reached the yard, Fletcher addressed Opal with brows raised. "Shall we tell them now or wait until after we eat?"

Curious, Lucy searched her mother's expression for a hint as to whether their information was good or ill.

Mama returned her gaze with a shrug and a smile. "What do you think?"

Lucy considered Fletcher, who appeared relaxed. Hopefully, that meant whatever they had to share was good. "If you have news, I'd prefer to hear it now. Did you receive my telegram?"

Fletcher shook his head. "When did you send it?"

"Yesterday."

Katie supplied, "We were already on our way here by then."

Of course. Lucy refrained from smacking her forehead. There wouldn't have been time for them to receive her telegram and travel all this way. "Then, why have you come?"

Opal's brow crinkled as she faced Biddie. "Didn't you tell her I was coming?"

"I did and...I've already given her your gift. I hope that's all right. After everything she'd been through, I thought—"

"What do you mean? What happened?" Opal searched Lucy head to toe and spotted the scabs circling her wrists. She grasped Lucy's forearm, careful not to touch the wounds. "Saville did this, didn't he?" Her hand went to her mouth. "This is all my fault. The man at the store in Campo said Saville had threatened you, but he didn't say you were injured. Are you hurt anywhere else?"

Lucy frowned at Mama. "Who's Saville?"

Fletcher responded. "Senator Garfield Saville is the man you know as Dr. Smith. On our way here, we crossed paths with Luman Gaskill who was carting the man to San Diego's jail. I wouldn't have recognized Saville with all that facial hair and wearing those ratty clothes, but when I told Luman we were coming to see you, he felt the need to warn us that you may not be up for receiving company. He explained that the man he was escorting to jail had been brought in for making vile threats and attacking you. So, of course, I took a closer look at him." He reached into the saddle on his horse and withdrew a small stack of paper clippings. He held them up, showing that they'd been cut from a newspaper. The headline of the first read, *Reginald Green and son arrested on charges of fraud— Accomplice, Senator Garfield Saville, still at large.*

Lucy snatched the paper from Fletcher's grasp, reading of how a newspaper article printed in *The Chicago Weekly Bulletin* had unveiled the fraudulent scheme that Green, his son, and Senator Saville had been running, leading to warrants being issued for their arrests. Reginald Green and Junior had been apprehended the same day the article was printed, but no one seemed to know where Senator Saville had gone. Originally rumored to be enjoying a long visit to the Continent, that information had since been proven false. There were additional accusations that the men had been involved in multiple murders and the arson of San Francisco's *The Daily Chronicle.* There'd been a run on the bank Reginald Green had been president of, forcing its temporary closure. The reporter went on to speculate what the events meant for the completion of Green's railroad and the second hotel, which had been scheduled to open in two weeks.

Lucy didn't realize she'd started shaking until Preston's arm came around her shoulders, steadying her. "You should sit." He guided her to the nearest boulder around the fire, and everyone else followed, taking seats on the various rocks and crates circled there.

Mama's curious gaze bounced between the two of them, but Lucy's mind was too full of relief to answer the unspoken question. She found Fletcher's gaze. "Are you saying the man who attacked me was a senator?"

"Yes, and I'm sorry we didn't get here sooner, but at least now I can assure you that every threat has been stopped. You're safe." Fletcher turned his gaze to Mama. "And so is your mother."

Lucy's relief was short-lived as she realized what the end of Green's scheme meant for the Davidsons. "Is there any chance of the investors getting their money back?"

Fletcher's expression was grim. "There's nothing left in Green's accounts. He wasn't actually investing money in profitable businesses. Or rather, he had at one point, but when those businesses failed to turn the profits he expected, he resorted to less honest ways of fulfilling the promises he'd made to his investors."

Mama's hands twisted in her lap. "From what I could understand of the papers I found, and what Fletcher confirmed for me, Mr. Green's been making payments to prior investors with the funds from new investors for a long time. Possibly years."

Fletcher leaned forward. "But with the economic turmoil of late, he's been struggling to find new investors. If we hadn't exposed him now, it's likely he'd have been forced to declare bankruptcy within the month." Biddie gasped as Fletcher continued, "It's an unusual fraud, but not unheard of. My editor friend in Chicago let me know of a Mrs. Nancy Clem who was arrested for murder and who was suspected of running a similar scheme a few years back in Indiana."

Lucy blinked. "Then it was you who wrote the article printed in *The Chicago Weekly Bulletin?*"

Katie ginned proudly from her seat on a crate near Fletcher's. "Aye. He's been writing articles in secret for years now, exposing the filthy underbelly of our government."

Fletcher's eyes narrowed. "I tried to have my article published in *The Daily Chronicle*, but you read what happened to them."

Lucy's breath caught. "The fire?"

"Happened right after I submitted my report and before it could go to print. Somehow, Saville and Green must've found out. So I decided it'd be safer to try again in Chicago, where those two didn't have as much say so. But my editor friend there never would have printed what I wrote without the evidence your mother stole from Green's office." He gestured toward Mama, who'd taken a seat on a stump nearby. "Of course, we turned over to the law everything we had, once we were sure there'd been too much attention drawn for Saville and the Greens' crimes to be swept under the rug."

"Wait. What evidence?" Lucy shifted toward Mama. "You mentioned papers. Was there a ledger?"

Mama's eyes widened. "How'd you know?"

Lucy explained how the man she now knew to be Senator Garfield had kidnapped and threatened her, believing she had hidden the ledger.

Mama apologized again, horrified that her gift had brought such danger to her daughter.

"Please, stop apologizing. There's no way you could have known. And God watched over me." She reached across, taking Mama's hand in hers. "We're safe now."

Biddie added, "And please don't worry about my parents or The Home. God is watching out for them. If He wants The Home to stay open and my parents to keep their businesses, He'll provide a way. If not, He'll guide and comfort them through the losses. We have to trust that He loves us and His ways are wiser than we can sometimes comprehend."

Fletcher grinned at her. "You sound like Katie."

Mama shifted on her stump, her attention still on Lucy. "Would it be all right to give you the other part of my gift now? I'd planned on saving it for your actual birthday, but..." Her words trailed off and she shrugged.

"There's more? But Mama, that doll must have taken you so long to make. You don't need to give me more. I'm just glad to have you with me."

"Then you like it?"

"Of course. I can't believe you even remembered the polka dot dress."

Mama rose and moved toward the main house. While the rest of them were talking, Gideon had quietly taken care of the horses and left the satchels in a neat pile near the front door. Mama stooped and opened one. After a moment, she rose, carrying a fabric-wrapped bundle. She placed the package in Lucy's lap. "I didn't have the money or time to purchase these until after the Greens were arrested, or I would have sent them with the doll."

Carefully, Lucy unwrapped the gift and gasped at the two beautiful, matching teacups nestled within.

"They aren't new. I purchased them secondhand, and there's a small chip in the bottom of one, but I hoped you'd like them, anyway. They were the finest I could afford and..." Mama's voice lowered to a whisper. "I hoped we might have tea together. Just you and me, the way we used to." She glanced at Preston. "Or you could invite your young man, if he's a mind to join us."

Overwhelmed by the goodness suddenly pouring into her life, Lucy couldn't speak for a moment. Her mind filled with praise for the God who'd given her more blessing than she ever could have imagined. Then she shook herself and gently shifted the cups, still cradled in their fabric nest, to one hand so she could reach for Preston with the other. "Mama, this is Preston—the man I'm going to marry."

CHAPTER 33

MARCH 10, 1874
CAMPO, CALIFORNIA

*L*ucy stood in the Gaskills' store considering the limited selection of fabrics. Her work dress needed patching where the fabric had snagged on shrubs during their long drive to bring most of what was left of Ginny's herd to market. Lucy debated which of the two shades of brown would be less conspicuous.

Biddie's squeal interrupted her silent debate.

Lucy turned to where her friend stood at the front counter. "What is it?"

"John Jacob Astor III, the grandson of Father's old friend, has agreed to donate enough funds to keep The Home open for the next two years." Biddie waved her letter like a flag. "They'll still need to sell most of their real estate and two businesses to recoup their personal losses, but that's so much better than selling everything to keep The Home open as they'd been preparing to do."

Lucy gaped at her friend. "It feels like a miracle."

Biddie nodded. "God is so good." She whirled toward the door. "I have to tell Gideon."

Lucy followed her outside, eager to share the news with Preston

~

A cold wind threatened to tug the letter from Preston's hand as he stood outside the Campo store. He read its contents again, thoughts racing. Harvey was offering him a raise and a promotion, to be the top-billed act in Harvey Arbuckle's Show of Wonders. The offer was contingent on Preston's return by the end of March, just three weeks away.

He silently thanked the Lord that they'd driven the herd to market last week instead of waiting until the end of April as they'd originally planned. With the continuing drought causing more ranchers to sell off stock they couldn't feed, Ginny's cattle fetched a much lower price than she'd hoped—less than she'd originally said she needed to make it another year. When he learned this, Preston vowed to stay until next spring, but Ginny insisted she'd be fine without him. It seemed Biddie's baking brought in more than Preston would have guessed, and Ginny was convinced that with a few adjustments to their budget, they'd be all right. She'd insisted that Preston had sacrificed enough and should return to the life he loved.

Preston had been torn over the decision, but with this new offer in hand, his mind filled with visions of his name at the top of every poster. He'd have second choice, after Harvey, of where to set up his tent each time they moved to a new city. Best of all, a raise like this would mean enough money to support a wife, maybe even children. He could picture Lucy waiting in his tent after his performances, a warm meal ready and a little girl with brown hair settled on her hip. The image was everything he wanted. But would Lucy be happy with such a life?

He remembered the complaints of the other wives who'd married men in the show. The dirt, the constant packing and unpacking, the inability to enroll their children in school—it all became too much for the women. The last thing he wanted was to drag Lucy into a life that would make her miserable. And she seemed content here, with her friends. Was it fair to even ask her to consider leaving them behind?

Preston set his jaw. He could make a life here, with her. It wouldn't be the same, but he could be happy so long as she was happy. He folded the letter and started to tuck it in his pocket.

"What's that?" Lucy stepped around him, grinning. "Did you receive a letter too?"

He jammed the letter deeper into his pocket. "What did Biddie's letter say?"

"I'll tell you after you share your news." She tipped her head with a frown. "We promised each other no more secrets."

He cringed. She was right. Despite his misgivings, she had a right to know and decide for herself. Not that the conclusion of the matter would be any different. "It's from Harvey."

"Oh? What did he say?"

He pulled the letter free and offered it to her. "You can read it."

Her eyes widened as she read. After a minute, she looked up at him, eyes sparkling over a wide grin. "This is wonderful! You've always wanted top billing. And a raise. How exciting."

He frowned. Didn't she understand? "I'm not accepting the offer."

Her brows furrowed. "What? Why not?"

He snatched the hat from his head, ran his hand through his hair, and replaced the hat. "Because you're more important. And you like it here, with Biddie and everyone. I won't make you leave all this for a life sleeping in tents, never knowing where we'll go next or if the show will get rained out. It's no life for a family."

"But you said, there were other women and even children who traveled with the show."

"And they always leave, eventually. It's...not having a home is hard on them. I won't do that to you."

"But I think joining the show sounds like a wonderful adventure." He opened his mouth to protest, but she wasn't finished. "I've slept under enough tents to know it'll have its drawbacks. But traveling with the show, with you, would be different than riding on a cattle drive. For one thing, there won't be any smelly cows. And we won't just be going from one grassy patch to the next. We'll be traveling from city to city. I'll get to see parts of the world I've never seen before." She took his hands. "And now that I don't have to hide anymore, I think I might like being married to the famous Preston Baker, best trick shot sharpshooter in the world."

Laughing, Preston scooped her into his arms and kissed her. When he pulled back, he stared down into her chocolate-brown eyes. "Are you sure?"

She nodded, still grinning. "Take me on an adventure, my love."

EPILOGUE

FEBRUARY 27, 1875

a bit dazed, Lucy bid the doctor farewell and sank onto the cot inside the tent she and Preston had called home for almost a year. Outside, hooves thundered across the show's new performance arena as Preston's shots pinged through tin cans to the cheers of the crowd. He was nearly finished with today's performance.

Her hand settled over her flat stomach. How should she tell him? He'd been so worried about the nausea that had begun two weeks ago and seemed in no hurry to leave. It had been his idea to send for the doctor, and he'd almost refused to go on stage, anxious to hear what the doctor had to say. But she'd convinced him she'd be all right and nothing would change in the few minutes he'd be gone.

Yet now...everything was about to change.

Something scraped across the outside of the canvas, and she smirked with suspicion. "You may come in, Scrapper." She'd sent him out with the promise of a peppermint candy if he behaved while the doctor was there.

The almost-eleven-year-old poked his head through the tent flaps, though his eyes were closed. "Are you decent?"

Lucy swallowed a chuckle. "Yes, come on in."

Scrapper opened his eyes and stepped inside, his expression unusually somber. As he drew near, lantern light reflected off an unusual sheen on his cheeks, as if he'd been crying. "What's wrong?" She took his hands and tugged him to sit beside her.

He sniffled and wiped his nose with the back of his hand, then straightened, his expression hardening. "Nothing."

She stroked his thick blond hair. "Come now, don't you trust me?"

For a moment, his expression didn't change, then it crumpled. "I heard the doctor say you're gonna have a baby." His voice trembled. "So...I guess if it's a boy, you won't need me anymore. But that's all right. I'm used to doing for myself. I knew when you adopted me, it wasn't forever."

"Oh, Scrapper, no!" Heart breaking for the tough little boy who'd been through so much, she pulled him into a hug. "No matter what happens, nothing will change the way Preston and I feel about you. We love you, and we will always want you as our son." She leaned back and captured his tear-streaked face in her hands so she could hold his gaze. "Always. Do you understand? Nothing will ever change that."

Scrapper nodded, his body relaxing and she tucked him back under her arm.

Preston burst through the tent flap. "What did the doctor say?"

He took in the sight of them, obviously noting Scrapper's tears, and the color drained from his face. He staggered back. "No."

Before Lucy could say anything, Scrapper jumped up. "Don't worry, Preston. Lucy says the baby won't change how much she loves us."

Preston blinked. Then his face split with a goofy grin. "A baby?" His delighted gaze found Lucy's. "Is it true?"

She nodded as she stood.

With a whoop, he swept her into his arms and kissed her.

"Eww," Scrapper complained and darted from the tent.

Lucy laughed against Preston's lips.

He pulled back. "How do you feel? Is your stomach still unsettled?"

She knocked the hat from his head and raked her fingers through his hair. "At the moment, I'm feeling pretty wonderful." Then she pulled him in for another kiss. One she hoped conveyed how happy and blessed she was to call him her husband.

Did you enjoy this book? We hope so!
Would you take a quick minute to leave a review where you purchased the book?
It doesn't have to be long. Just a sentence or two telling what you liked about the story!

Receive a FREE ebook and get updates when new Wild Heart books release: https://wildheartbooks.org/newsletter

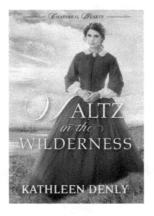

Book 1: Waltz in the Wilderness

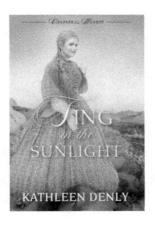

Book 2: Sing in the Sunlight

Book 3: *Harmony on the Horizon*

Book 4: *Murmur in the Mud Caves*

FROM THE AUTHOR

Dear Reader,

This book turned out to be the most difficult I have ever written. Not only did I write this novel during the darkest period of my life, the story addresses topics that are personally raw and real for me. In the spring of 2022 I sustained an injury which profoundly changed my life forever. Although the physical injury is finally on the mend, the medical complications—both physical and mental—will be with me for the rest of my life.

In this novel, Lucy, Preston, and Opal all struggle with allowing fear to control their lives. In Lucy's case, her fear of rejection drives her to keep secrets as a way of protecting herself. For Preston, it's a fear of failing to protect the women he loves that transforms his righteous anger into senseless rage. Meanwhile, Opal's fear of pain—both physical and mental—drives her to seek oblivion through an abuse of medication. In the end, they all must learn to put their faith and trust in God —the one who loves us always, loves those we love more than we do, and carries us through the darkest places. Beyond this, I hope the story also shows how we all need the people God places in our lives. We are not meant to journey the hard roads alone.

While I have not lived the lives of my characters, I have experienced parts of each of their stories in different ways. I have experienced rejection by those I trusted, failed to keep loved ones safe, and endured chronic, life debilitating pain. I think we all know the pain of broken relationships—of discovering that those we thought would have our backs, don't actually value us enough to stay, listen, and try to understand us, to forgive our mistakes and accept our differences. The pain of learning that a loved one has suffered unspeakable tragedy and there is nothing you can say or do to rewind time and prevent what happened is beyond what words can describe. Though I have thankfully never struggled with drug addiction, I do understand the overwhelming temptation to "make the pain stop" at any cost, and I have walked alongside those close to me as they battled addiction.

Among many other health issues that were raging at the time I was working on this novel, I was told that I was suffering from Post Traumatic Stress Disorder. For me, the symptoms included heightened levels of anxiety, numerous panic attacks, and emotional flashbacks. It also included severe and almost unending nightmares that woke me several times a night—sometimes screaming. They occurred every night for months, from the time I finally fell asleep until I quit trying to seek rest and just got out of bed.

Worst of all, however, are what I call the "full body flashbacks." When these strike I wind up reliving the worst day of the pain I experienced due to my injury. I see that day as if someone has placed a transparency image over my eyes, blocking my current circumstances and transporting me back to that place and time. I hear myself screaming and the sounds of travel as my husband desperately tried to get me to the hospital. I smell our van, feel the rumble of the tires along the road, hear the door slam as he runs inside to get medical staff to help me out of our van. And I feel the pain like ghost pains taking over my body. My heart races and I lose all clarity of thought until the only thing left is pain.

These symptoms can be triggered by anything from a smell that my brain associates with that day, to being in a place that I was in that day (my bedroom, my yard, my van, driving down the road to town, etc.), to a re-aggravation of my still recovering injured muscles which triggers a deep fear of reliving what I went through.

Thankfully, I have modern medication and have learned many therapeutic skills and tips to help me manage through these events. My character, Opal, wasn't as fortunate. In her time, there was very little understanding of post traumatic stress disorder. There was some vague understanding of a connection between Civil War experiences and what they then termed "soldier's heart" but that was about as far as it went. No one, except Opal herself, would have recognized what Opal was going through mentally as being largely a result of the attack by her "husband." Nor would she have had the knowledge to fully understand what it was she was experiencing or how to manage it. In her time, many would have considered her to be "losing her mind."

Addiction as a result of what we now know as PTSD was very common in those days. Add in chronic pain due to injury, and it was almost guaranteed since the methods of pain management at that time were so limited and nearly all were potentially addictive. There are many documented cases where the struggle began with a prescription for laudanum (opium) or morphine. So it made sense that Opal found herself in the situation she did. That isn't to say she had no choice or that her life couldn't have been different, only to say that her character is modeled after the true lives of people from her era. (For an interesting read on nineteenth century opium addiction and one man's attempt to escape it, I suggest *The Opium Habit* by Coleridge published in 1868 and freely available to read through the U.S. Library of Congress.)

No doubt some of you are wondering about the mysterious Chinese medicine I had Fletcher give Opal. Yes, the medicine did and does exist, though few western physicians were aware of it at the time and modern doctors are still conducting research to understand how it works. That's why it made the most sense to have Fletcher—or rather, his wife, Katie—be the one aware of the medicine. If you've read *Harmony on the Horizon*, you'll better understand that Katie is the character with the most reason and opportunity for knowing about this medication's existence. If you'd like to learn more about this medicine, try searching the internet for the traditional uses of and analgesic properties of *Corydalis yanhusuo* (a flowering plant long used in traditional Chinese medicine).

The crimes and characters of Mr. Green, Junior, and Senator Saville, though not based on specific individuals, were inspired by a combination of three sets of real people.

The first inspiration came from *The Notorious Mrs. Clem: Murder and Money in the Gilded Age* by Wendy Gamber, a fascinating account of the first occurrence of a "Ponzi scheme" before it became known as such.

Second, I considered our more contemporary example of Bernie Madoff—how he ran his scheme, what appeared to motivate him, and what ultimately brought him down.

The third inspiration came from the historical figures of William Chapman Ralston and Senator William Sharon and the financial scandal and collapse that occurred just before the opening of The Palace Hotel in San Francisco (still operating today, having been rebuilt after the 1906 earthquake). To learn more about these men and the history of this beautiful hotel, visit https://thepalacehotel.org/

To be clear, I found no evidence that either Ralston or Sharon were actual criminals (though I will say Sharon isn't someone I would want to call friend). Instead, I asked myself, "What if they had been running a Ponzi scheme in the midst of the financial scandal and economic panic that lead to Ralston's ruin and they had the ruthlessness of Mrs. Clem and her associates?" Many of the economic factors which lead to

Madoff's ruin were in place at the time of Ralston's downfall and, on the surface at least, there were some similarities to their personalities if you believe certain parts of their official stories. Thus, the criminal element for this novel was born.

The spessartite garnet mine Lucy and Preston work on Lupine Valley Ranch isn't based on an actual discovery. Instead, it is based on the fact that such discoveries were made in that area several decades later and the question, "What if they'd been discovered sooner?"

The wedding scene with its competitions, details about set up and meals, and the controversy over waltzing, are all based on actual local historical events. Though waltzing was accepted and common in most metropolitan areas by this time, it remained controversial with older citizens and in some remote areas such as the setting of this book.

Regarding the Gaskill Brothers: They are somewhat controversial historical figures, who did own the tiny town of Campo, including its store, blacksmith, and small hotel. Luman Gaskill was the Justice of the Peace for the Campo area and Silas Gaskill was known for his doctoring skills although he was not a doctor. Both were known to be kind and ruthless depending on the occasion. I've chosen to share their more favorable attributes in my novels.

Finally, I'd like to point out some fun easter eggs that I hid in this novel for those who've been following the Chaparral Hearts series:

First, in the scenes of Fletcher and Opal's escape from San Francisco, I specify that the storekeeper's wife is named Janie because she is the secondary character who helped both Fletcher and Katie in *Harmony on the Horizon*. I thought readers would like knowing that she has since married and risen in the world from her position as a maid.

Second, the hole in the hedge that leads to a garden behind a school where Fletcher and Opal hide from Chiv King are throwbacks to the earliest scenes from *Sing in the Sunlight* and how Clarinda managed secret rendezvous while attending The Young Ladies Seminary of Benicia (which would have been known as Mills College by the time Opal and Fletcher ducked inside the garden).

Lastly, you may have noticed the very brief mention that on their journey to Lupine Valley Ranch, Lei Yan recognized the teacher at the Stevenses' ranch and that Gideon considered the encounter a miracle. If so, I'd like to confirm that Lei Yan is the young Chinese girl from the opening scene of *Harmony on the Horizon* about whose fate so many readers wondered. I plan to write a short story of this reunion and add it to the Freebie Library available exclusively to my Kathleen's Readers' Subscribers. If you're not already a member, I encourage you to visit www.KathleenDenly.com and join today.

I love hearing from my readers, so please feel welcomed to reach out with your thoughts and questions at writeKathleenDenly@gmail.com.

Thank you for reading!

Kathleen

ABOUT THE AUTHOR

Kathleen Denly lives in sunny California with her loving husband, four children, two dogs, and ten cats. As a member of the adoption and foster community, children in need are a cause dear to her heart and she finds they make frequent appearances in her stories. When she isn't writing, researching, or caring for children, Kathleen spends her time reading, visiting historical sites, hiking, and crafting.

ACKNOWLEDGMENTS

This novel would not have been possible without the unconditional love of both my God and my husband, for which I am forever grateful. As always, I am grateful for the support, encouragement, and feedback of my mother for being my first reader, and of my beta readers who patiently read different iterations of this story and answered my many questions in order to bring this story to what it is today. I would also be remiss if I didn't thank my publisher for her patient understanding, wisdom, and encouragement. Additionally, I'd like to thank Julia, Ana, Cecilia, Ivan, Sally, Priscilla, Donna, Pam, and Peggy. You know why. May God bless each of you.